RAMON SENDER

THE

AFFABLE

HANGMAN

LAS AMERICAS PUBLISHING COMPANY
NEW YORK   1963

863
Se 5a
62175
July 1968

Ramon Sender

THE AFFABLE HANGMAN

Published and distributed by

LAS AMERICAS PUBLISHING COMPANY
152 East 23rd Street
New York 10

Printed in the United States of America
by Charles Press, Inc.

I sometimes think that there is only one man who lives the truth and who, furthermore, deserves the gratitude of all the rest and does not ask for it: the hangman. Upon his head rests all the social order known until today, and still the hangman, aware of it, offers himself as a propitious object for the scorn, fear, and moral repugnance of all. Here is the martyr and hero . . .

1

DECORATIVELY set in the walls were rows of glass aquaria full of colored fish and seaweed. Wherever a person's eyes fell they discovered something surprising. Nothing was still. Nothing could serve as a point of reference for the movement of anything else.

I had asked my friend to meet me here because when deciding on a place this had struck me as the least appropriate. I have frequently in my life made decisions like this. I go hunting difficulties so as to provoke some kind of effort unconsciously—what kind I almost never know. This effort is something like a set of inner gymnastics that tones me up.

The man I was waiting for was not really a friend of mine. I had met him only a few hours before. But I had immediately realized that he felt real gratitude toward me because I had offered him my hand, knowing that he was a hangman. He looked quite common and ordinary to me. I only remembered his face as a pink spot in the air. I was almost sure, however, that I would recognize him when he entered, though I could not say how, having forgotten even the color of his hair.

I glanced toward the distant door of the café where an employee was busy taking the coats and hats of the new arrivals. I asked the waiter for a newspaper. He brought me mine—the newspaper on which I worked, I mean to say. Inside my head everything was soft and shifting like the little spots of color—the fish—moving around me at all heights and distances. I first read what I myself had written. Two news dispatches, a short commentary, and the section of latest news covering the events of the early morning. Heading this section was the story of the execution of four condemned men. I was deliberately laconic because our newspaper scorned sensationalism. This is what it said:

'At five-thirty the garrottes were ready in a moat of the Model Prison. Here the death sentence of the four criminals convicted of murder in connection with the robbery of the Transcontinental Bank was to be executed.

'The condemned men, who had spent the entire night in the chapel, assisted by Father R., devoted most of their time to writing letters. Not one of them seemed to lose his presence of mind.

'The order of the execution was as follows: First the so-called Sevilla, who was seated on the garrotte at 6.13, just before daybreak. The coroner certified his death eighteen minutes later. Piqueras followed, taking twenty minutes to die. Then Banzo, who expired in three minutes, and finally Navarrete, in five. At seven o'clock the black flag was hoisted above the main prison gate, indicating that the sentences had been executed.

'The Brothers of Peace and Charity removed the bodies from the garrottes and placed them in coffins.

'The executioners from Ocaña and Burgos officiated, having arrived in the city for that purpose twenty-four hours before.

'The lawyers for the defense and the official prison functionaries, besides the mandatory witnesses required by law, were present.'

I had been one of the 'mandatory witnesses'.

Information regarding these executions was given to the public by order of the Office of Press Censorship. In this way the people thought that the rumors of other secret executions must be false.

The café was full of well-dressed middle-class people. Too well-dressed. Why are men and women so fussy about the way they dress nowadays?

I looked at the people around me, involuntarily staring at the nape of their necks. Some of them looked at me also. No one could imagine that a few hours before I had been watching four men seated and tied to posts being killed. I did not know if the hangman I was expecting came from Burgos or Ocaña, but I was inclined to believe from Burgos for I associated his physical appearance, in which there was a certain distinction, with the famous cathedral. The other executioner, gruff and taciturn, was probably from Ocaña. The one I was waiting for must have spent

8

already some years in that sad profession. I realize that 'sad' is not the right word. The law terms the process of execution by the garrotte 'vile garrotting.' The profession was not sad but vile. Yet that man had the reassuring expression of an honest citizen. 'I myself,' I thought, 'have more of a hangman's look.'

I remembered the condemned men with superstitious respect. From the moment they are sentenced and accept the idea of imminent death they acquire, in our eyes, an incredibly heroic prestige which, after the execution, borders on the miraculous. I recalled the four executions, but the details were mingled and confused. Over the memory of it all there was something like a fog of violent lights. The scene had been excessively bright with arc lights and reflectors.

The hangman would be arriving any moment. I did not know how he usually dressed when not wearing his professional clothing. The idea that a waiter was going to take his coat, call him 'sir' and show him to a table (I would stand up so he would see me) amused me. No one could imagine that he was an executioner.

I took another sip of wine, and with the newspaper in front of me started recalling the past night. I did not have to remember anything, really, for I was still living through it. Meanwhile, as I put my impressions in order, through a glass wall full of graceful fish I saw people walking along the street. It was still cold. The preceding night had been even colder.

My editor and I had started out for the prison in those last hours of the night before sun-up. Every night, near dawn, he seemed to be drunk, not on wine but on coffee, which he drank in enormous quantities. I admired that strange man who, it seemed to me, had won the important post he held by dint of skepticism and laziness.

As I said before, I was going to jail as a witness. It was the first time that a civil personality had been conferred upon me. I represented the city. The city merely required a passive attitude of me. To be there and look. When the editor told me about it I was somewhat perplexed.

9

Even though I represented the city, at no time did I identify myself with the citizens sleeping soundly in their beds, but with the condemned men. I considered them fallen to a fate that could very well have been mine. Although my conduct has always been if not exemplary at least discreetly honest, I knew that I was closer to the condemned men than to the judges, and which position I was in seemed to me to depend on fortuitous circumstances.

We reached the jail an hour before sunrise. The gate was closed and the editor of my newspaper said to the chauffeur:

'Wait until they open the gate and drive on in.'

Since the officer on guard did not permit this, we had to get out. Set in the immense gate was a small door barely large enough for a man to pass through, and we entered one after the other. We crossed an open patio with a garden in the middle. Then they opened a grating that gave on to a long corridor with an arched ceiling. On one side were stone steps leading to the warden's apartments. Other persons were there, but no introductions were made. The warden exchanged a few words with my editor and I saw that they were old acquaintances. We signed a register and sat down to wait. The warden walked about on the carpet with such elastic movements that one could have said he had prehensile toes that grasped the floor with every step. He was bulky and pot-bellied and had blue circles under his eyes. He sat down behind the glass-covered table presiding over the room. On the wall, above his head, was a photograph of the *Caudillo* with the eyes of a pensive gazelle. How is it possible for a dictator who has seized power by accumulating crimes to have the eyes of a gazelle?

The warden took a handful of Havana cigars out of a drawer and looked at those present one by one, recalling who smoked and who did not. I was thinking: 'That cigar business is more appropriate for baptisms and weddings.' Other people were arriving, among them a personage dressed in black, wearing an overcoat with silk lapels. He was tall and had the fresh face of one who has slept well. My editor and I, faded and tired, left the

10

initiative of the conversation to the others and found it easy to agree with them. A lawyer came toward us. He was disconsolate at having to witness the executions. Listening to him one had the impression that the poor men condemned to death ought to apologize and console him. The warden counted the cigars again. Finally he put them all in his pocket and started playing with a pencil.

In a few moments he came toward us, said something to the editor, and the three of us left. We returned to the wide corridor and kept on walking until we came to an armored door. The warden opened a small blind window with a telephone inside. He picked it up, spoke a few words, and without waiting for a reply replaced the telephone in its niche. Immediately the armored door began to swing open mysteriously while somewhere an electric motor hummed. We went in and the warden said:

'Now you are at my mercy.'

This was an old joke he repeated with his guests. He laughed more than was called for. We were in the middle of a glass rotunda on which five galleries converged. We crossed the rotunda where there was an officer with several telephones and small machines, like a pilot on the bridge of his ship, and crossed one of the galleries. Through another armored door we entered an open patio. At the back there was a wall some fifty feet high with a sentinel's stone sentry-box on top. At the foot of the wall was a door. The fresh air was pleasant. We went forward in silence. I was concentrating on the surprise waiting for us, perhaps, on the other side of the wall flooded with a glaring light. The warden turning toward me asked:

'Have you never seen an execution?'

Intimidated, I did not answer. Who has not seen executions in our time? Although a legal quadruple execution, with judges and sentences, defense lawyer and witnesses, no, I had never seen that.

The small door opened. On the other side there was an excessively brilliant light comparable only to that used in cinema studios or circus rings. Seeing my hesitancy the editor led the

11

way. The warden followed and I went last. At that moment I had the fear that some neurotics have of light. The warden, impressed by the fact that I had not answered his question, spoke to me again:

'This is the inner moat.'

I supposed that there must be another moat, the outer one. I asked about it and the warden seemed pleased.

'Yes,' he said. 'Behind this moat is another.'

He talked about inclined planes, dead angles, enfilades, sentries. In the harsh light flooding the moat I discovered that the circles under the warden's eyes were not yellow or blue or violet, but brick-colored. In spite of the harshness of the light the warden's pupils did not contract, nor did he squint. My editor, accustomed to shun the daylight and live by night, was foundering in that sea of brilliance. One of the arc lights was constantly changing intensity and making a hissing sound.

I walked about reconnoitering the place. There were two parallel walls, quite high, not very far apart. The ground was covered with yellow sand. Driven into the ground rather close together were four unpainted wooden posts, no taller than a man. I looked without understanding and said to myself: 'The garrotte must be in the second moat,' but then I soon realized that these were the execution posts. There were no other objects around except two tool boxes like those regularly used by plumbers—on the ground, near the wall—and near the first post a chair. An ordinary and innocent chair. Two men were taking nails and screws out of the boxes and slowly revolving about the second and fourth posts. They were in shirtsleeves and their collars and cuffs were starched. Both of them wore correctly pressed striped trousers. One of them had loose silver cuff-links that made a little tinkling sound. They looked like business men on a holiday.

The one with the loose cuff-links was humming softly to himself and I caught a few words:

The evening sun is dying . . .

I could not imagine these men, so correctly dressed—their

12

black coats were hanging one above the other on the back of the chair—working like two laborers. I asked the editor about them and he said that they were the hangmen. From then on I was aware that they filled the moat with their presence and especially their silence. I kept on asking questions, fascinated. The editor warned:

'Don't use the word *"hangman"* here.'

The warden heard him and clarified:

'They are *executers of justice.*'

I looked at the chair, a chair full of allusions to everyday life, and I had an almost tender feeling toward it. I kept watching the hangmen's movements. I was amazed that I had looked at these two men, before knowing who they were, without misgiving or reserve, just as we normally look at any fellow-creatures. Pursuing this thought made my head swim.

No sooner had they said that I should avoid the word 'hangman' than I saw taboos and prohibitions everywhere. Facing the small posts was a door. The chapel door. The condemned men were probably in there. Whenever one of the executioners dropped the top of the tool box, making a muffled sound, I clenched my teeth and the editor's jaw-muscle stood out in his cheek. Now and then one of the hangmen, with a small hammer, struck the clamps of the garrotting apparatus screwed into each of the posts, and though this made less noise than the falling box lid, it would be more significant for the condemned men, if they heard it. The warden made professional observations:

'The posts were set up yesterday afternoon.'

No one said a word. High above us, on the wall, the sentry's pacing could be heard, and outside the jail a barking dog. It sounded like the cheerful bark of a playful puppy. The warden added:

'The wages of the carpenters have gone up, but as you can imagine we never haggle over prices in this very special kind of work.'

At a convenient height the posts had a little seat where the condemned man was to sit. It was merely a plank reinforced underneath with metal supports. At the height of the neck, each post had two steel clamps fastened with thick screws. These clamps held the garrotting device, which looked like a fox trap, only smaller. Seeing that the executers of justice had finished the first part of their chore and were trying out the instruments, I approached. The one attending to the nearest posts looked at me, and after a moment's hesitation smiled. I also smiled and offered him my hand, introducing myself: 'Juan Echenique, editorial staff of *El Nacional*.' He looked very surprised, but finally shook hands with me, after wiping off the remains of grease with a rag. Then, not knowing what to do, he offered me the only chair. I sat down, careful not to crease the coats hanging on the back of the chair, but I felt that I was in such a ridiculous position that I got up again. Looking at the hangman I struggled between repugnance and curiosity. He was solid and massive. He put on his coat. His face had the expression of a frustrated family man.

I understood the mechanism of the garrotte when I saw it close at hand. It had two small rectangular metal frames cushioned with leather. These details which the hangmen arranged for the comfort of the condemned men—the cushioned iron collar, the little seat—absorbed all my attention. The front pieces of the collar could be opened by a spring, allowing the condemned man's neck to slip inside. Then they were again closed, and when the screw in the back of the post was turned one of the frames, or wings, of the iron collar delicately slid over the other, squeezing the necks until strangulation was produced, sometimes even disarticulating the cervical vertebrae.

The other hangman kept on humming softly:

> ...ungrateful fortune
> carried off my faithful lover...

Then he stopped. They were both silent and their silence was so impressive that when the rest of us spoke we whispered. The hangman I had greeted worked the garrotting device once more so that I could see it—he called it 'the cravat'—and I was gazing like one obsessed when the editor came up, took me by the arm, and led me away. The hangman looked at the two of us—it was a look lasting the fraction of a second—as if he had been surprised in something improper.

We came to a bulge in the moat where we saw four coffins lined up on the ground, open. The covers were leaning against the wall and numbers in white chalk were written on the black cloth. The editor asked:

'Do you want to go into the chapel to see the condemned men?'

No. I was afraid to meet their gaze. It would have been difficult to look at them. If my look were indifferent it would degrade them. If compassionate it would humiliate them. If simply curious it would hurt them. Furthermore the condemned men had lost a great deal of their importance for me and for the moment the hangmen were the heroes. I glanced at the other one, the one who was humming to himself, wondering: 'What kind of speaking voice does he have?' For he sang in a falsetto. He looked like the typical hangman in medieval tales.

The executioners were behind the first and third posts, waiting. 'They dress up in their best,' I was thinking, 'out of respect for the condemned men. Or out of respect for the mystery of death, perhaps.' The editor again suggested entering the chapel.

Glancing towards the door he added that before long now they would bring out the first one. I wished I could leave. I could not imagine myself seeing the executions. 'But by leaving,' I reflected, 'I won't change anything for they will kill those poor devils just the same.' Just then a corporal and two soldiers appeared on the wall to relieve the two sentinels. The relieved sentinel said to the corporal:

'Don't relieve me.'

I thought: 'That soldier wants to see the executions, or *the show*, as the corporal called it.' For the corporal had asked him:

'Do you want to see *the show?*"

I raised my head when I heard it.

I had not realized that they were bringing out the first condemned man. I wondered how it could be so undramatic. A little group of men walking. That was all. In the middle they had the so-called Sevilla.

In a monotonous voice someone was repeating words in Latin—a kind of litany. I stood on tiptoe to see the condemned man. The defense attorney was in the group that had just left the chapel. In front, walking backwards, was a brother of Peace and Charity carrying a rather large crucifix. The defense attorney offered Sevilla his arm, which the condemned man refused. Above the shoulder of the brother of Peace and Charity, who was trying to obstruct his view, the condemned man could see the posts. He looked at them one by one, from the first to the fourth. Then he looked up, but the bright lights made him blink his eyes. His hair was short but long in front and fell over his forehead. Something about him suggested the dryness of cork, and he seemed indifferent. He looked over the priest's shoulder again at the posts with the quickness of a bird: then at the defense attorney, as if he had never seen him before. All were silent except the priest muttering his prayers in a convalescent's tone as he continued to walk backward. At that moment I was thinking: 'The hangman is the only true priest for me now. He is the priest of an ancient rite still unexplained and not understood.'

Those surrounding the condemned man gave the impression that they wished to help him. They all treated him kindly and yet were leading him to death. In the gestures of the criminal there was a suggestion of virile modesty before that incongruity. When they stopped in front of the garrotte the priest stood to one side. The condemned man looked at the small device which the hangman was manipulating skilfully to open the clamps in front.

In his hand the hangman held two broad leather straps. He invited Sevilla to be seated. Sevilla remained standing, looking at the 'cravat' and saying nothing. The hangman continued pointing to the little seat. The condemned man, with a corner of his mouth twisted, tried to smile. Hangman and condemned man

16

looked at each other as father and son, or brothers, are wont to do. In the condemned there was the confidence of a common man who sees his own face in a mirror. The executioner said softly:

'Have a seat.'

'After you, sir,' the condemned man replied.

The joke sounded improper, but no one said a word. The hinted mocking of the executioner wounded us all. But the hangman said nothing. The other executioner came up, each of them took the condemned man by an arm, and between the two of them they obliged him gently to sit down. He was no sooner seated than the hangman with whom I had been talking put the leather strap around his waist, catching both of his arms with it and tying him to the post. Then he did the same thing to his feet.

All those accompanying the condemned man withdrew to one side except the priest, who continued holding the crucifix in front of him. The hangman pushed Sevilla's head back with a barber's gesture and the spring of the metallic clamp snapped shut in front. I was thinking: 'There he is. No one can save him now.' The condemned man's neck inside the trap, the executioner threw a black handkerchief over his head. At that moment the priest holding the crucifix withdrew and stood beside us next to the wall, praying softly.

The hangman took his place behind the post, and grasping the screw with both hands turned it. The condemned man shuddered as his head bent to one side, while under the handkerchief a snoring sound was heard. Sevilla's foot dug into the sand. Then the other executioner came up, put his hands on his colleague's, and continued the interrupted movement. The condemned man's shudder made the post creak. With gratitude my friend looked at his colleague who at once moved to the side of the third post with an expression of wounded dignity. Sevilla was still struggling on the garrotte. My eyes were fixed on the black handkerchief covering his head. All was still. One of the arc lights hissed, flashing slightly.

The hangman—my friend—remained beside the post, waiting.

17

Near me the priest was praying: 'Requiem aeternam...' The condemned man stirred. In the editor's cheek the large jaw-muscle was still prominent.

Some minutes later Sevilla appeared to be motionless and the prison physician came forward and took his hand in his. He shook his head. A moment later when he again felt Sevilla's pulse the middle finger quivered, and the doctor nodded. The hangman cleared his throat as if he were going to speak.

The priest with four or five others entered the chapel again, returning shortly with Piqueras, a stout man of grave, inborn solemnity. His profile was reminiscent of Roman medals. Just as he appeared the executioner spread a sheet over the dead Sevilla, covering the post completely and forming on the sand an immaculate cone of the height of a man. On the tip of the cone someone hung a small rosary. The nickel cross sparkled in the light. Then the hangman went to the second post and stood beside it. The front cross-pieces of the iron collar were already open. Piqueras, like Sevilla, felt obliged to make a show of cold curiosity, and after looking at the white cone asked:

'What day is today?'

'Monday,' the defense attorney told him.

Piqueras raised his right eyebrow before saying:

'And a fine way for the week to begin.'

But he was white as a sheet of paper. The priest walked backward muttering the prayers of the death agony. Piqueras, with his indifferent and joking air, seemed to want to pardon all of us. He looked at the hangman, surprised at the severe suit he was wearing. Recovering from his surprise he said jocosely:

'Well now, see you do a good job.'

Every word seemed incredibly significant. When the hangman was tying up Piqueras he noticed that the condemned man was trying to take something out of his coat pocket, and loosened the strap to help him. Piqueras hesitated an instant, then shrugged indifferently and said:

'What's the use? Go ahead.'

There was a strange composure in his tone. I supposed that he

18

had wanted to take out a woman's photograph. I was also thinking: 'His neck looks even stronger than Sevilla's and this is going to be more difficult.' The hangman pulled the strap tight against the post to make the buckle reach the necessary hole. Then he put the second strap around the condemned man's feet. Just as he had done with Sevilla he pushed Piqueras' head back, making his neck fit inside the little iron square, and when this was closed —into all these movements the hangman put a calculated rapidity —he covered his head with the black handkerchief. At once he turned the screw, but not so hard as before. Distrustful and ready to intervene if necessary, the other executioner watched. He approached, looked at the apparatus behind, and whispered something. Then he went to the tool box, took out a metallic goad-shaped hook, slipped the curved part behind the condemned man's knees and pulled hard. Piqueras' body slumped forward on the little seat and his neck slipped down a little. At that instant a sigh was heard. The hangman gave half a turn to the right, and we heard a nasal moan surprisingly delicate in a human mass like Piqueras. The condemned man took a long time to die. Three times the physician went to feel his pulse, always shaking his head.

I looked at the priest still muttering his prayers. Under the blue sky of the dawn the arc lights and reflectors were an extravagant luxury. The hangman continued to look 'nowhere'. At each creaking of the post the other executioner turned his head with a half indolent, half prudent gesture.

When the physician declared that death had come Piqueras had been on the garrotte twenty minutes. The hangman verified it with his watch and from his box took a sheet, unfolded it slowly, and covered the body and the post. Instead of one white cone there were two. The priest hung another little rosary on top and the light played delicately on the metal settings.

Some time elapsed before they brought out the third, Banzo. Amidst so much kind attention Banzo, who was small and weak, like the others felt the need to show his unconcern. His carelessness also had something clownish about it. He did not look at the image of Jesus held in front of him by the priest, but at the base of the cross, which was wide and polished with a small rectangular mirror set in a narrow golden frame. When he reached the post the executioner—the other one, to whom I had not spoken —put his hands on the condemned man's shoulders and obliged him to be seated. He had barely done so when his feet and waist were bound to the post, and as his head was about to be covered he asked for something. The executioner, impatient, asked:

'What do you want?'

'The crucifix closer.'

The priest went up to the condemned man who kissed the foot of the cross. In the little mirror with the golden frame he kissed his own mouth with a bitter gesture. The priest said to him:

'Sinner, ask God for forgiveness.'

'If I were God,' said Banzo smiling, 'and He were in my place, I would easily forgive Him.'

The hangman covered his head with the handkerchief and gave a complete turn to the screw. The seat creaked and the condemned man must have died almost instantly. The prison physician pronounced him dead three minutes later.

The priest had not had time to finish his prayers when the post was covered with the white sheet, forming a third white cone against the wall of reddish brick. Having caught the executioner's haste he hurriedly put the rosary on top of the cone and withdrew. The tip of the rosary, with the little white cross, dangled over a wrinkle in the sheet swinging gently. Only the fourth post remained uncovered.

Navarrete came last. It was now broad daylight. Under the blue sky the arc lights were rose-colored. One of them continued hissing. Navarrete was a tall thin man who had lost the last remains of moral, and even physical, strength. Surrounded by the group that had accompanied the other three, and preceded by the same priest, Navarrete was panting with distress, like a fish out of water. He walked aimlessly, and when he reached the post he kept on walking, neither seeing the hangman nor realizing that the execution instrument was before him. The hangman took him by the arm, and put one foot behind his so that when he backed up he stumbled and fell on to the little seat. The priest with folded hands was saying: 'Miserere mei Domine...'

Before I realized what was happening the condemned man's head was covered with the black cloth. The strap around his waist was so tight he looked as if he were cut in two. Navarrete hardly moved. Soon afterwards the physician pronounced him dead and the executioner covered the post with the sheet upon which the priest placed the fourth rosary. Against the wall stood the four white cones, immaculate under the arc lights with their quick blue and rose flashes.

The Brothers of Peace and Charity carried the empty coffins one by one to the foot of the posts. The judge, the defense lawyers, and witnesses were taking leave of the warden with amiable phrases. The hangmen came out of the chapel where they had gone to pray. They uncovered the corpses. Above the iron collar of the garrotte the squeezed necks seemed to have formed double chins lapping over the ridge of the jawbone. Their eyes were open and bulging and the crossed retinas revealed two or three different colors. The Brothers of Peace and Charity took charge of the corpses.

Banzo and Navarrete had a small spot of blood on the front of their necks. When I mentioned this to the warden he explained that the Burgos hangman had invented a gadget considerably improving the iron collar. It was a kind of injection needle which, when the screw was turned, pierced the under side of the jaw, fixing the tongue inside the mouth. This executioner had the reputation of leaving his condemned men looking 'as if they were making a formal call,' correctly seated and without any signs of apparent violence. I was thinking, obsessed: 'None of the condemned men feared or hated the executioner. Not to fear or hate the one who is going to kill you is prodigiously noble.' Beside the condemned men and executioners we were ridiculous beings full of frivolous preoccupations and absurd interests.

The light of dawn and that of the arc lights mingled above the four coffins. My hangman friend was pale. I could not have looked any better. The editor looked as if he had been disinterred. I went up to the hangman and said to him, lowering my voice:

'I would like to have a more leisurely talk with you, if you don't mind. Can you meet me at the San Ginés café at three o'clock?'

'Yes, sir. I will be very happy to meet you there.'

I shook hands with him again and went out behind the editor, who was evidently scandalized.

'Man,' he said to me, 'that just isn't done.'

He was referring to my shaking hands with the executioner.

From a prison telephone I called my newspaper and dictated the report to a stenographer.

The editor stayed for breakfast with the warden. They had invited me, but the idea of eating in that place upset me. Although I tried to conceal my uneasiness with excuses the warden was aware of it and remarked that life was a series of uninterrupted harsh events, and that it would never be any better, adding with a certain satisfaction:

'In Spain, at least, the death penalty is inflicted without the shedding of blood.'

Then he went on at great length about the horrors of the French guillotine. I left. Out in the street I saw groups of curious people looking at the black flag hoisted above the stone arch of the main entrance. Then they looked at me, taking me for the hangman, perhaps. This did not offend me. I was only thinking that I was too young to be an executioner. And I said to myself: 'I have just seen four men legally killed. It is horrible, but also trivial. It would be useless for me to dramatize and speculate about it.'

I got into a taxi, stopped at a bar, and contrary to custom ordered black coffee. Home in bed, I tossed about with wide-open eyes until midday. About one I got up and prepared to keep my appointment. At half past two I was entering the San Ginés café by the Caballero de Gracia Street door. 'I must understand once for all the moral justification of hangmen,' I said to myself.

22

'The execution of one man, or four, is unimportant, but the hangman, no. If the hangman's existence is indefensible, we are all lost. But we may be lost anyway.'

In the café I looked around for pleasant objects, but even when my glance rested on the lips or eyes of a girl I saw only her neck and calculated the possibilities of breaking her spinal column or at least producing strangulation. I felt a certain curiosity about this preoccupation. When I was most abstracted I heard somebody drawing up a chair beside me.

I turned and found the hangman. He was wearing a grey suit, white shirt, black tie and hat. A woman gave him an approving glance. The hangman had shaved before coming in spite of the fact that his face was clean when I saw him at the prison. The personality of his face was in the eyebrows, in the firm and some-what prominent frontal lobes. As he talked he gave the impres-sion of a discreet, melancholy and affable man. He read the re-port of the executions in the paper. He said that he was worried, remembering the difficulties he had had.

'And yet,' he added, 'I should not be surprised, because in twenty years I have never succeeded in executing a single con-demned man by myself.'

He lowered his voice so no one would hear. He looked around somewhat uneasily. At the next table there were two women and a four-year-old boy who turned his face and stubbornly fixed his big blue eyes on the hangman.

'We must leave here,' he said. 'The children are staring at me. They always stare at me.'

We went out into the street in silence. As we walked along I realized that it was very comfortable to be able to talk without having to look at him directly. People were coming and going with that lightness of springtime, when they go out for the first time without wraps. It was a beautiful day, though not sunny. Lilacs perfumed the air, as always in the month of April in Madrid.

I again told the hangman my name and he revealed his to me. He *revealed* it because, as he warned me, he usually kept it a

23

secret. His name was Ramiro Vallemediano. I remembered having told him mine twice in the prison, but I supposed that he had not caught it either time. I told him that I very much wanted to hear him talk about himself.

'Me? Talk about myself?'

'Yes. I would like to know all about you.'

We sauntered along, unconsciously heading for a park close by. Dreamily the hangman repeated: 'Echenique, Juan Echenique. . . .'

I asked him where he came from. He told me that he came from a northern province and that he could remember the village house where he was born.

'But those details interest you?' he asked.

Listening to him talk about his village home I reconstructed it in my imagination. A large room on the ground floor, with a fireplace, and inside the fireplace, in the corners on both sides of the metal refractor, two windows. How strange! Two windows inside the fireplace. Both had the elongated form of castle embrasures, revealing the imposing thickness of the wall. Below and far away one could see the gray meanderings of two rivers among broad green and yellow meadows. The hangman related these details as if he would apologize for being prolix. The darkness of the fireplace made the tints of that landscape stand out and at times, depending on how the light fell, it was projected upside down on the opposite wall of the room. There were miniature ships and incrusted pilgrim shells on the consoles and other pieces of furniture.

The hangman wondered if I was paying attention and looked at me, saying:

'Pardon me, but before going on I would like to ask you a question. Were you able to sleep after seeing the executions?'

'No.'

'Thinking about the condemned men?'

'No. One execution, or four, are not important.'

'Of course,' said the hangman smiling. 'Every month there are hundreds of illegal executions. It's regrettable, but everyone gets

24

used to that. And will you be good enough to tell me what you were thinking about when you did not sleep?'

'About you.'

We were both silent. We continued walking and the people passed by our side without looking at us. The hangman, Ramiro Vallemediano, after a long pause said:

'My mother was unmarried when I was born.'

He glanced out of the corner of his eye trying to see what impression that made on me and added, smiling:

'You can imagine the scandal. You know how peasants are. Neither my grandmother nor my mother could stay in the village. They went to live with a relative in another province where my mother passed for a widow. But really, are you interested in all this?'

I was 'watching' him talk. There were times, I mean, when the sense of his words escaped me because I was concentrating on his gesture and tone of voice.

'To make matters worse,' the hangman continued, 'the family lost everything and when grandmother died my mother had to rely on her own resources. Unmindful of what people would say she returned to the village and sold the house, which was difficult because people had taken to saying that two rose-bushes growing in the garden distilled blood and talked through the night. Some relatives turned an old half-ruined house over to her and refused to have anything more to do with her.'

Ramiro Vallemediano—the hangman—went on talking and I did not lose the slightest nuance of his expression. Soon after settling in that house his mother renewed relations with her lover. Everybody knew it. He was a married man and had not recognized Ramiro as his son in the civil register. 'Neither the humility nor the good manners of my mother,' said the hangman, 'were of any avail and the "society" folks of the village definitely closed their doors to her. The peasants, naturally, took advantage of that opportunity to submit the descendant of a rich and noble house to constant humiliations.'

Ramiro was born on a day in March at three o'clock in the

morning. As he said, he liked to imagine that night. 'It must have been windy. I have a morbid preoccupation with the wind. Look there, look.' A gust of wind was whirling the dry leaves around the base of the statue of Carlos IV. The sound of the swishing leaves gave a certain depth to the evening silence. Ramiro Valle-mediano kept looking at the whirlwind. Finally the leaves came to rest under the basin of a marble fountain, but a little nearer another and smaller whirlwind formed and moved along towards the pool. Since the evening was disagreeable the avenues were deserted. A nurse passed quickly by, pushing a baby-carriage. A child a little over a year old turned to look at the executioner with growing attention. The nurse slowed down to ask us the time. The baby continued staring at the hangman with wide eyes.

After a while the hangman said:

'The peasants of my country are afraid of the wind. That's why they make the sign of the cross over their mouth when they yawn. Some say it's a medieval superstition, but I believe that this was done before the Christian era and that the cross is not a cross but a cabalistic sign.'

I looked at the hangman, surprised. He was evidently a cultivated man. Again he asked if these confidences did not bore me and I told him no.

'I hope,' said the hangman, 'that you are not one of those humanitarian writers who want to set the world right with comprehension, tolerance and love.'

I laughed and said nothing. The hangman waited for me to say something because, perhaps, he did not understand my curiosity. In fact, it would have been hard for me to explain it to myself. Then the hangman, turning up his coat collar, said:

'It's spring, but cold.'

Since I said nothing, he added:

'In recent years millions of beings have died like those four in the prison moat.'

There was another small and graceful whirlwind of dust beside the marble basin of the fountain. I watched until it dissolved. So did the hangman.

2

R AMIRO was quiet for a moment and then he said:
'When I was a child my mother told me tales that made me
cry with pain, and then she would tell everybody how tender-
hearted I was.'

Near the house where he was born was an immense rocky
ledge adjoining a cliff formed by the slow action of the rain. This
cliff was called 'the butte' and from the top of it suicides would
leap. Although the village was not very large never a year passed
without someone jumping off. Every suicide left his beret or cap
up there, on the edge of the precipice, with a stone on top to keep
the wind from blowing it away, and between the stone and cap
a half-smoked cigarette. No one ever failed to comply with this re-
quisite, which formed in some way part of the ritual, so far as
anyone could remember. 'I asked my mother,' said Ramiro,
'why men went up there and killed themselves and she answered:
"I don't know. But I have also had the idea at times." When
she told me this I was six or seven years old.'

Ramiro learned to assist at Mass and when he was eight years
old he asked his mother one day—in all childhood innocence—if
priests wore petticoats underneath their cassocks. 'My mother told
me that someone had taught me those saucy ways and that such
things were not to be thought, much less said. Then she laughed.
I had the impression that I had said something terribly improper, however, in spite of my mother's laugh.'

Among his favorite childhood images were angels, devils, and
God himself. He saw God once painted with a long white beard,
a golden triangle behind his head, and grave and gentle eyes.
This religious print made quite an impression on him. It made
him feel afraid, and protected as well. Ramiro looked at the sky
on cloudy and windy days and now and then thought he saw
God's beard. Or the triangle.

Life for him was a continuous miracle. When he was thirsty

27

and drank, he felt extraordinary pleasure. The same thing happened when he ate and went to bed after playing all day long. He believed that God gave these pleasures to him. Only to him. And as if that were not enough, he dreamed. Dreaming brought him new pleasures, which he considered exclusively his own. Sometimes he prayed and asked God for toys and gifts, as if He were his father. When it stormed and hail covered the orchards the peasants complained. The grape harvest, the apple crop, were ruined. But Ramiro found magic in that shower of little crystal balls that trembling melted in his hand. At his first communion he requested heavy hailstorms, his mother having told him that whatever he asked for as he received the Sacrament would be granted. He was hurt by the peasants' dismay but it was a grandiose spectacle. And God had granted it to him. The storm ended with a marvelous rainbow. To Ramiro this seemed proof of God's good will towards him.

He had the reputation of being a smart lad. His intelligence was beginning to be proverbial, which surprised no peasant, for a bastard had to be more intelligent than a legitimate son. Ramiro let the people say whatever they pleased and considered being a bastard—he did not know the meaning of the word—a privilege. At first his mother had told him his father was dead. Ramiro identified his father with God.

The hangman paused and I asked him who his father was.

'A farmer in a neighboring town reputedly handsome and fond of women. As soon as I learned to read I started devouring all the books that fell into my hands. The schoolmaster loaned me some, the priest others, and still others I picked up wherever I could. Novels, essays on agriculture, jurisprudence, poetry, the Zaragozan calendar, and prayers to Santa Rita.'

He remembered his mother coming home one day, sad and in tears, saying that she had met a petty nobleman in the plaza who upbraided her in a somewhat sarcastic tone:

'And a fine upbringing you're giving the little bastard, who only knows how to chatter and to boast. With the trade you're teaching him, how is he going to take care of you in your old age?'

28

Ramiro was then twelve years old. He told his mother that each day of the following week he would devote to learning a different trade, and that in a short time he would know them all. Monday weaving, Tuesday masonry, Wednesday wool-dressing, Thursday tailoring, Friday carpentry, Saturday the smith's trade. The next week he would learn six more: the cobbler's, harness-maker's, barber's, scissors-grinder's, glazier's and house-painter's. He already knew the sacristan's duties since he had learned to assist at Mass. His mother said that to learn each one of those trades months and maybe years were necessary. Ramiro denied this:

'That may be true for others, but not for me.'

Later he realized that his mother considered him inferior to the other children because of his being a bastard, as if she herself had had nothing to do with the bastardy. This reflection gave him a certain childish skepticism, but sharpened his wits. He began to do exactly as he had promised. Monday he went to a weaver's workshop, and at noon, after six hours of painstaking work, he knew how to weave 'for the rich' and 'for the poor,' making the woof much thicker for the rich. With the thick woof more thread was used, but it also made better cloth and fetched a higher price. The thick woof was made by stepping on the treadle three times and then rising on his toes and falling back on his heels twice for every back-and-forward movement of the shuttle. For the poor he only stepped on the treadle once and a half. It went faster, but the cloth was cheap.

The boy did all this with a secret joy. It had taken him three days to learn, however, and not one, as he had said. An old weaver had explained interesting things to him, among others the language of the looms. For the looms talked. Some in verse and others in prose. His sang a silly song:

> ... and the
> maiden was in the well,
> the Beautiful maiden ...

On Wednesday evening Ramiro took home to his mother half

29

a yard of cloth woven by himself. The next day he went to a wool-dresser's and at daybreak began to card and comb wool. The master also told him fables of his trade. About a sheep-shearer and a sheep that refused to be sheared, and the traveler in need of a mantle who in the end turned out to be an angel. The mantle had to be made of that particular sheep's wool, and the sheep, of course, was the devil.

It also took him longer to learn to card than he had counted on. But two months later, when the boy had learned all the village trades, his mother told him that she was astonished by his talents and would give him permission to do whatever he wanted to, so long as he was always a good boy. Ramiro did not know what to do: the weaver's trade was heavy and sad, in spite of the songs; the wool-dresser's healthy and happy, but not very productive; the mason's dirty; the tailor's more suitable for women. He decided that he did not want to work unless he had a more important purpose than earning his living.

'What kind of purpose?' asked his mother, without understanding.

'Oh well, something very good or very bad that makes people think.'

'Think what?'

His mother suddenly burst out laughing and hugged him saying: 'The tricks that you don't think up no one in the world will think of.' Then she added that Ramiro ought to go to Sigena and become the page of the abbess, a second cousin of hers. This convent was for women of the aristocracy, she said, and enjoyed royal privileges. Like all those who feel themselves disparaged, Ramiro's mother often spoke of her noble relatives.

Meanwhile, Ramiro was growing up. Seeing him so big his mother complained:

'Now you won't be able to be the abbess's page because you have surely lost your innocence.'

Ramiro supposed that she was referring to childish innocence in matters of love. He had naturally lost that some time ago. The boy considered it a matter of pride.

Ramiro continued borrowing books from the priest, from the schoolmaster, and from a rich family spending the summer there. He read everything, with no plan of any kind, and since he had no critical spirit he believed it all. This confused him at times, because the teacher's books did not always agree with the priest's. A book of the teacher's called *The Renaissance* discussed Popes who got drunk, had private hangmen and poisoned their rivals in love or politics. Ramiro told the priest. He found the priest's indignation with the schoolmaster so excessive, that he began to wonder if everything *The Renaissance* said might not be true. Ramiro realized that with this book he possessed secrets that increased his importance in the eyes of the priest. The priest remarked occasionally to the teacher when he met him on the street:

'Your books are sowing poison among the youth.'

About this time Ramiro, now fourteen years old, was dreaming of the apothecary's daughter. Very strange dreams they were. He saw her in the form of a wax doll, nude, melting and burning everything it touched. The melting wax boiled in tiny bubbles, making a light sputtering sound.

There was a very old hermitage in the village and the city council decided to have some frescoes painted on the vaulted ceiling and walls, and two or three oils for the altar screens in the chapels. They sent for a painter from the capital. His name was Don Raimundo, and he was a bilious and ill-tempered man. Ramiro went to see him and asked to be his apprentice, but the stranger refused. 'You bastards are rascals,' he said. Ramiro, who felt very superior to that man for some unknown reason, did not take offense, and promised to be faithful, humble and honest. This last was important because gold-dust was to be used on the tunics of several saints. Actually, the real gold was to be used only on the figures of Jesus and his immediate family. Imitation gilt would be used on Jesus' grandparents and the other saints. Don Raimundo did not want to take on Ramiro. Ramiro was sorry because he wanted, he said, to learn how to paint.

'You're not doing it to earn wages then?' the painter asked.

31

This put a different face on the matter and he accepted him. They set to work. Ramiro was thinking about the apothecary's daughter with melancholy and wondering: 'If I wrote her a letter, would she answer?' Meanwhile he devoted himself furiously to helping Don Raimundo.

In the chapel he watched the master work. How he used the oil, turpentine, what he did to paint in tempera and how he prepared the wall before applying the colors. In a few days he felt informed on these matters and began to ask more important questions. Why yellow and blue made a green color, why sienna and rose and white gave the tone of human flesh, which colors advanced and which ones receded. The painter, knowing that at heart Ramiro scorned him, seemed annoyed by his eager diligence. Sometimes, instead of answering, he threw a spatula at him from the scaffolding, or the stick on which he rested his hand and supported his wrist. But after dodging Ramiro would repeat the question, feigning a certain humility, and finally the painter could do nothing but say:

'I use that color because it is a cold color.'

Ramiro said to himself: 'I wonder what the warm colors are?' Linking one revelation to another he eventually succeeded in having complete ideas on the subject. He had bought himself pencils and a box of pastels and was practicing at home with success. Three weeks later he felt that he knew as much as his master, and even dared to give him advice. This infuriated Don Raimundo, who ironically said to him:

'Hush, Tintoretto. Shut up, Velázquez.'

When he went down town Ramiro looked up these names in the encyclopedia in the mayor's office, and read extraordinary things. Velázquez had been a painter of the King. Goya too. Tintoretto belonged to the school of Venice. Since Don Raimundo's name was not in the encyclopedia and, on the other hand, other living painters were listed, he decided that this ill-tempered artist could not be important. This coincided with his first impression of the painter. Ramiro became more and more contemptuous.

When they were ready to begin using the gold, the deputy mayor came in person with a small leather pouch full of the precious dust. He inspected the painter's work and seemed satisfied with his having put a grapevine and ripe grapes in the empty spaces of the two main chapels. But among the birds on the grapevine there was a crow. A crow sitting on a runner. The deputy mayor, scratching above his ear, said:

'Maestro Raimundo, I never saw a crow eating grapes.'

The painter told him that it was a vegetarian crow and that deputy mayors everywhere were ignoramuses. The peasant replied that he knew this but didn't like being reminded of it by others. Things did not go beyond that. Ramiro enjoyed these incidents, but he worked industriously at helping the painter just the same.

The deputy mayor held the little leather sack in his hand and the painter, every time he needed it, would take a little gold dust with the tip of his brush. The fact that they did not leave the little pouch with him was impertinent enough, but he said nothing and went on working. Three days after they had begun using the gold, the apprentice noticed that at the bottom of the glass containing the sticky mixture a yellow and rather thick sediment was being deposited. The sediment increased, and when it was about a centimetre thick it disappeared mysteriously. Possessor of this secret, Ramiro bided his time. The deputy mayor kept insisting that crows did not go to vineyards to eat grapes but to rubbish heaps to eat meat, and the apprentice chimed in:

'Besides, a crow weighs as much as a hen, and the runner he is sitting on couldn't support anything bigger than a lark.'

The painter threw his jar of brushes at Ramiro's head. The apprentice dodged and the jar smashed against a column. The deputy mayor said that such manners were savage and that he might have killed the boy.

'One bastard more or less, what difference would it make?' the painter retorted.

The deputy mayor retorted that the bastards of his town were worth more than the legitimate sons of neighboring towns, and

33

infinitely more than the roving artisans who didn't know what a crow or lark ate. The painter felt insulted at being called an artisan, and came down the ladder taking off his smock. He refused to continue painting. The apprentice offered to finish the two chapels and vaulted ceiling. The deputy mayor could not decide such an important question by himself and said that he would consult with the municipality. When Don Raimundo saw that the boy's offer was being taken seriously, he demanded that they pay him for the work done immediately, but the deputy mayor said that he could not decide this either, and that he was very much afraid his fellow aldermen would refuse, since the work was unfinished. At this the painter seemed to go mad. When his anger was at its height the apprentice added:

'Before claiming any salary it would be better to return the gold.'

He told what he had seen and the peasant had the painter imprisoned on the spot. From behind the bars of the jail facing the patio of the town hall the poor man cried that it was an affront to culture and that he had relatives who would appeal to the King. As was natural—out of community loyalty—the whole town took part in the incident, siding with Ramiro against the painter. Everyone, that is, except the boy's mother, who sympathized with the old painter and went to the jail to see him two or three times. Ramiro could not understand this.

The Council finally agreed to free the painter, who left town cursing. Ramiro was commissioned to finish the chapel, and the first thing he did was to erase the crow and put a lark in its place. The aldermen were well pleased. They had complete confidence in the bastard, though not so much that they left the little leather bag with him.

The work finished they paid Ramiro the amount promised to Don Raimundo, and the boy went to the priest and gave him half to send to the old painter. This gesture impressed the village very favorably, although Ramiro's mother was frantic. She went about the town saying that her son was her cross and her shame. When she saw that Ramiro was becoming important she

34

began to lift her head high and at the same time, out of a curious spirit of contradiction, to feel ashamed of him.

A celebration was being planned to inaugurate the hermitage and give the people from outside an opportunity to see the pictures, but the boy asked them to wait because he had heard Don Raimundo say that 'the best painter was time,' that with the passing of the days the colors blended, giving a finer tone to the whole. In his innocence Ramiro believed that two or three weeks would be enough to perform the miracle. Meanwhile the priest approved the entire work, gave it his blessing, and stated publicly that the lad had great talent. Ramiro felt so grateful to him that he finally declared that the vices of a sixteenth-century pope did not compromise religion, and especially in modern times. The priest wrote out some sentences in Latin for the young painter to put at the foot of the pediment in the main chapel. Translated they said: 'On the third day of July of this year of Grace, 19.., Ramiro Vallemediano, citizen of this town, fifteen years of age, finished painting the two chapels commissioned by the illustrious municipal government and the Holy Confraternity of the Rosary —*Laus Deo*.' The boy simulated a small marble plaque with four silver nails on which these words were written. At the foot of another retable he signed: *Ramiro Vallemediano fecit*.

On the day of the inauguration not only the villagers but people from other neighboring towns came. The only one who refused to attend was the boy's mother. He could not understand.

Nevertheless the celebration was a great success. But something unforeseen happened. Dominating the vault were several figures, and above them floated a very beautiful angel, with one leg naked halfway above the knee, and the opposite side of the shoulder and chest also bare. The angel's face was that of the apothecary's daughter. The girl's father, offended, asked the painter to lengthen the tunic and close it above, or else change the face. Ramiro said that the similarity was accidental, and that an angel is an angel.

The priest himself had to call the apothecary to the chapter house and tell him that, as St. Paul said, 'to the pure all things are pure.' The apothecary did not know exactly what the priest meant by that, but he kept quiet. When Ramiro learned of the priest's protection he decided not to divulge the life of Pope Alexander VI.

Later, in the background of the vineyard, half hidden behind a stone cross, a demon with the apothecary's face was discovered. But since it had two very visible horns, and the apothecary's wife—now dead—had caused some gossip, the model believed it more prudent to act as if he were in no way involved. As for his daughter, she was spending the vacation in the capital with her aunt and uncle. When she returned her friends told her what had happened and she went to see the hermitage, and felt quite flattered.

Ramiro, meanwhile, had painted three or four portraits of notable persons in the village who paid him well, and his house was swimming in abundance. One of those who paid best was the petty nobleman who had insulted his mother some years back. Ramiro, then, was reigning in the village and beginning to attract notice in the province. But his mother seemed exasperated and offended by it all.

Finally the boy met the apothecary's daughter at a birthday party. They were playing forfeits and the loser had to do what the others demanded. When it was the turn of the apothecary's daughter they agreed that she should dance in the middle of the group while the others sang 'La Tarara.' The girl was shy about dancing alone, so her friends ordered Ramiro to accompany her. The future hangman stepped out into the center of the group. When the girl saw him she backed away. They all protested and obliged her to be friendly and cordial. They clapped their hands in rhythm and sang:

> La Tarara has
> a silken shawl;
> she will show it off
> in the Rosaleda.
> La Tarara, yes,
> La Tarara, no;

36

With her arms raised, and remaining in the same spot, she made swaying movements, which could not fail to give a certain voluptuous impression. Her cheeks were flaming. She stopped suddenly, saying that Ramiro had looked at her in a special way. The boy stopped too. Everyone protested and to encourage them they pushed them towards each other and continued singing:

> La Tarara, yes,
> La Tarara, no;
> La Tarara, mother,
> I will dance it so.

When the dance was over the two of them had become friends and felt as if they had known each other all their lives. She took him aside:

'It seems all right to me,' she told him, 'for you to have painted me in the hermitage, but you shouldn't paint me "underneath." How do you know if my legs are pretty or not above the knee?'

Before Ramiro's beatific expression she put her hand over her mouth as if she wished—too late—to take back what she had said.

The boy looked around:

'What I would like is to be alone with you, to tell you something.'

'It can't be good, if you are afraid for others to hear,' she said nervously. But then she became very serious and added, lowering her voice:

'At two in the afternoon my father always has a nap and I keep shop alone in the pharmacy.'

She blushed, and realizing that Ramiro was looking at her forehead, her cheeks, she blushed all the more. She decided to leave, and the haste she put into her goodbyes to her friends showed Ramiro that their appointment was as important to her as to him.

Ramiro's mother was greedily hoarding all the money earned by her son while at the same time wearing an injured look.

During a quarrel she called him 'son-of-a-bitch,' which astonished the boy and then made him laugh.

Ramiro left to keep his appointment with the apothecary's daughter. Everything went as planned. The pharmacy was on one side of the plaza, very close to Ramiro's house. At one in the afternoon the streets were deserted. The pharmacy was full of large old earthen jars inscribed with Latin names. The wall facing the street was entirely taken up by the door and two show-windows, one on either side. In the one on the left there was an immense blue globe full of a greenish liquid. On the globe was the figure of a nude Mercury with wings on his feet and helmet, and a caduceus in his hand. In the other window there was a stone bust with the brain disclosed, several packages of gauze and cotton, and at the back a garland of scagliola flowers with a sign saying: *Mens sana in corpore sano.*

Ramiro offered her his hand. She put hers out of reach on her shoulder.

'I think,' she said, 'that it is very soon for you to give me your hand, but if you have come to make a declaration of love you can begin whenever you like.'

Ramiro did not know what to say. Finally he took a paper out of his pocket:

'I wrote you a poem.'

'Read it to me.'

'No. It will be better if you read it yourself when you are alone.'

'Then,' she said, tucking it in her bosom, 'make your declaration of love.'

He went towards her, and lowering his voice said:

'I am fonder of you than of life itself.'

She backed away:

'It looks as if you want to eat me up. Besides,' she added after a strained silence, 'you shouldn't say "I am fond of you" but "I love you." Because "I am fond of you," ' she insisted, "sounds as if you want to eat me up.'

She spoke with quickened breath. It looked as if there was

not room for so much emotion in her gently heaving breast. Ramiro asked:

'And you?'

'It's too soon for an answer. The most that I can do is let you kiss me.'

The boy took a step towards her and she, looking at the glass door worrying lest someone enter, became very nervous. She raised a hand to keep Ramiro back. Then she entered the little laboratory. Ramiro hesitated an instant, approached the green curtains covering the entrance, and finally went in too. He walked up to her and embraced her. As the girl drew away she leaned against a lower shelf full of wide-mouthed bottles with glass stoppers. Ramiro still held her in his arms and kissed her. He felt her tight warm lips. He went on kissing her. She squirmed without too much resistance. Both of them were breathing hard. Some of the little bottles behind her toppled over. Ramiro did not let go. When the girl could speak, she said:

'What a brute! Don't you think so? It looked as if you wanted to eat me up.'

On the shelf two bottles were overturned and open. Out of one had spilled granules of glycerine-phosphate and out of the other highly concentrated strychnine. Steps were heard on the inside stairs and Ramiro, making ready to fly, said:

'When you have read the poem, send me your answer.'

'Me? No. I can't write you. That would be a rendezvous.'

Ramiro left and the girl put the granules in the flasks, carelessly mixing them, and set the bottles back in place. The following week, before Ramiro could see her again, he learned that she was very ill, and then the same day heard that her father, the apothecary, was dead. It was tremendous and unexpected news. Precisely because Ramiro did not care for the apothecary, he felt more pained and guilty. As for the girl, she was still gravely ill, they said.

It so happened that the pharmacist was in the habit of giving his daughter, and taking himself, glycerine-phosphate of calcium. And instead of those granules they had taken strychnine.

39

The entire village made all sorts of conjectures and wild guesses, not knowing what to think. Ramiro did not go to bed for two nights. When he heard that the investigations revealed strychnine in the bottle of glycerine-phosphate he felt guilty and seriously considered going to the suicides' butte to jump off.

A circuit judge from outside the town arrived with two or three secretaries and detectives. They questioned Ramiro and Aurora, the apothecary's daughter. She denied having touched the bottles, but Ramiro confessed what had happened. They then locked the boy in the village jail. Ramiro's mother seemed pleased and spoke to the judge about her son's evil instincts.

The physician reported that Aurora was steadily improving. She would soon be well. Ramiro spent three days in jail before being released. This seemed to disappoint his mother.

Ramiro felt responsible for the apothecary's death. In vain he repeated to himself that she had turned over the bottles and mixed up the contents. 'But if I had not gone to the shop,' he thought, 'nothing would have happened.' For three weeks Ramiro did not answer his mother when she questioned him, brooding constantly, especially at dusk. He was thinking about God and religion. Watching the clouds over the butte he had the impression that from there the dead popes were looking down, upbraiding him. Aurora was still ill and people were saying that she had grown fat, bloated and ugly. Ramiro could not believe that beauty could disappear so easily.

Finally he left the house one day to stroll in the cemetery. Many graves had marble stones, but the pharmacist's had only a wooden cross. Looking at the heaped up earth forming the little mound, Ramiro said to himself: 'That earth on top is the earth that was left over, and it is outside because the place it had before is now occupied by the coffin.' And he stared until he saw the face of the old apothecary at the foot of the cross. All the other dead seemed really dead to him, all except the apothecary. Ramiro tried to imagine himself dead and buried, also, but he could not. 'We will never know what life is,' he murmured. 'Or death.' He heard a cheerful, jovial voice beside him. The grave-

40

digger. He was a peasant with merry little eyes, as the eyes of those employed in funeral tasks are wont to be, and he said:

'Now the husband and wife are reunited here.'

Then he added:

'They evidently didn't get along any too well in this life.'

Ramiro did not answer. As he left the cemetery he felt the soft earth, the hollow spaces under his feet. Outside he discovered three small sheets of paper in a pocket of his coat, the rough draft of the poem he had given Aurora a few weeks earlier. He tore it to shreds, tossing the pieces away into the air. Back in the village he went to see her. She was up now and being cared for by an aunt. What the people were saying was true. The girl was very fat, one of her eyebrows had almost disappeared, and the skin on her face was peeling. In some places it was red, in others white and shining like mother-of-pearl.

Ramiro left with a heavy heart. Soon after that he decided to leave the village. He asked his mother for money and she told him she had none. When she refused she blushed, and Ramiro pitied her for that blush.

Aware of his pity Ramiro's mother threw back her head and started calling him murderer and poisoner. Then she went out and started talking secretively in the neighboring houses. She was keeping the money hidden, she said, saving it up for the entrance dowry required in the convent of Sigena where she intended to take the veil.

A few days later something unexpected happened. Everybody was again beginning to talk about the poisonings in the apothecary's house as of a criminal act that had gone unpunished. A neighbor said that she had seen Ramiro enter the pharmacy 'many times' in the days preceding the tragedy. Ramiro, feeling guilty of the apothecary's death and Aurora's illness, considered himself lost. He did not know what might happen, but he had terrible premonitions.

He went to see Aurora and found her more bloated and ugly than before. But she had memorized the poem and recited it to him, saying afterwards, very seriously, in front of her aunt, that

41

Ramiro had poisoned her father and wanted to kill both of them. Very sad and utterly bewildered, Ramiro left.

People were saying that he was going to be put in prison again. One night he fled, walking by night and sleeping by day, as he had read in old stories. He recalled his mother's last words: "I don't know what happened in the apothecary's house, but if you go to the gallows some day I will be unable to do anything to save you.' He received the impression that his mother hoped he would end up on the gallows.

Walking by night Ramiro became familiar with the moon and stars. Sometimes he also walked by day and mingled with the people. But he was afraid. He saw something antagonistic, unknown and terrible in others.

When he walked by night and at daybreak saw the rose-colored sky and crystalline horizons, he remembered the apothecary's daughter who had the same coloring as the dawn. Like it the girl seemed to be inflated and filled with expanding rose and blue and nacre gases. 'Perhaps she will be beautiful again some day,' Ramiro thought.

He didn't wander very far from the town, not more than a two-day journey. He remarked to himself now and then: 'My mother is behaving like my worst enemy. Why? Am I not just the same as I always was? And am I not her son?' He could not comprehend exactly what it was that so offended her.

Recalling his mother's former suggestion he went to the convent of Sigena. It was in the center of a gray desert, surrounded by high walls, above which only the tips of the spires were visible. The very high walls had triangular buttresses of stone and a main entrance that opened not on to any covered place but directly on to the street.

Inside this enclosure it looked like a miniature city. To the right the massive bulk of the convent of Romanesque stone and Moorish brick, to the left houses of different styles and ages. In the rear a church with twin towers. Beside the houses seen from the entrance there were lanes intersecting the main avenue. The colors were uniform. Black for the eaves — those of the

42

convent richly carved — and different tones of sienna for the walls, with white borders on windows and doors.

The streets, the main avenue as well as the side streets, soon came to an end in the *Ronda* — a clearing between the little monastic city and the walls. The walls had the old iron color of the desert rocks themselves. Moss was growing in between the great stones, with here and there a sprig of hedge-mustard. Not a tree was visible for over two miles around.

Ramiro went to the convent, asked for the abbess, and when he stood before her in a high-ceilinged room with painted panels of the fourteenth or fifteenth century, he introduced himself. The abbess had a smiling and youthful appearance in spite of her fifty years.

'In short, my boy,' she said, addressing him in a kindly and familiar way, 'you have come here hiding from the police. You must be a shameless scamp. There has always been a black sheep in the Vallemediano family and now it is evidently you. What can you do?'

'Everything.'

'Come now. God made you modest. Something to be thankful for.'

She sent him to the convent kitchens.

Inside the walled enclosure every kind of craftsman was to be found. Cobblers, tailors, dressmakers, stonemasons, gardeners, bakers. It was like a small medieval city. For the moment Ramiro was appointed kitchen helper. This work seemed hard and sometimes ignominious to him. Occasionally he insinuated that he had other skills, but he did not mention his painter's gifts for fear they might set him to painting saints for the rest of his life. In the midst of his misery he smiled, remembering a half roguish and childish verse that the farmers of his district were fond of reciting:

> The nuns of Sigena
> have a cock
> that fetches water for them ...

43

They gave Ramiro a loft in the church itself as a bedroom. Through a window opening on to the inside of the temple he saw a cornice where bats were hanging by their feet to sleep during the day. He could also see a verger with his white wig and silver staff moving about.

The next day he made friends with the organist, a lame nun with two front teeth missing, and generally regarded as a real demon. This seemed to be because, as she explained, she was the only sincere one in the community. She was habitually accusing the others of hypocrisy, and had been on the point of leaving the convent once when, in response to a nun's having said that she was the bride of Christ, the organist marched off grumbling: 'Yes, bride of Christ, but at night you sleep alone and bitterly regret it.'

She now knew who Ramiro was and also who was his mother — they had talked about her a greal deal in the twenty-four hours since the boy's arrival — and the organist with a sudden burst of confidence said to him:

'You are a bastard. Don't let that frighten you. There's more than one nun here who doesn't know her father either. But oh yes, they are all very noble. Very noble. As the proverb says: "Harlots, friars and pages, all have highest lineages." '

Within two days they had become fast friends, the organist and Ramiro. Then on the third day the police arrived looking for the boy. The abbess had written to his mother and she — exercising her rights — Ramiro was not yet of age — had legally reclaimed him. The Civil Guard took him back to the town by ordinary conveyance, on foot, that is, along the highway. He entered the village like a criminal and at his mother's request was locked up again. There he spent three days and although no one accused him of anything, everybody connected his imprisonment with the apothecary's death. The boy reflected: 'A few weeks ago I was feted by the whole town and now. . . .'

'This is what you deserve. Prison. For having wronged your mother.'

'I did?'

'Yes. Who told you to go to Sigena to destroy my good reputation with the noble nuns?'

When at the end of three days Ramiro was released, he went to see Aurora, who was now living with two maiden aunts.

3

H E was hoping to find Aurora better, but even though she had recovered she still had her spongy fatness and the reddish splotches on her skin.

Aurora was unaware of her ugliness and appeared self-satisfied and arrogant. She accused him of having told the police that he had embraced her in the little laboratory at the back of the apothecary's shop. Her aunts, who were present, looked at Ramiro as if he were a monster, and he apologized and confessed that he had done wrong and deserved nothing but contempt. Nevertheless, toward the end of the interview, which had been very painful, Aurora again recited the poem, taking advantage of the absence from the room of one of her aunts. The other was deaf. As Aurora recited with her deformed and swollen lips Ramiro, who was not listening, was gazing at two Cuban aquarelles of negro children and palms that were hanging on the wall. The frames were of raffia prettily hand-woven by the maiden aunts.

Ramiro left more depressed than ever and when he reached home he found his mother crying and saying that she could not go on living with a son who called on the apothecary's old maid sisters, her greatest enemies. Besides, going to see the girl made the village people talk and fanned the flame of suspicion. She wound up by saying that she was a mother-martyr, and after that important statement decided that it was the right moment to faint. Ramiro put a pillow under her head and went off to see the priest.

The priest was the only one who treated Ramiro with tolerance and friendliness. He believed that the situation between

Ramiro and his mother was becoming more and more strained and he advised him to come and live at the abbey for a while. The sacristan and his family lived in the back of the church and in the garrets there was a room that he could use until his mother calmed down. Ramiro did not want to accept this offer but when he returned home and found the house full of neighbors waiting on his mother, as if she were dying, he changed his mind.

He moved into his new lodgings with the sacristan that night. The village people talked, and all were agreed that Ramiro's mother deserved a better fate, and that the boy, with all his bastard's talents — bastards, as is well known, being brighter than legitimate sons — was a disgrace to his family and the town. Out of Ramiro's vilification his mother was hoping to win, by way of contrast, some right to public esteem.

At the rear of the church was the old cemetery, no longer in use, called the graveyard of Santa Ana. The silence in that burying ground was impressive, and seemed even more profound when, in the calm of the night, the breeze made a swishing sound in the black branches of a cypress that reached almost up to his window. Above the graveyard, in the pure air that seemed colder because of the moon, a nightingale would sing occasionally. Every spring there was a nest of nightingales in the graveyard of Santa Ana. And when the nightingales sang Ramiro admitted that he was in love with the apothecary's daughter in spite of everything.

He could not sleep. He heard the sacristan dragging things about on the floor beneath him. And when quiet was restored he listened to the nightingale once more. 'Living is hard,' he was thinking, 'but life is beautiful.'

He felt guilty toward his mother and reckoned up the sum of money she must have hidden away, approximately a thousand pesetas. How much more would she need, he wondered, to be received by the Sigena nuns?

Again he heard the nightingale in the darkness. And it was as if the highest note trilled not outside, but inside his brain, transforming him, so that he was neither man nor bird, angel nor illusion, but all of these at the same time. And he went on listening, without sleeping, unwilling to sleep since sleep was unconsciousness, and he wanted complete awareness amidst all this wonder.

The next day he wrote a letter to the organist of Sigena asking how much his mother would need to enter the convent. The organist answered immediately but did not say a word about what most interested Ramiro. In four closely written pages she repeated that the nuns were a pack of hypocritical liars, and that to go to a convent fleeing from the world was like going to the mouth of Hell running away from the devil. She called the nuns by their nicknames. She had nicknamed them all, from the nunnery messenger, *Capagallos* — Sister Caponizer, to the mistress of novices, *La Coscona* — Mother Windbag, and the sacristan, *La Culiparda* — Sister Brownbottom. The abbess she called *La Gatasocarrada* — Mother Singed-Cat. 'Vanity,' she wrote, 'has them more subdued and enslaved than café-singers. They are never called to the locutory that they don't walk up and down in front of the mirror three times to see that their veil hangs and flutters just so, and their girdle, chain and scapulary say something appetizing to those looking at them, for with the habits between them the smell of their armpits is not so noticeable. As far as the flesh is concerned, as I told you before, it has just as bad inclinations here as outside, and people here are always more irritable. Sister Capagallos passes the leisure hours behind the service door sniffing the trousers going by in the street, which are always the same: the baker, wool-dresser, gardener, tailor. But even so, I, who take it like the breeze of a fan, would be a nun if I were born again, to spare men my eagerness, and also because I'm lazy and like music. And as for lying, there is not a single one who tells the truth. They lie more than at a village fair. And if one tells the truth she soon repents, because the mockery and scorn of all are heaped upon her. But I repeat, if this happens among the members of a single family, I don't know why it shouldn't happen in a convent.'

47

She went on like this for two more pages. Ramiro showed the letter to the priest, whom he expected to be scandalized. But the priest merely remarked:

'If your mother finds out about your writing to the convent, she's going to be furious.'

The priest's indifference to the organist's nonsense made Ramiro think that the priest was very wise and discreet, and life something complex and arduous, not only for illegitimate sons but for everyone.

He borrowed more books from the schoolmaster and read everything he could lay his hands on. Pérez Galdós seemed gentle and kind, and yet more skeptical than Baroja, who appeared to have a blind faith in the established order, just like his mother, and the sacristan's family with whom he lived. For Baroja the peasant was stupid, the worker wicked, the middle-class man ridiculous, unless he had money, in which case he began to be interesting, the rich industrialist, admirable, the marquise, adorable, and the cardinal, really semi-divine. This disappointed Ramiro because Baroja's style seemed to him to be that of a man beyond good and evil.

He read many other books. When those of the schoolmaster and priest gave out he started taking out volumes of the encyclopedia at the town hall. There he read European history, religion, philosophy, and learned about the social and political doctrines of the time.

He wanted to return to painting but he had no paints, nor money to buy them with.

One day the priest told him he could go back to his mother because he had talked to her and felt sure that she would give him a welcome. He returned home with some misgiving. It so happened that his mother did receive him just as if nothing had ever gone wrong. But during the night, when they were alone, she began to moan and bewail her fate. Her own fate, not her son's. She had come from a rich and noble family. She had always been good to everyone but society was cruel and unjust to her. She ended up by saying that only two ways were open to her, the suicides' butte or the convent of Sigena. She was not courageous enough for the first.

Ramiro told her that he would work for her, whereupon his mother seemed to return to her former intemperate attitude.

'You? Work? At what? Will you take a hoe and go off to the fields? Like a day laborer? That's what you'd like. To disgrace your mother still more.'

She added that his presence was an insult to her because it reminded her of the tragedy of her youth and her life's shame. Exasperated, Ramiro told her that he was not to blame for what she had done in her youth and his mother burst into tears screaming: 'That's the only thing left for me to hear. That's the last dagger thrust.'

That night he was a long time going to sleep, listening to his mother crying. And he remembered with nostalgia the nightingale in the graveyard of Santa Ana.

Winter soon arrived and with it the sadness of the cold and the trees without leaves. He read and vainly tried to paint. No one wanted him to do a portrait. With the few colors he found at home he painted desolate landscapes on the backs of doors. Since he had a tube of white paint left over he added skeletons and skulls.

He saw Aurora at Mass, large, fat and puffy like a woman fifty years old. Her black clothes gave her a spectral air. Recalling her at the birthday party — dancing *La Tarara* — he loved her still. Twice he went to see her, without his mother finding out. The girl was making lace with bobbins and since her aunts held her to a daily task, which she had to finish to avoid punishment, she never stopped working all the time he was there. If once in a while she interrupted her work to look at him, she kept moving the bobbins so that her aunts in the kitchen would hear the clicking. And when she got up to fetch a picture she had autographed and wished to give him, she asked him to keep the bobbins moving.

As she gave him the photograph Aurora said: 'If you think you ought to kiss me. I have nothing to say.' Ramiro gave her

49

a long kiss, in which he put no love at all. As he kissed her he left the bobbins quiet but she freed one hand and started moving them again so as to go on deceiving her aunts.

Then Ramiro sat down, gazing at the countryside through the window, and Aurora said:

'Even though you did kill my father, it doesn't matter, since you did it for me.'

Ramiro did not answer. His hand, inside his pocket, was holding the photograph he had not yet looked at. Through the window he saw the gray-tiled roofs, frost-covered on the north. On one of those roofs there was a black metal pipe from which a stream of thick white smoke was pouring. Behind it the countryside was visible, a gray and deserted landscape with distant gray hills. On one of those hills, the farthest one, he could see something in ruins. Could that be the castle of Rocafría his mother sometimes talked about? The castle where his ancestors exacted a tribute of twenty-five village maidens every year? If those times were to exist again Ramiro, perhaps, would be the lord of the castle and Aurora one of the maidens. He took out the photograph, glanced at it and put it back in his pocket, afraid the aunts would return. Aurora smiled at him, giving him a sidewise glance, constantly keeping the bobbins moving.

Ramiro had felt aversion when looking at the picture. It was a picture taken after her illness, and Aurora with her loose flowing hair and white dress — her mourning clothes had not yet been completed — was uglier than ever. Nevertheless she asked him contentedly:

'It's a nice picture, isn't it?'

She repeated that even though he had killed her father she didn't hold it against him. 'If I had killed yours,' she added, 'would you hate me?' Ramiro burst out laughing. It would be very hard to kill his father. First, he thought, it would be necessary to find out who he was. Hearing his laughter Aurora also laughed. They continued laughing for quite a while and finally Ramiro rose to leave.

'Write me another poem,' she asked.

Ramiro hesitated and she insisted:

'Even if it's in prose.'

Ramiro went to the kitchen door to say goodby to the maiden ladies, who answered him gruffly. Then he left, walking slowly.

The village was desolate in winter. He had tried to make friends with some poor relatives whose daughters he had played with as a child, but when he saw that they treated him with distrust and even fear, he never went back. He shut himself up in his house and, remembering the poem Aurora had asked him for, wondered if perhaps he had talent as a writer. Whenever he finished reading a book he would have a great yearning to write. Then one day he decided to try. 'It's enough to be sincere,' he told himself. 'Utterly sincere.' He recalled Rousseau's *Confessions*, which he had borrowed from the schoolmaster and repeated. 'Utterly sincere.' But at his age, even if sincere, what could he write?

For a while that winter he kept a kind of diary, more or less as follows:

'*December* 8. — I take a walk in the country. People with hateful expressions. I stroll about. Everybody is doing something. I don't look, but I see. What do I see? Low cloudy sky. Wind. The bell of the hermitage where I painted Aurora sounds mad. Who made life? Life is ugly. I am wicked, but so is my neighbor. God made life and it is ugly. Aurora is a caterpillar. No. An angel smashed by a gigantic foot. And she asks for poems.

'*December* 15. — Here is the poem. Aurora was an adorable girl. A bud. But even though she is still the same she is somebody else. We are all damned. Where is the Aurora who danced *La Tarara* with me? She swayed her hips underneath her dress. Round hips, and since she did not know that this was ugly, she did it very well. Now she is a smashed angel, with cotton in her ears. I kissed her the other day and the kiss smelled of melted wax. She is all melted wax. I don't want to write the poem. I don't know what I would like to do today. Kill her. That's it. Kill her and jump off the suicides' butte.

'*December* 20. — I started out for the butte thinking: I'm

51

going to give my mother a merry Christmas. My mother is an imbecile but doesn't know it. If I kill myself she will feel important again and worthy of compassion. I am also an imbecile. Perhaps everybody is and doesn't know it.

'But strange things have been happening to me. I went to the Valencian's shop and tavern, and sat down in a corner. A dog was lying nearby on the floor. A man who was having a drink and arguing with somebody said: "Don't come to me with those stories, for I'm a wise old dog." The dog turned its head and looked at him, its ears cocked. We all felt confused.

'I am going to give my mother a pleasant surprise.

'But not today. I was heading for the butte with that intention but I was too unhappy for anything like that. Besides, there was a mist rising.

'Another strange thing: I passed some yoked oxen. And I remembered that when I was a child going to school my mother would say: "If you don't study you'll be an ox-driver." And they were eyeing me — those oxen. And I looked at them. With melancholy.

'*December* 27. — I didn't give that pleasant surprise to my mother. I am damned. We all are. I am unhappier than ever and I am seeking the why without finding it. If I were to find it, what bliss! But there is not the slightest chance. Everything shut tight. Heaven, earth. Everything. And I am thinking about Aurora as one of those dough figures they take to the oven for baking.

'For she is really in the oven, with her aunts. They are the kind of people proud of having bought a Chippendale cabinet on the instalment plan. She is in her aunts' oven. I am in my mother's. And everbody is in God's, roasting over a slow fire. Our fat melts away and we have a foul smell. I can't find out why I am unhappy. I want to find out but my desire is unhappiness, my thought is unhappiness, and my whole life is the impossibility of finding out why.

'Well then, I won't go to the butte.

'*January* 1. — New Year's Day. I went to the Valencian's after stealing two pesetas from my mother. I am still thinking about giving my mother a pleasant surprise. For her birthday, maybe.

'In the tavern there was a Catalonian who has a salt business in these towns. Everybody knows that he mistreats his wife. At night he beats her up horribly. But he said to the Valencian, speaking of her:

' "That saintly woman I have at home. . . .!"

'When the Valencian heard this he winked at me slyly. A fine type, the Valencian. That wink did me a world of good and I'm not going to the butte. I am thinking of Aurora as a clay pig with a pink ribbon around its neck and another around its tail. And of having pictures of her made to enter in a contest. Still I love her. Why? I don't know. If I knew why I'm fond of her, my love would end.

'I went to see the priest. The church smells like Aurora, of melted wax.

'*January* 7.—The priest is a good man. He doesn't believe in anything. I told him so and he almost burst into tears. We are all damned. He doesn't believe, but he keeps up the faith of the others so that they won't go to the butte as I intend to do. Does he help them with this? I doubt it.

'*January* 8. — I went to the river. It is near. But that river of blue water, green stones and trout looks as if it belongs to a distant country. I heard the hermitage bell and thought about my pictures. Maybe I am an artist. I don't think so because I am indifferent to everything. Men, women, animals, things. God made them all. And yet . . .

'*January* 9. — I began the poem, but it is horrible: dogs barking on the dark horizons, low clouds, crushed insects on roads leading nowhere; a dead dog, beheaded beside a rose-lined path. A peasant with a small knife in his hand. A peasant who got ten cents from the dog's master for cutting off its head. I saw it thinking of you, Aurora. The peasant took out his knife and with his other hand knocked the little beast flat on its back, holding it to the ground on its chest. The peasant stuck his fingers between its front paws. The little animal moaned. It was

53

not easy; the dog wanted to defend itself without harming the peasant. It wanted to escape. With his left hand he held the dog by the chest and with the right struck it with the knife under the jaw. The little animal struggled and looked at me as if expecting my help. Then it vomited. Before dying it vomited. I went on towards the butte but this time only to leave the agonizing dog behind me. On the butte I thought about you. About the virgin of *La Tarara,* who is fat and bloated and will not allow me to be fond of her, but love her. She too is damned. If she wants to come with me to the butte we can go together and jump off into space, dancing *La Tarara* in the air. But then I came back. On the way I met no one. I would have liked to meet someone, the witch of the wading pools, for instance, but I only found the dead dog. By its side were visible traces of the peasant's knife which he had cleaned on the dry grass, there beside the animal. And the little dog which when alive looked gentle and innocent, now showed a tooth between its lips with a cynical expression. I thought about you, Aurora....

'If I gave this page to Aurora, what would happen?

'*January* 20. — It has snowed. Because of this I feel a kind of light joy. But the children of the town are sad. No one is playing in the snow.

'I make a big fire at home and my mother looks at me out of the corner of her eye. I must give her a nice surprise. Jumping off the butte.

'Or else, going away. "Mother," I said to her, "even though I'm not yet sixteen I'd like to go away."

' "You will do well to do so," she said. "For being far away, perhaps I'll be able to care for you a little."

'I am thinking about it seriously. Through the window I can see the butte. Through the door opposite the distant highway is visible, and a little white cottage which they call El Ventorrillo — the country inn. I want to jump off the butte but first I would like to see the ocean. And a city with workers. In the papers I read about the workers struggling and protesting. Their protests must be as simple as my own when I think that I can't imagine why I am unlucky. But I believe that I despise all humanity except the workers. And all of nature except the sea.

'*May* 6. — I never wrote anything else during the whole winter: or went to see Aurora again: or fought with my mother. The schoolmaster and priest look at me as if I were crazy. We all are; but some can explain their madness. I can't. The Valencian lent me his horse and I rode off through the mountains, towards the butte. The idea of jumping off the butte with the Valencian's horse bothered me, not because of the animal's life but of the money it's worth, and because my mother might have to pay for it afterward.

'Near the butte I met a young girl with a cow on her way home. She was quite pretty and was carrying a big bundle of grass under her arm.

' "What time is it?" I asked her.

'She glanced at the sky:

' "About four."

' "And what day of the month is it today?"

'The little girl looked at me vexed and said:

' "Does the gentleman think that I am a flower to be able to know everything?"

'She went on her way. Those words — *I am not a flower so as to know everything* — made me decide to get to know the sea before thinking seriously of anything else.

'On the other hand I doubt if anyone could think seriously about what I'm thinking now.'

Ramiro's notes ended here. The hangman sent them to me from Ocaña after our talk.

Toward the middle of May he got fifty pesetas from his mother on the promise of repaying her. Dressing in his best he set off without saying goodby to anyone.

Three kilometers away, at the Ventorrillo crossroads, he waited for the bus. It was a large and ramshackle vehicle bound for a small Mediterranean city beside the sea. He would spend the whole night in the bus, but he was sure that he would sleep on a seat as well as in his bed. A woman resembling the Sigena

55

organist sat down beside him, and he was not surprised when she proved herself to be a gossip and busybody.

Before seven o'clock in the morning they reached the end of the journey. Since Ramiro had no luggage he took a walk through the town. The first thing he noticed was how differently the village smelled from an inland town. Ramiro expected to find the sea around every corner. The day was golden and blue. There was a church in the plaza, and thinking that the best way to discover the sea would be to climb up to the tower, he entered.

The main altar was prepared for the celebration of the Mass, but the priest had not yet left the sacristy. Bells were calling the faithful. In the church there were only three women and two old men wearing fishing jackets. In that church and at that moment Ramiro believed that the Catholic religion was the truest, noblest, holiest and purest religion. In that clean air smelling of wax and wood he was deeply moved.

'Now that I'm no longer with her,' he was thinking, 'my mother has probably begun to care for me.' But this was really a matter of indifference to him.

Ramiro disappeared up the dark stairs to the tower, and after climbing more than seventy spiral steps he reached the top. He could not help being afraid when passing near the clock machinery, for he was reminded of childish terrors when he had climbed his village tower.

His view from the tower ranged out over the sea to a distance where, the water fusing with the sky, for the first time he had the physical sensation of the infinite. Like all impressions of natural grandeur, this left Ramiro with his imagination paralyzed. The water was bluer than the cloudless sky. He felt bewildered before so much beauty. Recovering from his astonishment he thought of the mystery of creation and of God. 'The one who made all this made me too,' he mused with a certain secret rapture, forgetting the precarious conditions of his life.

He stayed there for over an hour. He saw the beach, at the very edge of the town. From the beach to the tower where Ramiro was, he could only see narrow winding streets, with whitewashed buildings, red tile roofs and green borders. Ivy clung to some corners and rue was on many balconies. The sea was as tranquil as a lake, limpid as the sky.

He started down. As he reached the chapel he heard: '*Ad Deum qui laetificat juventutem meam.*' He went inside and knelt, thinking of Aurora and of his mother. He thanked God for having created a world so beautiful. Then he asked God to let him hear nightingales in the evening some time. He did not doubt that this God, Who in his childhood had given him hailstorms and rainbows, would also consider him worthy of hearing a nightingale once more. He also asked Him to kill Aurora. To kill her gently and painlessly. Then he felt confused, thinking that he was asking God for impossible things.

Looking around for a place to get breakfast he reached the outskirts of the town and discovered a traveling circus. Some twenty caravans were grouped around a large main tent, with a canvas top and a flag hoisted above it. This was a happy surprise. Having nothing better to do he set about investigating it all slowly.

Leading to the main entrance was an avenue lined on both sides with large cages. They were covered with tarpaulins but had signs on top. The first one said: 'The Sea Wolf'. And the last one: 'King of the Jungle'. He took for granted that this must be a lion.

He strolled over towards the large conical tent and while passing through an alley formed by two rows of caravans, he saw some colored swimming suits hanging on a line. He was regarding them when a girl about his age appeared. She had a white towel around her head, bare arms, and one side of her face was covered with cold cream, which gave her an unpleasant appearance though she was unmistakably pretty. When she saw Ramiro she started to run and hide, then stopped on the top step and, looking at him suspiciously, asked:

'What are you doing here? Why are you looking at those clothes hanging on the line?'

Ramiro was noticing her bare legs and feet, so white in contrast to her tanned face and arms. She added:

'I see. You wanted to steal something.'

Ramiro hastened to deny it, saying he needed to buy a bathing suit so he could go to the beach for a swim.

'Buy it where? In this village they surely don't have any.'

'Then ... would you sell me one of those?' Ramiro asked.

'How much would you pay?'

At that moment Ramiro realized that the girl had green eyebrows.

'I don't know. Around two or three pesetas.'

He saw that she had the same cream on her hands as on her face. What a pity, he thought, in such a pretty girl. She must have some skin disease. The girl was aware:

'Do you think I have the itch?'

'Oh no, no I don't,' he protested.

'We have lots of swimming trunks. Some old, some new. I'll give you an old pair.'

'Here,' he said, taking out his money.

'No. I don't want it. What am I going to do with money if I can't get out of here? But don't imagine that I'm going to give it to you for nothing. Go down into the town and in a grocer's sbop behind the church buy me half a pound of candied egg yolks and half a pound of chocolates, but be sure they have cream centers. Meanwhile I'll fix you up an old pair of trunks and when you come back I'll give them to you.'

Ramiro was nonplussed. His surprise was greater still when she came up to him and familiarly put a hand on each of his hips to measure the size of the trunks. Ramiro looked at the girl's cheek, covered with cream. He was still absorbed and hesitating when she said to him:

'Run along. If my father comes we won't be able to do the deal.'

'Where is your father?'

'He has gone to hunt dogs to feed the lion. My father is the tamer.'

Instead of half a pound Ramiro bought a pound each of candied egg yolks and chocolate creams. He came back almost at a run, remembering the lion-tamer. The girl took the sweets, gave him a pair of red swimming trunks and said:

'Why did you buy twice as much as I asked you for?'

Ramiro noticed that now she did not have the cream on her face but there were dry scabs on the places that before were covered.

He walked away slowly with the trunks in his hand. He went along thinking about the girl. Her bare legs, which had given him a delightful sensation of fragrance, had awakened in him an urgent desire to kiss her.

He went to the beach for over three hours, swimming a good deal of the time. He would have stayed there all day but he was hungry. He went to a tavern in the fishermen's district. Still he had not thought about where he would sleep. On the seashore the world seemed clean, warm and comfortable. More comfortable than the interiors of houses.

4

RAMIRO went to the circus, but neither saw nor heard anything. He was thinking about Aurora and his mother, about himself and life, which was carrying him along in such an arbitrary fashion. 'Six months ago or more I was a painter. In love with a girl, I almost killed her, and did kill her father unintentionally.'

The idea that he might be able to work in this circus, not as an artist but at some of the thousand odd jobs, stuck in his mind. Here they would not require identity papers, or notify the police as in Sigena. Recalling the pictures he had seen on the outside curtains of the cages and at the circus entrance, he knew that he could do much better.

As he left the circus he vaguely remembered a confusion of lights, laughter and colors, unable to say exactly what he had seen. He found an inn. They asked him for his identity papers, but for the moment were satisfied with his name. Since he had no luggage he paid for his room in advance and slept ten hours without waking. In the morning, rested and happy, he went to see the lion-tamer's daughter.

He found her on the little stairs of her caravan. The first thing Ramiro told her was that he wanted to work in the circus. She asked him:

'Are you an acrobat?'

She added that the acrobat was the most important artist in circuses. She seemed disappointed that he was not and advised him to see the agent.

'What's his name?'

'Monsieur Léonard.'

She told him where he could be found, warning him not to say that he wanted to work as a circus employee, but that he wished to learn the horizontal and parallel bars.

'Monsieur Léonard was a fine acrobat and very skilful on the bar,' she added, 'and he has a mania for teaching young men because he says it's an art that is disappearing.'

Ramiro asked what country Monsieur Léonard came from, and she told him that he was a Chilean, and talked 'like those people over yonder'. Then they looked at each other a while in silence and finally he said, almost in a whisper:

'I wish I could give you a kiss.'

She uttered a birdlike trill of laughter and ran inside. Ramiro went in search of Monsieur Léonard. He found him in his wagon, half of which was his office, the other half his bedroom. A red curtain divided it in two. On the wall an old poster showed the Chilean with his chest covered with decorations. Ramiro stood before him and the athlete raised his head, asking:

'Who are you?'

Just then a man in blue trousers and yellow knit shirt passed by the window, whistling to a small dog following along behind him. Léonard shouted to him, without waiting for Ramiro's reply:

'Where are you going with that toad? Your lion will swallow him in two chews.'

'Give me yours, Léonard,' said the man in the blue trousers.

'With your dog he'll have enough for four lunches.'

'I'd sooner give you the leg of Judas.'

He was referring to his game leg. Monsieur Léonard's dog was growling in the back of the wagon, and the old man explained to Ramiro:

'When the lion-tamer goes by, my dog cocks his ears and puts up his hackles, because he's very intelligent. Quick as a flash for scenting. And he knows very well what is going to happen to that one' — he pointed to the little dog following the trainer. 'He sniffs the blood basin.'

Monsieur Léonard glanced at the little dog that was disappearing with the tamer:

'It hurts you to see him so cool and collected.' Then he added:

'It's marvelous how the tamer loves a pack of cards.'

Ramiro realized that they were now friends and he was afraid of breaking the spell with some indiscretion. Monsieur Léonard asked:

'And you? Don't you like to sling a card now and then?'

'Yes, sir.'

'Then see here, young man. At your age I did more manly things. All by my lonesome I threw a young bull — and unmounted.'

After a pause he added:

'Still you haven't told me what it is that you can do for me, young man.'

'I would like to be a bar performer, but I recognize that I need training.'

Monsieur Léonard showed a certain agreeable surprise. But he checked it:

'You are very young. You don't have a single whisker. What do they call you?'

Ramiro told him his name and Monsieur Léonard continued:

61

'I don't have a single whisker either, but that is different. I'm part Indian and when I was a boy I pulled out the few whiskers I had by the roots.'

Ramiro did not know where Monsieur Léonard was going to stop. The athlete continued looking at him:

'If you now find me here a scribbler with ink on my fingers it is because of a fatality.'

It was difficult to engage this man in conversation. Ramiro insisted:

'I should like you to teach me the bar, Monsieur Léonard.'

'And you think you are going to begin with the bar?'

'I wouldn't mind doing any humble chore in the circus if I could work at the bar with you.'

'What can you do?'

'I can look after horses, mend a table or wagon, fix an axle, build a hut of stone or brick, paint ... I could paint all the signs for the cages and the main entrance to the circus much better than they are now.'

The old man looked at him with an indefinable expression. He asked him if he had references.

'No, sir. I don't come from around here.'

'I didn't have references when I began either. It doesn't matter. Your physique does not displease me, my boy. You have form. You're no dwarf. And what are your pretensions? Would you work for meals, room, and a little of the king's silver?'

'Yes, sir,' Ramiro answered, smiling.

The old man made a gesture as if he were brushing away a fly:

'Forget about the bar for the time being, my son. That is a science. Come with me, if you like.'

They started out together, but the Chilean suddenly turned back and tied the dog, that had wanted to follow him, to a strap fastened in the wall. The animal moaned, and Monsieur Léonard explained:

'It's a fact that even though the lion's cage is at the other end of the camp, it sniffs the blood basin from here.'

62

The manager of the circus was a Frenchman, with a drooping mustache and very unsteady, thin lips. Monsieur Léonard enumerated Ramiro's different skills. The manager, twisting his lips to the left until they touched the edge of his mustache, interrupted him:

'You know, Léonard, that I like to give you *plaisir. Prenez-le,* as second electrician.'

Ramiro was about to say that he knew nothing about electricity when the manager shook hands with him and turned his back, considering the matter settled. They both left, and Monsieur Léonard said:

'I will take you to the chief electrician. At the beginning you will stand the cramp as best you can.'

That expression — the cramp — referring to electrical things, amused Ramiro. Later he discovered that Monsieur Léonard used 'cramp' for every kind of difficulty.

They showed him the tool wagon where he could sleep. Ramiro was glad that he would live alone in this wagon. The walls were covered with hammers, tongs, pliers, carpenter's braces, rolls of wire, screws and hundreds of other things.

He had passed his sixteenth birthday and now had fuzz on his face. He shaved for the first time. Then he waited for the circus to open. Shortly before the performance began an employee came up to tell him that the manager was calling for him. The Frenchman received him less coolly, saying, as he showed him a typewritten sheet of paper:

'I have talked to Monsieur Léonard about you again. Do you wish to *signer* this contract?'

Ramiro supposed that it concerned his work as electrician, but saw that it referred to something entirely different. The contract obliged Ramiro to paint new posters and signs, as well as a monumental new front with gigantic figures. They promised him two thousand pesetas, out of which he would pay his assistant, if he needed one. The company would pay a carpenter to make the frames.

'*D'abord,*' said the manager, 'you must make the sketches and general plans. *Vous me les montrerez* as soon as possible. If *nous* are in agreement I will sign the duplicate. But you will have to work as second electrician besides.'

Ramiro signed the contract. The manager thanked him and Ramiro left trembling with emotion. Recalling that he had to paint all the animals, Ramiro visited the cages and, still unable really to believe in his good fortune, began to jot down notes and make rough sketches. In the last cage was a very long crocodile, asleep close to the bars. This took the most time. His sketches finished, Ramiro went inside the circus and sat down beside some other employees near where the ring communicated with the stables. There he found Monsieur Léonard, who took him by the arm, saying::

'Come with me right away.'

He left him in the hands of the chief electrician, and Ramiro began to listen to his instructions. He learned where the outlets were, which were the high tension cables, how a small transformer worked, what the insulators, binding-posts, and switch-boxes were. In spite of the fact that Ramiro had confessed his ignorance the boss did not seem impressed.

It was Saturday and the circus was full. The manager acted as ringmaster, and after the clowns he put on a comic number of animal imitations. He began roaring like a lion, with a glass tube like a lamp chimney. Then he imitated the pig, donkey and horse. The audience asked for more and the manager took out his special bag of tricks: the frog, dog, hen, rooster. Of course when he imitated the rooster his voice cracked, and a peasant called out from a distant seat:

'Hey, that rooster's a hen!'

The ringmaster, offended, shrieked three more 'cock-a-doodle-dos' that came out perfectly. Then he imitated the cow, sheep, and even a little newborn chick. This almost made the country-women hysterical with laughter. The manager pretended to be chasing it around the ring trying to catch it, and the cheeping became as anguished and tragic as if he really had the chicken in his hands. Afterward the audience clamored for the nightingale. The imitation was so perfect that Ramiro grew sad thinking about his village, the apothecary's daughter, and the graveyard of Santa Ana.

About to get ready for bed, he remembered that he had had no supper, and went to the fishermen's tavern. He was afraid he would be too late, but he found it open and full of clients. At a table nearby a group was playing cards. Another group on his left was playing dominoes. On the white wall was a tourist poster picturing wide beaches and curly waves. The cat was half asleep on top of a wine cask. Ramiro ate in silence.

The next day, impatient to finish his sketches for the new scenery, he got up very early. Before noon he had finished, and went to see the manager, who looked them over carefully, signed the copy of the contract which had already been signed by two others as witnesses, and gave it back together with a blue envelope containing ten one hundred peseta bills. He said that the rest of the stipulated sum would be paid when the work was finished.

Ramiro left with the sensation that he was walking on air. He found Monsieur Léonard, who congratulated him and went with him for a stroll on the beach.

'In Chile,' said the old man, 'when I was a boy I went to the beach to gather shell-fish, and later on I was a sailor for over ten years. This was the exercise that made me able-bodied and fit for the bar.'

Ramiro asked him what he thought of the manager of the circus. Monsieur Léonard seemed wary and said nothing. Then he began to talk about the lion. It was a very wise big cat, he said, and when they fed it they had to throw in the dog already drawn and quartered. Once they put a live dog in the cage, but the lion was quiet, eyeing it respectfully. Monsieur Léonard said that the lion was a gentleman and did not wish to molest his guest. For two days they lived together and nothing happened. The third day they took the dog out. It was the 'auburn' dog that lived in Monsieur Léonard's wagon and growled because it 'sniffed the blood basin'. When referring to the lion,

Monsieur Léonard never said 'the lion', but 'the big cat'. They separated and Ramiro went to the post office and sent his mother two hundred pesetas to help toward the dowry for the convent of the noble nuns. Then he went to inspect the coach-house where he intended to start working.

Ramiro ate in the circus restaurant and occasionally, at night, went to the little fishermen's tavern for a drink of wine or beer. He planned to invite the lion-tamer's daughter to go swimming with him. He confided his hopes to Monsieur Léonard, and the Chilean said:

'I see. But she is too young to be deflowered. Only three years ago I was still holding her on my knee.'

Ramiro told him that he was not thinking of that, but the Chilean paid no attention.

From the very first Ramiro had suspected that the artists of this company had long since renounced fame and glory. Even the animals impressed him as being in a state of ruin and decline.

Ramiro went about perplexed for several days. Then one evening the electrician sent for him. He had to be away for a time, and explained to Ramiro what should be done in his absence. If the fuses were blown, he could temporarily repair the damage by putting a copper object — a penny would do — in the blown fuse and later, after the performance, the regulation repairs could be made. He called his attention to other possible accidents, explaining in great detail what was to be done in each case. Ramiro was sure that he would not have any trouble.

The next evening, after a normal day's work, when the night performance was beginning, a circus fuse blew out. Ramiro put a copper coin in the old fuse and soon afterwards there was a short circuit behind the framework of the main entrance, and the flames invaded the stables and spread rapidly.

The fire destroyed even the dry alfalfa for the horses which was stored in the barns at the furthermost edge of the camp. At midnight, the peasants and fishermen, tired of battling the flames, let the fire consume everything, trying only to keep it

66

from spreading to the village and the dry wheat-fields then ripening. All the animals were burned in their cages except the lion, which escaped and, after running around the town with his mane on fire, died in the plaza beside the entrance to the City Hall. The peasants screamed:

'Watch out, the lion's loose!'

And Ramiro heard the manager say, with both tips of his mustache caught at the same time by his strong teeth:

'The only danger in *approcher* the lion would be to get one of his fleas.'

The village mayor threatened the manager with severe reprisals if the houses caught on fire. The manager looked disconsolate:

'*Quel malheur, mon Dieu!*'

Under the light, swiftly moving clouds, reddened by the immense bonfire, the fishermen went back and forth, trying to save something. The young ones, as usually happens, had taken the catastrophe as undramatically as possible and were walking about, very excited, exchanging jokes and laughing at the slightest pretext. Only two of the circus personnel were missing: the lion-tamer, and an old French equestrienne who had died trying to save her horse. About the tamer they were not sure, and everybody felt happy, and slightly disappointed, when he showed up safe and sound, repeating: :

'Poor Philip!'

Philip was the lion.

Ramiro watched the tremendous conflagration thinking about the equestrienne, whom he imagined standing on her horse with her white riding skirt in flames. He went to the inn where he had slept the first day, but instead of going to the room assigned to him, he went on upstairs to an open gallery facing the sea. There was no moon. When he became used to the darkness he could see the foam spreading over the beach in the distance. He stayed there several hours. Afraid of being surprised by the daylight, he went to his room shortly before dawn. All the rooms were occupied by the circus people.

He wrote a letter to Aurora, describing for her the death of the French equestrienne and her horse, whom she called *Chéri*. As he wrote Ramiro had the impression that it was Aurora whose skirts were on fire. He could smell the burning human flesh.

He also sent his mother a postcard filled with timidly presumptuous fibs. Then he sewed the eight hundred peseta bills inside the lining of his coat.

The next day he was summoned to make a deposition before the authorities. The circus manager was there, dwelling on the contract he had signed with Ramiro a few days before to redecorate the circus, and showing the receipt of the thousand pesetas advanced him. The representative of a fire insurance company was there taking note of the contract and receipt. Ramiro felt sure that the fire was of incendiary origin, its object being to collect the insurance, but he wasn't bold enough to say so to the authorities.

When it was dark he realized that he had not eaten for twenty-four hours. He was not hungry, but his stomach ached. He went to the fishermen's tavern, where they were still as excited and noisy as if it were a holiday.

Ramiro was thinking about the equestrienne as he ate. She had been burned alive with her *Chéri*. 'Perhaps,' he thought, 'without my contract and the receipt for the thousand pesetas the manager would not have dared to set fire to the circus. This did not leave him with a feeling of guilt, but a vague and somewhat shameful sense of well-being. Later, on the beach, his ideas began to change. He hated the French manager and thought: 'I have to get away.' He did not know where or what for. Perhaps to some large city full of indifferent people. When he reached the inn the circus manager came out to meet him.

'I hope,' he said, 'that if they call on you to testify again you will be *plus gentil. Il s'agit* of the life of the whole company.'

Ramiro looked at him, without speaking. The manager added:

'You said that you were going to accuse me. Of what? Of

68

having given you money? Of course,' he said in a conciliating tone, 'I only paid you half.'

He reached for his pocket book and Ramiro stopped him: 'Don't bother.'

The circus manager looked at him, serious and calm: 'Do you want the other thousand or not?'

'No.'

The manager left, asking him 'not to harm so many simple and innocent people who lived off the circus.' He said something about his 'delicate artist's conscience', but Ramiro was no longer paying any attention.

He went to bed sure that he would not sleep, but he dozed for four or five hours. He woke up early, and at daybreak prepared to leave the village. He did not wish to see anyone, or to go on breathing that air which smelled — or still seemed to smell — of burned flesh.

There was a railway station in the next town some two leagues away. He decided to go there on foot, and left without any baggage.

'I am a coward and a wretch,' he said to himself aloud, 'because I don't dare to denounce the circus manager to the authorities. Nor, on the other hand, do I dare to accept the thousand pesetas still owing me, according to the contract.' He also felt himself accused by the equestrienne who had called him *chéri*, just as she called her horse.

After wavering for a long while Ramiro went back to the village to see the circus manager, intending to ask him for the rest of the money. As he entered the inn he heard him arguing with someone and repeating:

'*C'est pas sérieux, ça. C'est pas sérieux.*'

He hesitated. Finally he left without seeing the circus manager.

69

5

HE reached the station, but instead of going inside he continued walking along the railway track until nightfall. The night was warm and crickets were chirping. Close by he saw a haystack and decided to spend the night there. He made himself comfortable on the far side — away from the highway, pulled out some clean straw for a pallet, rolled up his jacket for a pillow and, remembering that sewn in the lining were the eight hundred-peseta banknotes, lay down. A light breeze caressed his chest through his open shirt. When he was almost alseep he thought he heard his mother's voice saying: 'This unworthy son of mine poisoned the apothecary and his daughter.' With eyes closed Ramiro recalled the book on the Renaissance, which said that the popes sold Christian white slaves to Turkish sultans. Was that a sin? 'Probably,' he concluded, 'we have invented sin, knowing that no one can avoid the tremendous acts determining it. And we hate sin and we love it, we fear sin and at the same time profit by it, irremediably. Maybe the popes are more aware of this mystery than we are.' He fell asleep with the sensation that he was gently falling into a well of cotton.

He slept soundly until daylight. The straw beneath his body was warm. He got up feeling vigorous and strong, and made for the highway ravenously hungry. Noticing everything around him he could do no less than wonder. A libellula sitting on the twig of a bush looked at him with its big bulging eyes, in which three dew-drops trembling on a near-by leaf were reflected. The dew-drops moved with the breeze, and in the shifting light and shade the air was fresh and balmy. The libellula was pale green and seemed to belong more to the plant than to the animal world. Its eyes were full of images of Ramiro, multiplied and very, very small. The next village was not far, and he was famished.

In the plaza of the town he saw a little café which had just opened. It was full of mirrors covered with green tulle. A canary was singing in a corner, but no one seemed to be about. In a little doorway at the back, closed with double curtains, a girl appeared. Repressing a smile she came up to Ramiro. He asked her why she was laughing and she said:

'Look at yourself in the mirror.'

Ramiro saw that his hair was dishevelled. She offered him a small comb and went to fetch coffee. When she came back Ramiro returned the comb and caught her hand. She blushed.

'Where are you going?' she asked.

'To Madrid.'

'On foot?'

'A little while on foot and another little while walking.'

Ramiro devoured his breakfast, and she looked at him with a pleased expression.

'Did you have a fight with the railway?' she asked.

Ramiro told himself as he glanced around: 'If I stay here ten minutes longer, I will never leave.' He asked the girl her name. She answered:

'Mariquiña.'

She came from Galicia. 'But not on foot,' she explained, always smiling.

'It is possible,' said Ramiro, 'that I will never reach Madrid if on the way I find another girl like you.'

'Don't worry. There's no other like me.'

He went out rather bewildered. He did not know what happened to him when he encountered women. He was in love with all of them, before he ever laid eyes on them. But really loved only one. One who repelled him: Aurora. He saw her fat and pink, and still with cotton in her ears.

The sun was beginning to burn, and he must have walked for more than an hour in a state of pleasing numbness when a truck, coming up from behind, stopped at his side. The driver said:

'There's room for another here. Climb in.'

Ramiro looked at him, hesitating.

71

'It's free,' the driver insisted, smiling. 'I'm doing it only for friendship's sake.'

Comfortably seated, protected from the sun, Ramiro wiped his forehead with his handkerchief. The driver said:

'Mariquiña told me about you in the café. She said, says she, if you catch up with a young fellow going to Madrid who looks so-so, give him a ride in your truck. And I do what Mariquiña says. You'll probably say that's silly, but that's the way I am.'

'She's a very pretty girl,' said Ramiro.

'Who? Mariquiña? She's worth an empire. But I don't want to tell you everything she said about you.'

'Well, what could she say?'

'She said that you looked crack-brained. A man who walks to Madrid in this weather probably does seem crazy to Mariquiña.'

Ramiro laughed and said that he wished to pay something for his good turn. The driver refused:

'I told you I was doing it for friendship. Mariquiña and I are good friends. Three times a week, fifty-two weeks a year, I go to that café. Whatever she says, I do.'

He took a curve at terrific speed, and continued:

'Besides, if I charged you and the company found out, they'd fire me. I work for a company that delivers fresh fish to Madrid.

'Are you Mariquiña's sweetheart?'

'Yes and no. I'm not ready to get married yet. Those of us who move around have our hitching posts everywhere. In Madrid I get along fine. Better than fine. Holy God, what I've learned in that town! The women look for you and you just let yourself be loved. Especially in a house of girls where I go sometimes.

He burst out laughing, thinking that he had said something really witty.

'But I,' he added, 'play the monkey with them. That's the way they say it there. Play the monkey. Oh, I pay, sure. You have to be honest, or at least save your face. But then we play cards and I win it back again. That is, only in the cheap houses.

But sometimes I go to a high-class house, and no funny business goes there. The mistress of that house is called Paca la Encajera — the Lacemaker.'

Then he talked about his work. The company he worked for had a chain of fish-markets in Madrid. He earned good wages and worked only three days a week — Mondays, Wednesdays and Saturdays. It was not easy to get a job with this company. Before he started working they gave him many tests. After a long silence the driver added:

'In four hours we'll be in Madrid. It would have taken you over five days.'

He said his name was Victor. Ramiro found the driver's childish gaiety refreshing. The man talked without stopping. He apologized, saying that he did it to avoid falling asleep, since he had been at the wheel all night.

They reached Madrid on time, entering by the Prado. Ramiro got out, promising to meet his friend at eight in front of the Flor Bar in the Puerta del Sol.

'Don't forget my name,' he said. 'Victor. They call me Victor.'

Ramiro went up an intersecting avenue leading to the Retiro. 'I am in Madrid,' he said to himself happily. He sauntered aimlessly. A cicada was singing in the trunk of a tree, and Ramiro took it between two fingers, watching. The insect was still. He wanted to find out if the insects of Madrid reacted in the same way as those in his village, so he tapped its stomach with his finger. The insect began to sing again. Ramiro put it back in the tree thinking that this fat-bellied broad-faced insect looked like Aurora, and had the voice of the organist nun of Sigena.

The park was immense. A mild coolness pervaded everything. In the green shadows the song of a thrush was heard. Ramiro sat down on a marble bench, saying to himself that no better place in all the world was possible. Such would be the heaven in which the Sigena nuns believed. In a small formal garden he saw a marble fountain surrounded by roses. Standing on a graceful carved pediment was a siren revealing her soft white breasts on which the light reflected the yellow and red

73

tones of the roses. Ramiro sat down to gaze upon that fountain. Water from the jet was falling on the siren and she was vainly trying to cover herself with her hands. For she had hands, not fins. Her head was not deformed, and her hair was not green but the color of the marble, although in some corners where the water was slow to evaporate a little moss had grown.

Far away the bells of the tram-cars clanged and automobiles honked. 'I arrive in Madrid,' he thought, 'and make myself at home without care or uneasiness, as if I had been living in the city for years.' Yet he did not know where he would sleep that night or if he would eat at all the following day; for he had no intention of touching the eight hundred pesetas from the circus.

He got up and began retracing his steps. After walking for a little over half an hour he found himself beside a high iron grating tipped with gilded lance points. On the other side of the grating there was a wide street paved with rubble-stones, and four rows of trees. The houses, five or six stories high, revealed — beyond broad portals — carpeted marble stairs. At almost every house a man in livery stood at the door. Ramiro thought that the important people of the city must live here, and he remembered that he had a relative — a relative of his mother's — aristocratic and rich. He thought of him as one might think of the rings of Saturn.

Leaving the park he came to a building of red brick and gray stone, with a broad porch and double flight of stairs. On the façade he read: Museo del Prado. He had frequently come across allusions to the Prado Museum in the mayor's encyclopedia in his village, and he started up the stairs with almost religious emotion. A woman was selling prints and reproductions at a little stand.

He found himself in the middle of a gloomy rotunda with a very high ceiling and walls paneled in dark carved woods. It was like the entrance of a cathedral. At the back he could see a much lighter space where groups of visitors were coming and going, speaking in low tones. That was the central gallery, with large sky-lights through which the light entered, carefully gauged. His emotion grew as he walked through the gallery.

Both sides of the main gallery were covered with pictures of all sizes. Some were immense. These occupied the top places on the walls, and had monumental figures: an old man eating a nude child (Kronos devouring his children). Blue, rose, green, gray masses, surrounded by softer masses in gentle or violet contrasts, reflected the light, filling the air with floating forms. Ramiro did not know where to look. He would have liked to see all the pictures at once. When he was in front of one canvas, impatience to see the next kept him from concentrating. He sat down in front of a 'Venus' by Titian and stayed there for over an hour. At first he thought that this central gallery was all there was, but it was only a small part. On both sides spacious halls opened off, each one dedicated to a particular painter: Velázquez, El Greco, Murillo, Ribera, Zurbarán, Rubens, Goya. In the main gallery there were pictures by Veronese, Van Dyck, Raphael, and many others. He went down to the ground floor and saw classical sculptures, Greco-Roman marbles. He climbed another stair to a room full of Flemish primitives, and through it passed to another of Italian primitives. Returning to the central gallery, he looked once more into the Velázquez room, and then heard a distant bell as a guard in dark blue uniform and white gloves came to warn him that they were about to close. Several groups of visitors were moving towards the exit. Ramiro left feeling as if he were floating in the air. Remembering his own paintings in the village he said to himself: 'I will never touch a brush again.'

Once outside he began to think where he could sleep that night. Everything around him, in the streets, in the plazas, seemed new, rich, well organized. On the Castellana Boulevard there were processions of carriages of all kinds, old ladies in coaches drawn by horses in silver-embossed harness, limousines with elegantly dressed footmen.

At the hour agreed upon with the truck driver, Ramiro was

in front of the Flor Bar in the Puerta del Sol. So many people were passing through there that he would never have discovered his traveling companion if Victor had not suddenly presented himself and relieved Ramiro of his confusion, slapping him on the back. The truck driver was unrecognizable. He was so dressed up he looked like a manikin in a tailor's shop, and seemed especially pleased with his tie, green with golden flowers. He grabbed Ramiro by the arm and they got on a streetcar together. During the trip he related how he had stolen something from all the women he had known in Madrid: a brooch, lipstick, compact, and even an occasional garter. This arsenal helped him to put on airs in the village where he lived.

Victor treated Ramiro like a bashful boy in need of protection and told him that they were going to the house of Paca la Encajera.

When Ramiro confessed that he had never been in a house of prostitution Victor's enthusiasm increased:

'You've been lucky to find me. Don't think that the house we're going to is just any house. No. Not everybody goes there. Doña Paca is an old woman who knows lots of smart people. And a saint with her girls. Well, a mother, that's what I mean.'

The streetcar had left the center of Madrid and was going up the Calle de Alcalá. For Victor the entire city was one immense brothel. Ramiro realized that this could not be so, and the more enthusiastic Victor grew, the more silent and abstracted he became. He repeatedly asked himself: 'Why am I going with this fellow?'

The streetcar turned into an avenue. The Calle de Alcalá went on in another direction, disappearing into space. Finally they got off and went up an avenue with mansions on both sides, two- or three-story houses surrounded by gardens and iron gratings. They stopped in front of a gate. Victor pushed and saw that it was only partially closed. At the end of a gravel path was a marble porch. The door of the house was closed. An elderly servant woman appeared, looking at them distrustfully.

'The women are not in,' she hastened to say.

Victor explained to Ramiro:

'Here the girls go out at night, to the theatre, Andalusian taverns, cabarets.' Addressing the servant, he added: 'Don't leave us in the doorway. I am Victor.'

Once inside, he asked:

'Where is Doña Paca?'

'She has a headache. You, who are you?'

'I already told you that I am Victor, the fish trucker. Have you no memory?'

Losing his patience, he pulled out a handful of notes, held them under the servant's nose and said, nervously:

'Do you think I'm a nobody?'

Ramiro was shocked to see that the house looked like any other. There were religious prints in expensive frames on the walls, and a discreet silence throughout the house. Victor, in a courtly mood, insisted on paying his respects to Doña Paca, so the servant ushered them into a little parlor while she went to announce them. A pretty brunette appeared. When she saw that they were two she left without greeting them, and in a loud voice called: 'La Cañamón'. Another girl came almost at once. She was the daintiest doll imaginable. There was an air of nobility about her, like the Infantas in old engravings. Ramiro was tremendously impressed. She laughed and used tough street expressions, trying to give the impression that she was a very knowing little minx. Her fine oval face looked like wax and had a childlike mobility. Her eyes were small and rather deeply set, and Ramiro was surprised to discover that small and fugitive eyes could have a special beauty of their own.

La Cañamón wanted a glass of champagne, but Victor appeared not to heed. Ramiro thought of the money in the lining of his jacket. At that moment the servant announced that Doña Paca would see them. They went to another room, at the back of which was a glassed-in gallery facing a garden. There, seated in an armchair with many cushions, was Doña Paca. She nodded and pointed to the nearest chairs with her ivory-headed cane. Then, looking directly at Ramiro, she asked:

'Who is this young man?'

And a very strange thing happened. Doña Paca's eyes were riveted on Ramiro in an abnormal stare. Her hands opened and the cane fell to the carpeted floor with a soft thud. Doña Paca apparently wanted to speak and opened her mouth, unable to say a single word. Her hands waved about in the air, fluttering towards each other and then separating, with an accelerating movement like a palsied tremor. Then she fainted.

The girls ran for smelling-salts while the servant loosened Doña Paca's girdle and, raising her skirts, took off her garters. Ramiro was amazed at the youthfulness of the knees and thighs of this old woman. They returned to the little parlor. Victor was so impressed that he ordered champagne for La Cañamón. The brunette arrived shortly and said to Ramiro:

'You have evidently reminded Doña Paca of somebody important in her life.'

She looked at Ramiro admiringly. Ramiro offered La Cañamón a glass of champagne and kissed her lightly on the lips.

'This friend of mine is a romantic.'

'Why?'

'You don't kiss women in the profession on the lips,' he said in a doctoral tone.

The girls were offended and they protested. From Doña Paca's room a voice called, and the girls went to her. When the two men were alone, Victor asked:

'How are you set for money?'

'Bad. I don't intend to spend anything.'

'You could have said so before I ordered the bottle of champagne.'

A tense moment followed, but then Victor seemed to reconsider and recovered his good humor.

'Do you like La Cañamón?' he asked.

'Very much.'

'Really?'

'Yes. So much that I would marry her. Assuming she'd be willing.'

'That's the best joke I ever heard in a place like this. Marry a prostitute!'

Victor slapped his knee and roared. At that moment a queer type, affectedly dressed and with his hat on, with gray complexion and precise gestures, entered:

'Greetings to the gentlemen,' he said, touching his hat brim.

They offered him wine, but the stranger, after a glance at the bottle, refused:

'Thank you very much. But I never touch foreign brands.'

For an instant he seemed disposed to clarify his ideas on this subject, then refrained with a skeptical expression and disappeared into Doña Paca's room. Victor remarked:

'He must be Doña Paca's lover.'

The girls came back and the servant told Ramiro that Doña Paca wished to speak to him. Ramiro went, thinking: 'Now this imbecile will tell the girls that I want to marry La Cañamón.' He found the old woman alone. Beside her chair, on a small low table, was the bottle of smelling-salts which she sniffed occasionally. She invited Ramiro to sit near her and said to him:

'When young men come to these houses they lie and joke. If you prefer, don't tell me anything, but if you do tell me something, I beg you to tell the truth. Are you a relative of Prim's?'

Ramiro said yes, without knowing who Prim was. He could only recall having heard the girls in the park singing:

> In the Street of the Turk
> they assassinated Prim
> seated in his coach
> the Civil Guard with him.

Looking at Ramiro the old woman said she felt as if she were seeing General Prim brought back to life. 'He had a beard, but sometimes, to avoid persecution by the Queen in times of conspiracies, he disguised himself and shaved. Beardless, he was just like you. Don't think,' she added, that I am an old maniac — nymphomaniac, as they say now — and that I am going to drape myself around your neck. No. Nothing like that. I am

79

only a ridiculous old woman, long since ripe for the grave. But I would like to hear you talk, if you don't mind.'

'I . . .' Ramiro began.

'They killed him,' she interrupted. 'They killed him on the Calle del Marqués de Cubas, also called the Street of the Turk. It seems like yesterday, but it was in the year 1870.'

After a melancholy pause she continued:

'You are exactly like him. You have the same impetuousness. I don't know what you're like inside but Prim didn't believe in anything. Those who believe in nothing are, nevertheless, the only ones who in a given moment can believe in everything. He was nervous, too. And he didn't listen. At least he looked as if he didn't listen, but he never missed a single detail of anything going on around him. I think he had a sixth sense. He would have married me, and I was in love with him like a good girl. I couldn't marry him. You understand. I am a bad woman.'

Ramiro said nothing. He was thinking of La Cañamón, and as if the thought had awakened the same suggestion in the old woman, she said:

'La Cañamón is an angel. They told me that you like her. What do you see in her, if I may ask?'

And without waiting for Ramiro's answer, she added:

'Before you leave you must give me your address. Do you have a telephone?'

Ramiro told her that he had just arrived in Madrid and still had no address.

'Stay here tonight,' she said. 'Tomorrow we will talk more leisurely. As far as I'm concerned, if La Cañamón wishes, she can have a guest . . . Do you understand? Oh, youth! How good it is to be young!'

She looked as if she were going to faint again. Her hands began to tremble. Ramiro held the salts near her and made her sniff them. She said:

'Call Dorothea, please.'

Ramiro did not know who Dorothea was, but he returned to the parlor and asked for her. The brunette went to fetch her.

Victor had disappeared. At that moment the taciturn man came out and saluted:

'May the gentlemen find contentment.'

He went away through the opposite door. The brunette returned and Ramiro asked her about La Cañamón. She came in, too, and taking Ramiro by the hand led him to her room, a spacious and solemn bedroom with dark green rugs and curtains.

When Ramiro woke up it was mid-morning. La Cañamón was still asleep, with her little nose of purest wax against the pillow. Ramiro dressed without making a sound and stepped out into the hall. The house was still. The other girls were also sleeping. He found the servant, who told him that Victor had left shortly before, giving notice that he was not responsible for anyone's expenses. The servant added:

'I'm telling you so you'll know who you're dealing with.' She said also that Ramiro had nothing to pay.

Out in the street he felt sad and lonely. As he walked in the sun he saw a flower shop. He bought two dozen white carnations. Since he did not know La Cañamón's address, he delivered the carnations himself. He gave them to the servant, who looked at him with amazement and then smiled, saying that La Cañamón was not yet up.

Ramiro had no money left, that is to say only a few copper coins, since he had no intention of touching the circus money. He was hungry and he enjoyed feeling alone, poor and hungry, like the artists whose lives he had read. Thinking of La Cañamón, he believed himself in an intimate relation with a miraculous little being. For the first time he had had intercourse with a woman and he was dazzled. In his dazzled state he thought of the apothecary's orphan daughter, saying to himself:

'I ought to marry her.'

He felt in love with La Cañamón but obliged to marry Aurora.

He wished to return to the Museum, but wore himself out wandering about almost all day long without finding it. He was hungry. He covered the city, the old and the modern sections.

81

It was very late when finally he reached the Castellana. On one side of the broad avenue occasional streetcars passed with lighted signs saying: Hipódromo. He took one of them, wanting to get as far as possible from the center of Madrid. The car left the city, and half an hour later reached another urban district, like a small village. It was Chamartín de la Rosa. The streets were deserted. He crossed the village and struck out over the countryside, in the direction of some pine groves surrounding a large building of red brick and gray stones. Ramiro was thinking: 'That building must be a convent.' Inside the pine grove he went as far as possible from the building, and in a secluded and pleasant spot lay down at the foot of a tree. 'Wild animals, when they are going to die, run away to the forest to hide,' he recalled with a certain romanticism. He intended to look for work the next day and to find it somewhere. With a sensation of well-being, thinking of La Cañamón, he fell asleep.

He woke at dawn, walked to the village and caught a streetcar that left him near the Prado. But the Museum was not yet open. He went to the Retiro and sat down on a bench under the trees of a small garden enclosure. Finding an old newspaper in a waste-paper basket, he read it through, from the editorials to the last advertisement. He had the impression that life in the city was bewildering and difficult. The classified advertisements gave him little hope of finding work, but this didn't worry him at all, for he knew that in a few moments he would be surrounded by the paintings of Velázquez, El Greco, Goya. . .

With no hope of finding any mail he went to the main post office nearby and inquired at the General Delivery window. Some days before he had sent that address to Aurora. To his surprise, but without any pleasure, he saw that he had a letter. It was from her. She began: 'Esteemed Ramiro.' Every word seemed to be wrapped in cotton. As always the girl put on airs with him, but she sounded amorous.

Ramiro began to think of her as something distant, pure and unpleasant. Like his own childhood. The letter smelled of melted wax.

82

He went back to the Museum. It was open. In front of some pictures were copyists with easels and palettes. The place smelled of turpentine, and the odor revived Ramiro's memories of the hermitage in his village. He wondered if the copyists were making these reproductions to sell, or for themselves.

He sat down in front of the 'Meniñas' of Velázquez. He was weary and as a result of much looking and not comprehending, the fatigue was producing a heaviness that localized on the left side of his stomach. He stayed there all morning long. He watched foreigners with guide books in their hands file by, young men with bushy hair, smart-looking girls. About two in the afternoon a professor arrived with a group of students. The professor, in a doctoral tone, was declaring that the corporeality of the figures in that picture came from physical laws of light unknown in painting before Velázquez. He added the names of each of the figures, and when he said that the one dimly seen on the right was King Felipe III, Ramiro was again conscious of the social importance that a great artist could attain.

He continued gazing at the picture. The dwarf on the right looked like Aurora — after her illness — except that Aurora was large and blonde. Ramiro remembered that he was now seventeen and that she must be the same age. It would soon be time for them to marry, although Ramiro wanted to earn some money to help his mother enter the Sigena convent. But as he thought about that old woman who hated him, he found it pleasant to imagine the displeasure that he would cause her by marrying Aurora, for she considered the girl socially inferior.

He looked at the dwarf with a kind of repugnant relish. Marrying her would be somewhat like mocking life. This mocking of life struck him as appealing and worthy indeed of a bastard Vallemediano.

On his way out he again passed through the main gallery and saw a picture representing a medieval auto-da-fé. At the top was God himself, no less. The religious dignitaries on their thrones came next. Below them were the nude culprits burning at the stake, and at the very bottom the people. He went closer to see

83

the smallest figures. The only pure thing there, he reflected with sarcasm, was the executioner.

And he left thinking: 'Life is ugly. But it is the work of God. And we worship God for His work — His ugly work — what a contradiction!' He was very tired and sat down on a bench near the museum entrance. He wanted to recall pleasant things in his life but the only thing that brought him some kind of nostalgia was the sea. He got up and continued walking.

The fatigue had disappeared and in his imagination he was seeing the princess and the king of Velázquez's picture — not motionless, but moving, talking to each other, and looking at Ramiro. He noticed that two girls were coming towards him, half curious, half timidly. In faulty Spanish they asked him if he would be their guide and show them the city, but Ramiro told them that he had just arrived in Madrid where he was as much a foreigner as they. The girls went away a little confused, and in that confusion Ramiro was suddenly aware of erotic possibilities.

He was hungry and spent his last coins on food. Then he walked through the central streets past elegant shops. Disconcerted he started looking for the Retiro Park, supposing that he could spend the night there. He could not fix his attention on the anomaly of living without a home or money — he did not want to use what he had in the lining of his coat because of his feeling that this was the price of the life of the equestrienne and *Chéri*. He knew that without eating he could not live, but death did not frighten him; to see it coming in these conditions was almost a pleasure. In this pleasure there were cold and warm colors, and in them red, as in Titian, predominated. In the tones of Veronese and El Greco — livid greens and spectral yellows — he found an allusion to Aurora's kisses, which he had classified in a way that he himself did not understand: *chlorophyllic kisses*.

The evening was very different from the morning in the Retiro. Everything suggested romantic repose. Before long he saw some watchmen walking around sounding a small trumpet, warning the people before closing. But the park was immense and nothing would be easier than to hide. For more than an hour he walked in the same direction, avoiding the main avenues and discovering the gradually deepening silence. He happened on the meteorological observatory. It was surrounded by large clumps of bushes and leafy trees, with occasional secluded corners, and in these corners, fortunately, benches. He made himself comfortable on one of them. From there he could see a lighted window in the observatory. The open window had a white curtain fluttering lightly in the breeze.

Looking at the sky, which had green streaks like El Greco's, he felt that the only thing binding him to life was a certain rich unconsciousness, and in this thought he found a kind of pleasure similar to that of painting. A sumptuous unconsciousness and a weary disdain before other human beings. *Before* and not *against*. It wasn't worthwhile to be an enemy of men.

Fatigue was overcoming him and he stretched out on the bench and fell asleep. Next morning, with the first light of day, he was awake. The observatory window was still open and the white curtain waving like a flag. He wished to leave the park, but it was very early and the gates were closed. He washed in a fountain and drank from his cupped hands. He remembered that his shirt was rumpled, the collar really soiled, and that he could not buy another. 'I must look like a tramp,' he thought. But as soon as they opened the museum he was there. Impatiently he went from room to room, and each painter seemed to speak to him in a different tongue. Finally he settled down in front of the paintings of Goya. The old painter seemed to be saying to him: 'A man who starves to death with eight hundred pesetas in the lining of his coat is mad. Of course, everyone has a right to his own madness. But do you think that money is the price of the equestrienne's life? So what? That woman's life was worth no more than that of the circus lion or crocodile, also burned to death. It is true that you reach these extreme conclusions without ceasing to live outside of, and on the margin of what others call *"life"*. What would happen to you if you really entered into it?' Saying this, Goya laughed with his thin lips, and went on talking: 'I stole. And I killed. Not only a rival or enemy. I would have killed, and without the slightest remorse, that pretty nude creature they called the Duchess Cayetana whom you are contemplating now in my picture. I only admitted one norm in my life: to live and be in condition to paint, to express my life. What does the rest matter?'

Ramiro answered, talking to himself: 'Yes, but you entered into life. And I am not going to enter. I do not want to enter. Why? Ah, this I do not know although I can imagine.'

6

GOYA still seemed to be talking to him, whether in earnest or jestingly Ramiro did not know. 'We consume ourselves, burning. You have only begun to burn, and your fire is young. Take your money out of the lining of your jacket; eat, drink, and "burn"; and come to see me again tomorrow with your body and soul satisfied.'

At closing time Ramiro, wearier than ever, started walking along the Prado toward the Castellana. He saw the Chamartin streetcars and vainly searched his pockets for a coin so as to get out to the pine groves. It would have taken three hours on foot — too long after two days without food. He went to the Retiro, but the gates were closed. He felt no hunger — only a kind of intoxication which kept him from walking in a straight line. He considered himself the victim, not of society or men, but of fatality and God. And that was pleasant. He walked on, not daring to sit down on a bench for fear of falling asleep and being detained as a vagrant without proper identification papers. As he approached the Hipódromo the café terraces gradually gave way to little beer and *horchata* stands with several dozen tables scattered under the trees. Farther on they disappeared. Ramiro sat down on a bench and fell asleep, leaving his hat beside him. Two or three hours later he awoke to find his hat had been stolen. This amused him. The poor devil stealing his hat must have been a thief's apprentice, or an old and unsuccessful thief.

In either case it was touching. He felt well. But he was, he reflected, on the way to the end. He tried to see everything around him as a natural desert which he peopled to his liking with the images of the Museum. He got up and began strolling along, wandering idly until dawn.

In the early morning light the trees along the Castellana, full of birds, were fresh and moist. Every leaf gleamed like a gem. The joy animating the birds refreshed his soul, but he heard their chatter as a kind of music suggesting an immense and nonexistent innocence. 'Perhaps,' he thought, 'that innocence is in everything except men.' He felt neither sadness nor melancholy, but a somewhat painful stupor. The risk of dying of hunger seemed simple and natural to him. Nevertheless the possibility of losing consciousness and receiving first aid from the public health services was repellent. He felt important in his misfortune.

He started off in the direction of the Hipódromo as if he were going somewhere. Before reaching the end of the avenue he turned to the left, and by chance entered a very wide street where bedclothes and mattresses were draped over the balconies. He lost his way and when he tried to return to the Castellana realized that he was in a labyrinth of streets in a modern section of the city. The weight of his body pushed him to one side. He tried to look as if he were going somewhere, but his will failed him.

He happened to be in front of a building under construction where workers were arriving to begin their day's work. In the daylight the idea of dying, so natural at night, seemed extravagant and absurd. He went up to a foreman thinking: 'If they give me a job they won't pay till Saturday, and how will I live till Saturday?' The foreman told him he could not give him work and that he should see the delegate.

Ramiro went in where they were working, asked for the delegate, and was taken to him. He was a bourgeois-looking man.

'There is a job as substitute day-laborer,' he told him, 'at four pesetas a day.'

'All right.'

'Show me your union card.'

Ramiro had no union card, so the delegate shrugged his shoulders and turned his back. Beside him was a carpenter sawing a beam. He looked up, annoyed:

'You, give the man the job. If the union card's the trouble, he'll have it by noon.'

Ramiro waited. The delegate, raising his voice, said:

'Take that shovel and get to work with the mortar.'

Ramiro took off his jacket and began work. Realizing that he was not very proficient his fellow-workers sent him along with others to transport the mortar in a wheelbarrow. Ramiro was most careful to do it well. When he returned with the empty wheelbarrow they showed him how, if he wheeled it with his arms raised and bent, his hands at the height of his shoulders, he would tire himself less. When it was time to eat, the carpenter asked Ramiro to join him. Together they went to a place where they were in the habit of leaving their street clothes to change into overalls. The carpenter opened a drawer and took out some papers. He began putting down Ramiro's name and other details on a little card. Then he took a seal out of his pocket, glued it on, and on the seal put some initials. He seemed to carry all the tools of the secretariat on his person.

It was necessary to pay a few cents and Ramiro said he had no money. The carpenter hastened to reassure him:

'You can give it to me when you get paid. How long has it been since you've eaten?'

'Bah, that doesn't matter,' smiled Ramiro.

'What do you mean, it doesn't matter?' replied the astonished carpenter. His wife would be arriving any moment with food, and he invited Ramiro to join them.

The carpenter said his name was Graco. He was a journeyman and earned twelve pesetas. Graco's wife, whose name was Libertad, arrived. In this couple there was a natural delicacy with which they conquered Ramiro more than with their food. When the bell rang they went back to work. But Ramiro felt no happier. As he went back and forth with the wheelbarrow, he was thinking that the ideal would be to live in that light-headed and semi-fluid state of the man who has not eaten for two days. Sounds were purer, colors more delicate, odors more fragrant. And one did not feel hungry. He really wasn't hungry. The brain had a prodigious clarity.

At six the work-day ended. The delegate hunted up Ramiro, asked him for his union card, and said, disgruntled:

'Your wages will be five pesetas.'

He took note of the number and handed him back the card. Ramiro was leaving when he saw Graco coming up to him:

'Come home with me. We have room for you.'

They headed for Cuatro Caminos and soon were there. Graco lived in a one-story brick house, with geraniums in the windows. He showed Ramiro to his room. Graco and his wife went to a meeting and Ramiro dropped down on the bed. He tried to go on thinking about his situation but fell asleep. When Graco and Libertad returned they decided not to wake him up for supper. Ramiro slept until morning, woke up happy, had breakfast with his friends, and got ready to return to work. They both looked at him with quiet satisfaction. Ramiro felt obliged to promise to pay them as soon as he got his wages.

'Our house,' said Graco gravely, 'has one door, and the door has no lock. Anyone who likes may come in at any time of the day or night. Society is badly organized and we are all responsible.'

Ramiro was a little disappointed when he realized they had not done all this for him, but out of loyalty to their principles.

He was thinking about La Cañamón. He had no desire to go to see her — the Infanta, as he sometimes called her, the nickname 'La Cañamón' — 'Birdseed' — striking him as unjustly vulgar, because the idea that she would give herself to any man, to the first-comer, after having been his, drove him to despair.

Graco had friends who came to see him. and he introduced Ramiro as a 'comrade'. At the meetings he sometimes met young people who spoke several languages. They did not smoke, drink, or eat meat. They invariably had a lot of hair, a healthy sunburnt color, and wore open sandals on their sockless feet. To

Ramiro they looked like ancient prophets. Very beautiful girls were occasionally among them. One day he saw a young man with Graco who was rejecting their doctrines and shouting:

'No, no. I admit that the Spaniard who at twenty is not an anarchist is a poor devil, but the one who is still an anarchist after thirty is an idiot.'

Ramiro listened to everything that was said, not daring to form an opinion. He was aware that these men were trying to change the moral order of the world. Libertad and Graco had come to seem like his own brother and sister, and in the ease with which he had accepted this feeling he saw something miraculous beyond his power to understand.

Now and then Graco would take an ill-humored dig at Ramiro:

'What kind of bird are you, anyway?' he would ask, looking at him in amazement.

Ramiro laughed and said that the only thing he could tell about himself was his name. He was ignorant of all the rest. No one really knows anything essential about himself. Why should he? Libertad would laugh hard and take her husband's part, saying:

'Graco's right. You are like a friar.'

'A cracked friar,' added Graco, very serious.

Ramiro laughed and protested:

'No, not crazy. There you're wrong, Graco. A little nervous, maybe. But what can a fellow do?'

Then alone he would say to himself: 'The trouble with me is that I can't enter into life. I listen and don't believe what I hear. I look and don't believe what I see. I speak and my words sound as if they were spoken by another and do not deserve to be taken very seriously.' Precisely because of this — his unwillingness to enter into life — he refused to abandon himself to anything spontaneous. He was in love with La Cañamón and was still thinking about marrying Aurora. He hated his mother and sent her money. He had plenty of money on him and had been on the point of starving. 'Surely,' he thought, 'there must be a place for people like me. For people who don't want to take part in the game.'

Some months later Graco arrived home one night very worried, saying that the next day he had to leave on a trip. Libertad did not conceal her concern either. Thinking that there must be some danger behind all this, Ramiro offered to accompany his friend.

'You?' Graco replied. 'What for? The fewer the better on these missions,' he added.

Graco left, and two days later the papers published the account of a bank robbery in a northern city. The hold-up men had escaped with almost three million pesetas. A bank employee had been wounded, and in the fight with the police Graco had been killed. The others had been able to flee with the money.

Libertad moved like a phantom through the house. She did not cry.

'The police will come,' she said. 'I am surprised they've not been here already.'

Ramiro admired her serenity, which he found natural and at the same time monstrous, though he could not have said why. He asked:

'The money taken from the bank . . . is it for the organization?'

'Yes. Who else could it be for? You must get out of here at once, because the police will come.'

She was gazing at a newspaper photograph that had been published with the story of the theft. There was a street, a handsome building in the background, and a man dead on the sidewalk. The man was Graco. And Libertad remained dry-eyed. Ramiro could not understand why she did not cry.

'The terrible thing is,' said Libertad in a weak and trembling voice, 'that when people see a man dead like this they think that he is not like other men, but a beast.'

Ramiro had thought the same thing when he first saw the picture. They were quiet for a long while. Ramiro asked:

91

'And you, what are you going to do?'

'I will go to live with some friends. The police have not yet identified Graco. As soon as they do they'll come here.'

Ramiro said that he would wait for the police. Since he was innocent there could be no danger. Libertad told him that the police only needed a suspicion to ruin a man. But Ramiro insisted on staying — at heart he wanted to be arrested — and she picked up a small bag in which she had packed some clothing and left.

That same night the police arrived with an impressive display of strength. They surrounded the house and arrested Ramiro. Since he did not give his real name, and also lied about his birthplace, which the police disproved by telephone, they became gravely suspicious. For two days Ramiro had nothing to eat or drink. Again he felt that inner fluidity already familiar to him, but this time it was not pleasant. At the end of the second day he confessed his real identity. As soon as this was verified he was fed and taken to the Model Jail.

Ramiro's arrest had awakened curiosity, and the newspapers were devoting a great deal of space to him. The news about Graco exhausted, they exploited any accessory detail. The police never found the other assailants. When Ramiro was identified some of the incidents in his life, including the apothecary's death, came to light. Everything was published. With cold humor Ramiro reflected that in jail he was expiating the deaths of the apothecary and the equestrienne. Jail seemed like a school to him. He felt happy and tried to recognize his happiness as the same kind that he had noticed in Graco before whom he had sometimes asked himself: 'Why do *they* want to make a revolution? They don't need it. They are the happiest beings in the universe.' And this happiness, incomprehensible at first, he was beginning to feel. To be like Graco seemed to him the end of a complicated process not attainable by everyone. 'If I could eventually become one of them ...' he pondered, fascinated. Graco's death did not strike him as a tragedy, or even a misfortune, but simply an accident. 'I too would know how to die like that,' he thought. The

92

usefulness of his death did not matter. A preoccupation of that nature could not occur to anyone. There are no useful deaths. But there could be a certain glory in dying like Graco. The bad thing about it was that to leave life as Graco had done, you first had to enter into it. And Ramiro had not entered into it. Perhaps he never would.

They had taken him to prison at night. Groping his way around in the dark cell he found a straw mattress, lay down and was soon asleep. In the morning he stretched, and having nothing to do, began to read the scribblings on the walls. The bolts on the three floors of every gallery clanged, and the metal plates of the armored doors echoed the sound, increasing it in the hollow spaces. One of the scribblings said: 'The Burgos hangman is the best,' and someone had written underneath: '. . . welcome to him, you bastard.' Meanwhile Ramiro was thinking: 'I am in jail,' and feeling himself to be interesting. He noticed bullet marks here and there. 'Those bullets,' he thought, 'came through the window.' The one who had been in the cell before him, he found out later, was bored, and some nights played at escaping. He would take off his jacket, hang it by a string out of the window, and pull it up and down the wall. One shot would ring out, then another. Then perhaps a heavy discharge. The old man would pull up his jacket riddled with bullets, count the bulletholes, sigh, and say:

'Premature.'

Ramiro examined the long, cold cell. 'If this is all . . .' he thought. When he was searched the first time they took away all his papers. The second time, they took his last week's wages, almost intact, and gave him a receipt for the money. Then during another search in the gallery, his shoe-laces, belt and tie. In the lining of his jacket he still had the eight one hundred peseta bills.

The sound of bolts being drawn that had been coming nearer now rang out at his cell. The door opened and a sombre fellow appeared with a hunk of bread which he left on a stool.

'Are you in for swindling?' he asked.

93

'No,' said Ramiro.

'Robbery?'

'No.'

'Blood?'

'No.'

'White-slaving? Gambling?'

Ramiro shook his head. The stranger gave him a disdainful glance and said:

'I see. Public order. Another one of those who want to reform the world.'

He spat out of the corner of his mouth, looked him over again slowly, and added:

'In that case El Piculín will come.'

Alone again Ramiro sat down on the cot. A gust of fresh air blew in at the window, and when Ramiro felt it on his forehead he had the physical evidence of freedom. The wind embodied that dangerous abstraction: freedom. He started remembering. He was saved from this peril for the moment by the presence of a strange individual who came in and introduced himself as 'El Piculín'. He had an enormous head which was very evidently good for nothing. He was small, beardless, and getting along in years. He only knew how to steal the bottles of milk left in doorways, and since in this field he had no competitors the police would go and pick him up immediately whenever they received a complaint of this kind. El Piculín returned to prison very content. Here he had food, room, tips. Ramiro gave him a look, and asked:

'Why don't you think up something else?'

'I've been brooding over that particular for years, but haven't happened on to anything worthwhile. Now if I was like Mangas ... Mangas earns as much as he wants by puncturing tires in parking lots and then helping to change the wheel. Rare is the fellow that doesn't give him a peseta.'

Ramiro lay back on the straw mattress again. Meanwhile El Piculín said that he would sweep the cell. 'What you give me later, when they give you vouchers for the money they took away from you in the office, will be for the other orderly who exploits me. He's exploiting me and three others who work in the second gallery.'

El Piculín talked like a mechanical head without arms or legs. He also asked Ramiro if he was in jail for swindling, and when he found out he was not he seemed vexed.

Since Ramiro had nothing to say, he added:

'Swindling is the most distinguished business here.'

Through the window came a monotonous noise, like the scraping of the edges of a tin can on the stones of the wall.

'That's a professor,' explained El Piculín, 'who is busy in the patio making a cup for you. A drinking-cup. Out of an empty can. He makes one for all the new prisoners. He's a little...'

He touched his temple with one finger.

Ramiro wanted to go out into the patio like the others, but he was in solitary confinement and, as El Piculín told him, he would not be able to go out until the judge had heard his deposition. El Piculín knew many little things about prison life. He went away. The wind blew louder and louder on the roof-tiles, and in the groves of the park close by. In the wind Ramiro imagined he detected a voice. Was it Graco? Once he thought so. Ramiro really believed he heard his friend saying:

'You see? El Piculín prefers to live inside these walls. Freedom is not in the street. You have freedom with you. You are locked up with all your immense freedom. And you say you don't wish to enter into life?'

Since Ramiro could not go out to the patio during the exercise hours he entertained himself listening to the wind. He also recalled the incidents with the police. During the first questioning they made the following observation: 'He is very young and inexperienced.' This humiliated Ramiro. He wanted to tell them that he needed no experience, because experience only makes skeptics, egoists and embittered people.

Ramiro was taken to the court to make his deposition. The judge was a gloomy man, well along in years. A stenographer took down Ramiro's testimony and when the prisoner had signed his statement, the judge told him that he was no longer incommunicado. Ramiro returned to his cell. Early that same afternoon the door opened and a head wearing a uniform cap peered in:

'At the first note of the bugle,' it told him, 'open the door wide, go out into the gallery, and stand at attention. Then do like everybody else.'

The man disappeared, leaving the door ajar. It was the first degree of liberty inside the prison. Ramiro could go to the patio, talk with the other prisoners, and walk more than six paces in the same direction. When he heard the bugle he went out. His next-door neighbor, who was also in front of his door, was talking to himself and looking at his wrists:

'Well, if I'm not in fine shape for the trip to the pen!'

Later Ramiro's partner in line, he told him that his aorta was inflamed. Since the doctor had told him this, he had been repeating it to everyone with a certain satisfaction.

'Now you'll see,' he added. 'day after tomorrow I leave for Dueso with two Sisters of Charity.'

He meant two Civil Guards.

Ramiro went out to the patio with curiosity. On one side of the triangular courtyard was a high wall. On the other two sides were the walls of two galleries, covered with barred windows. On top of the wall a sentinel in his box was on guard. Seated in the sand against the wall, most of the inmates of the first gallery were smoking and chatting. Groups of three or four walked the length of the patio, arguing. A middle-aged man with gray hair, gold-rimmed glasses and embroidered slippers, came up to Ramiro. In his hand he was carrying an empty can. It was 'the professor'. They called him this because of his conventional and, at the same time, eccentric air.

'Are you,' he asked Ramiro, 'the one occupying cell sixty-five?'

'Yes, sir.'

The professor said that he had made him a drinking-cup and that tin cups were very practical in jail, where glasses were forbidden. The can passed into Ramiro's keeping. Ramiro thanked him, but was impatient. He had spotted an acquaintance he had met in Graco's house. Ramiro was admiring the cup that glimmered in the sun when the professor suddenly saw some imperfection and took it back again, went to a corner, and began to scrape it rhythmically against the stones. The cup moved back and forth with a sharp shrill sound that filled the patio. A gipsy walked about with twitching hands, and looking fiercely at the professor exclaimed:

'That fellow, he brings me the evil eye with his tinny noise!'

The breeze formed graceful whirlwinds and swept a paper into the corner where it was storing up dry leaves. The professor arrived, wiping the can on the inside of his jacket. The wind — Graco? — said in Ramiro's ear: 'I killed for love, you through error, others because of hate. Most of those still on the outside kill through omission. Through omission, understand? They are the worst criminals, those who risk nothing. And Cojo? Ask Cojo why he killed the cardinal. And after talking to him perhaps you'll decide to intervene in what you call *life*, even though you still don't know what it is.'

Ramiro returned to his cell without having had the opportunity to talk to Cojo. The cell window faced east and every day the first rays of the sun were projected inside on the wall. Since he went to bed very early he was often awake before it was light. At this hour he felt safer, more serene, and happier than when he was free. Some days the limpid cold of the morning, the smell of iron and cement, plus an easy conscience, made Ramiro think that life in jail can be pleasant. After a while he would go out into the sandy gray patio. Every day when they broke ranks some new individual would approach Ramiro. This morning, walking lightly in spite of his peg-leg, there was Cojo, the Hobbler. He was a young man of quiet appearance. He smiled, revealing very white teeth, and asked Ramiro if he had been living in Graco's house at the time of the bank affair.

Before replying, Ramiro gave Cojo a long look. That man had been implicated in the death of Cardinal Soldevilla. The police only suspected Cojo, evidently, but soon after the crime he arrived at the jail, marking his way with precise dots. He was indicted, but no one could prove anything against him. Cojo was periodically transferred from one prison to another, and appeared in the patios of all of them tranquil and smiling.

They walked back and forth, turning around in the middle of the patio so as not to frighten six or eight sparrows pecking at a piece of bread on the ground.

Throughout the morning Cojo spoke only in vague generalities about the regime inside the prison. This jail was a place of privilege where few had the good fortune to go. Cojo, full of curiosity, was trying to make Ramiro talk. Near them was a financier who had come to grief with a scheme to raise money for cheap building construction. Two pickpockets and three swindlers were listening to him like pupils in a class. The light in the patio was honey-colored. The wind promised storms. In fact the storm was already breaking.

Ramiro put a friendly hand on Cojo's shoulder and asked, pointing to a spectral type walking along with a notebook under his arm:

'Who is that?'

'The librarian.'

The librarian passed among the groups of men with a timid air. He seemed to be saying: 'I beg your pardon, gentlemen murderers and thieves, I am unworthy to figure among this selection of heroes.' He was carrying a notebook and whenever someone would ask him for a book he jotted the title down. Lightning rasped in his voice as in a telephone receiver. The professional murderers were the aristocracy in the patio. They frequently asked for the *Portfolio of the Artistic Nude*.

The first thunder rolled and a few raindrops fell. The librarian marched off, but not without first giving Ramiro a card on which he read: 'Herminio Fernández Plat. — Just a man.' With this in his hand Ramiro got into the line that was forming by the wall, under the orders of the guard. The line was now crawling at the foot of the cube of brick and cement. Cojo smiled and accommodated his wooden leg to the normal step of the rest. The professor had turned up his coat lapels to protect his starched collar. As always, the Andalusian behind him stepped on both his heels, and the bourgeois protested, smiling:

'For heaven's sake, my dear sir. The same old thing every single day.'

Ramiro became acquainted with another Andalusian, known as El Tripa. He was a character who spoke about his trial with indignation because, as he said, he had had two prosecutors and only one defense attorney. He was a guitar player and illiterate. Of gipsy origin he was a relative, like all gipsies, of Pastora Imperio, El Gallo, Montoya. He hated political prisoners, and they responded to his hatred with a jocose congeniálity that exasperated him. His hatred was compatible with a mysterious respect for Cojo. A respect of indiscernible origins.

There was a fat and frowning killer in the patio who paced nervously and opened his arms wide, talking to himself. Every morning he went out to the patio with a big hunk of dry bread that he put to soak. When it was soft he took it to one end of the patio and began calling the sparrows. The wall and sentry-box soon filled with birds and then Curro — for this was his name — returned to his place beside the veranda. The killer gave a belly-laugh and said:

'Poor birds. If I didn't look after them. . . .'

When someone, strolling, went close to where the sparrows were eating and frightened them, Curro looked daggers at the impertinent fellow. One day Ramiro told him that he could not understand those old maid's sentiments of his, and Curro said:

'Why not? Can't you see that they are innocent little animals?'

Ah, innocent. In jail the spectacle of innocence was a pleasure for the criminals, a pleasure that Ramiro could not understand. Maybe he would never be able to understand. Ramiro was not innocent. What could he be, he, Ramiro? He wished that he could see inside himself with some clarity.

99

7

CURRO, with his left cheek wrinkled up and one eye closed was repeating:

'They are innocent.'

And he added, looking at Ceneque:

'What've you got to say, you son of a bitch?'

Ceneque smiled.

'All the logic in the world's on your side, Curro.'

Curro continued to look at him bitterly:

'Are you serious or joking? Because if you're joking I'll smash one of your horns for you.'

Then they went on talking about their crimes as if they were natural, unimportant things.

Ramiro was pacing up and down with Cojo, trying to become his friend. But Cojo, apparently simple and trusting, was always on guard and listened to Ramiro's confidences with only one ear. Ramiro wished to make him talk, but Cojo was silent or vague, and in turn questioned him about his friendship with Graco. It was a friendship whose social background he could not comprehend. The game of evasions sometimes annoyed Ramiro and he would leave Cojo and seek the company of the professional thieves. Cojo said goodbye with his friendly expression, his smile revealing fine white teeth. The calm and balance of that murderer of cardinals vexed Ramiro. Recalling the book on the Renaissance he thought of other cardinals murdered by pontiffs. And of Pope John XVI who, tortured by the cardinal who was to succeed him on the throne, with his eyes torn out, with his mutilated half-tongue repeated the words dictated to him by his successor: 'It is just for you to treat me as you do; I deserve nothing else. It is just for you to treat me as you do; I deserve nothing else. . . .' For hours on end he chanted those words with his bleeding mouth.

The terrible punishment cells were in the dungeon of the prison. Near them were several shower baths used only by some prisoners. They asked for permission to bathe and when they received it could go alone or together, without being under guard. Thirty minutes later they all had to be back in the patio. The underground part of the jail was humid and dark. The floor, of clayey earth, had something about it reminiscent of the cellar under a theater stage, or a ship's hold. Great waste spaces, small beams and columns, a black corridor lined with punishment cells on both sides. Near the showers there was also a bath-tub, with now and then a little water in it cooling bottles of wine.

'The orderlies' wine,' someone said.

One day Curro also went down to the showers, very suspiciously, looking all around. He was afraid to go down to the dungeon, but he needed to have a private talk with someone, and he had asked permission to take a shower. Seeing the others under the spray he shivered and sneezed like a cat.

It was a cloudy day. The wind was still beating upon the galleries, stealing in through doors and windows. Ramiro thought he heard Graco's voice: 'I held up the bank. Everything went well, even my death. If I had only been wounded, the police might have got confessions and information out of me. Not because I am capable of talking out of cowardice, but because they employ chemical means, drugs that destroy the will. My victory was just one rung on the ladder of everyone's failure. Because we all fail. You all fail. Everything that lives seeks its own destruction. Through pleasure, or pain, just the same as through indifference. The only interesting thing in all this is your resistance to getting into it all.'

The wind quieted and Ramiro got up and started pacing back and forth, alone. Cojo came up to ask him if he knew who the other two companions were who had worked with Graco on the bank hold-up. Ramiro was on the point of saying yes, just to presume a bit, but he did not know how to lie. He said no. This reply seemed to reassure Cojo, who commented:

'It was a clever job. A pity Graco fell.'

In the afternoon an incident of a rather serious nature oc-

101

curred. Someone insulted a guard who answered with a blow, and a crowd of prisoners gathered round to protest.

Ramiro felt that any man imprisoned should protest, no matter what the reason, and he cried out louder than the others.

Shortly afterward all who had protested were put in solitary confinement. 'I am playing Don Quixote stupidly,' Ramiro told himself, in the dungeon.

The cells had no windows and the doors with large peepholes opened upon a passageway which was equally dark.

Straining his eyes to see in the darkness, Ramiro noticed the little square of light cast on the floor by the peephole through which the guards looked from time to time. At that very moment someone was there. Smiling. His teeth looked like piano keys. 'He has already been where I am,' Ramiro reflected, 'and is a victim of authority's need for histrionic simplicity.' What authority? 'Always there is an authority — civil, military, religious, financial. And it behaves with a truly admirable histrionic simplicity.' That head had the hiccoughs.

Ramiro did not know what to do, say, or think. In this state of indecision, conscious of the fresh and slightly irritating saltpetre odor, he fell asleep. When he awoke he did not know what time it was — not even if it was day or night. Contrary to his custom, he was thinking about his mother, although with no emotion of any kind. He supposed that she still bore him a grudge for being a bastard.

Silence seemed to drip through a thousand stalactites. His heart, Ramiro's only watch, ticked off the minutes. Distant shots were heard. From them he judged that it was night. During the day the sentries did not fire. At night they were afraid and sometimes fired at any dubious shadow. He looked through the peephole and shouted for the guard. When he arrived — he was likewise a prisoner — Ramiro asked him the time.

'What's that to you? Or do you have an appointment?'

The guard marched off. Ramiro's eyes had become accustomed to the darkness. His dilated pupils perceived the shades of black, as shades of white or green may be distinguished in the

102

light. By the end of the third day nervous depression, inactivity, made it impossible for him to sleep. The dungeon air was foul. There was no ventilation. Pickled human flesh. The devil would surely buy it for his caldrons. Among the prisoners there was actually one who was afraid to open his mouth in the patio when there was a gusty wind because, he said, demons wandered around loose in the wind looking for open mouths to enter, seeking a new dwelling place. He must have been a peasant. Only peasants believed in such things. Ramiro was also a peasant in some ways.

The wind was whirling through the dungeon. They had left a window open somewhere and the wind rose to the ceiling, clawed at a cobweb, shook another. Then it went to peer into a punishment cell. The wind was full of parasites. Ramiro believed it was so out of boredom. If most of the great mysteries as well as most of the little actual things of life were unexplainable — one of them being why he was in that particular spot — it was necessary to believe everything. Or nothing. It made no difference which. The wind was carrying demons from the rites of exorcism — major and minor — incubi and succubi. It also carried thistledown that wheeled through the air floating gracefully here and there, looking for the verdant seductions of Moncloa Park. Among the major demons were the Latin scholar and the fool. If the prisoner had the misfortune to swallow the scholar he would break out talking Latin, which would leave the jailers stupified. The other, the fool, would probably be a reasoning, egotistical demon, and a good citizen.

The Latinist demon was in the passage way. He went about wearing a skullcap and carrying a kind of salmon-colored stick like a crosier. Tied to the end of his tail was an iron triangle that clanked against the pavement. Ramiro wanted to ask him something when he saw him peering through the peephole, but since it is impossible to ask demons questions, one must wait for them to speak. The demon introduced himself with a famous line:

E no lases juvate....

Ramiro protested and the demon insisted, mockingly:

'We come here representing patrician truth and the Roman *juri*. My Latin is lay and pagan. It is not used in the churches but in the academies of jurisprudence. The right to possess is not divine, for that would be little. It is something more: it is demonic. In life we always win. God tossed us into the world and things didn't go badly for us because we are footloose, free to go very much as we please in the temporal, while all He has left is the eternal. I am the patrician demon who leaves the Christian refuge to his subjects for their consolation. These cells are an invention of ours. A little narrow, eh? But there's no other way. On the Roman *juri* my vast universe is organized. What does Cojo think? It isn't easy to find out, is it? But that doesn't matter. Look at life. It is an exciting and noble spectacle. Men exchange blows for a hunk of bread. They overwork and struggle, jumbling together God, honesty, intelligence, and good — in books, tribunals, newspapers — to justify and assure a piece of bread. In all this I command. I have a set of Latin bylaws governing all temporal forms: the idylls of youth, gold markets, church morality, the order in which politicians glory in newspaper editorials. I am the obscure dictatorship of Latin in the sacristy and academy and I have also invented a useful thing called democracy of the toga, which has a very impressive motto: *Vox populi suprema lex*, in which no one believes and by which all abide.'

He said many other things but Ramiro was not listening. That was probably what Victor the truck driver would have said, if he were able to express what he felt. But another demon was approaching. A minor demon. He burst out laughing, holding his protruding little belly. He chided some one in Latin and laughed again.

'Laughter,' he said, choking, 'laughter is my element.'

Then he raised his hand as if he were leading off an orchestra and, lifting his head very high, queried:

'Good breeding?'

He answered himself with a coarse noise that did not, to

be precise, come from his mouth. Ramiro withdrew to the back of the cell and Curro protested, thinking it was a guard:

'Swine! If I get out of here some day you're going to find out who I am!'

But the minor demon was also peering into Ramiro's cell and trying to see inside:

'You're withdrawing? Of course, you are in your castle. In your Boobyland castle. You love innocence. Like Curro. That mania of innocence is, nevertheless, the greatest crime and because of it you come to our camp. You are like us and I have therefore permitted myself something nasty in confidence. But the truth is that I am a pig and an ignoramus. I salute you and am at your service. Ha, ha, ha! I have many companions among people like you. Fools, pigs, ignoramuses. Stupefied fools, filthy pigs, brutish ignoramuses, as that sombre and stubborn heretic Unamuno, who is so afraid of us, would say. I've already said that I have friends among you. And among your enemies. With general acquiescence or protest all of you watch sin passing and become part of it. With the hymn to innocence you sing your own servitude to crime. Forgive me if I insist on this, but I have not been out of here for six hundred years. Not out of this countersense which no one will ever be able to unriddle. You will not achieve anything either by staying on the margin. On the margin of what? Of life? And you, what do you know about where the margin of life is?'

Ramiro was going to answer but the demon had made off. Behind that demon the female demons had emerged stretching out in vague spectral forms. One for every cell. Their faces were greenish and their hands long and cold like algae. Curro shouted and an orderly came. He wanted the doctor. But when the orderly guard looked through the peephole Curro stared at him, exclaiming:

'What a beautiful face you have for a good slap!'

'Do you want anything or not?' The guard impatiently asked.

'What for? They'll prescribe some little camphor pills for me like they did before when what I need is a female.'

Again the corridor was still. Through the peephole Ramiro saw some thistledown floating outside. The thistledown was seeking love, like Curro. It belonged to another kingdom and was seeking forests and riverbanks. The wind tried to get it out through the roof, through the walls, but could not. The wind became furious and the thistledown lightly skimmed the ground, flew up into a corner and caught on a cobweb. The spider hurried out and grabbed it. The spider must have been soft and cold, the female demon of the white thistledown.

Ramiro called through the peephole, hurling his voice outside, but no one came. A new neighbor answered, who introduced himself, saying:

'I'm Chino. Who are you? I'm Chino.'

He added that they had taken him directly to the punitive dungeon from the street 'with notorious arbitrariness,' and that was why he did not know who was in the galleries. Chino said he didn't mind the punitive cell. It was a quiet and cosy place. But he needed to know if Cojo, Romerito, and other friends and co-religionists of his were there. Ramiro told him that Cojo was in the dungeon cell beside him and that he had heard of Romerito but did not know him. Chino said that he wished to file a complaint against a general who had been governor of Barcelona and had just been dropped from the new ministerial cabinet after a government crisis.

'If we had a light here I'd read you the most important part of my writ,' he said.

Ramiro wondered how he had been able to conceal those papers from the police who searched him. He liked having this new neighbor although in his voice he sensed an excessive faith in life. A faith that might be called obvious.

The third day after Chino's arrival the prisoners were taken out of the dungeon and back to the ordinary cells.

Ramiro received a letter from Aurora. She had learned about his being in jail and said: 'You have relatives in Madrid who are watching out for you and you won't be in the ergastulum much longer.' Ramiro repeated: 'Ergastulum? Where did she dig up that word?' Ramiro did not know that Aurora wrote to him surrounded by dictionaries. The girl did not appear frightened by the idea of his being in jail and this was what most astonished Ramiro. As for the important *relatives in Madrid,* he tried to guess if it could be the Duke of L. or the Marqués of U., both cousins of his mother's, of whom he had heard. Yet Ramiro was sure that neither of them would do anything for him.

Chino appeared in the patio. Ramiro wanted to see his face to confirm or rectify the impression he had received from his nickname and voice in the darkness of the dungeon. At first glance Chino looked timid, but underneath one sensed an inner strength and cold calm that did, in fact, remind one of the Chinese. Together they went to look for Romerito and Cojo. Romerito was very young and always loquacious and gay.

Chino had written up the facts upon which, as he said, he would later have to base his complaint against General M. A., whom he called 'ex-murderer chamberlain of the King.' Ramiro listened to the reading, impatient and bored. The narrative was colorless and dull, although it had a strong note of sincerity: 'I, Ricardo Perín Gonzáles, alias Chino, of age, residing . . . etc., do hereby accuse General M. A., in my own name and in that of hundreds of comrades who have lost their lives because of him, of being a murderer, as I will prove with names and dates in the course of the present writ.'

He cited many circumstances — names, places, witnesses: 'November 7th, 1920, the undersigned being in bed at his home, the policemen L. O. and F. B. arrived and made me get up and took me and my consort bound through the street, to the office of the Commissioner of Police. The undersigned saw three pistols on the Commissioner's desk, two hand grenades, and several printed sheets of instructions from my union. The chief told me that the police had found all this in my house. It was not true because in my house there was no weapon of any kind and when I said so one of the policemen struck me and knocked me down with notorious arbitrariness.'

Chino was growing weary and interrupted the reading, saying that it was a rough draft and that later he would copy it clean. The professor and Copón were approaching. In another group close by Curro was saying that he did not want to go to the visitors' room where his relatives were waiting for him, and that he would only go and see them in the attorney's office, which had a window with a single instead of double grating, through which he would be able to knock out his brother-in-law's teeth. Laughter gave a certain cruelty to the parenthesis in Chino's reading.

Chino began reading again: 'Then the policeman L. O. and two others put me in an automobile and we left for the outskirts of the city, going toward Montjuich. Along the way they handcuffed me. When we had left the city, another policeman I did not know, and who I found out later was from the commissariat of the fifth district, said.

' "Shoot him now, because it's late, and my sweetheart's waiting for me." '

Ramiro, listening, said to himself: 'Yes, we know. They tried to kill you.' The dullness of Chino's narrative made Ramiro impatient. Chino stated that he had only put down the initials of the guilty parties because it seemed to him imprudent to reveal their names before filing the formal accusation. Then he went on:

'The others searched me and left in my pockets my union card and other papers that I, with my hands tied, could not verify. They also left me a pistol, and the policeman F. B. said:

' "Don't forget that you must untie his hands afterward." '

Again Chino paused. Other prisoners had come to swell the group. Most of them listened to a few words and walked away, unconcerned. Chino went on:

'The undersigned was now ready to endure anything. The policeman F. B. insulted me and stuck the pistol butt into my ribs. We must have walked some ten steps when N. R. V. said: "Let's finish him." And he shot me with notorious arbitrariness. The undersigned leaned against another policeman who drew away and fired two more shots at me, one in the head. The undersigned kept on walking with the three policemen behind, firing. I fell to the ground and F. B. said to the others who were leaving: "Wait, I still have two left," and bending over he fired two more shots into my chest. Then they left. I lay on the ground without entirely losing consciousness. Later some guards came up and glanced at me from a distance, saying that since I was dead there was nothing to be done but notify the court of justice.

'Thus the undersigned lay for six hours, at the end of which two guards with the same F. B. came and stuck a lighted match in my mouth. I was able to hold my breath and endure the pain caused by the burning match, and to this is due the fact that the undersigned is still alive. They took me to a hospital and the prison physician, a certain Don M. L. de R., ordered two young physicians to allow no one in the room without his permission. To these altruistic doctors the undersigned owes his life, and bases his opinion on these facts to formulate the accusation against General M. A., trusting that justice . . . .', etc. etc.

Once again Chino stated that this was only the rough draft and asked if they thought that it was well worded. As he read he had emphasized the expressions that sounded legalistic to him, like *the undersigned*. Chino, in spite of everything that had happened to him, still had faith in justice, even in the justice of the monarchy. And he was appealing to it. This gave him a somewhat ridiculous but moving innocence.

Chino had two bullet scars on his neck, two on one cheek. Through his open shirt he pointed to five more on his chest, where he also revealed a floating rib. His left arm had two more scars. The prisoners looked at Chino, more intrigued by the fact that he could live with so many lesions than by the injustice and barbarousness of the attacks. Poor Chino needed the encouragement of the others to make his accusations against General M. A., and when he saw it was not forthcoming he felt that his case must be less important than he had believed. With a skeptical air he said to Ramiro:

'I know now that whether they kill me or no it's not really

109

important outside the range of my own personal and private interests. But even so ...'

These words produced a slight shudder in Ramiro.

The next day Ramiro received a letter from his mother saying that he would be leaving jail very soon, and that as soon as he was out he should call and thank the Duke of L. She also said that her presentiment of some time back had come true and that she was becoming fond of him again, now that he was far away and separated from her.

8

THAT night Ramiro scarcely slept, kept awake by a strong wind blowing outside. At times there was a lull, then once more the wind was howling against the chimneys. Toward dawn he fell into a deep sleep and when he awoke it was broad daylight.

On the following day Ramiro was released. In the office he was given another letter from his mother, which he decided not to read until he could be alone somewhere.

His immediate problem was to find a room, and since he had nowhere else to go, he took a streetcar which would set him down at Graco's house.

A strange woman opened the door. When Ramiro introduced himself, she told him she took in roomers and that he could be put up for a day or two. As could be expected, Graco's widow had been arrested, but the woman was unable or unwilling to give further news. Ramiro decided to accept the invitation and to remain here temporarily until he could make other arrangements.

When he was alone he read his letter. In it his mother reminded him to call on the Duke of L. She added that this aristocrat was a powerful and honest man. Ramiro did not know whether to ascribe his mother's confidence to childishness or senility, but that same evening he telephoned the Duke's house. The majordomo said that his master would expect him at seven.

Ramiro, after putting on a clean shirt and a tie, presented himself at the Duke's palace, near the Museo del Prado. It had an imposing seventeenth-century façade — gray stone and pink marble columns — hidden from the street by a high wall and a park.

It annoyed Ramiro to be received in the presence of other callers, among them a priest — a canon, judging from the mauve binding on the edge of his cassock opening. This priest had the noblest mien Ramiro had ever seen: tall, lean, with composed and intelligent features revealing a complex inner life. His gaze slid discreetly over persons and things, without lingering on them. There was something of Cojo's natural calm about him. The Duke called him Father Anglada and treated him with respectful familiarity.

The Duke made a rather odd impression. At first glance he looked like a weak man. Thin — you always seemed to see his profile, regardless of the angle from which you looked at him — and slightly asthmatic. He must have been about sixty years old. His asthma was chronic, and when he became excited it was not uncommon to hear the wheezing bellows of his lungs. Ramiro felt that he was facing a simple and cordial man. The canon was evidently deaf, for he was wearing a hearing apparatus, barely visible, in his left ear.

There was a third person with the Duke and priest who, without being a servant, revealed a position of dependence on the aristocrat. He must have been his lawyer or financial agent.

Ramiro was sitting in a large uncomfortable armchair upholstered in red silk. When he saw that the lawyer was getting to his feet, he thought that finally he would be alone with the aristocrat. After having been in jail that very morning with common criminals, he could not get over the strangeness of finding himself in this place. 'If this good priest knew . . .' he mused. But then he added: 'Perhaps he does. Maybe he intervened in the negotiations that finally set me free.' The priest shortly took his leave. The Duke accompanied him to the door, returned, breathing somewhat laboriously, sat down beside Ramiro, noisily blew his nose, and said:

111

'So you have turned out to be a real rascal, it seems.'

Ramiro looked at him as if he did not understand. 'He's talking to me as to one of his own family,' he said to himself.

'What do you mean?' Ramiro asked.

'No,' said the Duke, 'I'm not accusing you. Every man for himself. The only thing I wish to know is whether or not you did take part in the bank hold-up.'

Ramiro shook his head.

A servant wearing a dress-coat entered with a tray on which a silver object was emitting a thread of smoke. This smoke gave off the fragrance of eucalyptus. The servant set the tray on a tabouret near the Duke and left. The Duke waited until he had disappeared before continuing:

'If you get into serious trouble again, don't count on my help. Getting you out of jail once is all right. But don't forget that I will not do it again, even though all your family pleads on bended knees.'

'I didn't ask you to get me out of jail,' said Ramiro.

The Duke paused, looking at him:

'That arrogance will get you nothing if you find yourself in trouble again.'

Ramiro was silent and the Duke explained further:

'What I have done for you I did not do for you or even your mother, who is an unfortunate person, but for your grandmother. For her and for myself.'

Ramiro smiled with a certain ironic humor which alarmed the Duke somewhat. Ramiro was gazing at the Duke's nose in which he saw race and breeding. It was delicate and almost transparent. 'The plebeian,' he was thinking, 'is the pug nose, and the aristocratic the Hellenic.' The Duke's, however, was not Hellenic, but aquiline.

'Yes, sir, for myself,' continued the Duke. 'You don't have to thank me for anything. It's a fine thing to do good. God gave me life to help the humble. My only mission is to be an arm of Providence for the relieving of human miseries, to the extent that my means permit. What I have done for you is insignificant, since we are relatives. But what would happen to so many poor devils if they didn't have their wages paid them by my administrators? And then people talk. What do they know? I have paid out more than a million in wages to put the manorial domain of Roncesvalles and Granada de Ega under cultivation.'

He said it so sincerely that Ramiro felt disconcerted. In his own way the Duke could be as innocent as Chino. The Duke was talking, and aware that he was not impressing Ramiro with these arguments, he changed his approach:

'There will be time enough to preach you a sermon. Tell me, what are you planning to do now? Once the legal business is settled, why don't you return to your village? Or do you have other plans?'

'I prefer to stay in Madrid, near the Museo del Prado. Painting . . .'

The Duke interrupted him:

'They told me you have ability and that you painted the hermitage of Santa Ursula very nicely.'

'I did my best. I would do better today. But that doesn't mean that I regard myself as a painter. No. Nor am I interested in proving whether I am or not.'

'What, then, is important for you?'

'Nothing. In reality, nothing.'

Ramiro's replies lacked the tone of submission the Duke was accustomed to hear and was expecting from a bastard relative he had just got out of jail. He asked him for his address, and Ramiro wrote Graco's address on a piece of paper.

'Do you have means of livelihood?'

'Before going to prison I worked as an unskilled mason. I can find a similar job again.'

'Unskilled mason. What the Vallemedianos have come to!'

He pointed to a picture on the wall. A small painting.

'Are you capable of painting that?'

'Do you mean, would I be able to copy it?'

'No Could you paint another and different one of the same value?'

113

'No. I don't think so. The author is an artist of genius.'

'What genius is that?'

'Zurbarán.'

It was the first time the Duke had heard the name, he confessed. He knew there was a Zurbarán Street in Madrid, but he supposed that it was named for some politician of the last century. Ramiro briefly explained who the painter was. Then he asked him if he had many old paintings, and the Duke said that he had his worst pictures in Madrid, that there were better ones, he had been told, in his houses in Navarra and Vizcaya.

'Why don't you make a catalogue?' Ramiro ventured.

The Duke seemed to have found the solution:

'Good. *You* are going to make the catalogue. I will let you see a pile of parchments that no one has ever read. There you will find the history of each canvas. If I am not mistaken, there must be about a hundred.'

Ramiro gave him to understand that he would need the help of a specialist.

'All right,' said the Duke. 'Find him and pay him for me, but you must make all the arrangements. I don't want to see him.'

Then he rose, as if he considered the interview finished, and said something surprising:

'Tomorrow in the servants' pavilion you will have a room with an independent door and stairs. Well, not with the servants, but with the employees who live apart. I will give you a salary of three hundred pesetas, and lodgings, until you finish the catalogue. Don't hurry. Do it slowly and well. Do you have anything to say?'

Ramiro remembered that the palace was near the Museum, but all this was so unexpected that he did not know if he should accept or not.

'I'll give you my answer tomorrow,' he said.

The Duke, who was doubtless expecting an explosion of gratitude, looked at him thoughtfully and said:

114

'You are mad. Your mother warned me that you were half-mad.'

Ramiro was almost happy when he left, but he put himself on guard against his optimism. His stay in prison had changed the order of his thinking.

It was not that he believed himself to be a kind of revolutionary. For that he would have to enter into the current. And he continued on the margin, his only ambition to watch others live. All night long in Graco's house he was thinking that being at liberty did not make him happy, and that the Duke's appearance on the scene was merely a picturesque incident.'

When he got up in the morning he went to the Museum. Everything seemed a little different after his stay in jail. Goya had still more harsh and severe things to say to him. And he listened and answered them and allowed himself to laugh inwardly at Goya whom he considered trapped by all the tricks: love, social importance, beauty, religious faith, maybe. Goya's nose was also broad and flat.

He stopped in front of an easel where a painter was copying a Rubens. The painter himself looked like a type out of a Flemish picture. Blond and rosy, with partially white hair, he seemed to be some fifty years old. He was wearing gold-rimmed glasses, striped trousers, a braid-trimmed black coat, stiff shirt, wing collar, and a large cravat with a romantic cameo in the centre. He handled brushes and tubes with such neatness and deftness that even if he had been painting for years on end not a single stain would be visible on his hands. He was the kind of copyist Rubens deserved.

Ramiro moved along and asked a guard who the painter was. The guard replied:

'Don't you know him? That is Mr. Santolalla, of the Royal Academy of Fine Arts of San Fernando.'

This Santolalla could be a valuable aid in making the catalogue. Ramiro went up to him and asked:

'Can you leave your work for a moment?'

115

Santolalla turned his face, surprised. Seeing that Ramiro was regarding his formal clothes, he explained.

'At five I have to attend an exposition in the name of the Academia de San Fernando. But tell me. What is it about?'

'The catalogue of the Duke of L.'s gallery.'

The painter cleaned his glasses with the corner of a handkerchief and said:

'I have a great deal of work just now. The Academia has appointed me to represent it this month at all public functions. I don't even have time to sneeze.'

Ramiro smiled:

'Supposing you were to accept, your only mission would be to see some doubtful pictures and tell me if my opinion is correct.'

Santolalla listened with some misgiving:

'In any case, before accepting I would have to see the Duke himself.'

'No, sir. Your relation with the Duke would be through me. But the Duke authorizes me to pay you.'

Santolalla looked at Ramiro, hesitant.

'Are you a member of the household staff of the palace of E.?'

'No. No indeed.'

Ramiro asked Santolalla when he intended to stop work.

'About twelve.'

'I will return then and we will talk more leisurely, if you have no objection.'

Ramiro looked for a telephone and called the Duke's house. The major-domo, who sounded as if he had been expecting the call, told him that his room was ready and that he could come at that very moment. Ramiro felt that the major-domo treated him with a certain mechanical courtesy in which there was a complete lack of esteem. He did not mind. The disdain or admiration of others had never worried him. He decided to go to the Duke's palace then and there. The major-domo had told him that his rooms were reached by a different stairway from the main entrance and on another street.

Ramiro's lodgings were almost sumptuous. He had two rooms and a bath. Ramiro was more surprised than pleased. On a divan were two used suits and several pairs of shoes. There was also a chest with shirts and underwear. The Duke was his own size and Ramiro thought, puzzled: 'Can this be the Duke's own clothing?'

'Is this all for me?' he asked the servant.

'That is what the major-domo said, sir.'

Ramiro tried on one of the suits, which looked as if it had been tailored precisely for him. The waistline of the trousers was a little large, but he drew it in with a belt.

On a small table there was a leather notecase, and underneath it a receipt. The servant said:

'Will the gentleman sign the receipt?'

Ramiro signed. The receipt was for a hundred pesetas. He was sure that the money must be inside the notecase, but he preferred not to verify it in front of the servant.

'Are you going to stay in my service?' he asked.

'I am sorry to tell you, sir, that those are not my orders.'

In the servant's courtesy there was also something like a derisive undertone. When he was gone Ramiro opened the notecase and saw that he had not been mistaken. He took the hundred peseta notes out of the lining of his jacket and put them in the note-case. Looking in the mirror he found himself so changed that he murmured:

'I must go and see Santolalla immediately. If he sees me so well-dressed, he will accept.'

He had left him barely an hour before, but the artist was already putting away his tubes of paint. Santolalla said that since he did not have much free time, it would be well to have lunch together.

The went to a nearby café full of mirrors and red velvet lounge seats. Pulling at his coat sleeve, Santolalla asked:

'How do you address the Duke?'

Ramiro did not understand. Santolalla explained:

'Do you call him Excellency, I mean, when you speak to him?'

Ramiro smiled to himself, thinking: 'This little bourgeois in his tail coat and gold-rimmed glasses wants to know up to what point he can feel honored by my company. City people must be like that.' But he, too, feigned absent-mindedness:

'No, no. I just call him Duke. What difference does it make'?

This, instead of satisfying the painter's curiosity, whetted it. Since it was understood that Santolalla was going to pay for the meal, Ramiro offered him an apéritif, and when he took out the wallet given him by the Duke, which had stamped in a corner, on the black leather, a tiny gold crown, Santolalla was vanquished then and there, and gave him a card of admission to the exhibition, remarking that when the King attended the invitations were terribly restricted.

'But is the King going?' Ramiro asked.

'Oh, I don't know. That is never known, you understand.'

Ramiro thanked him for the invitation, thinking: 'If Cojo could imagine that the day after getting out of jail I would be under the same roof as the King of Spain, what would he say?' The painter whose work they were going to see was very well known, and Santolalla asked him if he had seen any of his pictures. Ramiro shook his head.

As they finished their luncheon Santolalla looked at the clock, alarmed. He had to leave. In an effort to find out if he intended to accept the work or not, Ramiro asked him what his fee would be.

'That will depend,' the painter replied, 'on how much time it takes. Rather than cash remuneration I would prefer the Duke's permission to publish a monograph, if the discoveries are really worthwhile.

Ramiro realized that Santolalla was interested in establishing some personal relationship with the Duke. 'He wishes to make a conquest of him with a monograph,' he reflected, and the idea seemed absurd, taking into account the Duke's indifference to the world of art.

When he was alone, he thought: 'If Cojo were in my place, it is likely that there would be one king less in the world this eve-

118

ning.' For a second he himself thought about killing the King, but he observed: 'What for? It would be an unnecessary act and without consequences. Tomorrow they would crown another and everything would be reduced to a useless scandal.' Taking up the telephone, he called the house of Paca la Encajera. He asked for La Cañamón and was told she was not yet up. He put down the receiver thinking: 'Oh, the little animal of pleasure goes to bed late. I wonder who she slept with.' But he was muttering to himself in this way without ceasing to feel a natural respect for the girl. He took Aurora's picture out of his pocket. 'She has the face of a wife. Of a faithful and prayerful and sensual wife.' He felt a certain tenderness.

Again he thought of his opportunity to kill the King. He smiled, imagining what would happen after the assault, and said to himself: 'Here I am with the King's life in my hands, but also poor Santolalla's, whom they would consider an accomplice, and perhaps the Duke of L. as well.' These observations amused him, but thinking of the practical aspect of the crime he looked at his empty hands and muttered:

'With what?'

The afternoon was sunny and with time to spare until the opening of the exhibition, he went for a stroll. The streets were thronged, and he observed the people's faces with interest. 'They are hateful,' he thought, 'and charming. And the sun warms their blood and gives them the same joy of living that the moon gives to cats.' A beautiful girl attracted him. He followed her until he saw that she was conscious of being followed when, feeling rather ridiculous, he went off in another direction.

At five o'clock he arrived at the Museum of Modern Art. A carpet had been laid from the vestibule to the very edge of the pavement. Near the entrance several men in dark clothes were discreetly keeping watch. Feeling that he was being observed, Ramiro went in, and someone took down his name and the number of his admission-card. Fifty or so people had already arrived, among them quite a few women wearing furs — the mid-autumn weather was turning cold. To escape attention, Ramiro

119

looked at the pictures and consulted the catalogue. Glancing at the crowd now and then he soon realized that the painter was a small man who seemed to know everyone there, for he spoke to various groups of people, always making them laugh although his features expressed the utmost seriousness. Obviously he had the clown's gift and this, perhaps, was the secret of his success as a painter.

The pictures had an amazing wealth of light; their glow illumined the room, veiling it in a golden penumbra. This was painting to delight the eyes, thought Ramiro. At first glance it could be more pleasing than Velázquez, but it had no staying power; looked at a second time, these paintings were irritatingly empty or inane.

Ramiro became conscious that someone was staring at him. He turned, and saw two young women looking at him from the opposite end of the hall. Both were endowed with a warm and quiet beauty. The younger of the two was sun-tanned, as if she had recently been at the seashore. There was something rather aggressive and masculine about the other's appearance. 'Ladies of the court, probably,' he thought. He was intent on a picture of a nude woman when someone touched his arm. He turned around, surprised, and saw before him a mature man, also formally dressed, who spoke to him in a patronizing way:

'Pardon me, young man,' he said to him. 'Who are you? Do you have identification?'

'And if I do,' said Ramiro quietly, 'I don't show it to everyone.'

He could imagine that this man belonged to the secret service, but he was not sure. At that moment Santolalla came up with the painter.

'This young man,' he said, 'belongs to the family of the Duke of L.'

The secret service agent looked at both of them.

'He is Don Ramiro de Vallemediano,' said Santolalla.

Ramiro smiled at the 'de' Santolalla had placed between his first and family names.

'Yes, sir,' intervened the Andalusian painter. 'He is a friend of mine. You can leave the boy in peace. I answer for him and Santolalla answers for me.'

Ramiro could not get over his astonishment at hearing the painter call him 'the boy'. Then he realized that he treated everyone in this way. 'These Andalusians,' thought Ramiro, 'all act like gipsies. And when they're not imitating gipsies they don't know what to do.'

Santolalla was taken aside by the secret service agent and they talked for two or three minutes. Ramiro felt nervous. When Santolalla returned he said:

'Don't you know that gentleman? He is the Director General of Police. You evidently treated him too casually.'

'If I had known who he was, I would have treated him worse'.

Santolalla laughed:

'It is true that he has a bad reputation.'

The King arrived just then, without any ceremony. The Andalusian painter went to receive him accompanied by others, among them Santolalla. The rest remained where they were, facing the entrance. The King took in all the room at a glance. As his gaze passed over the guests, they, with their heels together, bent their heads and bowed slightly. Ramiro continued gazing directly at the King thinking that to greet, even with a gesture, someone who had not been introduced, would be grotesque. He did not know if this attitude was arrogance or timidity. Besides, he liked the King as a spectacle and did not want to lose a single detail.

The King proceeded along the right side of the gallery. Around him the painter revolved, repeating: 'Sire ... Sire ...' Ramiro thought that the monarch had the most impersonal expression he had ever seen; but in his smile, in his manner of bending over to listen to someone — the King was the tallest person there — he had a majestic and stately air. His was a Hellenic and slightly curved nose, quite the opposite of Chino's.

Photographs were taken in front of some pictures. The King passed near Ramiro, accompanied by the reception committee.

Between Don Alfonso and Ramiro was the Director General of Police with his right hand in his pocket. Ramiro said to himself: 'He has a pistol in that pocket.'

When the group moved on Ramiro breathed freely. The King left a wake of pompous brilliance. From his face one could guess that he had never read a book or known any circumstance in life that obliged him to meditate upon himself seriously. He lived on the surface, enjoying and accepting in a sporting manner the good luck of having been born King of Spain. 'If I were king,' thought Ramiro, 'I wouldn't be like that. I would take the greatest pains to be the exact opposite.' This idea, however, did not strike him as very inviting.

Again he saw, at the far end of the hall, the two girls who seemed to be ogling him. He went toward them, pretending to be looking at the pictures. The younger said:

'At last I have seen a real monarch.'

She spoke with a South American accent, probably Argentine. Ramiro looked at her and she gave him the suggestion of a smile. Ramiro smiled frankly and she went up to him:

'Introduce me to the painter,' she said.

Ramiro looked for Santolalla, who called the painter and presented him. Accustomed to homage, the painter bowed and said to the Argentinian:

'Thank you very much for taking the trouble to come and see my pictures.'

She made it clear that she had only come to the exhibition to see the King. Her ambassador had given her the invitation. The painter accepted the slight. The young lady glanced at the pictures and said:

'It's incredible that you all still paint like this. All this is too *pompier*.'

The painter, with some resentment, commented:

'I would be curious to know what some persons understand by painting.'

And since no one answered, he added, addressing the Argentinian:

'I beg your pardon, madame, but to speak *ex-cathedra* it is not enough to be a beautiful woman.'

Ramiro commented dryly:

'It is enough and more than enough, especially if I am present.'

Santolalla was frightened, the painter silent, and the Argentinian said to Ramiro:

'Thank you, handsome paladin.'

Everyone laughed, even the painter, who snatched at the opportunity to try to put himself above the incident. Ramiro felt that his position was ridiculous, but he liked the feeling. Santolalla asked the beautiful Argentinian if she was a painter, and she said no, that she wrote poetry. Then she took Ramiro by the arm, remarking:

'You must be a great painter.'

'Well,' he said, 'you are a great poetess and I am a great painter.'

The Argentinian's friend was beginning to show impatience:

'Let's go,' she said.

They started toward the entrance, where they saw a sign with gilt letters announcing an exhibition of sculpture in an adjoining room. The beautiful Argentinian kept on talking about the King with enthusiasm.

'He strikes me as vulgar,' Ramiro remarked.

'Yes, but his is a royal and august vulgarity.'

Ramiro was surprised to find himself on familiar terms with the young lady, but he realized that she was the one who had taken the initiative in that familiarity. Santolalla came up to say goodbye, and Ramiro asked him what he thought of the exhibition.

'Oh, the painter is a good friend of mine and I fear that friendships influence my opinions,' said the copyist of Rubens on the defensive.

'Confess that what our friend said is true.'

'Since you are present,' he said, throwing it off as a joke, 'there is nothing to do but to say the lady is right.'

He went off laughing. Ramiro said that he was leaving, too, and the Argentinian looked disappointed:

'You are the first Spanish hidalgo I have met and you're leaving us?'

She insisted that he accompany them, and the three of them got into her car. They took the friend home. She said goodbye with a look of reproof that did not escape Ramiro. The Argentinian replied, with a birdlike quickness:

'Are you thinking that I'm going to deceive Estrugo?'

The friend left with an expression of comic desperation. The Argentinian explained:

'Estrugo is my husband.'

'I supposed as much,' Ramiro answered, smiling.

'He might be my lover. You can deceive lovers, too.'

Ramiro looked at her with astonishment. She asked:

'What do you think of me? That I am mad?'

'No. I think that you are a beautiful woman and so friendly that any man would be filled with hope. But I also think that this appearance could be deceiving and lead one into a false situation. Am I right or not?'

Then he repented of having spoken so candidly. She turned toward him:

'Do you believe that I am a light woman?'

'I believe whatever you want me to believe. I've already told you that you are one of those who are always right.'

'That's what they say of madmen.'

Then, without waiting for a reply, she added:

'It's true. I am a little mad. My poor husband tolerates it because it is a madness that harms no one but myself. In Buenos Aires I was beginning to have a bad reputation. And when I saw that it was inevitable I planned to enjoy it to the utmost.'

Then, before Ramiro had spoken again, she asked:

'Where do you want me to leave you?'

'Don't worry about me,' said Ramiro, as if he were waking up. 'Here will do.'

'No. I'll take you home.'

124

Ramiro gave his address to the chauffeur and she went on talking:

'It is strange,' she said. 'A man spends his life looking for a woman. A woman devotes her life looking for a man. And no one ever finds the one he is looking for.'

Then, realizing that all this was depressing and somewhat out of place, she asked Ramiro with a gay expression:

'Do you paint?'

'Occasionally.'

'Are your pictures as bad as those we have just seen?'

'No. They are worse.'

He said it with conviction and she seemed agreeably surprised. Ramiro, in spite of the fact that he felt attracted to her, did not know what to do or say, because it was the first time he had ever been in this situation. When they arrived she offered him her hand. Ramiro kissed it, thanked her, and went in the gate. The gate-keeper met him with a letter. It was a note from the Duke asking him to appear at nine o'clock.

A disturbing impression of the beautiful Argentinian lingered with him. He found her adorable, but did not understand her. 'Perhaps she is very rich,' he thought, 'or it may be a way of affecting a certain kind of wealth in her country.' He decided to forget her, and did so easily. 'I am potentially in love with all women and when I find one I only isolate a part of my desire,' he reflected. But all that desire came from the obscure depths in which the memory of the apothecary's daughter, before her illness, was slumbering. As for La Cañamón, he made an effort not to think of her, which was like thinking twice over. 'I am in love with all of them,' he repeated. 'But I will marry Aurora, because in that way I'll be faithful to the idea I had of myself when I was a boy, and furthermore, I'll be able to enter into the current without accepting the game.'

Trying to find his bearings in the labyrinth of immediate things, he thought: 'The secret lies in holding oneself aloof and on the margin, if possible, of this living dream — going to the museum every day, reading some interesting book or other at

125

home, and finding a woman once in a while.' But he was aware
that the memories of Graco seemed to offer him a kind of moral
example. Cojo, Romerito, Graco, Chino had accepted the game
and become involved in it. In that he considered them incau-
tious, weak, and in a certain way innocent. That innocence was
a sign of inferiority.

There were still two hours to kill before his interview with
the Duke. In an effort to divert his mind to other things, he
took out Aurora's picture and stuck it above the mirror on the
wall. Gazing at it with a half smile on his lips, he muttered:
'She is a virgin, but the strychnine in her body has given her the
look of a woman who has given birth to two or three children.'
And he laughed aloud at the thought of her in a white wedding
gown and veil standing at his side before the altar.

9

AT nine o'clock Ramiro was received by the Duke, who was
in evening dress and wearing the little golden lamb of
the Toison d'Or on his chest. He was going to some reception or other. Ramiro told him that he had begun work, and
that he had found a collaborator, a specialist who would solve
the difficult problems. But the Duke was not listening.

'Sit down,' he said.

Ramiro realized that there was something else on his mind.
The Duke, after making sure of the flexibility of his nostrils,
pinching them three times between his index finger and thumb,
said:

'You were at an exposition of painting today attended by the
King, and behaved in an outrageous manner. On the day after
your release they find you waiting for the King in the Museum
of Modern Art. Such things can bring much greater difficulties
than any you had heretofore.'

Ramiro was disconcerted by the rapidity and accuracy of the
Duke's information. The Duke added in the same accusing tone:

126

'You said that you were a relative of mine.'

'No, that isn't true.'

'All right. You permitted someone else to say so. But I understand. I called you to say ...'

'That you don't want me to make the catalogue.'

'No. To say that I will only help you in the measure you deserve. And not for you, but out of respect for your poor grandmother.'

Ramiro made a gesture of incomprehension and the Duke went on:

'For your grandmother, the most unfortunate woman who ever walked the earth. You have something of her in your face, and your mother has written me things that have reminded me of the fatality which for centuries has been hounding that branch of the Vallemedianos. However that may be, you have my blood. I am not a man of prejudices. I occupy too high a position to need prejudices. Understand? There have always been bastards in the family, and I don't like to judge the weaknesses of others because I have enough of my own. In any case, the bastards on the feminine side are more likely to be relatives than the others. God will judge all of us; the only thing I ask of you is caution.'

'But ...'

'I don't want you to defend yourself, Ramiro. Just listen. Your indiscretions don't harm me, but in spite of that — listen carefully — in spite of that I must tell you that if you fall into evil ways again, I will not help you.'

Ramiro did not answer. The Duke approached him and looked into his face:

'I will not help you, and you must realize that you will have to rely solely on yourself. Is it true that you go around with tramps and murderers?

Ramiro hesitated a moment before answering:

'I don't know exactly what you mean. When I reached Madrid the only people who helped me were some simple and honest men. One, my best friend, was killed shortly afterwards. They put me in prison. In prison I met others.

'What do you think of them?'

'They are simple and heroic men.'

'Are they heroic because they throw bombs? Don't say they don't. They all throw bombs. Twenty years ago, when the King was married, they threw a bomb in the Calle Mayor and a shell fragment came within an inch of my nose.'

Ramiro was looking at the Duke's nose — so fragile — with a certain tenderness. Again the Duke gently squeezed his nostrils between his index finger and thumb and asked.

'That friend of yours they killed was one of those who held up the Vigo bank?'

'Yes.'

'A thief.'

'He wasn't stealing for himself.'

'What did he live by then?'

'The union paid him the wages he regularly earned at his job on those days, in addition to his traveling expenses.'

Ramiro surprised himself by defending those men whom he remembered in a distant and picturesque existence that seemed to belong to another planet. To another constellation. The Duke looked at him with curiosity:

'Are you seriously implicated in all this?'

'I? No. But they are people who risk their lives for their convictions, just as your ancestors did in the fifteenth century. With the difference that your ancestors, when they stole, stole for themselves.'

The Duke looked uncomfortable:

'My ancestors, no. Our ancestors.'

Ramiro clarified modestly:

'In my case, only on the maternal side.'

The Duke smiled. Ramiro, encouraged by this smile, added that he did not believe in the noble origins of the aristocracy. The Duke agreed with him, and said that the aristocracy was only distinguished from the other social classes by the habit of privilege cultivated through the centuries. Finally this situation had actually created a form of superiority in some way. He also

128

said that a little idealism in a member of the poor branch of the family was not a bad thing, but that he should not forget that misfortune had been pursuing that branch since the fourteenth century, and that every time Providence concerned itself with that part of the family it was only to send it horrible trials. Of this there was no doubt at all. The facts had proved it again and again since time immemorial.

'You see that I don't know you,' he added, 'and that nevertheless I do concern myself with you. Why? At times, remembering your family, I tremble. Your grandmother's misfortune — may she rest in peace — is only one link in the horrifying chain.'

Ramiro wondered, but without any curiosity, what had happened to his grandmother. He said that he was ready for everything, without fear and without hope of any particular kind.

'Without fear and without hope,' said the Duke, concentrating. 'That is tremendous. And how could you have reached such conclusions so young?'

'Young?' said Ramiro. 'I sometimes believe that I have lived a thousand years.'

The Duke gave a hearty laugh and got up. Then he became dramatic and sad:

'Not a thousand. Two thousand. Ten thousand years. We have all lived as long as the world. I must go now, but I shall call you tonight on my return. We still have a great deal to talk about.'

He left. Two liveried footmen were waiting for him at the French doors opening on to the garden. When Ramiro heard the car start off he returned to his apartment. He passed through a wide corridor paneled in dark woods smelling of wax, and hung with large paintings, portraits of medieval types in court dress or hunting costume.

He came to a landing on the secondary stairs leading to his rooms, surprised to have found his way so easily. Thinking of the Duke with a certain friendly complacency, he remembered some of his phrases, unable to understand him. He could not explain to himself why 'a little idealism' in the poor branch of the family seemed like a good thing to the Duke. 'Perhaps he considers idealism in the rich a hypocritical attitude,' he concluded. 'Or at least not very intelligent.' He put the telephone on the night table beside his bed, and lay down, fully dressed.

He fell asleep and dreamed that King Alfonso XIII had ordered him to be beheaded. The scaffold was covered with black velvet, a coat of arms embroidered on the background, with a half moon of silver. Looking around, Ramiro saw a post, also covered with velvet, at a corner of the scaffold, and in the middle of the post, plainly visible, a hook like those sometimes seen in butcher-shops. The hangman's arms were crossed, and he was leaning on an enormous axe. Ramiro asked him:

'What's that hook for?'

'Sir . . . to hang your head on after it's cut off.'

When Ramiro woke up he remembered that the executioner had the face of the Duke. This detail made him think that really the society he knew could be classified in two groups: hangmen and victims. His friend Graco had been executed by the servants of the King, that is, of the Duke. By people like the Director General of Police. The persons he had seen at the exposition could be classified with the hangmen, perhaps, even the painter, the bad painter. Even, he added, the gentle Santolalla. All conformists shared in the complicity, in that complicity of the scaffold. Was he a conformist too? Or a victim of those who argue and protest? He could not say. Both things seemed unjustifiable to him, and slightly ludicrous.

He was thinking about all this when the telephone rang. The major-domo told him that the Duke preferred to postpone the interview until the following day.

The next days passed without anything of note happening. The Duke forgot to call him and Ramiro felt he had no right to remind him of it. He went to the Museum where he found Santolalla still copying the Rubens. They had become real friends. Ramiro told him he was sure that in the Duke's collection there were at least three paintings by Velázquez and six

130

Goyas, besides some Grecos. Santolalla shook his head with a half admiring, half reproving expression. Reproving, because these pictures were in private galleries, inaccessible to the public.

It bothered Ramiro to keep the circus money in his notecase, so he went to the post office and sent it all to his mother, together with a little note saying that now she would probably have sufficient to enter the convent of the noble nuns. She answered by return saying that whether she went to Sigena or not was a question for her to decide, and was no concern of his or anybody else.

At dusk Ramiro usually stayed in his rooms waiting for the Duke's call. As his apartment was at the top of that section of the palace, he sometimes heard the wind, but it was not the same as in the jail.

Finally the Duke called him one night, about eleven o'clock, when Ramiro was already in bed. He dressed, and left his room thinking that his relations with the old aristocrat were not very comfortable. The Duke received him with his customary familiarity.

'Remember what I told you a few days ago?' he asked him.

'Yes. Imagine what an impression it made on me, for that night I dreamed the King ordered me to be beheaded.'

The Duke seemed interested and Ramiro told the entire dream, concealing, however, the detail about the executioner having the Duke's face. He listened attentively and asked him if he had read anything about Alvaro de Luna, the nephew of the anti-pope Luna of Avignon.

'No.'

'You haven't heard how he died?'

The Duke went to a bookshelf and took out a book. He looked for something, then came to Ramiro with the book open. It was a chronicle of the execution of the Lord High Constable Alvaro de Luna. The Duke said that the narrative was taken from an account attested to before the King, Juan II, in 1453. The fact that Ramiro and the executioner had repeated the same dialogue in a dream five centuries later made the Duke

131

uneasy. He added that in the portfolio beside him were documents Ramiro might be interested in examining. Ramírez, he said, had classified all these papers, and it occurred to Ramiro that Ramírez might be a distant relative of his, since the name Ramiro was traditional in his family, and the suffix 'ez,' in the primitive Iberian, meant 'son of'. The hypothesis was unfounded and absurd, but it had been spontaneous. He supposed he was one of the secretaries of the Duke. To know all the family and servants of the Duke's household would have been a vast undertaking. The Duke said:

'I believe that the misfortune of this branch of the family can be traced to the schism of Avignon itself.'

The Duke roughly sketched the life of the Constable of Castilla, in reality the true king for more than thirty years, whom Juan II had arrested and imprisoned one night without any warning, accusing him, among other things, of having bewitched him. The whole court was against him and this was the cause of his downfall. The Lord High Constable defended himself, sword and shield in hand, and finally surrendered to the King in person. Shortly thereafter he was beheaded.

The Lord High Constable's descendants had continued to know misfortune and the greatest misery. There had been a little of everything: rebellions, crimes, sporadic heresy. In the middle of the seventeenth century there were two Vallemedianos defending the quietist doctrine of Miguel de Molinos before Pope Innocent II. One of these Vallemedianos was burned at the stake by the Inquisition. When the Duke was about to tell other lamentable episodes, Ramiro asked:

'What was that doctrine of Molinos about?'

The Duke seemed annoyed because this question obliged him to explain something he did not understand:

'Canon Anglada explained it to me once, but I don't remember. In any case it is something satanic.'

Glancing through the portfolio Ramiro saw a book entitled *Le quiétiste espagnol Miguel de Molinos*. Overwhelmed by a kind of retrospective terror, the Duke added:

'A strong tendency to fight the royal house has lingered on in that branch of the family. The Bourbons of today are in no way to blame for the actions of Juan II, you know that. Nor the Austrians.'

He looked at the clock. In spite of his impatience, he continued:

'The last four generations of your family have been isolated in the village in the shadow of a castle in ruins. The castle Rocafría. But even so, remember what happened to your grandmother. It wasn't enough for her to renounce everything and hide away in a corner of the mountain. The monster went to look for her there.'

'What monster?'

'Why, you know. Fatality. In this case it was all the accumulated horrors. And she, as I told you, was the purest woman imaginable.'

Ramiro was silent. He knew nothing about his grandmother. Nor was he curious. The Duke added:

'All right. Everything seems casual when Providence so wills, but catastrophe lies at the very heart of chance. Don't worry. I will help you. But you must accept my decisions with closed eyes.'

Ramiro nodded, without great conviction. The Duke then asked:

'What do you think about my sending you abroad to a good university?'

So many arguments, so many allusions to history and destiny to end up here? Ramiro shook his head and smiled. The Duke gave him a long look and said with a tone of desolation:

'You are the image of my cousin Xavier.'

It was not the first time that the Duke had spoken of his 'cousin Xavier'. Every time the Duke made this innocent reflection, Ramiro mused: 'In spite of my indifference to social hierarchies, at heart this similarity to the mysterious cousin Xavier flatters me.' He was aware of there being something sordid in all these reflections, and thinking of Graco he felt ashamed. Yet

133

the sense of shame gave him a certain voluptuous pleasure. He asked the Duke if he wished to know what had happened to him since he left the village. The Duke looked at him, yawned, and said:

'All right, tell me.'

Ramiro told him everything. Finally he spoke of his visit to Madrid and of his life as a tramp. The Duke asked:

'Did you finally have intimate relations with the apothecary's girl?'

Ramiro thought he detected an erotic curiosity in the question. He said no. Then he was sorry. He should have said yes, even if it was a lie. But would the Duke have believed him? Did he believe him when he told the truth? The Duke seemed disappointed in Ramiro's story. He yawned again, and rose, saying:

'If you need anything, speak to the major-domo, who has orders regarding you. And don't go about with those people you met in jail. That's idiotic romanticism.'

Ramiro took the portfolio with all its documents and went to his room. It was very late, but he began to glance through it with a certain curiosity. He read the general record of proceedings of the council of Constance in 1414, where they agreed to dethrone the pope Luna.

In the portfolio there was a genealogical tree he found incomprehensible. The reading of the execution of the Lord High Constable of Castilla left him cold and indifferent, although the similarity of the hangman's words to those he had heard in his dream seemed magical to him. He recalled that the Duke had remarked to him casually:

'You are almost a child, but your experiences have made you mature precociously.'

This made him laugh. Mature. What could that be about maturing? And when is maturity tardy, and when premature. To mature it was first necessary to get into the game, into the dance, besides. Had he done so?

As he looked through the papers, something referring to

Miguel de Molinos attracted his attention. He discovered curious data which began to illuminate the corners of his mind concerning the gravest problem he had faced in his life since the deaths of the apothecary and the equestrienne, as well as Graco. Inevitable crime and natural salvation. The problem seemed to him hideous and angelical at the same time.

The book said the Molinosista doctrine had had considerable influence in the French church. This doctrine advised inner non-resistance to evil, tranquil debasement through acceptance of all miseries which come to the soul from without, until it reaches an 'unbreathable solitude' in which the surrendered soul is gradually annihilated. 'When that annihilation is almost complete,' Molinos says, 'a very profound inner peace is created in which, perhaps, merciful God descends to us with His grace.' The expression 'quietism' referred, then, to an atony of the will which isolated man until it enclosed him in the castle of his own misery. Neither good nor evil. Once there he remained motionless, without the will to virtue, waiting for the help of God. Conscious of his own insignificance, of his natural bestiality, of his criminality, with his soul deaf and mute, with his spirit inert as a rock, man awaited God, if He wished to come. Ramiro thought he heard Molinos say:

'And if He doesn't come, so much the worse for Him, because He Himself will be lost in man's perdition.'

Ramiro liked that. He repeated to himself: 'Life is not our business but His. All for Him, then.' But he kept on reading: in *quietism* the evidence of misery blinded all the soul's powers, except those giving heed to the infinite of one's own non-being, for in theology sin exists only in the form of *non-being*, in negation of being, and in being useless and powerless to do anything before others or oneself except renounce even the idea of recognizing oneself in shame. When that state is reached, after a long and delicate process the word *virtue* is as devoid of meaning as *vice*.

Ramiro again thought that there was a powerful background of truth in all this. Evidently quietism was widely diffused in

Europe during the seventeenth century. The Roman nobility practiced quietism. Likewise a part of the society of Paris, and of the courts of kingdoms such as Austria and Sweden.

Any kind of debasement was acceptable amid 'quietude of spirit', since the greatest depravity was still too noble a state for the natural misery of our being. 'It is an aristocratic and decadent doctrine,' Ramiro told himself.

Reading the history of the charges against the Padre Miguel de Molinos, and his condemnation, Ramiro discovered the following practices to have been indulged in by Molinos and his closest adepts—according to the testimony of several witnesses: kissing, embraces, immodest contacts followed by pollutions, lewd abuses with the servants, strolls in the nude: while in a state similar to ecstasy one declared the commiting of no sin, since the spirit was in a state of quietude, and matter abandoned to its natural misery.

Inside the book he found a typewritten critical summary of masochism. Ramiro said to himself: 'Yes, this is true.' But the quietism of Miguel de Molinos, with or without masochism, seemed to him to illuminate interesting zones of a mystery more profound than any perversion classified and defined by the psychologists. He considered the facts which in their continuity and co-ordination made up the totality of his life, thinking: 'I am a vile man; it can be said *a priori* that I am, in so far as proving it is concerned, and yet there is nothing easier than to prove my innocence.' He realized that he had religious faith, but still his faith did not save him in his own eyes. Above his acts there was something pure and immaculate. To wish to make his behavior agree with *that*—he did not know what it was—seemed to him impossible. Every time he attempted it, he stumbled on the depravity of others pushing him towards the ambit of his own depravity and wishing to enclose him in it. And when he had the impression that they were succeeding, he felt that he as well as the others were rather ludicrous.

He concluded, saying: 'All this is unnecessary and idle. I am, and tomorrow I will not be. And no one consulted me before bringing me into life, nor will anyone consult me before taking me out of it.'

Then he began to doubt: take him out of life? How were they going to take him out of life if he had never entered into it? 'Oh, I entered like a cat or bird, but refuse to enter like a man,' he said to himself. 'I refuse to enter a place from which I know they will drag me some day by force. I refuse to believe, since that faith will be of no use to me.'

His indifference toward everything that lives (every living thing, by the mere fact of living is condemned to disappear some day) was greater than ever. 'I must be careful,' he told himself, 'and not try to offend anyone with my way of feeling.'

10

RAMIRO resisted the temptation to go and see La Cañamón. Instead, one day he telephoned the number given him by the Argentinian. Her friend answered. She seemed pleased to hear Ramiro's voice and said that they had frequently spoken of him. Ramiro promised to call.

Two days later he went. The beautiful Argentinian was in the home of her friend, a luxurious apartment in the Salamanca section of the city. Ramiro sensed something strange in the air when he entered. The young women's eyes had no lustre, their expression was uncertain, their movements of a soft and imprecise harmony. The Argentinian asked:

'And where has my paladin been hiding for such a long time?'

She looked at her friend in silence. This silence of theirs was full of impertinent secret understandings which Ramiro perceived at once but could not qualify. The Argentinian again spoke:

'Tell my friend that we didn't deceive Estrugo at all that day.'

Ramiro looked first at one and then the other, confused.

He realized that they had talked about him since their meeting. The Argentinian left the room and returned with a glass half filled with a liquid that looked like whisky. She offered it to Ramiro and he smelled it, without tasting it. He had never taken whisky.

'Don't you drink?' she asked.

She lighted a cigarette and inhaled the smoke. Then she blew it out slowly as she said:

'Do you think it's poisoned? Isn't it true, hidalgo, that you think there's poison in it?'

Ramiro, still holding the glass in his hand, said nothing.

'Aren't you my paladin?'

Ramiro continued silent, not understanding.

'Aren't you in love with me?'

'No, but you do interest me more than any other woman I know, that's certain.'

'Well, that's that,' said the Argentinian's friend.

The outrageous questions of the one and the impertinence of the other's comments left Ramiro more and more disconcerted. What offended him in these women was the complete lack of coquetry, of feminine desire to please.

Ramiro was sure that they had something up their sleeve with regard to him, something specific and unfriendly. The Argentinian said:

'Andalusians are more gallant than Castilians.'

'Why?' Ramiro asked.

'Because there is a popular refrain that says: "Poison would you give me, poison would I take." '

They both watched him anxiously and Ramiro said to the Argentinian, looking at her lips:

'But that is different. If you gave it to me with your lips, I would drink it too. I suppose the song means that.'

She took the glass from Ramiro, sipped, and offered him her lips. Ramiro kissed her and they both drank. As Ramiro drew away he saw the other woman, suddenly pale, approaching the Argentinian. And without saying a word, she slapped her. The

Argentinian burst into tears. Ramiro stepped between them when he saw that her friend was going to slap her again, but the aggressor, with a strange fire in her eyes, said to him:

'Get away from there or I'll smash your face too.'

Ramiro not only moved away but left the room, looking for the stair door. He walked on tiptoe, and behind him heard the Argentinian's weeping and the tender expressions of the other treating her as if she were a child. Ramiro perceived something comical in all this. Especially in his own retreat. He was afraid, not of the masculine woman, nor of the glass with the strange liquid, but of his own confusion, for he was completely in the dark about it all.

In the street he felt liberated. Yet he still liked the Argentinian. And he was sure of possessing her some day, any day, if he happened to find her alone somewhere. He sauntered along, feeling an odd inner placidity.

Never before had he met homosexuals—for these women were obviously Lesbians. Somehow he could accept the fact of homosexuality in women, could condone it; but masculine homosexuality was beyond his comprehension.

At a loss where to go, he finally thought of looking up some acquaintances who might he able to give him news of those he had left in jail, and he turned his footsteps in the direction of a building where the C. N. T. had its headquarters, which he had not visited since Graco's death.

It was an old palace, containing reminders of its former splendor. In almost unfurnished rooms there were still gilt cornices, fine mosaic floors, and Gothic fireplaces. On some of the monumental fireplaces were long green boxes of filing cards. He passed down hallways where the bevelled glass doors bore signs reading: 'Union of Cooks and Kitchen Help.' 'Union of Plumbers', 'Delegation of the First International'. He entered one large room where a pine table and a dozen chairs scattered haphazardly about were the only pieces of furniture.

Upon inquiring about his imprisoned friends he was surprised to learn that Cojo had been released and indeed was expected to arrive here at any minute. As he waited, he wondered how Cojo's case could be dismissed so lightly if the acts ascribed to him were true. As he ruminated, Cojo arrived, smiling as usual. He greeted Ramiro affectionately, then remarked that he ought to join a union. Ramiro reminded him that he did belong to the mason's union.

They were interrupted by the arrival of an athletic looking young man. When Cojo introduced them and Ramiro heard the new arrival's name, Alvarez de Villanúa, he recognized a fellow countryman, a man from his own province. While Alvarez talked with Cojo, Ramiro's mind wandered and he recalled again that the King had been within his grasp and at his mercy only a few days before this, an incident that still seemed unreal to him and certainly one he would not want to mention in this place. Hearing Alvarez speak of the necessity of direct action, he suddenly realized that this man doubtless knew his family, at least by name, and hoped that Alvarez would not be able to identify him as the bastard son who had caused so much talk in the district. After a long pause, Cojo asked Ramiro:

'Have you ever played an active part?'

'In acts of violence? I offered to accompany Graco on that bank affair, but he refused to let me.'

Cojo shook his head:

'It isn't necessary. Neither you nor Alvarez should play an active part.'

Alvarez left shortly, and Ramiro remained alone with Cojo who said, lowering his voice:

'We are studying a "Graco plan" of peasant agitation.'

He spoke in vague generalities and Ramiro asked no more questions, certain that even if he did he would get no concrete information. They left, starting down towards the Gran Vía, talking of Graco with respect and admiration, but taking for granted that nothing else could have happened to him. 'All these men,' said Ramiro, 'are fleeing from the peril of idle sentiments. I don't have to flee. I've never had any.'

They said goodbye and Ramiro let several days pass without visiting the clubrooms. One evening he was called to the telephone. It was the Argentinian. She apologized for what had happened in her friend's home and asked him to call on her. She added that she was alone and that her husband had gone to Paris on business. Ramiro was filled with misgivings:

'Are you really alone? Where?'

As he was going up to the house it occurred to him that he should have taken some precaution. Just what, he did not know.

The house was luxurious. For Ramiro things began to be luxurious when the stair carpeting covered the landings and continued on into the apartment, and when inside the apartment the rooms had no communicating doors, but arches leading from one room to another. An elegant house would only have doors for the bedrooms and baths.

The beautiful Argentinian was charming in sheer black pajamas very cool to the touch. When he entered she threw her arms around his neck and kissed him. Ramiro noticed that her eyes looked drowsy.

'Are you a Lesbian?'

'No, but she is and she is in love with me. I'm not a Lesbian for I have always thought that between women and women something is lacking for making love.'

She was talking quite seriously, and realizing this Ramiro managed with difficulty to hold back his laughter.

'Don't scold me,' she said, 'for what happened the other day.'

Ramiro, with the pretext of seeing the apartment, opened the clothes-closets and was finally convinced that no one was around. He had not had a woman in his arms for some time. He liked the Argentinian, but he especially liked her passive and tranquil. Before he had looked over the house they had fallen on to a divan in the bedroom—she had pushed him down—and after some caresses the girl had got up, saying: 'You are suspicious. You have no confidence in me. Go on, examine the house carefully. Look under the rugs.'

141

When his momentary distrust was past Ramiro gave way to his desire, and they devoted the long evening passionately to each other. Between two voluptuous yawns Ramiro said:

'What a pity I didn't know you before!'

He meant 'before she was married, before she knew her friend, before becoming, in short, what she was'. She gave him a hard look:

'I am sick and tired of hearing that,' she said.

She smoked and drank. Ramiro only drank. With the first whiskies he realized that she had put something into them. After observing him a moment the Argentinian said, carried away by a childish enthusiasm:

'You are a pure being, an infant. And I am a hopeless and perverted decadent. That's why we make such a good pair. You don't love me, I know it. But I don't care either. My husband loves me and that's enough for me. He's an extraordinary man who sees through my eyes. A man of half virtues—harmonious, discreet, prudent. And really intelligent. Any other woman would adore him. But don't think that I don't love him in my own way. I care more for him than many a faithful wife cares for her husband.'

Ramiro was silent, and listening to her he felt a certain natural respect for the husband. But suddenly she said she wanted to . . . . —she used the lewd verb—in the Spanish, not Argentine, way, and Ramiro, excited by this word he had never heard on the lips of a woman, not even in the house of Paca la Encajera, did not need to have it repeated.

Afterwards they drank some more and she smoked.

'Why did you say you would like to have known me before and not now?' she asked.

Ramiro did not answer, realizing that she was greatly interested in the question. He had said it, in fact, just for the sake of talking. It had been a chain of meaningless associations. He had thought: 'She is beautiful. And rich. She is perhaps intelligent. I might be able to live with her. If I were capable of entering the contest between faith and the longing for

142

pleasure. But I met her too late.' Still he did not answer. He looked at the time. He wanted to dress but she took his clothing, locked it in a wardrobe, threw the key into the toilet and flushed it. She said that she had foreseen everything, and brought out of the kitchen ham, candied egg yolks, bread, coffee and cream. Amidst jesting and her extravagant questions they ate. She seemed slightly drunk.

In the early morning hours they went to sleep. Then Ramiro suddenly woke up. Sexual indulgence refreshed him as if that form of pleasure had the restoring effect that sleep was supposed to have.

She woke toward midmorning and said, drowsily, unaware or feigning unawareness:

'Dear little one, why don't you challenge Estrugo? I adore Estrugo, but I would like a Spanish gentleman to kill him in a duel.'

Ramiro kissed her. She laughed with an expression sometimes angelic and sometimes reckless.

The telephone rang and she answered:

'Mais non, mais non,' she said in French. 'Je n'ai besoin de rien. J'espère que vous allez me f.... la paix... Comment? .... Non, non. Si j'en ai besoin je vous appellerai.'

She hung up the receiver and said:

'The porter is French. In these equivocal houses the porter is always French.'

Ramiro could not see clearly into this girl. Her crude expressions sounded like part of an unbecoming disguise. 'Can it be the fashion to behave like this?' he wondered.

At noon she closed the windows and turned on all the lights, remarking that she liked an eternal night. The air was dense with cigarette smoke. She served more whisky and Ramiro, after two glasses, realized that he was feeling the effects of some drug. He had thought about getting away, but he did not see how to manage it. In doubt, with passive and quiet spirit, he let his flesh sink into the mystery of sex, attentive to his reactions. She recited Baudelaire, looking Ramiro in the eyes:

'Je te frapperai sans colère — et sans haine, comme un boucher....'

Ramiro was losing consciousness of the world around him and a series of lights and forms became visible in his imagination. He saw himself entering a neutral world, which interested only the most superficial part of his curiosity, in spite of the fact that the things he saw had extraordinary power. 'Is it true,' he wondered, 'that drugs cause visions?' And he saw all this conscious of his own state, and at the same time attentive to the physical phenomenon of the drug and images. 'All this is interesting, but I will escape as soon as possible, and avoid such things in the future.' He saw himself in a place where he had never been before. The landscape was vast and in the distance the horizon seemed to be closed off by immense funereal tapestries, in which there were odd signs. Ramiro heard someone say:

'She is dangerous. A little dangerous.'

He was in a cold grey landscape. Above the city a weak sun was floating, in the midst of dissolving yellowish clouds. From the distant station-yards came muffled sounds and the whistle of a locomotive. Snow was melting and pools forming. The place was like a cemetery bathed in yellowish light. The snow was rapidly dissolving and disappearing between the graves. A stone slab in a corner reappeared—washed clean. There were traces of iron rust where the metal letters and long screw for the cross at the head had been. The hole for the screw pierced the slab. And Ramiro wondered: 'Who is there behind that slab? The apothecary? The equestrienne?'

Four ragged boys, eight or ten years old, stopped beside the adobe walls. They tried to persuade one to go in, but no one dared. Finally the four entered holding hands. Ramiro thought that perhaps they were the orphan children of executed workers. They went to the big slab in the corner and threw little pebbles into the hole, holding their breath to hear them fall. Then for some secret reason they became frightened, as birds sometimes do. They left at a run, but hovered near the walls.

144

From some direction came the voice of the beautiful Argentinian:

'Don't leave bruises on my shoulder or breast. No marks must be left on a married woman.'

A freezing little gust of wind laced the sunlight. Cojo's shadow remarked:

'We are not alive. A donkey, a fish, a bird experience life, but without knowing it, of course.'

'That's why, that's precisely the reason why,' commented Ramiro. 'The one who becomes aware no longer lives.'

A great cloud of smoke blew over them. The horizon was reddening in the west and on the opposite side of the city at the same time. Flocks of birds were fleeing before the clouds of smoke. One was very beautiful. The Argentinian muttered:

'That colored bird is death. I recognize it.'

A big red moon appeared on the horizon. Cojo looked at it and said:

'That is the last moon of the Christian era.'

Ramiro wondered: 'Why? The Christian era was not so bad, with its jealous acts, its petty crimes, its theoretical virtues, its hidden sacrileges, and its genuine hope. It wasn't so bad. Everybody was hoping for something, and everyone was afraid his hope would not materialize.'

In the growing darkness Ramiro's and Cojo's shadows had spread out over the cemetery and covered the landscape. Reflections from the flaming horizon made the shadows quiver. Beside the cemetery walls a bucket of machine-gun shells and four pairs of silver candelabra came tumbling down, hurled by a water-spout, which then turned back toward the city, dropping other objects. Among them three human heads.

'Those are the first,' said Cojo, 'of the hundred we can expect.'

One of the heads belonged to a high ecclesiastic. It repeated over and over:

'I am the victim of an error!'

He was evidently at that age when the inertia of dehumanized old habits is all that is left. The eyes saw only errors all around. 'I am the biggest error,' he said to himself, and added: 'There were a hundred persons who thought about killing me but no one did—no one did for fear of that pyramid of the law on whose apex the hangman waits.'

Ramiro thought he was waking. He saw himself beside the beautiful Argentinian, sound asleep. She was nude and seemed to be breathing with difficulty. In a voice that did not sound like his Ramiro murmured:

'For ten thousand years I have been trying to learn to kill and to die, in vain. But that isn't so. I'm lying. I am lying with dream words, which are not mine. Why do I lie?'

'You have with you,' a voice replied, 'the melancholy of the crimes you did not commit and of the deaths you will not know how to face.'

Awake, Ramiro looked at the nude girl thinking: 'She has a marmoreal beauty steeped in oils. She reserves prolonged and exciting tendernesses for me. But she loves her husband. She loves her husband too much.'

Gentle breezes came in from outside, appeals of the daytime. Ramiro said to himself: 'This is my second moral nature talking. I wonder what the third one can be?' He was still for a long time, attentive to his own silence, then continued: 'I shall have to go away. The trees outside are shouting, calling me. How will I get away? It is not so easy.' Ramiro was still aware of the play of shadows between the window and the curtain edge, as if someone might be hiding there. :The elevator in this building has wooden and opaque glass walls. Eyes cannot see through that glass. This is important and I don't know why. Maybe because then they won't see me. Who could see me? The Argentinian's girl friend? I admit that I am afraid of her. Of her and not Estrugo. She seems very intelligent. Lesbians always seem very intelligent. But I am much more intelligent. It's the truth that all my imagination is new and untried. My imagination, I mean, is used up during the day but renews itself at night and every morning is virginal again. She has already spent her

146

imagination and has no more. Although I have no desire to get into the game, what I am saying is true. I can be a negative being and still tell the truth. Why not?'

Ramiro went on musing: 'There are yellow haloes everywhere. By day in the curtains and at night in the zone separating the luminous circle and the shadow under the lamp. I could be happy, but, unfortunately, happiness is not enough. That's another reason why I don't plunge into the convivial world. She is still asleep. I did not want to ask her about her past. She would not tell me the truth about the only things that interest me in her, the erotic things: and when she lies, the way all women do when speaking of sex, she tells boring things, because her reality is all fantasy and imagination, while she lies with reason alone.' Ramiro was surprised to feel more intelligent and inspired than usual, and ascribed it to the drug. He continued: 'For some weeks now I have not had the slightest material preoccupation. But have I really ever had any? No. Not in the village or in Madrid. In Madrid I was hungry, hungry as a stray dog, but still without material preoccupations. Am I also eliminating moral preoccupations? I am now near equilibrium. I believe that I will find it on a plane similar to that of the absolute quietude of Miguel de Molinos. But none of that matters. Today must be a golden, cool and humid day. I see myself in my most febrile anxieties as God must see me. But I cannot smile with full consciousness of my secret joy, and since leaving jail I have never ceased to feel an urgent need to find out if there is a place for me on earth and what that place may be. It's the truth that all forms of greatness seem somewhat ludicrous to me. To smile at oneself it is necessary to have developed structures higher than one's life, and on that plane I have no structures, only mysteries. Only mysteries.' Ramiro was still. He saw people ill dressed, unshaved men. With closed eyes he had voluntary hallucinations. He only had to close his eyes to have them. Outside the clouds could be heard passing by. The moon peered through a clearing in the clouds, sliding down its own reflections over the cemetery. It fell outside the walls.

Thirty more heads were being gently deposited on the ground. Since their bodies had remained behind in the city, the women could affect a virginal air with impunity. The most vicious did so. The authentic virgins stubbornly insisted on appearing cynical and corrupted. Not far away someone was singing:

> Ay, my sweet love,
> if you do come to see me,
> ay, my sweet love,
> if you know how to love me. . . .

A toothless head raised its voice nearby:

'Those young girls! They don't know how to wash their ears yet and there they are talking about love.'

These words came from an old fortune-teller who had *grace,* or the gifts of divination, perhaps, because, as she said, she was the daughter of a canon. Superstitious people went to her house with their problems. The old woman said that love was something to be savored with wisdom and art after the age of fifty. And Ramiro said to himself: 'Estrugo must be about fifty now.'

Another woman's head turned on its broken neck:

'White bears wandering in great herds through the deserts of the moon. Three men are tied to me: the Genteel One, the Sad One and the Strong One, who travel the highways of the world, their only mission being to win the right to go on destroying me with their caresses. Their faith is apparently very strong, but weakens when they see me laugh. My laughter is a joy concealing a mystery, and that mystery alienates them. I have them tied with the false promise of my martyrdom. White Bears of the moon, keep fear and hope afire in the Genteel One, the Sad One, and the Strong One.'

Several heads were floating in the air over the cemetery. One complained:

'How sad the flesh! How painful to see that the lie of beauty is not enough and that it nevertheless must be enough, since there is no other!'

The heads of a country physician and priest were arguing,

148

uninterested in their surroundings. The physician said that, tortured by the anxieties of his time, he had performed experiments like the following: one day, after analysing the gastric juice of the son of the housekeeper, he placed in a retort a composition of pancreatin, acids and lymph exactly like the boy's. He submitted it to the same natural temperature of the stomach. Under these conditions he gave the boy food and at the same time threw into the retort equal portions, ground up and moistened with a liquid similar to saliva. Gradually he increased the temperature of the retort. Digestion began in both at the same time. All the phenomena of digestion were accurately reproduced in the retort, but suddenly the physician stepped outside and returned with an alarmed expression:

'Boy,' he said to him, 'your mother is dead.'

The boy's digestion was cut off and it was necessary to make him vomit. Then the physician repeated again and again before the retort: 'Your mother is dead,' but the digestion in the retort proceeded undisturbed. The physician added:

'When they explain this to me I will then see if I am a materialist or not.'

A slick plastered-down head arrived, with side-whiskers, mustache, and glossy hair parted in the middle:

'Everything is lost, comrades.'

Another head, hanging by its hair from a bramble, monologued, indifferent to everything:

'Who am I? As the philosopher says, for the universe I am nothing. For me, I am everything. But the fact remains that I am this everything and inside it — inside the consciousness of that same universe for which I am nothing. This is brought to my reason by an organ foreign to my faculty of knowing. I am not I, but it. Who?'

A melancholy voice beside it answered:

'You are nobody. You are everyone. I do not dream, or when awake, try to be different from the rest. I refuse to make myself conspicuous. Carlyle's hero dies more intensely the more he individualizes himself, and the taller the supports raising him above his time. On the other hand, man, plain man, dies less the more impersonal he is, and comes to live eternally when he attains that sincere and profound sympathy of the nameless universal, the anonymous absolute. Merging with elemental man-ness. Are you nobody? You are each and every one.'

A head with flaming hair and beard flew through the air and finally smashed against the wall. Everyone had recognized it where the bigger pieces fell. Cojo said that he knew the man whose head had just crashed. He had filled out a filing card for him, as for so many others with whom he had had dealings.

'For me, too?' Ramiro asked.

Cojo laughed and did not answer. The previous head's filing card read as follows:

AGE — Forty-six.

STATURE — Normal.

GAIT — Sure and slow. He had an unconscious tendency to orient himself toward the north. He was one of the few men to see which way the birds were flying before leaving home. Also, when a piece of glass seemed to catch fire in the sun — as he lingered at the dinner table on his terrace — he looked at the flame and analysed it without blinking. 'It is curious,' he would occasionally remark. 'That spark is and is not the sun.'

GESTURES — Gesticulating, he frequently opened both arms in an apparent eagerness to embrace or squander himself on every-thing. When he folded his arms his stomach rumbled.

FAMILY — He married a very common woman, but at the end of a year of intimacy she proved to be extraordinary. In her there was only what one wished to put in.

LUXURIES — In the mornings he attended to his errands on foot. Sometimes he did not answer when spoken to. If he went out at night, in dress clothes, he stopped at corners to urinate. He had not read Dante and confessed it simply, along with his ignorance of contemporaries like Kafka and Joyce.

The beautiful Argentinian became visible in the corner of the old cemetery.

'What's going on here?' she asked.

'These are my hundred heads,' Cojo replied.

'You have a hundred heads? Are you a hydra?'

Ramiro heard them, thinking: 'I drank a lot of whisky and it was drugged. That was unnecessary, because my nerves can enter into any situation, however extemporaneous, without the need of drugs.' But he wished to sleep and could not. He knew that he would continue in this stupor, which was neither dreaming nor waking. His attention was drawn to the new heads and he saw a very mournful one arrive. When it struck the earth the face came off and another, very different, appeared underneath, radiant with happiness.

'My joy wounded others,' it said. 'People cannot tolerate happiness except in persons by nature inaccessible to them: a millionaire, a Hindu monarch, etc. I had to use this mask of grief. Then they trusted me.'

Beside it were other heads: the intelligent man who disguised himself as a fool because he put everybody too much on guard; the courageous man who had to feign cowardice so as not to seem insolent; and the simpleton who had prepared for himself the silent mask of an intriguer so that people would not come to plunder him because of this simplicity.

'Sometimes there is nothing better than to suggest the truth,' said the simpleton, 'because that is what most easily throws people off the track. A fool who plays the fool often passes for an exceptional intelligence. A weakling playing the weakling is sometimes regarded with certainty as a strong man.'

'Then the simple truth is best?'

'No, gentlemen, by no means. If the simple truth is not covered with a made up truth, it has no effect.'

Ramiro said to himself: 'Poor people. They are all afraid. Of what? Why? If one accepts death from the beginning, why be afraid? But, ah, they all want to have the right to hope and that must be paid for. I do not live, that is, I perceive myself in the disdain that life provokes in me.'

The skull of the provincial professor, from its modest corner, said:

'Here I am, my poor brothers. I am Pánfilo.'

A *pánfilo,* according to the people, is a simpleton. According to the Greek etymology, he is the one who loves everything. But this Pánfilo loved the criminal who kills and the hangman who executes, and had for everything surrounding him a gentle look of tolerance. His tender outpourings of humanity came one after the other, every day, before any manifestation of the extraordinary. When three million beings in the world repeated the difficult phrase: 'Love your enemies,' and did so sweating a cold and viscous liquid and making mistakes in pronunciation, he kept on smiling, impassive. Animals and plants he called 'creatures of the Lord'. Like the poor little one of Assisi, however, he called men 'poor sinners'. But he loved them also, not for their graces, like the flower or fish, but for the weakness they revealed in the fatality of their sins.

This head reminded Ramiro of his village priest. Cojo commented:

'To love men out of compassion for their sins is frightful arrogance.'

Lightning flashed. A head streaked with grey hair blinked its eyes and shrieked comically. Every time the lightning flashed it shrieked again. On the wind a crowd of screaming heads came blowing in. They all wanted to express a desire of long standing: the death of their wives. Or husbands. Of the 'adored wife'. Of the 'beloved husband'. They dared do nothing to satisfy the desire, which had become a necessity, and for the moment resigned themselves to cause only pain. Delectable pain. Succulent. Someone said, as if reciting a parable:

'When the cat has wounded the mouse and it cannot escape, he begins to play with it. It is not just, however, to accuse the cat of cruelty. The sustained fear in the mouse before the cold ferocity of the cat produces a large amount of albumin in the little rodent which makes it more tasty and appetizing. It is merely a question of the palate.

One of the recently arrived heads spoke of its repeated exercise of virility. The old lady, who said she was the daughter of a canon, ventured some advice:

'One must be careful. My grandmother — may she rest in peace — said that once is niggardliness, twice courtesy, three times courage, but four, four is villainy. And my grandmother was in the intimate circle of the Empress Eugénie.

The sadist wished to go on excusing himself:

'It is not the individual himself who can determine his own inclinations.'

The old woman tried to calm him down:

'Bah, husband's pain. It hurts a lot but doesn't last long.'

In the silence following these words a song was heard. The refrain ran:

> Marry, Marieta,
> marry and you will see;
> the sleep of early dawn
> no more for you will be.

Two young heads, a man's and a woman's, were conversing softly when a strange alabaster image fell beside them: a nude man in an attitude of prayer. Another head — Ramiro recognized Santolalla — shifted to one side to keep from being smashed. It contemplated the image, saying:

'It's a St. Jerome. Have you noticed how little imagination image-makers have? There is sculpture that has been copied thousands of times. This St. Jerome, with small modifications, is Gaspar Becerra's, and he, in turn, copied it from Michelangelo or Vasari, and it is the only one known to Christianity throughout the world.'

'Oh,' the Argentinian recalled. 'I met you the same day as King Alfonso.'

She got down on all fours to kiss him. Ramiro stirred in his bed. Cojo laughed, seeing Ramiro's nettled nonconformity. 'The little bourgeois buck,' he said. And still laughing, he added: 'The young buck.' His laughter was drowned by another screaming head:

'They gave me life without my asking for it. But what do you really wish to kill, killing me? The *zoon politicon* of Aristotle? The so-called rational animal? Am I the *homo sapiens* of Linnaeus? Or the *power man* of Machiavelli? In that case, are you killing me for revenge? Am I the *homo economicus* of Marx? Are you killing me to rob me? Nietzsche's *superman*? In this case murdering me, are you adoring me in your own image? Am I the *Dionysian man* of Klages? The *libido man* of Freud? The positivist *homo faber,* the unfeathered biped, the vertical mammal? What do you want to kill, by killing me?'

All were silent. So much and such fluent erudition intimidated them. Someone was weeping in a corner. Ramiro said to himself: 'They are all afraid. All have had an immense fear of life. Why did they participate? Who ordered them to?' The head that wished to find out whether or not he was the *homo sapiens* of Linnaeus said:

'Hush, everybody. Paca la Encajera wants to speak.'

And wearing her white coif she said:

'I failed in life, but I did teach my science to young girls. Poor little doves of mine! For less than five hundred pesetas, not one of them would undress.'

Again the song was heard in the shadows:

> Marry, Marieta,
> marry and you will see...

The old woman waited, commenting at the end:

'Poor little girl with the wedding mania. Obviously she is not over fifteen and does not know what a man is. By the voice I can tell her age, stature, and even the color of her hair. Her pronunciation reveals that she has all her teeth, and none of them is loose. I would have made a person of her.' She was still for a moment, the song was heard again and, giving a great tenderness to her voice, she called: 'My daughter, don't think of marriage. Man will put a chain around your foot. Do not work. The bosses will exploit you in offices as well as bedrooms. Look to your interests and advantage. Remember that you have a treasure and

154

that you must know how to manage it. There is nothing worse for good management than attachments, especially when they come early. My daughter, I have made more princesses than all the kings of the world together. You are of the age to begin. Open your eyes. Pay no attention to aristocrats or blazons. Dukes must be made to pay in advance. Rich merchants and farmers are better. Among them are some capable of ruining themselves a hundred times so long as they can pass as richer than their neighbor. You will be a princess and empress if you know how to resist in such a way that when a man comes to your bedroom he believes that he has had to conquer all the legions of hell; if you know how to be a little simpleton on the outside and cunning inside, a coquette on the street and a prude in the bedroom. Don't forget that little simpletons attract, coquettes amuse, and prudes bind and hold. Have no character. All your character must consist in moulding yourself just enough for the enemy to discover his own. And don't tether anyone short, unless he's an Indian maharajah, or let anyone become too fond of you. If someone does really fall in love with you, contrive to let him go. Those are sad little animals who profit no one and frighten away the others to boot. Be very careful with writers. They are the people who make a false show and have nothing. They will pour out verses to you and trick you out of the peseta honestly earned. Also beware of soldiers, men of little pay and much venereal disease. If you find a man like Prim ... but no. There are no men like him.'

The old woman paused before going on with her advice:

'If you have a rich lover who keeps you, don't hesitate to cheat him from time to time. This business of infidelity is a sickness of the soul that kills nobody and makes more than one live. But let them always be good opportunities. Between fifteen and forty-five there is one thing you must not forget and that is that the house as well as dress and kitchen must be of the best, but you must never pay a cent for them. Nor for the car or other services. To pay out of her pocket for a single pin or ribbon must fill any self-respecting woman with shame.'

Another toothless old woman howled near by:

'Ay, dear God! That is good advice! If only I had had a guide like that in life!'

And Ramiro was reflecting that those people had gone into the game, in their own way. The beautiful Argentinian also? He could not say whether she had or not.

'I must find out, if I can. I wonder if it will be possible to discover something so vague and undefined.'

11

RAMIRO knew that he was awake and yet he kept on seeing the cemetery instead of the beautiful Argentinian's bedroom. Behind the cemetery the earth was catching fire. First the shrubs, then the earth itself. Cojo's shadow and his own were dancing in the reflections. Then gradually the flames died out, and the meadow reappeared flooded with moonlight. Three nude men came into view, carrying a large rectangular stone slab. They climbed to the top of a hill and left the stone in a perpendicular position. They went away and then returned, again carrying a stone slab which they set down perpendicularly close to the other. Then they sat down, waiting. Something about the hill reminded Ramiro of the suicides' butte.

Now a tractor appeared, towing a double trailer with a crane, from which another stone slab of the same proportion was suspended. It was a caterpillar tractor and left the road easily. The crane raised the stone slab high, then deposited it horizontally upon the two perpendicular stones, thus making a dolmen. One of the men took a piece of charcoal and started to write something on top of it.

'What for?' the others asked.

'So that men will know that we are beginning all over again, and that our brother was called Pascual Floren.'

'But that's only his name. It's unnecessary.'

'Then what shall we write?'

hands, top hats, daggers in their belts. The clear strong voice continued:

'Man, father of man, is the beginning of all things. And the end. But since things have neither beginning nor end, nameless man is infinite. Let us proclaim man-ness master of space, master of time, fused with the very substance of the eternal. The man who carves a rock, sings a song, drives a trolley, or builds an airplane, subdues the infinite and gives proportion to it. But only so long as he conserves his man-ness in purity, without the corruption of the old acquired and artificial personality, without the childish madness for differentiation.'

A luminous mist rose over the hill. Down below, the flames were reappearing. The fire made no sound, completely enveloping the hill. Neither the dolmen nor its builders were now visible, but the same voice could still be heard:

'For the nameless man! For the inexpressible man!'

The fire lasted for almost an hour. Finally the hill was again visible, covered with ashes. Standing on the hilltop, the dolmen remained intact. The grey ash had a metallic sheen. Great crevices were again opening between the rocks. Tiaras, crosiers, broken teeth, everyday hats above empty eye-sockets — all reappeared, phosphorescent. Around the dolmen the nude men were silent, waiting. A professor's skull said:

'Some of these beings could not live because of the intoxicating consciousness of being; others because of the certitude of absolute non-being, to which they could not grow accustomed. Still others, having come to feel the plenitude of their own person — defined and made sublime — acquired on this summit a horror of the emptiness on the other side. And the majority found living intolerable because they desired to kill and could not. Or, trying to avoid it, they had fallen into crime. An indefinable crime which did not give them away, but which was ever present in their person. And Ramiro? What about the case of Ramiro Vallemediano?'

A chorus of guffaws answered that question. The poet, politician, merchant, prostitute, financier, employee roared with

159

laughter. Individuals. Individuals full of hatred and fear, and the hysterical need to laugh.

The dolmen was still standing. On the horizontal stone the naked young man cried:

'Let our acts be the only things influencing our spirit, and let them be living acts without conclusions. Human acts, simple and universal, from which no one will ever be able to derive an experience that could be transformed into doctrine, or a doctrine capable of crystallizing into law.'

Incredulous, Ramiro said to himself: 'But can all this be possible? Isn't it too fantastic and Utopian?' He opened his eyes. At his side he saw the nude girl, without knowing who she was or why she was there. Nor did he give any erotic meaning to her nudity. He sat up. She did not seem to be sound asleep, and muttered:

'Are you leaving?'

This question fully roused Ramiro and sowed a definite intention in his mind: 'I must get away.' He wanted to leave at once. He answered:

'Yes. I am leaving.'

'So am I,' she said with closed eyes.

He had a premonition. An alarming apprehension. He got up and looked for his clothing. He remembered that she had locked it in a wardrobe, which he vainly tried to open. Through a window he could see that it was night. Looking for a lever to force the wardrobe door, he said to himself: 'I ought to express everything I have seen.' And he dreamed of some day painting a picture in the manner of Bosch. 'The hardest thing would be to make the cold breezes circulate among the figures of the nude men. But it would also be the most significant.' He pried off the lock, took his clothes and finished dressing. As he combed his hair in front of a mirror in the bathroom he saw that his pupils were dilated and opaque. His hand trembled when he raised it to his head.

He had intended to leave by the main door, but he was afraid of the soft carpet, the lift, and the night watchman. As he passed by the bedroom he entered again. She was still nude, lying in the same position, breathing with a heavy snoring sound. Thinking that this was due to the position of her head, Ramiro gently removed one of the pillows and, with her head lower, the Argentinian breathed more easily. The air in the room was very thick. 'We must have been here for more than forty hours, with the windows closed,' thought Ramiro. There in the bedroom once again he felt something inside him wishing to sink back into lethargy and voluntary hallucination. But he realized that if the Argentinian woke up it would be difficult to get away, so he left hastily by the service stairs.

In the vestibule he found that the door could be opened from the inside, even though it was locked. He went out, walking briskly toward his house.

Fortunately he had the key in his pocket. The carpet muffled his steps on the stairs, and once in his rooms he took a deep breath and said to himself: 'Am I crazy or drunk?' He felt sleepy but knew he would not sleep. He lay down, undressing again to feel the coolness of the sheets on his skin. He had no sooner closed his eyes than he saw that the images of the previous waking dreams were still alive. He was not displeased to find them again, if with them came the sensation of fluidity and incorporeity.

A voice within the dream said: 'I have heard that life is a vale of tears. It is true. Miguel de Molinos thought so too. Then someone tells me that life is good and one must rejoice in it, and I feel that this is also true, and what Alvaro de Luna must have believed. If I am alone I end up by wondering: why do I believe in two contrary attitudes? In doubt I try to quiet my spirit and give entrance to sin, if it wishes to come. Thinking of my aversion to violence, I ask: Can I be a virtuous man? The truth is that I never know how I am going to act in a certain situation, since I don't know what kind of moral nature I have. Miguel de Molinos' quietude would be best, attained in full consciousness. But . . . how can I attain it if my imagination is full of visions?'

161

In the brief pause following these reflections a scream was heard, and someone said:

'Doubt is the bad thing. Sex is the only certainty. Sex. But sex is only an accident, at least for me.'

Another young head fell beside it. It was disheveled and without make-up.

'I arrived late,' it said.

'Ah, is it you?' the previous head asked.

'No. I don't want to be me. I hate the concrete.'

Ramiro said to himself: 'This woman talks like the beautiful Argentinian. One day she will be still, like Graco.' The waterspout was growing again. The cargo of heads and inert objects was more abundant. Skulls — sometimes clean, sometimes covered with magnificent flowing hair, almost always afire — fell in a heap. The first of the new series said:

'I was affable with the humble, dignified with the haughty. I thought I was generous without ostentation, industrious without greed, proud without presumptuousness, forward without vanity, timid without pusillanimity, intelligent without arrogance, tolerant without meanness, valiant without insolence....'

It went on defining itself by its good qualities, in an endless chain. Everything it said was true. Nobody could ever put a blemish on it. But nobody loved it and Cojo spoke up to say: 'Perfection does not inspire love but admiration, and man does not like to admire. Each of the beings you have known looked for some flaw in you. Women in your body perhaps, men in your conduct. Had they found it they would have revealed it, to make you accept it also. Admitting it, you would give them a part of what constitutes your intimate *raison d'être*. You would stop presenting yourself as worthy of admiration. Then the others would begin to understand and pardon your defect. In that moment you would have attained love. As soon as a defect is understood and forgiven, true love begins. We love for defects, not perfections. Besides....'

Cojo was silent. A breeze, moist and salty with blood, was blowing. Cojo concluded:

162

'Besides, man is constantly beginning, he wants to have, beyond every goal, still another long road to travel.'

With the first light of day came the calm. Ramiro realized that his eyes were open. The breeze from the city was clean. The cement of the tall towers freshly washed by the rain smelled good. Sunlight capped the highest part of the buildings. A dewy calm rose from the green earth of the parks, from the fallen autumn leaves, and the wrought iron flowers of the street lamps. Everything had the cleanness, strength, and fragrance of a healthy awakening.

From his bed Ramiro saw the day as if he were floating over the streets, the distant avenues, and the sterile landscapes of the city's outskirts. Far away was the snowcapped blue Guadarrama. A shadow passed without really taking form. Ramiro finally thought he saw his nightmare landscape. The bell of a distant hermitage rang out summoning the peasants.

Then everything was interrupted because it seemed to grow dark again. A lead-gray cloud sailed by. Or else Ramiro had simply closed his eyes. A voice cried out on high:

'Yes, quietude of the soul. And below, chaos stirring like a nest of sanguinary larvae futilely trying to speak.'

The posts of the Carabanchel wireless station looked taller. The dolmen was visible. There was something new in the cemetery, and he did not understand it. Bees were flying about. They hovered over the wild flowers whose stems bent slightly under their weight. Ramiro, who had read Virgil, said to himself: 'Bees and graves have been friends since Mount Hymettus. Bees on the gravestones represent immortality. These peasants know nothing about the funeral rites in the Orient where they sprinkled the dead with wax and honey, and engraved dozens of bees on the tombstones.' Ramiro did not understand this either, and when he thought he understood he asked himself: 'Can that be the way of escape from life for those who, like me, have never entered into it?'

With open eyes Ramiro continued to see his nightmare landscape. The bees were flying about in the cemetery. They drank in the neighboring streams and gathered their pollen from the multi-colored flowers on the graves. In the distance the chimneys were smoking again. Ramiro muttered: 'This is impossible. Since I have been living here ... in the Duke's house ...' But he did not know how to go on.

He had a warm bath and went to bed again. He slept and when he woke it was night. His head ached and he was hungry. He tried to remember what he had seen but could not. It was like trying to think about life on a plane that was not life.

He went out to eat, and with his stomach full he felt like sleeping again. He bought a newspaper and returned home. In the paper he saw the photograph of a woman resembling the beautiful Argentinian. He read with indifference, then curiosity, then avidity. It was she. Suicide was mentioned, possible murder. The French porter of the *maison meublée*, not having seen the Argentinian for three days, had entered the apartment and found her on the floor, naked and unconscious. He notified the police, who took her to the hospital. When Ramiro reached the last line and saw that she was alive and out of danger he sighed with relief. Deep in his heart, however, he felt slightly disappointed. In the apartment the suspicions of the police had been aroused by the broken lock of a wardrobe. Ramiro was alarmed. In the news report certain details were hushed out of delicacy. At the end it stated that Señor Estrugo, the husband, who was in Paris, had been in touch with the physician on duty at the hospital, and was flying home. Ramiro was surprised at his own indifference. With the newspaper before him Ramiro felt that the most important thing in all this was his discovery that her first name was Lydia.

He began to study the problem calmly, and the danger that it could mean for him. He wondered if Lydia's friend — he did not know her name, either — would mention him to the police. Ramiro was sure that if his name were mixed up in the affair he would lose the Duke's protection, but he did not really care about this because he was beginning to feel something awkward and grudging in that protection. 'How much happier I was in

164

Graco's house,' he thought. And he added: 'There were no *persons* there. *Death* did not exist there, in spite of the bullets and police.'

The next day Ramiro got up early and bought all the newspapers. They only repeated the news of the night before. He went to the Museum. Santolalla was not there. He wandered through the main gallery, reflecting on how calm he felt amidst the consternation caused him by Lydia's accident. 'I left her house when I sensed death in the bedroom. Death came in and I saw it. That was when I decided to leave Lydia alone.

Two days later Lydia testified that she had taken sleeping drugs, nothing more. The husband insisted that investigations be dropped. One of the biggest problems had been created by the French porter, who stubbornly insisted on talking about 'amour' and the 'éternel féminin.'

A few days later the Duke sent for Ramiro, who went with some diffidence, fearing that he had also found out about this adventure. The Duke said:

'I have learned that you keep getting into trouble. You know that I don't like it.'

Ramiro was slow to realize that he was talking about the people of the CNT.

'But that is not true,' he said. 'In recent weeks I have limited myself to visiting the Museum.'

The Duke assumed a conciliating attitude:

'Let's see, Ramiro. Would you be capable of telling me everything you have done, now that you are giving me an account of your actions?'

'No,' replied Ramiro, annoyed. 'We all do things that are of no interest to others.'

He was recalling, with a feeling of intimate security, that no newspaper had mentioned his name in connection with Lydia. But even so, the Duke never read newspapers. This lack of interest of the Duke in the press, the radio and the cinema had always astonished Ramiro.

The Duke then remarked in a friendly manner:

'All right. The idea of seeing myself again involved in your difficulties bothers me, and if you are going to continue in the same way it will be better for you to leave my house.'

Now the one who had to master surprise was Ramiro. He got up, walked over to the window. The Duke's respiration was audible some distance away. Ramiro said that he would leave the house the next day. The Duke nodded and added:

'I will pay you your salary until the catalogue is finished.'

Then he looked at the clock and calmly and silently returned Ramiro's nervous look. Ramiro realized that the Duke considered the interview over. He left, thinking that the decision which had been reached with apparent casualness had probably been most carefully prepared by the Duke. 'Perhaps the Duke does know something about the Lydia affair,' he reflected. The fact that the Duke, knowing about it, had not said a word, could signify his determination to break a relationship which, with the explanations and counter-explanations, would have acquired new and uncomfortable rights of intimacy. But Ramiro could not overcome his amazement and repeated to himself in the innermost part of his consciousness: 'This man is taking on a threateningly familiar and omnipotent significance in my life.'

Ramiro no longer laughed at himself so often. He remembered the sea, the prison, the dolmen, and the immortality of the bees, thinking that perhaps there was a solution. That he could, after all, get into the great game. But the ways of these people were of no use to him. What could his way be? Again he thought of Miguel de Molinos. About the friar who said to God: 'Here I am. Here you have your handiwork. Let's see what you can do with it, your work. And what for.'

He took a small furnished apartment in Covarrubias Street and moved his scanty luggage there. The following day, in accordance with the Duke's request, he sent the major-domo his new address. Ramiro's apartment was on the top floor, and had a little terrace with two or three weatherbeaten pieces of garden furniture. There was a lift. At night Ramiro felt more isolated than in the Duke's house. And he was not tranquil. He tried to forget Lydia, but it was not easy.

He wrote Aurora a letter. A love letter. A sincere love letter, because everything he said was untrue. From the salutation 'Dearest Aurora,' until the end, where he proposed that she come to Madrid with one of her aunts and that they marry as soon as she arrived. When he posted it he was thinking: 'I will be an ideal husband.' To be what people call *an ideal husband* it was best to marry in that way, without love. Ramiro knew that he was capable of it. But chance decided otherwise.

Her aunts answered his letter. Both of them, one signature under the other. The envelope was thick with soft things inside that he pulled out with difficulty. A lock of hair, his poem — the one he had given her the day he first kissed her in the laboratory of the apothecary shop — and some white silk fringe with dangling white pearls. 'From the coffin,' he said to himself, before reading the letter. 'She is dead and they are sending me this fringe they cut from her white virgin's coffin as a souvenir.' Or from his mother's coffin, perhaps? He read the letter intently. No. It was not Aurora. A cousin of his he scarcely knew had died. But why were they sending him a lock of her hair? And a piece of the fringe from her coffin? Aurora's aunts told him that it had been the girl's express desire. They were also sending some short prayers of intercession for her soul for him to recite on Fridays.

Ramiro could hardly remember that cousin. He had the impression that he had suddenly discovered something authentic in his own life. As for the poem dedicated to Aurora, they were returning it because his old childhood sweetheart had married and did not think it proper to keep it. 'Why didn't she tear it up?' Ramiro wondered.

These two pieces of news together gave him a vague and secret satisfaction. But how much sadness can joy contain? In that case he might also ask how much joy can misfortune hold? Ramiro was enjoying his confusion.

With the coffin fringe, the lock of hair, the poem and the prayers in his hands, he did not know what to do. He was on the point of throwing them in the waste basket but kept the coffin fringe, not because the memory of the girl meant anything to him, or because of superstitiousness regarding funeral customs, but because that piece of cloth with the dangling fringe was so white and neat that it deserved some kind of respect.

As for Aurora, she had gone with her husband to live in a neighboring village. Her aunts did not say what village, perhaps out of prudence and decorum — they were women respectful of the *sacrament of marriage* — and Ramiro, imagining Aurora in the arms of another, considered himself slighted in spite of his remembering the girl as ugly, fat, and still with cotton in her ears.

Ramiro slept badly. He thought of the serenity of those first days in Madrid — when he knew Graco — and would have returned to them gladly, hunger and all. He began to feel more acutely conscious of Lydia's memory. The physical desire for a woman was anguishing at times, and he would have gone to look for her, had he known where to find her. He did see La Cañamón occasionally. She seemed more pure and worthy of respect than Lydia, although he could not have said why. He sent her flowers once in a while.

He began frequenting a literary club called the Ateneo. He liked the Ateneo. He was attracted by that confusion of genius, roguery, austerity, and charlatanism impossible to find elsewhere. Ignacio de Juan, a taciturn youth, son of an adjutant colonel in the ministry of war, was a congenial companion. Ignacio looked like a timid boy, but he had a passion for adventure. He was always in need of money for his amorous enterprises and was a specialist in pawnshop speculations. Furtively he took pawnable objects out of his house and pawned them. Among them the dress uniforms of his father, with gold aiguillettes, silver spurs, parade belts and swords. He always carried a calendar where the dates of official celebrations at court, which his father had to attend in full dress, were marked with red crosses. Two days

168

before these dates he went around gloomy and worried, muttering to his friends, from whom he obtained small sums which he added up on a piece of paper. One day he had to go into bankruptcy, and his family discovered everything. The scandal had epic proportions. His father decided to send him to a brother of his who owned a cigarette factory in the Philippines.

Ramiro made new friends. One day he was walking along the street with González Arrieta, a non-practicing physician who used his professional position to buy morphine, to which he was addicted. Ramiro did not know this at the time and ascribed his friend's pallor to sexual disorders. Arrieta was constantly going to the café lavatories to give himself an injection, and Ramiro in his ignorance said to him ingenuously:

'You are like the dogs that have to urinate everywhere.'

They went into the Granja del Henar and Ramiro sat down in the columned patio at the back of the café. While waiting for Arrieta he saw La Cañamón enter. She was alone and seemed to be looking for someone. Ramiro stood up so she would see him. She came toward him with a radiant expression. She sat down, took off her gloves, and said:

'I can't stay long. I was looking for La Manolo to go to Rector's, but first we have to go home to dress.'

'You don't have time for me, that's evident.'

'Hush, you. You are the one who runs away. Why don't you come to see me? Doña Paca often speaks of you.'

'And you?'

'You're right. We don't talk about what really interests us, you know. Ah, and thank you for the flowers. You're crazy, but I don't mind. I'm crazy, too. Why don't you come and see me?'

'Because I like you too much.'

'Too much? Can you like somebody too much?'

'Yes, If I come to see you, even if I stay all night, I have to go away the next day and leave my place to another. And that is too sad.'

'Don't talk like that. Don't mock. No one loves women like me. We please or not, that's all.'

169

'You may be right, but you said before that I'm crazy. It's true. In that sense it is true.'

She laughed, and touched his foot under the table.

'You're more solemn than a judge. You don't know how to joke. You're not the type.'

'If you'll have me as a husband,' said Ramiro, 'we can marry whenever you say.'

She looked at him with misgiving. There might be some truth in all this, but she said:

'Be careful. People at the next tables heard you and are laughing. Don't you see they all know me? Would you marry a woman of the streets?'

'All women are women of the streets in some way.'

She became sad. Finally, she said:

'If that's true, let's marry and go away to some other country to live. Eh? What do you say? Are you sorry? I knew you were going to be sorry.'

She had lowered her voice and this detail made Ramiro think that she was in earnest.

'Maybe it's a good idea,' he said, 'but I'm afraid of good ideas.'

'How afraid?'

'I don't know. I'm not afraid of misfortune or death, but happiness is not natural. That illusion of happiness is where we all get trapped. I don't try to be happy.'

La Cañamón took a sip of Ramiro's beer and said:

'Trying to be happy is useless. Only those are happy who can be.'

'You may be right,' he said. 'There is something outside our life that sees us live and sometimes does tremendous things to us. I don't mind,' he added. 'Happiness and unhappiness have nothing to do with my real life. Don't look at me like that. I'm serious.'

'Where is that life, then?'

'I don't know. In the sacrifice I make, I believe.'

'What sacrifice?'

170

'The sacrifice of you, for instance. There is where I feel myself living in a more complete way.'

Her eyes were moist. Ramiro was aware of people looking at them.

'Let's go,' she said.

But at that instant Arrieta arrived, and sat down beside La Cañamón, after having been introduced by Ramiro, Arrieta, with the morphine in his blood, was loquacious:

'I have seen you,' he said, 'somewhere.'

He clapped his hand to his forehead and began to tell how Paca la Encajera had gone to bed with all Madrid at the turn of the century. Thinking that he was being witty, he added:

'I haven't gone to Paca la Encajera's house for years because only French prostitutes interest me. Look here at La Cañamón. She looks like a schoolgirl. But there are vicious schoolgirls. Are you very vicious, Cañamón?'

'Go away,' Ramiro said to him very gravely. 'Leave us alone.'

'What will happen if I stay?'

'I'll smash your face.'

Arrieta reached for the water-bottle, and as he lifted it to strike Ramiro the water spilled over his own head and shoulders. This shower had immediate effects on the neurotic. He turned livid while the people at the neighboring tables laughed. Ramiro took La Cañamón by the arm and left. When they reached the arch connecting the rotunda with the rest of the café, Ramiro remembered that he had not paid, stopped and looked around for the waiter. As he turned he saw Arrieta trying to dry himself with his handkerchief. Arrieta, in a friendly attitude, said:

'Don't worry, I will pay.'

Out in the street La Cañamón said to Ramiro:

'Is that fellow crazy?'

'A little. No more than you and I, but in a different way.'

She said that she would give up going to Rector's if he wished to devote the night to her. Ramiro took her to Doña Paca's and left her at the door after having kissed her, as he would a sweet-heart. He returned to the Ateneo in the same taxi, thinking:

'Why didn't I stay with her? Definitely Arrieta is crazy, but I am not very sane either.'

Cojo found Ramiro's address which was unknown to the police convenient. Gatherings in his apartment became very frequent. Cojo considered Ramiro as a sympathizer he could trust.

'You romantic bourgeois,' he said to him one day, 'are at times more reliable than revolutionaries.'

Ramiro thought: 'I am neither bourgeois nor romantic.' In reality Ramiro was rather a man of feudal and peasant roots. But he was not annoyed with Cojo, to whom he was bound by the powerful fraternity of the dungeon cells. At those meetings they talked about the *Graco plan*. Everything referring to his dead friend seemed worthy of respect to Ramiro. Shortly before his death Graco had outlined a plan and proposed it to the National Committee, a plan on which they had been working ever since.

Ramiro, not well informed on social problems, nevertheless remembered the peasants of his village, and it was enough for him to know that the Graco plan was against rural feudalism to support it with enthusiasm. The contact with the multitudes and the danger of playing an active part excited him. At one meeting he spoke of the threat of police repression. Cojo said there was no struggle without victims, and Ramiro added, to himself: 'Also there is no peace without victims, and still we don't know which crimes are the most inhuman, those of peace or war.' Being in on the secret of the Graco plan obliged him to meet other persons and go all over Madrid helping to wind up secondary details, because in the important ones he had no part. One day he was with Cojo and two others in the door of the Ateneo arguing about the legal committees and their re-placement by clandestine ones, in case the legal committeemen were arrested. Cojo said that with committees or without them, he was sure of spontaneous popular movements of revenge after

172

the defeat, if this occurred. One of these reactions, the most common, was likely to be an attack upon the convents. While turning these ideas over in his mind Ramiro saw a robed priest pass by, leisurely and grave. When he saw Ramiro the priest tipped his hat and greeted him very courteously. In his courtesy there was great respect. Cojo and his companion looked at each other without comprehending and Ramiro, who did not recall the priest—it was Father Anglada, the canon he had seen once at the Duke's—could not explain it either. They agreed that the greeting was for Ramiro and they laughed. Ramiro did not share the laughter of his companions and was silent.

When he went to the Ateneo again he ran into the old theosophist Roso de Luna, and the son of the poet Valle Inclán, a boy sixteen years old.

In those days he argued a great deal with Roso de Luna and others—theosophists, poets, sociologists, mystics—about all kinds of problems, especially religious and metaphysical ones. Ramiro preferred to listen and in general limited himself to stimulating talk in others. He therefore frequently took contradictory points of view and when they called it to his attention he said:

'I don't contradict myself. What I mean to say is that my persevering in contradiction represents as logical a continuity as any other. Nature is an immense contradiction: life-death, being-non-being. But no one dares to accuse nature of being illogical. You take a single term: life. I take them all at the same time.'

Since he said so humbly and affably, they believed him.

12

SOMETIMES Ramiro felt such contempt for himself that his excessive scorn was shed upon others. Easily he let all his relationships cool. He scorned Santolalla, looked on the people of the Ateneo with critical indifference, inwardly jeered at the

Duke who helped him, and at Lydia whom he would have liked to possess again in spite of everything. He only loved La Caña-món. In her he saw something dead and yet adorable.

He found a note from Cojo under his door, reminding him of a meeting that night in the 'unaccustomed' place. After long hesitation, Ramiro decided not to go. But about nine o'clock the telephone rang. He answered thinking it might be Lydia, but it was Cojo asking him to come at once.

The meeting was held in an inside room of a tavern, around a large table. The room was brightly illuminated, the bare walls violently reflecting the light from a horizontal crown-like hoop suspended from the ceiling by three copper chains. In that torrent of light some of the unshaved faces looked very pathetic. One of the committee members demanded 'comrade Valle-mediano's' credentials, but Cojo said that Ramiro did not need credentials since he represented no one.

It concerned nothing less than the final agreement on the 'Graco plan'. Ramiro was assigned a definite mission: to telephone Sevilla and give this exact message to an individual whose name and number he was given: 'The prices in the catalogue of thresh-ing machines were to be taken as F.O.B. in all the province of Cádiz.' Ramiro was to do this immediately when ordered to do so, hence he was to be at home every evening from six until midnight. The day and hour had strategic importance. Ramiro, who accepted with a secret enthusiasm, liked to feel himself pushed by some kind of urgency. Someone objected to entrusting missions of such importance to persons who did not belong to the organization.

Two days later Ramiro received Cojo's call telling him to transmit the message that night. Ramiro did so. During the next few days he saw none of his friends. The earth seemed to have swallowed them up. News of unrest in the Andalusian country-side began to appear in the newspapers. Not knowing exactly what was going to happen, Ramiro expected sensational develop-ments. Some newspapers devoted long articles to a study of the problem from the angle of enlightened and complex sociology.

Every time the telephone rang Ramiro answered, hoping it was Lydia. Instead of Lydia, Emilia called one night to ask if he had seen the Argentinian. Ramiro answered curtly:

'No.'

'Really, you and Lydia haven't seen each other?'

'No.'

Ramiro wanted to ask her if Lydia was in Madrid, if her husband had returned to Paris, but refrained. The curtness of his replies made Emilia suspect the opposite.

The next day the newspapers came out with more news of the situation in different regions of Spain, especially in the Cádiz countryside, and just after noon someone whose voice he could not identify called and asked him to come to a subway station. He had used the formula agreed upon, and Ramiro went. There he met Cojo, who said to him:

'Take your paint-box and get on the night train to Sevilla. You will be there before noon tomorrow. In the afternoon go to Jérez. As soon as you arrive start painting out in the open between the old cemetery and an olive mill. Someone will come up to you and say: "Do you like the landscape?" This sentence is a countersign and the one who says it will be a delegate from the district committee.'

'How will I know the place?'

Cojo gave him a photograph. There was the mill.

'The companion approaching you will bring resolutions from the district of Jérez that must be carried out. You must sacrifice everything to the need to carry out those resolutions.'

Ramiro hesitated before accepting, and Cojo asked:

'Are you afraid?'

'No. But I would like to know who named me.'

'I proposed you and the committee approved.'

There were so many committees that Ramiro never really understood which one it might be, nor did he care to ask, because his ignorance was perhaps a factor they had taken into account. He accepted, thinking that he had no time for anything, since the train left at midnight. On his return home he

175

found the Duke's cheque. Cojo had given him two hundred pesetas besides. They had said goodbye to each other confident that Ramiro would be in Jérez the next morning.

The telephone was ringing as he entered his apartment. He ran to aswer, but too late. He was undecided and depressed. A moment later it rang again. It was Lydia, saying she wished to see him. Ramiro hesitated. Finally he told her that she should come as soon as possible because they could not be together very long.

Twenty minutes later Lydia arrived. She nosed about the apartment and said that it was very ugly but seemed ideal for clandestine meetings. 'That is just what Cojo says,' he thought amused. Ramiro helped her undress, and after their lovemaking, he suddenly asked:

'Did you really try to commit suicide?'

She said nothing and her silence alarmed Ramiro, who said to himself: 'If she doesn't dare to answer it must be because she is still full of her old suicidal plans.'

Lydia finally said:

'It will be better if you don't mention that again.'

A moment later when she went to the bathroom Ramiro looked for her purse, and not finding it he returned to the bed thinking that she must have taken it with her. Then he raised a corner of the mattress at the head of the bed and saw a small object of blue leather and black satin. He opened it. Inside were two little cardboard boxes with three glass tubes in each. He took them to the adjoining room and left them in a pocket of his coat. When she returned the purse was in its place. Lydia said:

'Do you know your little house isn't so bad? I believe that I could live in a place like this, too.'

Ramiro was thinking about the accident in the *maison meublée*:

'What a scare you gave me! At first I thought you had killed yourself.'

She smiled sadly:

'But you, Ramiro, you ran away and left me alone.'

'What did you want me to do?'

Ramiro told her that she was living in chaos. Lydia yawned and declared in a sorrowful voice that in abandoning oneself to chaos there were exquisite pleasures as well as frightful dangers. Ramiro said that it was necessary to return to chaos perhaps, so as to organize everything all over again. She nodded and said:

'If you find a way, count on me. I will be your first adept. But I believe that it would be better to return to chaos forever, never to leave it again.'

Then she looked under the mattress and poked about in her purse. She was pensive for a moment, got up and left the room. Ramiro said to himself: 'She thinks she left her drugs in the bathroom.' He heard her prowling about. She came back quite preoccupied and asked:

'Have you gone through my purse?'

'No. Why?'

She was still nude, standing. She rested her weight on one foot, making her right hip curve out gracefully. She said nothing. She came up to Ramiro and lay down beside him. Ramiro could not explain the beauty of this woman, always fragrant and constant in spite of alcohol, drugs and every excess. She was one of those beauties who continue to have an adolescent freshness far into middle age, and who, perhaps, suddenly become lamentably old one day, without transition. Ramiro's curiosity, however, was still alive:

'What did you tell your husband about the mishap?'

'That it was accidental. The poor dear believes everything I say.'

Ramiro thought: 'Ah, now she said so. It was attempted suicide.' She realized it too late. 'She has youth, fortune, beauty, love. Why commit suicide?' Ramiro wondered. He decided not to ask her any more questions, since it is useless to try to find out what has passed through the mind of a frustrated suicide. He looked at her eyes, and she asked him:

'Didn't you ever think about it?'

'No. Why kill yourself when it is so easy to die without planning it?'

'Eh?' she said, surprised.

'Yes. It is so easy to get killed.'

Ramiro was thinking of the dangers of his mission to Andalusia. She laughed:

'Who's going to kill you, my darling?'

Lydia knew that laughter vexed Ramiro, but she could not hold it in. It spilled over in her throat, nose, eyes. Seeing her laugh Ramiro said to himself: 'She thinks that I am afraid of her husband.' The heaving of Lydia's breast and the deep sound of her laughter made her desirable and they abandoned themselves to each other. When Ramiro looked at the clock he saw that he could not now catch the train. It was ten minutes before midnight. 'Bah,' he thought, 'there will be another tomorrow.' But then he could not be in Jérez at the proper time. He closed his eyes.

Amorous excess left him in a lassitude deep within which reality seemed to change its nature. He was barely aware of physical contacts and felt himself floating in a dense but fresh atmosphere, where sounds in their different intensities revealed the quality of each layer of air through which they passed. Ramiro thought of the immense physical happiness of which man is capable. He believed that man drew this happiness, as all other kinds, out of chaos. And he said to himself:

'What has happened in the life of this woman? What is it that is broken inside her?' He could not find out, but he refused to give up trying. Finally they went to sleep, and Ramiro woke with the first morning light. Very uneasy, he telephoned the Mediodía Station. The first train for Sevilla left at eleven, and would not arrive until late at night. At that moment he hated Lydia, but then, as he watched her sleep with her childlike face on the pillow, his hatred changed to tenderness.

He called the airport. A plane left at ten and reached Sevilla at noon. The ticket cost a hundred and fifty pesetas. He would

178

cash the Duke's cheque. If he wished to get there in time he could dally no longer.

The telephone had awakened Lydia. When Ramiro told her that he was catching a plane immediately for a distant place, she insisted on going with him. Ramiro said to her:

'The police may be waiting for me at the aerodrome.'

This seemed to frighten her, and since she knew nothing of Ramiro's private life she began to see dangers and shadows everywhere. Ramiro could not understand. 'She is ready for suicide, but the idea of the police frightens her.'

He decided that the surest way to free himself of her—because in spite of the danger she repeated that she wished to go with him—was to urge her to make the trip. Ramiro put too much eagerness into this.

'No. no,' she answered. 'There's someone who would miss me."

'Estruguito?'

'Yes. You must be very careful with my husband. That's no joke. He carries a revolver.'

Speaking in a grotesque and melodramatic tone Ramiro said that if he did happen to be murdered by Estrugo it would be a sweet and glorious death. She laughed as falsely as he had spoken. In the falseness of it all there was a great sadness. Ramiro promised her to return as soon as possible. She suddenly appeared preoccupied by the insecurity of plane flights, and when she said so Ramiro roared with laughter:

'You sound like an adoring wife.'

'Don't you believe it. The adoring wife would be wanting the accident to happen.'

'Don't say such outrageous things!'

Ramiro insisted she dress quickly. She protested:

'Can't I stay on here in your house? Don't force me to go out in the street faded and dishevelled. I'll be ready to leave in an hour.'

Ramiro kissed her and left in a hurry, thinking: 'The only

thing binding me to Lydia is the flesh. But isn't that kind of attraction the strongest?'

He took a taxi and hurried to the bank. He was carrying a paint-box in which he had put two shirts and some socks. Before leaving he had warned Lydia not to answer the telephone if it rang.

He cashed the cheque and went to the air company offices where he bought his ticket. A fat, tired-looking man, wearing a leather jacket and carrying papers in his hands, was pacing back and forth in the office. He signed something and gave it to a secretary. Then he looked at Ramiro and the other two passengers and said:

'Whenever you like.'

The pilot did not have a very reassuring air. They climbed into a waiting car. The aerodrome was quite far. When they arrived Ramiro noticed several planes on the ground, the motors covered with leather sheaths. They all looked safe and powerful except one whose fuselage had dubious colored patches, worn by wind and rain. This was the only plane that looked unsafe to him. And this was the one in service.

There were only three passengers. Ramiro followed the pilot inside. He made himself comfortable, and when he saw the propellers turning he realized that they were about to take off. Seconds later he saw that they were air-borne. Ramiro isolated himself, lost in thought. Through the little windows the ochre steppes of La Mancha were filing by. The River Tajo, Orgaz, appeared. Traveling south is depressing; on the other hand, traveling north stimulates and heartens.

Ciudad Real, Almadén, Puertollano. Mines and miners. Summits black with coal. They had been flying for over an hour, and Ramiro felt himself rocked by the old plane and deafened by the roaring of the motors. He occasionally opened and closed his jaws to relieve his ears. Between Córdoba and Lora del Río, just behind the mountain of Almadén, he began to feel sleepy. He spent the last half-hour of the journey dozing. The sensation of descent awakened him. They were above Sevilla. The plane came down in widening circles, capriciously raising or lowering the horizons.

They left the aerodrome in a company car. Soon afterwards Ramiro was seated on the terrace of a café with a glass of manzanilla before him, talking to a bootblack.

'How does it happen,' he asked, 'that they call the main street the Street of the Serpent, if they're so superstitious in Sevilla?'

'Well, that's why. People play with the things that scare them most.'

He said that he was not from the city but the mountain, and that he had come to Sevilla because the countryside was up in arms.

Ramiro bought a canvas and a folding easel. Then he inquired about transport to Jérez, attending to these errands in a mechanical and indolent way. He boarded a bus which dropped him in the plaza of the little city at three o'clock. He realized that the box and easel made an inoffensive tourist of him. The presence in the countryside of pairs of Civil Guards at regular intervals revealed unrest.

Ramiro soon found the place indicated between the old cemetery and the mill. The mill was a gloomy old building with moss and weeds growing on the tiles. He started painting and when he had despaired of anyone approaching him an indifferent-looking man appeared.

'Do you like the landscape?' he asked.

Ramiro identified himself and the stranger said:

'Follow me at a distance and don't lose sight of me. I will stop in front of the door of a house and light a cigarette. Then I'll go on my way. You must go in that house. They are expecting you.'

'Who is expecting me?'

'You'll see.'

He started walking. The man was wearing a sheepskin hunting-jacket and corduroy trousers. Ramiro picked up his belongings and followed some fifty paces behind him. From the rear his guide did not look like a peasant; nor like a worker either. He could be just artisan, potter, or cobbler. There was something comical about his walk. Broad-shouldered and short-legged, he moved with a fleet-footedness out of keeping with his imposing chest and shoulders. Twice Ramiro lost sight of him when turning a corner and quickened his pace. Finally he saw him stop in front of a door and light a cigarette. Then the man quickly disappeared, his mission performed.

Ramiro entered the house. A woman about thirty years old, wearing a flower in her hair, met him asking:

'Are you the one from Madrid?'

'Yes.'

The woman looked at Ramiro with a certain curiosity, not hostile but not friendly either. She took him to a room on the first floor where there were two rocking-chairs with cane backs and seats, a lamp stand like those used in spiritualistic séances, and flower-pots blooming in the corners. In the centre hung a chandelier with a square silk shade, with bead tassels at the four corners. Ramiro sat down and waited. In a moment Cojo appeared. When Ramiro saw him he felt in some way like one who is contemplating a clever sleight of hand performance. Cojo smiled:

'You weren't expecting to see me, were you? Well, here I am. I wasn't sure of finding you either, since you didn't catch the train last night. How did you get here?'

'By plane.'

'Dangerous. There are more police around aerodromes than at other stations.'

'I doubt it. I think there are probably fewer. In any case, here I am. What do I have to do?'

Cojo emptied his pipe striking it on his wooden leg.

'Don't be in a hurry. There are two or three centers of action in the south, the strongest at Medina Sidonia. Things are moving along.'

'Well?'

'Could be better.'

He smiled. Cojo was always smiling. You couldn't tell any-

182

thing by his expression because it never changed, in good luck or bad. Ramiro asked:

'Did you think yesterday I had deserted?'

'Well, not exactly. But then, anything's possible.'

'Don't you think I'm a trustworthy man?'

'Who knows? Do you think so?'

Ramiro looked at him squarely and hesitated. Finally he shook his head.

'Then,' Cojo said, 'you're not going to ask me to have more faith in you than you yourself have.'

Ramiro put his outstretched hand on the lamp stand. He noticed that the nail of one finger was fringed with black. And he remarked, also smiling:

'Hasn't it ever occurred to you that there are many Catholic priests who have no faith and yet perform their duties as well as the others?'

'Naturally,' Cojo said, 'and probably better.'

A cat peered in the door, looked at Ramiro and Cojo, seemed satisfied with its inspection, and left. Ramiro asked:

'Am I going to stay here or do I have to go somewhere?'

'You will go to Medina Sidonia but there is no bus until early tomorrow.'

'And what will I do in Medina Sidonia?'

Cojo refilled his pipe slowly:

'They'll tell you there.'

'Don't you know?'

'No.'

Ramiro supposed that Cojo was lying. He looked at his pipe, his wooden leg, his hands which were broad and strong but at the same time seemed transparent like glass. Cojo smiled and said:

'I see what you're thinking. You're thinking that since I came to Jérez I could also go to Medina. But I have a physical handicap.'

He was referring to his game leg. Ramiro said:

'Your lameness didn't keep you from killing the cardinal.'

'Nonsense. I had no part in the cardinal affair.'

Changing the subject, he added:

'Do you know how I lost my leg? I worked on the railway and had an accident. A train ran over me. Since then I've been collecting disability insurance. Life has strange quirks. I live on the income from my leg. My capital is my left leg. There are many kinds of capitalists, aren't there?'

'You had something to do with the cardinal affair,' Ramiro insisted. 'There's something about you of a murderer of cardinals.'

Somewhere in the house a child was crying. Ramiro was always taken aback and surprised to see the natural order of daily life going on around men like Cojo. Cojo got up and left the room. He returned shortly with half a bottle of wine and two glasses. He went on talking as he poured out the wine:

'Do you say that because of the way I look? Nothing we see is ever true. It's not untrue, either. But among the different things that we imagine we always choose the most absurd. It's natural because we are all tired of truth.'

'What truth?'

'Oh, who knows. We are alive. In spite of everything, life is good. Everything that lives wants to go on living. We must live better, and more, if we can. Listen to me. I'm not talking about the life that can be improved with money and stupid vanities. No. Neither you nor I are that kind. I'm talking about the simple art of living. To breathe, walk, be what one is.'

'I don't feel that need.'

'I know. That's why, when I didn't see you in the station last night, I thought: "This fellow is letting us down." And that's why I'm here. I answered for you, to the committee. You are a vacillating type. Rootless.'

'Something might have happened to me. Why didn't you call me at my house?'

'The police have been tapping your phone since yesterday.'

'How do you know?'

'We have companions in the telephone exchange who keep

us informed. And how did you happen to miss the train? Been drinking?'

Ramiro shook his head.

'A woman?'

'Yes. A woman.'

'I supposed so. Good. The fact is that here we are and nothing's lost. You look worried. Are you afraid?'

'I don't think so.'

An old man, gray and tired-looking, came in. Lowering his voice, he said:

'They've struck out for the mountain.'

"Is Gallinito with them?' Cojo asked.

'Yes.'

Looking at those two men Ramiro thought that there could be no co-ordination between them. Before speaking the old man seemed to make an effort of his will and to concentrate it all on his words in a false and insincere way. Cojo gave the impression of making the same effort to say meaningless words. 'I don't believe in either of them,' he thought, 'and they don't believe in me, and maybe they don't believe in each other, either. Yet here we are all three, and what is stranger still, here I am ready to go to Medina, where I have never been and know no one, to do something, and I don't even know what.' Thinking about this and about the name Gallinito, which struck him as funny, he could not help laughing. The other two glanced at him, surprised, and Cojo filled the glasses again.

'Did La Zumaya come?' he asked.

'Yes, but there are Hungarians along the river bank.'

'Then she's hiding out?'

'No, not she. It's her father who's gone into hiding.'

For Ramiro those unintelligible words were not even mysterious. With the comicality of Gallinito's name in his ears he said to himself: 'La Zumaya must be a woman. But why does she have to go into hiding when there are Hungarians along the river?' He decided they must be talking about gipsies. Whenever he saw or heard of something unusual among Andalusians he blamed it on to gipsy customs. He was not interested in gipsies. He found neither grace nor mystery in them. They seemed picturesque, but made him uncomfortable. Everything was contradiction in them. They were cowards, always going around with knives stuck in their belts. They were dirty and ragged and everything in them was converted into gaudiness and presumptuousness. They lived by thieving, but their thefts were ridiculous petty stealings. Their most-hated enemies were the Civil Guards but there was no case on record of a gipsy ever daring to kill one of them. They felt themselves to be the descendants of kings, and sometimes called themselves Pharaohs, but they bowed and scraped to the most stupid little bourgeois and flattered him like slaves. Ramiro felt too contemptuous of gipsies to hate them. But Cojo went on talking with the old man in cabalistic terms:

'Is La Zumaya getting old?' he asked.

'No. She keeps her form: and her daughter's a rosebud. But there are Hungarians along the river. With bears. When a bear shows up around here, we know. The earth swallows up old Zumaya.'

'And so?' asked Cojo, not in the least interested.

'It seems that the folks from Perpignan have sworn by her head.'

Voices were heard in the hall. Cojo evidently recognized someone he was expecting and hurried out; so quickly that he knocked into a chair and stumbled. Ramiro stayed with the old man, of whom he asked:

'Does Cojo come from this country?'

The old man seemed surprised that Ramiro did not know all the details of Cojo's life. He took a drink and poured Ramiro another. Finally he answered:

'I don't think so. But he comes making the rounds once in a while on business for the organization. There's a lot to be done in this part of Cádiz. A big lot to be done. Ten like Cojo wouldn't be enough. And Cojo is a man .... yes sir, a real man.'

They were silent. After a long pause the old man added.

186

'Every inch a man.'

Again they were silent. In the hall there was not a sound. Cojo and the newcomers must have gone to another part of the house so as not to be overheard. The cat peered in at the door again. In a corner there was an old mirror, splotchy where the quicksilver had worn off.

Ramiro looked out of the uncurtained window at a prickly pear with a red flower at the tip of one of its broad flat leaves. A premature flower. Ramiro thought: 'That flower will freeze one of these nights.' The danger the flower was in seemed more important to him than his own mission. Then Cojo suddenly returned and said:

'You won't have to go to Medina Sidonia.'

'Why not?'

'It's not necessary,' he said, avoiding longer explanations and added, turning to the old man: 'Take him to see La Zumaya tonight. Say I sent you. And you, Ramiro, you can go back to Madrid tomorrow if you like.

'Why not today?'

'Well . . .' said Cojo. 'What's your hurry? I'd rather you waited a day. Something new can turn up and I like the idea of being able to count on you. I say . . . if that's all right with you.'

That evening Ramiro walked through the town with the old man, whose name was Julian. Ramiro was more interested in Julian than in any excitement the town might offer, but his companion was not very talkative. They went to a tavern and had their drinks in silence. Julian evidently suffered from some liver complaint and every time he asked for a glass of wine he would look at Ramiro and say: 'I'm killing myself.' But this thought did not keep him from draining the glass and ordering another.

When it was dark they headed for the edge of the city. They walked out into the darkness by a winding street and after a quarter of an hour Ramiro asked where they were going. 'To the Zumayas,' said Julian. Ramiro had the feeling that they

187

were being watched. He stopped twice, having heard a metallic sound in the shadows, like that of a clasp knife opening. Afterwards he thought he heard steps. Julian, also pricking up his ears, asked:

'Are you loaded?'

'Are you asking if I'm carrying arms? No. Why?'

'Curses. I left the iron at home, too.'

A little farther on they saw a light, a little light waving in the air.

'There,' said Julian, 'is where La Zumaya lives.'

They went on walking and before long saw two men waiting for them in the middle of the road. Ramiro supposed that besides these two men others were lying in ambush. The tallest one said:

'From Perpignan?'

'No,' Julian replied, 'from Jérez.'

He pronounced it *Kérez* instead of Jérez. The shorter man said, suddenly calm:

'It's Julian. Let'em go, it's Julian with a gentleman.'

The men disappeared silently. Julian said:

'They have sentries and scouts out because there are bears on the banks of the Gaudalete.'

Finally they stopped in front of some shacks at the foot of a hill, beside an old tile-kiln and several caves. A light shone occasionally in the darkness. Someone was peering out of a door or passing by a window. Julian knocked and a strange cry was heard inside, like that of a wounded bird. When all was quiet Julian called:

'Hercules. Hey, Hercules. We've come in the name of the Niño de Arcos — the Arcos Kid.'

No one answered. They heard a dog being called and tied up. Then a little window opened in the door and there was a light and a face with a pair of very black eyes.

'Back up, so I can see you,' said the man in the little window. Julian backed away and the light from the window fell on his face. Ramiro wondered who the Niño de Arcos might be, in whose name they were calling. Cojo perhaps? Ramiro was becoming interested in these mysteries, even though they still struck him as absurd. The Niño de Arcos. Why should they call Cojo the Niño de Arcos? The door opened. The gipsy had one hand in his pocket and carried an oil lantern in the other. They went in and the door closed again. A hoarse voice said in the darkness:

'They come in the name of the Niño de Arcos.'

A very old white-haired woman came out. She was wearing a flower at the top of her high hair-do and had a smiling face and blue eyes. A gipsy with eyes of that color was really a novelty.

'You're Julian,' she said, 'Loba's son-in-law. Come in, you're just in time. This is Hercules and this other one'—and she pointed to a ten-year-old boy peering like a rat around a corner of the corridor cut into the living rock—'this is his son, Herculito. Come on boy, say hello.'

The old woman laughed, asked Hercules to lift up the lantern so she could see Ramiro better, and exclaimed:

'This is the bogeyman of Holy Friday, the one who sold Our Lord. But welcome.'

After saying this she touched the metal lantern to conjure away some danger she apparently saw in Ramiro and went inside. Julian and Ramiro followed her into an enormous place ill lighted with three or four oil lanterns. No one was there. The old woman had disappeared behind a matting curtain. Ramiro sat down on a low chair wondering why he had come.

Julian saw a guitar on the floor leaning against the wall and with the back of his hand he brushed the strings, which continued vibrating for quite a while. Then he sat down and said:

'La Zumaya must have gone to tell the girls.'

Ramiro looked at the whitewashed stone walls and ceiling. At the back there was a kind of small stage. Wicker baskets leaned against the wall. Julian looked at Ramiro trying to find something in his face to justify the *bogeyman* and said:

189

'If they bring bottles, since I don't know what to say to a treat, I will drink and like God make a grand coup.'

Changing the subject he added:

'Did you see the old Zumaya? Later you'll see the young one. Isn't it a shock to find blonde gipsies? But they're terrified because there's a tribe of Hungarians about. These folks here despise them but they have a feud of iron and blood on. That's all I know. Gipsies are very secretive.'

Before long the old woman reappeared with a bottle and glasses. Before pouring out the wine she hesitated:

'I'm taking for granted, my sons, that you have the grace of God in your pockets.'

A cavernous voice rang out near one of the doors. It was Hercules:

'That bottle's paid for by the Niño de Arcos. Naturally.'

The old woman smiled, wrinkling up both cheeks and said:

'That's another story. Hurrah for the little carousal!'

Julian started to take one of the glasses and the old woman said:

'Wait to clink glasses with me.'

Ramiro asked why she had called him bogeyman and La Zumaya, after looking at him silently, as if she were calculating whether or not it was worth while answering him, said:

'Did they ever read your hand?'

'No.'

Ramiro stretched out his right hand, palm upturned:

'You read it. I would like someone to tell me what's going to become of my life.'

'If you knew you'd hang yourself like Zacarías Col de Jou. And you'd say that I'm to blame, just as if I had seen it.'

The old woman shook her green skirts with red flounces looking for something in a pocket where thimbles, copper coins and amulets jingled. Then, putting her hands on her hips, she said:

'Why did you come here a night like tonight?'

'What's wrong with tonight?' asked Julian, to make her talk.

'You can feel crows in the air.'

'Is that all?' asked Ramiro.

'What else do you want me to tell you, *Marquesón?*'

Ramiro hesitated a moment and finally said:

'It looks like there are bears on the river-bank, or so I've heard.'

The old woman looked at him, intrigued and suspicious:

'This one knows the doctrine. I hope he won't turn out to be a spying dog, but if he does he'll not leave this house in one piece. Hercules! Have a good look at this fellow, so his mug will stick in your mind. Because the darling boy doesn't come from this country.'

The gipsy—small and lemon-colored—had nothing Herculean about him.

'I'm at my post,' he said, 'and can't leave because tonight the shadows are growing beards. Do you hear? The shadows are growing beards. Naturally.'

The old woman made a wry face and set about trimming the lamps, saying: 'I see. Fear watches over the vineyard.' Ramiro asked who was Zacarías Col de Jou and Julian also listened attentively for the reply. The old woman again spoke of Perpignan, of hanging or not hanging, and that she was not to blame. At the end Ramiro was as confused as at first. The old woman asked him, with a suddenly flattering expression, if he had five little coins to adorn the *little feet of the night* that was coming, now that *the heart of the day* had passed into silence and gloom. Mechanically Ramiro pulled out a bill. The old woman shrieked like a wounded bird — that was the way she laughed — went out and returned in a moment with a guitar player who complained that his hands were cold and he didn't know if he could play or not. He reeked of stale tobacco smoke. He sat down with the guitar on his knees, got up again, found a stool for his foot, began to tune up, pushed the stool away and looked for another. Again he complained about his cold hands and called out:

'Niño!'

Julian appeared to come to life and said in a low voice: 'The little carousal is beginning. A day like today it'll be good because the Zumayos are in a fog. Scared. Showing the white feather.' A young man came out adjusting his short little jacket and dancing with his clicking heels. 'Here comes my darling with his little cardinal's slippers,' said the old woman. This allusion to the cardinal reminded Ramiro of Cojo. He could not imagine Cojo's being on familiar terms with these people although he remembered that there were two gipsies in the Madrid jail who treated him with mysterious respect and submissiveness. The lad continued tugging at his jacket and looking solemnly at the right lapel, then the left, as he went on with his complicated heel-work. In all this there was a sad and feminine petulance. Ramiro heard flourishes, muffled clapping on wood and hoarse vibrations, discords, and laments coming from the guitar. Everything struck him as excessively and disagreeably romantic. But just in case something might be lacking the guitarist exclaimed:

'Olé tus c— —'

This praise of the dancer's virile glands made Ramiro burst out laughing. It was a sarcastic laugh that spoiled the guitarist's inspiration, as the musician himself said, grumbling, and made the dancer go into a frenzy of gestures, turns and twists, and redoubling of his heel-tapping on the low platform.

'The niño has form,' said Julian.

The guitarist seemed to be apologizing for him with his expression. 'He's not in his faculties today.' But he put more power into his hands, more style into his chords, and more muffled beating on the body of his guitar. The dancer continued, but finally fell into a chair, disgusted.

'You're not dancing well, Niño,' the guitarist said.

The 'Niño' offered his excuses, stoically raising his eyebrows and crossing his arms:

'How do you expect me to dance with my flesh torn and bleeding?'

The old woman, who was still busy with the lamps, said:

'The Niño has a cold, hasn't he? Say that you have a cold, my darling.'

'Torn and bleeding. Today I wouldn't even dance for the lofty pontiff of Rome, because my flesh is torn and bleeding.'

Then the guitarist started playing again. Ramiro was beginning to see everything from a grotesque angle. Aware of his repressed laughter, for gipsies have an almost feline sensitivity for such things, the dancer assumed a distant expression. Ramiro kept wondering what the story of the hanged man of Perpignan might be, but he could not imagine. The old woman was clapping her hands in rhythm and the boy tapped his heels. The guitar player raised his long nose as if he were going to let out a howl and sang:

> Path of my love
> who knows if the little plant
> budded forth again....

Then a shot was heard outside. The guitarist stopped playing, the dancer stood still with his arms raised in the air. La Zumaya cocked her ear. Just to be saying something, Ramiro remarked:

'There is Zacarías Col de Jou.'

The old woman jumped to her feet, crying out:

'Where?'

Ramiro made a vague gesture. He meant to indicate the countryside, the highway, the night, but unconsciously he pointed to a corner of the room.

'There.'

The old woman screamed:

'Holy Christ of the little petticoats!'

'He was talking just to be talking, Zumaya,' said Julian, 'you don't have to take it like that.'

The old woman repeated: 'He saw him. How did you see him? With the rope around his neck? Because Zacarías Col de Jou hanged himself. Tell me what you saw, my darling.'

193

Ramiro, seeing the old woman's excitement, was silent.

'Tell me, illuminated *payo,* and I'll put on a bang-up carouse for you at friends' prices. I myself will shake my heels for your little weasel eyes.'

Ramiro, to see how far the joke would go, said that he had seen him in a corner of the room. Before he had finished saying so, Hercules, with Herculito behind him, appeared, surprised. The old woman pointed to the corner, stammering: 'He saw Zacarías there,' and left the room with dramatic determination. The guitarist continued looking alternately at Ramiro and Hercules, nonplussed. Hercules spoke with aversion:

'No guards, shrill whistles or lamps can save us from a dead man. We put scouts out on the roads and naturally we have him right here in plain sight tied to La Zumaya's shank.'

Ramiro had said 'There is Zacarías' as a joke. It was like saying 'Danger stalks the river bank.' He had said it to see how the old woman would react, and she had understood that Ramiro was seeing Zacarías inside the room.

La Zumaya came back leading by the hand a muscular bushy-haired man about sixty years old. His very black beard joined jet-black side-whiskers and hair. He was a big man and with his hairiness reminded one of the sketches of Samson in sacred history books. He came in trailing his sash, hanging loose at one side, and repeating over and over in a thunderous voice:

'Where is he? Where do the boys say Zacarías my pal is?'

He seemed to hesitate, fearful, when he reached the centre of the room, looking at the corner where the old woman was pointing. He pulled up his shirt, showing his bare side with its long scar, and said, addressing the phantom:

'Zacarías, if you hanged yourself it isn't anybody's fault. Look at your flourish and signature here.'

Turning toward the old woman, he added:

'Blessed be your dead. If he comes back let him find us all the best of friends and let the dead of Zacarías see that they are in good company, with joy all around.'

But he didn't seem entirely reassured. He started shouting,

194

calling inside, and old men with blue shirts and Andalusian hats, young men with black jackets with big jet buttons, came out. They looked at the corner and then at Ramiro, a little fearful. Samson leaned toward the outside listening. Finally he said:

'If Zacarías's folks come here let them find us in friendly mood. If blood's what they want, blood will flow, and if wine's what they want, wine. We're not short of bottles or knives. Let them choose, and the sea swallow up the one who can't swim, and misery swallow up the one who can't find a good word.'

Turning to Ramiro he added:

'What do you say, gentleman? Did I miss anybody?'

Ramiro raised his glass and drank to his health. La Zumaya looked at Ramiro approvingly and he thought: 'All this because of a misunderstood word, a joke.'

He then imagined that these people were obsessed with Zacarías and that his mentioning that name had materialized all their fear. They were ready to sing and dance, pray and drink, to that fear. Someone advised:

'The *cuadro,* girls. Get together over there. Take your places. And let the racket and grace of God come. You have to dance, too, Zumaya, so that they can see the style of our time when you and I were sweet on each other.'

Ramiro wondered where so many people were coming from. Hercules seemed to have no personal interest in the fiesta and went out. The guitarist cleared his throat and started playing with flourishes. He sang:

> Dark are the shadows of grave-diggers,
> Dark are the shadows of the living,
> But white are the shadows of the dead.

On the platform Ramiro saw a young and really beautiful woman, probably La Zumaya's daughter. The old woman talked to her for a moment and then went out shouting, asking for *la gallisa.* Someone brought the old woman a glass containing a cube of wax with a lighted wick in the centre. The old woman

195

took the little light to the corner where she thought Ramiro had seen the dead man. A gipsy called Samson returned to the middle of the room, pulled out a long knife, opened it making the spring sound like a ratch, and kissed the blade.

'If iron is what you want, here it is. If wine is what you want, the house is well stocked. The gentlemen from Perpignan have only to ask.'

Julian whispered to Ramiro that the hairy muscular man was chief of the Ronda gipsies and that in France the dead Zacarías had been something like the king of the tribes of the lower part of the mountains, called there *les gaves*.

'Two or three years ago Zacarías and El Zumayo quarreled and soon afterwards I don't know what happened, but Zacarías who was the best bear-trainer in Hungary and Austria, hanged himself. The bear-people evidently blame the Zumayos and last year there were two or three pitched battles. This is what I say. How are the Zumayos to be blamed because he hanged himself? That's what I say. Now it looks like the *zacachos* or *zacajones*, as they call the Perpignan folks, are waiting for them on the river bank and the Zumayos are wondering whether to fight or not.'

The hairy Zumayo wore a ring of iron or old oxidized silver, almost black, on his ring finger. According to Julian, la Zumaya made him wear it in times of danger. Ramiro was no longer listening to Julian. He was looking at the platform with the dancing girls. The young Zumaya looked very beautiful—at a distance and in the dim light—and was dancing in the centre in rhythm with the clapping of the others. The rhythm of the clapping was so fast and nervous that the guitar itself could hardly be heard above it. Fear of the black and moonless night seemed to animate them all. The old Zumaya had put the third *gallisa* in the phantom's corner and the three little flames were flickering with the breeze made by the dancer's skirts every time she turned. Ramiro wondered: 'Why did Cojo send me here?' As if he had heard the question Julian replied in a mournful voice:

'You know that there are police in Jérez, and whenever a

foreigner comes it attracts attention if he doesn't go looking for gipsies and carousing. Especially in times like these.'

He added that he wouldn't be surprised if Cojo himself dropped in. Just then the guitarist shouted, encouraging the ballerina:

'Olé, little new moon of the Zumayos.'

Without taking his eyes off the ballerina, Ramiro asked:

'I keep hearing about the Niño de Arcos. Who is he?'

'Come on now,' said Julian laughing. 'Are you acting the fool?'

That reply made Ramiro suspect once more that this was what they called Cojo. He could never have imagined that Cojo was an Andalusian. He spoke with a Madrid accent and his manners did not have the extravagant picturesqueness of the south.

'Why do they call him that?'

'He was born at Arcos de la Frontera. He's a relative of the Zumayos. Didn't you know?'

'And his leg? How did he lose his leg?' ventured Ramiro.

'That was seven or eight years ago. In a fight. Before becoming a cripple he was a very terrible man. Now he has become more reasonable.'

This discovery completely changed Ramiro's conception of Cojo. Not only was Cojo the Niño de Arcos, but he had lied to him, saying that he had lost his leg in a railroad accident and lived off the insurance. These discoveries made Ramiro gay and light-hearted. It seemed strange that Cojo would so easily let him go around with people who could tell him the truth about those big or little lies. In any case it was pleasant to trap Cojo in something irregular. And as he started imagining outrageous things it occurred to him that perhaps Cojo had not come to Jérez to fill his post but to join the Zumayos in their peril. Maybe he didn't care about what was happening in Medina Sidonia, but about what might happen on the banks of the Guadalete. This idea opened up vast and complicated new perspectives. Any parallel between the Graco plan and the dangers from the *zacajones*, however, seemed thoroughly base to Ramiro.

Meanwhile the young Zumaya girl was dancing on the platform and the old woman was putting the fourth *gallisa* in the corner, beside the others. The dance finished, some of the men and women came down from the platform. Ramiro looked for the old Samson and asked Julian what had become of him.

'Who? El Zumayo? I would swear,' said Julian, 'that he is somewhere about inside with the Niño de Arcos.'

La Zumaya came up to Ramiro who again stretched out his hand for her to tell his fortune. The old gipsy stopped, frightened.

'You don't know what you're asking,' she told him, very gravely.

At that moment Ramiro felt a hand on his shoulder and heard Cojo's voice saying:

'No. Not Zumaya. Don't ask her to tell your fortune.'

Ramiro stood up. Cojo's hand was still on his shoulder. He saw that the old Zumaya was looking at both of them, amused.

'Now you know,' she said. 'Don't ask me to tell your fortune. That's what the Niño de Arcos says. But I say yes. I do. Give me your hand, and a silver coin to make the cross.'

Cojo burst out laughing and sat down beside the two of them. The old woman pretended to read Ramiro's hand and told him a pack of lies amidst laughter and joking. Cojo said:

'Don't pay any attention, Ramiro. All this is pure fantasy and a stupid joke.'

Then he ordered the old woman, with a certain curtness, to take the silver coin and go away and leave them alone. Ramiro was surprised to see that she obeyed without a murmur. Samson appeared a little tipsy, with two other men, and wanted to ask Cojo something about the *zacajones*. Cojo pushed him aside, but since Samson insisted Cojo answered, raising his voice so that all would hear:

'What I had to say on that subject I've already said once before. I didn't come here to fight with anyone, and I don't care whether you all fight or not. The Perpignan folk are down there. Are you waiting for the new moon to go down to the river?

198

All right. Tear each other's insides out like you've been doing in recent years. I don't want to know anything about it. I came to see you and be with my friend a while.'

Samson interrupted:

'No one asks you for anything but advice.'

Cojo said in a friendly tone:

'If you don't go down to the river, Zacarías's men will come up here. By twos, by fours, at night, like foxes. And one day they'll fall on you and not leave a single one alive.'

'That's so. We'll have to beat them to it,' said the old Zumaya.

Cojo went on:

'You'll have to beat them to it, but here the men are looking at each other's noses, with sentinels on the road and lamps in the windows. If you, Zumayo, were not a coward, the bears would have disappeared from the river bank days ago.'

'The bears on the river bank?'

'Yes.'

'And me a coward?'

'Yes. You're a coward. If not, why do you get drunk on a day like today? Come on, Zumayo, the drinking's over. At least in front of me.'

Samson staggered and murmered:

'You say that to the son of my mother? My dead little mother knows very well that I take what the Niño de Arcos said because I know what I know, and because before she died my poor little mother crossed my heart with a silver thimble and told me: 'Don't turn against your own, for the blood of the Zumayos is yours.' And I promised, and now the Niño de Arcos calls me a coward and my insides come up in my throat, and if I don't get a drink something's going to happen to me. Thanks, *Niña*. But I swear by this cross'— and he kissed the cross formed by his thumb and forefinger—'that the son of my little mother promised not to turn against his blood, or else the doctor from Ecija would be here now winding up guts and fitting bones together. Because I. . . .'

He cried and talked and drank. Cojo paid no attention to

199

him and the women went on consoling the bearded old man and saying that he was a lion. Again Samson showed his scar, lifting up his shirt with an obscene gesture.

Ramiro wanted to laugh, but Cojo nudged him and discreetly whispered:

'Don't laugh.'

The guitarist played and old Samson, pushed by the women, climbed on to the platform and started to dance, still moaning. Cojo told Ramiro that La Zumaya had very strange qualities and that sometimes she really foretold the future. He did not believe in such nonsense, but he had to accept the facts sometimes without trying to understand them. The truth was that years back, while the bearded old man was in hospital recuperating from the wounds received from Zacarías, the French gipsy had hastened to seek the homage and submission of the old Zumaya and ask for the young girl in marriage. The old woman received Zacarías as if nothing had happened, even with extreme show of friendship and love, and offered him kind words but no hope. Then she read his hand. La Zumaya was as famous for her divining virtue in the gipsy world as Zacarías was for his knife. And she told him what was going to happen to him throughout his life with minuteness of detail and utter clarity. She laid his future before him just as she saw it. The only thing she refused to predict was his end. La Zumaya refused to tell him how he would die. 'I know and I see it,' she said, looking at his throat, but I will not tell because God does not permit that.' She added that if Zacarías knew how and when he was going to die he wouldn't be able to sleep a single night for the rest of his life. And she kept the secret, because she loved her enemies as the holy Christ of the little petticoats commanded. But she told the others the secret which promptly reached the ears of Zacharías.

La Zumaya's words began to come true the very next day, for she had announced that a relative of the Zumayos would save him from the Civil Guard and leave him on the frontier. And so it had happened. All this seemed proof of the submission of the Zumayos to Zacarías Col de Jou, but the accuracy with which the prophecy was fulfilled began to make him uneasy. Three months later Zacarías was sure that he could anticipate his own future. He did not forget a single incident foretold by La Zumaya and the future seemed to him like a long rosary of days, foreseen and known, which he always wore hanging around his neck. Zacarías fell in love with the one La Zumaya said he would, and the woman betrayed him as La Zumaya had predicted. He quarrelled, spilled blood, and gave his own just as he had the presentiment, because of having listened to La Zumaya.

One day, half crazy, he ran away and lived for several weeks in a cave, without telling anyone, but suddenly he realized that La Zumaya had foretold it. Then he returned, locked himself up in his house and refused to go out, but the old woman had also announced this to him. And when he did not know how to escape from that chain of foreseen things in which it was impossible to move or even breathe, Zacarías hanged himself. And he hanged himself on precisely the day that the last incident prophesied by the old woman was fulfilled.

And now the folks from Perpignan were accusing La Zumaya of having bewitched and murdered him. And young Zumaya was dancing with Samson who was still opening his hands, and spreading out his fingers, and moaning, because they had called him a coward. Ramiro was impressed and said: 'I wish that the blue-eyed old woman would read my hand, too: like she did for Zacarías Col de Jou:'

Cojo shook his head and said:

'If you knew your future life you wouln't be able to live. You, or anyone else, Ramiro. Know today what is going to happen to you until the last day? Also know when and how that last day will come? Come on, no human being can stand that.'

Ramiro thought: 'Cojo knows. He knows what is going to happen to him, day by day, until his death. And he lives, in spite of it all. And that is where his inner calm and that superhuman serenity I sometimes sense in him come from. Cojo knows.' Then suddenly he had his doubts. Cojo might be right, and it would be impossible to live knowing everything that the future has in store for us. But Ramiro would have liked to make the experiment and he looked at La Zumaya with a curiosity mingled with temptation and relish.

At that moment Samson shouted and three women held him fast. Samson said that if the one from Perpignan hanged himself the Zumayos were not to blame, and that La Zumaya had only read the lines in his hand. He had wanted her to and La Zumaya had courteously complied. 'That was no reason for seeking blood vengeance.' But if they went on with their provocations he would go down to the river, all by himself, to take on all the *zacachos*, shooting. Cojo said to Ramiro:

'He does a lot of shouting, but don't worry about his doing anything. It's fear. The first degree of fear, one might say. It will grow and when it finally blinds him, they will all go down to the river.'

Then he looked squarely at Ramiro:

'Are you ready to leave tomorrow?'

'Yes. For Madrid.'

'No, no. You must go to Medina Sidonia.'

'Just where do we stand, anyway?'

It occurred to Ramiro that Cojo had perhaps been making an experiment when he told him a few hours before that he would not have to go to the place of danger. He wanted to find out if he was glad or disappointed, and in this way discover his secret state of mind. Ramiro doubted that Cojo had discovered anything, but he understood that he should take precautions.

13

RAMIRO liked having discovered something false in Cojo's character, and he remembered, with amusement, the *income from his leg*. The next day he left Jérez in the autobus, more attentive to the landscape and the novelty of the places than to any possible dangers. He saw nothing dramatic in what he was doing. He actually had the impression that he had never yet found anything dangerous in life, dangerous for him, that is to say. Nor did he see anything really disturbing in the gipsies, and their problems with the gipsies of Perpignan.

The peasants had vanished. The fields looked deserted. Half an hour after leaving Jérez he began to see, on both sides of the road, the high wire fences that enclosed the pastures of the fighting bulls.

By noon they were in Medina Sidonia, a white and green city where, as in the twelfth century, a Zegri or Abencerraje tribe seemed to be living still. It was very clean and full of white surfaces and eight-sided bay windows. It looked new, with a newness over three thousand years old. Mist was falling. 'In this town,' Ramiro was thinking, 'it doesn't rain ordinary water, but holy water for the delicate torso of María Mármol.' And who was María Mármol?

'There she is,' said a little girl of twelve or thirteen to Ramiro. 'Always quiet, waiting for her sweetheart.'

She was a graceful Phoenician statue standing on a grey stone column in a niche in the truncated corner of a building. María Mármol.

A porter had picked up Ramiro's box as he left the bus and was silently accompanying him to the inn. In the lobby, he waited for more than two hours in a large wicker armchair. He watched the rain, a fine, subtle and persistent rain. He found the streets of the city modest and intimate, with their low stone houses and dripping balconies. 'I could stay here for ever,' he thought.

A respectable looking middle-aged man, who had just shaved and still had white powder on one side of his face, arrived.

'Are you Ramiro the painter?' he asked.

'Yes.'

'You must go to Benalup at once.'

'Where is that?'

'Two hours by road towards the Ronda Sierra.'

'Are the Civil Guards out?'

'Not many. The worst is over.'

'How do you know that I must go to Benalup?'

'The district delegate told me so.'

'But aren't you the delegate?'

'No. He is in the mountain with the fugitives.'

'Can I see him today?'

'It's not certain. Start painting on the edge of the town, near the river, and he will send someone to you, because today he will know without fail that you are here.'

'Won't they be suspicious if they see me roaming about?'

'They'll be more suspicious if they don't see you. They know that you are here and now they need to see what you are doing.'

Ramiro, his easel under his arm, started for the edge of the town near a river or stream. The Gothic king Don Rodrigo must have wandered through here, he thought, after his sad defeat at Guadalete. The phantom delegate did not show up, or send anyone. Not a peasant or worker was to be seen anywhere. Before nightfall Ramiro returned to the inn. There he found the delegate. He was the agent of a wine exporting house, accustomed to going about the region visiting the wine growers. But now he seemed uneasy and to be on guard. He had a toothpick between his teeth. He told Ramiro that for the moment he could not go to Benalup. Perhaps in a few days it would be possible.

'And what am I going to do there?'

'A report, on what happened there.'

Ramiro was somewhat disappointed, thinking that a mission like this did not justify such a journey.

'Can you get along with priests?' the delegate asked.

'Yes. Well enough.'

'I will introduce you to a priest who is a relative of the priest in Benalup. The rest is up to you, but be careful. You're risking your neck.'

That night they went to see the priest, an old man of kindly and rude aspect. Before replying to the delegate's greeting, he said nervously:

'Have you heard the latest news? God have mercy on us! Five hundred day-laborers from Benalup are up in arms out in the countryside.'

'I heard something,' the delegate replied, 'but they say they are out to escape punishment.'

The priest, afraid of that peasant mass, seemed to grow bolder:

'They may escape the punishment of men, but not God's.'

Ramiro was thinking: 'This good man looks on God as a kind of chief of police in charge of assuring his private tranquillity. He doesn't know that what God wants, in all probability, is for everyone to live in peace and friendship in this prodigious corner where, with the natural resources equitably distributed, even those of the priest, it would be almost impossible not to be happy.' But what he said to the priest was:

'Nor will they be able to escape legal punishment, if there is justice in the world.'

They became friends. Ramiro exhausted his knowledge of religion, citing the encyclicals *De rerum novarum* and *Quadragesimo anno,* and the priest, enthusiastic, wrote a letter of introduction to his relative, saying, among other things: 'Only benefits for the social order can come from the mission of this friend who represents, perhaps, the highest interests of the court.' Ramiro had been careful to drop the Duke's name casually into the conversation, and in so doing he kindled the priest's imagination. The priest also told him that it was important for him to maintain the discreet and confidential nature of his task, and that the facts should not be misrepresented out of considerations of ill understood respect for the feelings of those for whom his report was destined.

Early the next day Ramiro took the mail bus to Benalup. Their route lay through low hills studded with immense prickly pears. Still he saw no danger, enjoying the surprises of a humid landscape. The temperature must have been like that in greenhouses where plants are artificially cultivated. He was thinking about Zacarías, the French gipsy, who had hanged himself.

They arrived in two hours, and Ramiro went directly to the parish house. The streets were empty except for an occasional Civil Guard. He realized that they were spying on him from some windows. 'If they killed me here,' he was thinking, 'death could have some enjoyable quality about it.'

The Benalup priest was very young, and looked like a good man distressed by the recent events. He seemed to be satisfied with the victory of the forces of order, while at the same time anxious about the proportions the repression was taking. As he spoke he frequently repeated the expression 'out of God's goodness', and Ramiro decided that for him God was not a kind of police chief, as for his uncle, but more like a kind housekeeper. Ramiro sensed the failure of the Graco plan in everything, and realized that the peasants were living their bitter hours of expiation. The priest of Benalup — this name, with its Arabic-Roman etymology, could mean 'wolf's son'—seemed surprised and pleased with his uncle's letter. He looked at Ramiro somewhat disconcerted. Ramiro made himself at home in the abbey, and through the priest easily reconstructed the events that had taken place three days before. Introduced by the priest, he won the confidence of the officers of the Civil Guard, who spoke to him without reticence.

Apart from the abbey, barracks, and three houses belonging to modest proprietors who passed for rich men in the village, there were no real buildings in Benalup. The people lived in huts of mud, or stone. In the long winters the peasants went out with nets and ropes hunting wolves or foxes and selling the pelts. In summer they harvested the wheat. With the wages of the short summer season they bought provisions, and some of them gunpowder for hunting, since the more fortunate had old shotguns.

The poverty of the landless peasants was frightening. Ramiro, observing the lay of the land around Benalup, said to himself: 'This is an artificial town, like half of those in Spain. In the Roman period and Middle Ages it had military expediency. Here, at the time of the wars between Rome and Carthage,

206

perhaps, they built a castle to guard the entrance to the Ronda Sierra. Artisans and shepherds came to live around the castle. When the reasons for military vigilance ceased to exist, artisans and shepherds stayed on. There is no reason whatsoever for them to live here now, nor any natural wealth on which to live.'

At night he shut himself up in his room and by the light of a candle, since the electricity was not working, he wrote down his observations. When he blew out the candle to go to sleep he listened to the last sounds of the village and sometimes thought he heard distant wails. He could not tell if they came from animals or people. He also had the feeling that again he was following the line of least resistance, not knowing exactly what he was doing, or what he wanted. Yet his aimless rambling brought him occasional pleasures of an undiscernible quality. And he thought of the Niño de Arcos and La Zumaya with amusement. He planned to see those gipsies again. He wanted the blue-eyed old gipsy to tell his fortune.

In the morning the little curate seemed less nervous, as if the day were dawning full of purity, forgiveness and clean breezes. He spoke of the excesses of the police force, although he understood that the rebel peasants had deserved some punishment. Recalling his pious readings, Ramiro said:

'Punishment? And who are we men to mete out punishment?'

This disconcerted the priest. Ramiro was conscious of the presence of sinister shadows in the village. Dogs with hair on end were seen now and then evasively crossing the street. The curate said:

'Those dogs have been feeding on human flesh for days.'

Ramiro was by now wholly immersed in this atmosphere of violence.

'How can you live here?' he asked the priest.

The priest said that life was sad everywhere. Ramiro did not agree. The bad thing was that the good life offered was not enough. He knew beforehand that all the happiness in the world would not be enough for him, supposing he could attain it some day. Then why look for it? He realized that these were extravagant ideas, however, and that he should not talk like this in front of the priest, because when ordinary people witness unusual behavior they put themselves on guard. And for him it would be dangerous for the little curate to put himself on guard.

Since the atmosphere depressed him he wrote two letters: to Lydia and La Cañamón. But then he dared not post them. The one to Lydia said:

'Life is sometimes amusing in its utter meaninglessness. Dear Lydia, what I remember best about our long interview is what the nude men at the foot of the dolmen said about immortality. I can no longer be like them, anonymous and impersonal. I am a person, a corrupt and individualized man. You don't know anything about that. Really, everything is extraordinary and fragile. I like you, and at the same time you repel me. But let us not lose the thread. I can no longer be immortal like the men of the dolmen. I have no salvation. And I go through the world hoping to find some pretext from time to time in order to justify this anguish of a man on the margin. I have not entered the game. I will never get into it. You are an abject and yet adorable woman, like life itself. I think that you are as confused as I am, even though you live for pleasure and believe you find in it something more than intoxication of the senses. When I am on the point of getting into the game, I stop and look at myself. And I see myself so loath to enter and so conscious of the senselessness of entering, or staying on the outside, that I decide to back out once again and live a marginal life.

'When I was leaving home yesterday morning I remembered your body with pleasure, and at the same time I felt like spitting, and the saliva that came to my mouth was repugnant. Yet I had kissed you with more than desire, with a frenzy in which *my margin* also intervened. If you don't mind, I will tell you again that I wish I had known you before. Before what? Before you became what you are? Not only that. Also, perhaps, before I became what I am. Although it is quite true that I would be embarrassed if I had to explain who I am. And you?

What would you say about me? Several times I have heard you say that I am a pure man. If there is some purity in me it is only that of the man on the margin. And maybe you don't know that I can see everything from that margin without any curiosity whatever. Everything. I can see you agonizing, poisoned with narcotics, and wait to see what happens to you, without feeling compassion of any kind. I can see a mad dog devouring a child, without doing a thing to stop it. I can laugh at the pain of others, but also at my own. Hasn't it ever occurred to you, when we say *the pain of my body,* or *the sadness of my soul,* or *the obscurity of my spirit,* that this *my* denotes possession? When we say *my* body, *my* soul, *my* spirit, who is the proprietor? And where is he? On the margin. That's where I am. And from there the only thing I see is that everyone is unhappy and everyone wants to go on living — in inevitable unhappiness — just the same. Isn't it grotesque? If one sees the number of absurd contradictions surrounding us he cannot help snatching at that margin the way the lizard on the rock makes for the sun. That marginal business is the only privilege we have. Nature does not place us in life, but on the margin of life, and then we do or do not enter into it. I have not entered yet. Will I some day? With whom? With a woman? With a friend? In any case it will be neither woman nor friend, but the illusion of friend or woman.

'I am in an Andalusian village now. Dogs are going by underneath my window. The old oil motor of a bakery is sputtering—it is certainly the only engine in the village — and the air is filled with the smell of blood. They have told me that I am risking my neck coming here and yet I don't feel the slightest danger and I am trying to discover some facts about which I do not care.

'About the facts themselves, I do not care. But from the margin I open my eyes eager to see everything in front of me. Why? Neither the dogs, nor the bakery motor, nor the priest, are in the least interesting in themselves. But there must be a truth, a shadow truth — a shadow would be enough for me — because things exist for some reason. It is the *for* I do not see. Ever since I was born people have been talking about justice, in order to punish the weak. Wouldn't it be better to say: let us kill the weak? They talk about love, to justify its different gradations: rancor, distrust, lack of confidence, fear, and above all else the reverse of love which is not hatred but indifference.

'I sometimes think that there is only one man who lives the truth and who, furthermore, deserves the gratitude of all the rest and does not ask for it: the hangman. Upon his head rests all the social order known until today, and still the hangman, aware of it, offers himself as a propitious object for the scorn, fear, and moral repugnance of all. Here is the martyr and hero, and the man who can be a smiling hero and martyr, because he has found the truth. The curious thing is that he found it on the margin, with no need to get into the game. From the margin I am also looking for another truth. Will I find it? I don't know. I do nothing but open my eyes and look. Is that enough? You have not helped me. What I remember about you most often is that warning, repeated again and again with the voice of a spoiled child: "Don't leave any telltale marks on me. You mustn't leave any marks on married women." But remembering it, I desire you, Lydia. And that desire is compatible with the scorn and even a certain moral repugnance which at this very moment chills me. I must return to the margin, there to find some warmth, like a hen soaking up the winter sun.'

The letter to La Cañamón said:

'I was going to write you a love letter, but it would be false. I love you because with you no illusions are possible, but if there aren't any, naturally I cannot really love you. How can one love without illusions? Do you understand me? Then my love is a mess. That doesn't keep me from dreaming about you. Always. Even when I am with someone else. An Andalusian song says:

> You will endure the torment
> of sleeping with somebody else
> and dreaming of me.

210

'It is not such a terrible punishment, really. I am happy with you and with my memory of you. Yesterday I was with some gipsies and I wanted them to tell my fortune just to see if you would appear in their prophecies. They didn't say anything about you. But it was all taken as a joke and when I go back there again they will read my hand in earnest. I am sure that in that future of mine you will appear. How? I don't know. I am an inferior man in many ways and perhaps superior in others. I don't know in what. You don't know either, but you women have a kind of wisdom for such things, and because of that possible superiority, perhaps, you accepted me and will accept me again.' Ramiro closed with some endearing expressions. The letters finished, he read them over and again felt that he was still on the shore of a river. 'Our lives are the rivers — flowing into the sea — which is death.' If he did not enter the river the sea could not claim him. But that was not why he refused to enter. He was also indifferent to the threat of the sea.

Then, what did Ramiro care about?

Thinking about these things, without coming to any definite conclusion, he mentally reconstructed what had happened in Benalup some days before.

Until a few days ago there had been a union of peasants in Benalup. Their headquarters were in a little white one-story house near the plaza. News reached the office. News from the committee, and in a certain way, from Graco — now dead — and from Cojo — still alive.

One of the peasants on the committee was Curro Cruz. He was already in his seventies, and when he reached the offices on the morning of that day he raised his head with difficulty to look at a wooden jamb-post jutting from the roof of the building. The old man spoke with the quavering tone of one of his age:

'You who have better eyes, go up to the top of the ridge and see if the trains are running.'

The trains passed by some distance away from the village. It was almost impossible to see them from there. Through an open window behind an iron grating, in the plaza, came the

211

music of a gramophone. Also the 'chas-chas-chas' of the motor at the bakery.

In mid-afternoon the issuing of ammunition began. Tullido's son had hoisted the black and red banner above the headquarters' door. In the council room Curro Cruz could not understand why the trains were still running as had been reported. Although it was only a committee meeting, other people were gathering and by night the place was full. Curro Cruz said that it was necessary to join in the general strike. Hearing them talk about strikes, anyone would imagine they worked all year long. The old man read a small printed sheet which had come with the letter from the district committee of Jérez. It spoke of the need of radical change in the feudal system of landownership. As Ramiro read it afterwards to himself, he said: 'Here is Graco.' He thought he had heard Graco repeating those words. The peasant organizations were going to declare a general strike in conjunction with the unions in the cities.

After the reading Curro Cruz stated:

'We have agreed that a commission should go to parley with the Civil Guard to avoid bloodshed.'

Mariquilla Silva Cruz — Ramiro took the names down carefully — the fourteen-year-old granddaughter of Curro Cruz, a little brunette and sprightly as a lark, was talking in the doorway with her sweetheart, Manuel Cabañas. As Ramiro put these data in order he realized that each detail, if it was to be trustworthy, would cost him investigations and verifications.

When Curro Cruz left the union offices for his hut he was accompanied by his sons Francisco and Pedro, taller than he and with all the vigor of their young manhood. His granddaughter Mariquilla, with Manuel, followed, whispering and laughing. Behind them Mariquilla's father, José Silva; a woman neighbor, Josefa Franco; another neighbor, Francisco Lago Gutiérrez and his daughter Francisca Lago Estudillo, a girl eighteen years old, mature, with a grave and serene grace. Ramiro was tempted to describe each one of these people and reveal the differentiating traits of their personalities just as he imagined them, but in a task so serious as his report, he did not wish to leave anything to the imagination. The details given him by the priest were confused, as far as their personalities were concerned. He realized how difficult it was to write a narrative.

In the ravine beyond the plaza the shadows were no longer those of the village, but of open country, with gusts of wind smelling of the mountains. But one could still hear the measured explosions of the motor at the bakery in the plaza, always weary and always working. The citizens of Benalup could not conceive of night without that motor, which could be heard everywhere and was like the throbbing heart of the village.

The hut of Curro Cruz adjoined a small yard surrounded by a low wall of stone and mortar. Curro and one of his sons lived here alone. The cone-shaped roof was of straw and dry branches, supported by two wooden cross-beams. The hut, however, was square, about seven yards across. A piece of mended sacking nailed to a post divided the room in two. Behind the curtain was an iron bed.

In the free space between the bed and the wall there was a linen chest with hunting cartridges on top. Curro took more cartridges out of the chest. In other huts the same thing was happening. Peasants were going out with shot-guns slung over their shoulders.

The men were coming to ask Curro what ought to be done and the old man asked in his turn, with a taciturn expression:

'Is the telephone line to Medina Sidonia cut?'

Someone answered yes, and the old man added:

'Eight of you go to the highway with picks and dig a ditch from side to side that automobiles cannot cross.'

The union rooms had filled with men, many of them armed. Curro Cruz, accompanied by the committee, had returned to declare that still the only will in Benalup was that of the people gathered together there. The commission to notify the mayor and Civil Guard of their dismissal was appointed.

Soon word came that the mayor had resigned and, accompained by the commission, was on his way down to the plaza to ask the Civil Guards to surrender their arms. The news was received with huzzas. Some were surprised and disappointed that it was all going so easily. An impatient voice said that no one knew what would have to be done to the proprietors, and that the Duke's own administrator was still undisturbed in his home. Curro Cruz, with great difficulty, wrote a communication asking the district committee of Jérez for work horses and implements, with which to put the untilled lands under cultivation. In the silence of the night the explosions of the motor still were sounding, when suddenly two sharp and clear rifle shots rang out: the rifles of the Civil Guard.

Curro Cruz got up first and went out. In the darkness everybody was going down toward the plaza. The roosters answered each other from yard to yard. After the shots of the Civil Guard the silence in the plaza was menacing.

Presently the sky began to brighten. The light made the white of the walls stand out, and the windows of the barracks of the Civil Guard were neatly outlined. Curro Cruz concealed his shot-gun behind a parapet on the corner and waited silently. Then he fired. The panes of a window shattered, and on the other side they could see a Civil Guard falling, his head split open. 'It's the sergeant,' was shouted here and there.

In spite of his age and poor vision which did not allow him to see a train passing several miles away, Curro, a great hunter, could recognize the shadow of a Civil Guard behind a window pane. He was a primitive, with the violence and virtues that such types frequently have. Calm, sinister and grave, he had never found a master who did not treat him with distrust. His companions were apt to love him, but his superiors were more apt to see in him an enemy to be avoided or destroyed.

'Now, there is blood!' Curro was saying, 'and blood calls for blood!'

Then things began to happen fast.

The committee of peasants wrote a proclamation declaring the expropriation of the lands of the Duke of Medina Sidonia and claiming sole authority in the town.

All day long armed men came and went, but with no more violence. The bakery engine kept on working, asthmatic and stubborn.

The Civil Guards did not surrender.

More shooting broke out and another guard was wounded. The following day and night passed quietly. But at dawn armed forces arrived, and from the western side of the village came two long and loud reports whose echo rebounded on the farthest huts, ricocheting through the plaza and along the high barren ground. Some of the peasants thought it was cannon-shot. Then they learned that it was the forces of the rural Civil Guards and State Police who, before entering the town, fired in the air to announce their arrival to the Guards locked up in the barracks. Curro Cruz declared:

'The comrades have not been able to do anything in Medina Sidonia or Jérez. Let everyone watch out for his own life.'

At the entrance to the town the section of the Civil Guard and two companies of State Police who had arrived in buses fanned out, two hundred and thirty men in all. They entered the village from different sides. Not a soul could be seen in the streets: the Guards looked cautiously at the doors and windows, ready to fire. As they turned a corner they saw an armed peasant, ten yards away. Raising his rifle a Guard ordered:

'Go inside your house and shut your door.'

As the farmer turned his back a shot was heard and he fell, wounded. The bullet pierced his side, between his ribs and thigh. They did not pick him up until many hours later.

The plaza was empty. They went to the barracks and gave aid to the injured Guards. Then they started up toward the huts on the top of the hill. As they passed the union headquarters they tore off the red and black banner. They saw another peasant in the door of his house, unarmed. Three Guards took aim and fired. The peasant, Andrés Montiano, died on the spot.

It was five o'clock and the sun had moved from the bald summit of the ridge to the crests of the Ronda Sierra. In the dread-filled silence of the town the Guards felt something mysterious and threatening. The three who were wounded (two Guards and a peasant) had been evacuated to Cádiz, but the dead man, Andrés Montiano, still lay where he had fallen.

They began to search some of the houses. Manuel Quijada was taken out of his hut and made to walk in front of them, hand-cuffed, so that he would show them where Curro Cruz lived. As they climbed, the road became rougher. When Quijada finally refused to go on, they beat him with their rifles. He continued walking, with a fractured ankle. Along this stretch there were no huts. Then they came to a stone fence that had belonged to a hut torn down long ago, next to the house of Curro Cruz. His family used the enclosure as a corral. In it there was a small gray donkey with white ears. It belonged to Francisco Lago, and the eight or ten neighboring families used it for carrying water. Inside the hut of Curro Cruz there were, besides Curro himself, the following members of his family: his son-in-law José Silva, grieving over the loss of his gun in the skirmish on the highway and feeling ashamed and guilty; Curro's sons, Pedro and Paco, more worried about their father than themselves; the neighbor and cousin Francisco Lago; his daughter Paca Lago, eighteen years old; Josefa Franco, daughter-in-law of Curro Cruz, a widow, and her two children, Mariquilla, fourteen, and her little brother, ten. No one thought of self-defense. If they had they would not have stayed there with only two shotguns, and they would have made the three women and boy leave. They were awaiting developments, sure that they would be taken out of there manacled, bound for the Medina Sidonia jail.

Mariquilla was looking at her broken *alpargatas* through which her bare toes, red with cold, stuck out. She laughed and cheered up her relatives.

The voices of the Guards came closer, and as Curro Cruz went to open the door two shots were heard. He said dryly:

'Everything is lost.'

In that small space there was barely enough room for nine people, sitting on the floor. Curro Cruz bolted the door. They

216

were in the dark, but dared not make a light. Curro insisted that the women and boy leave by the little yard at the side, but no one moved.

The hut was surrounded by hills on three sides. Curro Cruz had seen the Guards take up positions, the farthest thirty yards away. 'They can destroy the house with stones,' he thought. Guards came up to the door. The boards creaked with the blow from the butt of a gun. With the second blow the door burst open. José Silva and the old man fired, with no time for aiming. One of the Guards fell. The hut filled with powder smoke. The old man went out, picked up the Guard's rifle, tried to take off the cartridge belt, but finding it difficult, dragged the wounded man inside. He shut the door again. There was no room on the floor so they put him on the chest. Josefa Franco took the bullets out of his cartridge belts and placed them on the floor. A profound silence had followed the shots outside. Mariquilla, very pale, looked at the policeman and said:

'He's dead. He must be dead, Father, because he's not breathing.'

Curro, who had reloaded his gun, looked through the loophole once more. Then he pulled the two mattresses from the bed and put them against the door. He stroked his chin, tugged at the few hairs on his chin, repeating:

'Everything's lost, but we must fight. Blood calls for blood.'

Discharges sounded outside and the roof shuddered. The women were still huddled on the floor.

The Guards now occupied the immediate heights. Their fire was coming from two sides, the bullets crossing over the roof. Since they did not know that the floor of the hut was below the ground level, they could not understand how, after two hours of firing, the people inside were still alive. In the intervals between shots the noise of the bakery motor could be heard.

Two Guards tried to enter the hut by the small entrance opening on to the little corral at the side. They jumped over the fence, but Curro and his son fired. One of the Guards was

217

able to escape. The other fell in the corral, wounded in the shoulder. No one was aware of this at first, the shadows were so thick. Later they heard cries, and moaning appeals for help. The firing ceased and the wounded Guard cried out:

'Don't shoot, or you'll kill me. Come and talk to them. They'll surrender.'

Two Guards were distrustful. They thought it was a trick.

'Who are you?'

The Guard gave his name. They asked him the names of his officers and he told them. Then they detached Manuel Quijada, who approached the hut still handcuffed, and limping on his broken ankle. Curro Cruz requested that the women and boy be allowed to leave in return for permitting the wounded Guard in the corral to be rescued. The Guards refused. As Quijada returned he fell, wounded by a volley fired by the Guards. Firing recommenced with the same tenacity. From the hut they were shooting less frequently. The wounded Guard still screamed:

'Attack the house. If you go on this way you're going to kill me.'

They tried to attack, but fell back before the fire of Curro and his son. Before midnight the firing on both sides had slackened Then rifle shots were heard outside the hut and Fidel Madras, a Civil Guard, received a bullet wound in his right arm. They blamed the shot on some peasant in the neighborhood. A patrol searched the surrounding houses and rounded up young men who were led as prisoners to the thick of the fighting. There they were killed. The first two were José Toro and Manuel Pinto, the latter the son of an old woman of eighty.

The Civil Guard wanted to liquidate the whole affair before daybreak. By midnight four shotguns, instead of two, were firing from the hut, not counting the dead Guard's little carbine. The girl Paca Lago had succeeded in slipping out and getting back in with two more shotguns. Shortly after midnight they had two casualties: Pedro Cruz, with a bullet wound in his head, and Josefa Franco, with her left breast seared by a

rebounding shot. Francisca Lago had said when she returned:
'The Guard on the fence has died, Father.'

Pedro stayed on the floor, curled up into a little heap, his
head bloody. When his niece, Curro's granddaughter, went to
bandage him she saw that he was dead. Since the corpse made
movements difficult, the Guard's body was removed and left
hanging over the stone fence of the corral. The other Guards
thinking it was someone trying to escape, fired on it furiously.
Pedro's body now occupied the place on the chest where the
Guard's body had been. The women and boy tried to flee, but
the attackers, who had focused two or three searchlights on the
hut, saw them and increased their fire. In spite of what Francisca Lago had reported, the wounded Guard in the corral continued to scream and cry for help. Again Curro Cruz proposed
that the women and boy be allowed to leave, but they would
only consent to the boy's leaving because as they said, the
women could be part of a ruse for everyone's escape.

The boy left, jumped over the fence without any difficulty,
and ran down towards the town. The old man said: 'The
family won't be entirely wiped out.' Then he pushed
Mariquilla:

'You go, too.'

Mariquilla went outside, and seeing flashes of light all around
ran for safety to the side of the little burro. The Guards fired
but she was able to get away. The poor animal was riddled
with bullets.

From this point on Ramiro could give no further details in
his report of what happened inside the hut, for there were no
surviving witnesses. The previous data he had collected from
Mariquilla Cruz and her little brother, who only remembered
details of secondary concern, as when a bullet wounded his
Aunt Josefa in the breast and blood splashed on his lips. From
here on Ramiro could only take note of what happened outside
the hut. That explains why, when he reached this point in
his report, he had the impression that he was losing touch with
Curro Cruz and his sons for ever.

219

Newly arrived reinforcements stole about in the darkness with misgiving, until they were also well protected behind parapets. The attack recommenced. More than three hundred rifles were firing on a miserable hut of mud and branches, but the night advanced and Curro's resistance never weakened. The Guards hesitated to use hand grenades for fear they would open a breach somewhere and the besieged be able to escape. Finally they started throwing some on the roof. The grenades burst on the roof, projecting the charge down vertically. Two bombs opened a wide breach in the wall and the Guards set up a machine gun to make flight through there futile. Since light was needed for loading the gun, they turned a pocket flashlight off and on. The two machine gunners were wounded by a single shot.

The roof was almost destroyed. The Guards threw cotton wads soaked in gasoline, and set them on fire with grenades. A woman's screams were heard inside. All of them were surely wounded by now. Then the firing ceased. The hut burned like an enormous torch, lighting up the dead little burro in the corral and the corpse of the Guard. The billowing smoke, red at first, turned grey, finally mingling with the black vault of the night. Shots rang out again inside the hut, but the Guards, with their machine guns and hand grenades ready, did not reply. More than three hundred men silently witnessed the spectacle. Francisca Lago peered out through the flames for an instant, then climbed up to the little side entrance and crept out on all fours, her clothing and hair aflame. The machine gun got her some ten feet away from the hut. Her father, Francisco Lago, also tried to flee, but as he peered out he folded up beneath the machine-gun bullets, while the roof burned and fell on him in fragments. Still three more shots were heard, inside. The Guards answered, with more grenades. Then, to the smell of burning wood was added that of flesh, and the smoke became more dense and compact. The moans and firing ceased. Four men and a woman were burning in the pyre. Everything was over.

It was starting to grow light. Francisca Lago's body was still smoking. They went up to her to make sure she was dead. Guards threw on the pyre the bodies of three more peasants they had shot. It was a sunless dawn. Two Guards were carrying the corpse of another peasant with difficulty, their feet slipping in the gravel. Once or twice they dropped the body to keep from falling. Now beside the hut they threw it over the ruined fence. It fell into the middle of the fire, raising a great column of sparks.

Most of them started down toward the center of the village. Sentinels stayed near the hut to keep the townspeople off. With the wood of the roof consumed, as well as the beams and cross-pieces, the pine table and chairs, the breeches of the guns, mattresses, and the little fat on the bodies of the besieged, the fire was dying out. The walls had disappeared. Only the base, a rim framing the human remains and ashes, was visible. In the ashes, burned and twisted, the metal arches of the head and foot of the bed stood out, that bed which was the only luxury of the family of Curro Cruz.

The cloud of smoke still rising from the top of the hill slung a black diagonal sash across the village sky. All the dwellings were closed. An officer said, looking at his watch:

'We have just an hour for an exemplary punishment.'

They broke ranks and the Guards spread out towards the ravine. A ten-year-old boy, Salvador del Río Barberán, was looking out the door of a hut. He had an exploded rifle cartridge in his hand. The Guards said, laughing:

'Throw that away, boy.'

Then they pushed open the door. Old Antonio Barberán appeared, asking what they wanted. They shot and killed him. He lay there all day long in his own blood, forgotten.

During the night most of the peasants had fled. Among those still left in the village not more than two or three members of the organization could be found. Ramiro could not understand what happened next. He went on taking notes and muttering to himself, sometimes sarcastically.

One of the State troopers, accompanied by a Civil Guard of the permanent detachment in Benalup, knocked down the door of Juan Silva González's hut. He protested, saying that he would have opened it willingly. They aimed their guns at him and made him come out with his arms upraised. The Civil Guard, whose name was Salvá, spoke up to say that this man had not taken any part in the affair, whereupon the State trooper reminded him that this was no time for weakness or indulgence, and that he should think carefully about what he was saying. The Guard insisted that the peasant was innocent, and they let him go back inside his house. A woman neighbor ascribed what followed to Juan's rather bold manner when he reproached the police for having battered down his door. A quarter of an hour later three State troopers returned, shouting to Juan Silvá:

'Come outside.'

'Didn't you hear that my husband is not to blame for anything?' his wife warned.

'No matter. It's only for a deposition.'

He obeyed and they took him to the burned out hut of Curro Cruz. Another group of State police and an officer were there. Pointing to the smoking ruins, the officer ordered the prisoner:

'Go in there.'

'But how?' asked Juan. 'Don't you see it's all on fire?'

The still smoking corpse of Francisca Lago, his niece, lay near by. A Guard was losing his patience:

'Get along, go on in.'

'But how can you want me to go in if I'm going to burn up?'

Juan went towards the fire, and as he was making ready to hide behind the fence the Guards fired on him and he fell into the smoking ruins. Then, according to a woman who saw it, and who was afterwards driven off at rifle point, they put a pistol to his temple and 'blew off his head.' As Juan Silva fell four more handcuffed peasants were climbing the hill.

At the same time that Ramiro was trying to discover what had happened in Benalup, secret investigations by government agents were being made, and through the little priest who folded his hands and said that 'the goodness of God' was inscrutable and that He sometimes permitted innocent men to die, Ramiro was able to see the depositions of the surviving peasants. He copied parts of them. The depositions of the mothers of Juan Grimaldi, José Toro, Juan and Manuel García Benítez, went like this:

'Dolores Benítez, forty-seven years old, married, with seven children. Correct this number: *Five, I say, for they killed two of them* for me. Her sons Juan and Manuel, twenty-two and twenty-one years of age, went to bed together in their mother's bed. At about twelve at night they got up and made a fire, because with all the shooting going on it was impossible to sleep. They were beside the hearth with their mother when, in the early hours before daylight, she saw the hut of Curro Cruz burning in the distance. She called her older sons to help her keep watch, so the fire would not spread, and this is how they were when at daybreak a loud noise was heard at the door and several Guards entered, saying:

' "Have the men get up and come outside." '

Her sons went out, the mother continued, 'and when the older son saw her crying he told her to be calm because he who has done nothing has nothing to fear. The witness added that the two left and that she followed them but had to turn back under the threats of the Guards. She stayed near by and heard shouting and then many shots. Later she went up to the hut of Curro Cruz and found the *corpses of her sons, crossed one over the other, and there was a huge pool of blood, and nowhere to put one's feet. The old one's head was blown off and the other one she could not see because in her suffering the world disappeared from her sight.*'

'Maria Villanueva, seventy years old, married, very weary and excited, said that she was with her child Juan Grimaldi (she explains that for a mother a son is always a child), who was the one they killed. He was at home about eight o'clock in the morning when a crowd of State police arrived and said:

Men, outside. The father and son went out with arms raised against the sky. A Guard, with the butt of his rifle, turned the bed over looking, he said, for arms. He found none. An officer, seeing her cry and embrace her son, told her not to worry because they were only taking him away for a deposition. They took her son to the side of the hut of Curro Cruz and there killed him and the whole town knows that her son had never meddled in politics.'

Ramiro could have taken notes from all the depositions, for the priest supplied him with the reports, but he only jotted down a few more.

'María Toro, forty years old, widow, said that her only son of twenty-three, who was ill, was taken by the Guards at seven in the morning. When he did not return she went up toward where she heard shots and saw her dead son with a great wound in his head. Her hands were covered with blood when she tried to embrace him. They had done *a very bad thing to the child of her heart.*'

The Guards also entered a house where there were no men. An old woman named Joaquina Jiménez was alone. The Guards asked for her son, not knowing if she had one or not. She confessed that he had 'fled to the country.' Then they beat the old woman so that she died the next day. The one later making the deposition was her nephew, Francisco Jiménez. In the house next door lived a sick old man, Manuel Benítez. The Guards ordered Manuel to get up and go out with them. Manuel Benítez walked with difficulty. The Guards had to help him climb the hill. When they reached the smoking ruins Manuel saw a pile of fresh corpses and some peasants still standing around, among them Juan Cantero, almost a child, and Fernando Lago, now full-grown. Both were handcuffed. When the Guards saw them they suddenly remembered that Manuel's hands were still free, and tied them also. He reminded the Guards that he had been ill in bed for five days and they told the officer, who said:

'I have definite orders.'

224

But when they saw that the arrested man's appearance was really that of a sick man, they told him to sit down on a mound of earth. The officer said to the arrested men:

'Go in the corral to see the Guard's corpse.'

Two went towards the ruins. Manuel Benítez only turned his head. Then the officer gave the order to fire, and several rounds were discharged until all three were dead.

While Ramiro was taking down all these particulars he was thinking: 'When we have blood before us, innocent human blood, it is hard to escape from reality, and it is impossible to stay in it.' He spent two days in silent bewilderment. 'Nothing easier,' he reflected, 'than conversation with these poor peasants. Then why do they kill them?' But everything Ramiro saw, thought and said was *from the margin*. Without leaving the *shore*.

Every evening in the abbey, before going to bed, he had a talk with the priest. At the thought of those men murdered and stacked up in the corral or in the burned hut, the priest sighed and said that it was all natural.

'Could you yourself fall into such crimes?' Ramiro asked.

'Into those and others much more horrifying. I, and you, and everyone.'

'Then crime is inevitable?'

'Without God, yes.'

Ramiro was thinking: 'That is also the basis of the doctrine of Miguel de Molinos. The difference lies in that fact that Molinos leaves all the initiative for the exercise of the good in the hands of God.' He told the priest that there was something contradictory in religion. Everybody considers life horrible and yet everybody worships the author of life, God, whom they know only by His work. It was an incomprehensible, vicious circle. The priest said:

'Precisely. Behind every vicious circle, incomprehensible, is God.'

This impressed Ramiro.

One night Ramiro let himself fall into a waking dream, a hallucinative vision; he saw the smoking hut of Curro Cruz and on both sides of the pile of corpses, the stone slabs of the dolmen. The dolmen was blackened with smoke so thick it hid the horizontal stone on top. The fallen were the same that he had seen before, only now they were dressed and bloody. Ramiro was looking at them and meditating: 'It is natural, but it is cruel. Life should be something else, but it never will be.' No guard was in sight, and the smoke smelt of burned flesh. When the wind blew it toward Ramiro he felt that he would choke. Behind the dolmen nothing was visible. The back of the landscape was fluid, without mountains or plains or anything definite, as if the world ended there. Curro Cruz got up, completely charred. He tried to climb on to the top of the dolmen but his body was disintegrating, and in a knee and elbow the naked bones, also blackened by the fire, were plainly seen. Ramiro said:

'Men will some day see life as it is, although they may not profit by the experience or be better. And to last until that day it is first necessary to go through all of this. But is it worth the effort? Meanwhile where is the nameless man, the inexpressible man? Where is that man they were talking about the night of the hundred heads?'

Curro Cruz replied:

'He has gone. As you advance he moves on ahead. He is in a place that no one will ever reach. But no matter.'

Curro Cruz was still trying to climb on top of the dolmen, and rubbing against the stone he lost the last of his charred flesh. He was finally able to reach it, but his skeleton was now clean and naked. Ramiro asked him a question but Curro Cruz evidently did not hear. At the foot of the dolmen there were men, some rich, some poor — not utterly poor, but belonging to that middle class which is the social foundation of Spanish cities. Ramiro told them what had happened on this hill some days before, and a carefully dressed man shrugged his shoulders and remarked:

226

'So what? It's always been like that and always will be with those who enter into life.'

Behind him other men and women were setting up little sheds, something like shops, or little temples or money exchanges. They looked at the dead near by, at the burned out hut, and laughed at their own savagery. Ramiro was indignant:

'Why are you laughing? What is there to laugh at? You have got into the game and because of that you do not have the right to laughter.'

But no one answered him. Women and men of honest and diligent appearance — they might have been merchants, lawyers, physicians — looked at the bodies of the fallen and shook their heads with pity, but still smiling. One old man said to another:

'These men burned in the hut lived the way the *homo gibraltarensis* lived twenty thousand years ago.'

The women looked at themselves in their little hand mirrors, running the tips of their tongues over their lips. Some were arranging vases of flowers. Ramiro did not know exactly what they were selling. One of them looked like Lydia, another like La Cañamón, and Ramiro desired them.

The next day, at breakfast, the priest continued his pious commentaries. The fall into sin was fatal and one had to be resigned to it. Ramiro said, following his histrionic plan, that he sometimes felt the need of protest and revenge, and that he realized he could fall into 'error' through desperation. The priest reassured him, declaring that the same thing happened to him, and that after the recent events he had lapsed into such crises that twice he had gone to Medina Sidonia for confession. Then he gave Ramiro more data gathered from secret official information. Ramiro felt a grateful friendliness toward the young priest. And he thought that if he had wished to unmask and try to convince him that Curro Cruz was right, he might have succeeded. But was Curro Cruz right? he wondered, without being in the least interested in trying to find out.

Here is the testimony given by María Cruz Gracia, forty-three, mother of ten children 'and counting the one killed, eleven'. Her dead son's name was Andrés; he was twenty. He was in his grandfather's house together with Israel Montiano's son, who was also killed. With the 'lights of day' the State Police came and took away her son and Isabel's 'for a deposition'. Seeing that they tarried, her sister-in-law Isabel went to the hut of Curro Cruz where she had seen them being led, and found them 'thrown down on their backs'. She returned and said, weeping: 'They've killed them for us.' The two women went to the hut. No Guards were about, and there were rivers of blood which the dogs were drinking up. The poor boys were 'thrown down' on the ground like 'poor little innocent creatures'.

Diego Fernández, on the other hand, expressed himself in a laconic manner: 'Between seven and eight in the morning they took my son to the hut of Curro Cruz where they tied a rope around his hands and shot him.'

Ramiro could not go on taking notes. These depositions, always the same, insisting on the same details over and over again, and the final shot, produced in him a moral fatigue that disarmed him before the very society that Graco had been fighting.

As the sun rose over the Ronda Sierra — about eight in the morning of that sinister day — the Guards heard the chiefs say:

'That's enough for now.'

They went back down to the plaza. In a nearby alley several Guards appeared, prodding along two handcuffed peasants. Instead of being taken to the hut of Curro Cruz they were added to the string of prisoners being sent to the Medina Sidonia jail. Twenty-three dead men were in the ruins of the smoking hut. Two more of Curro's family were half-burned — Manuela's clothes were still smoking — and six totally charred. The Guards had shot the peasants on the ruins of the hut because they felt that by so doing they made the act a better example, and also because the bodies left there could be confused with those who had offered armed resistance.

Ramiro was very tired, and slept badly the first nights. He

thought of Lydia now and then. He desired her more than ever, and at the same time resolved never to see her again. Death, blood, the peculiar danger in which he found himself stimulated his desire, and in this fact he sensed another mystery. When death is hovering near, instinct urges us to reproduce because the species does not want to disappear. He intended to leave Benalup as soon as possible, fearing he would not be able to keep up the pretense for more than three or four days. He calculated how long it would take the priest to begin to be suspicious, but he knew that his suspicions would first lead him to talk with the parish priest of Medina Sidonia, without whose advice he would do nothing, and the little curate could not leave Benalup without Ramiro's knowledge. Although Ramiro was easily reassured, he never lost sight of the danger.

He kept one of the small printed sheets with which the peasant agitation had begun. He read it so many times he knew it almost by heart. 'I wonder if Cojo edited it?' In the confusion of those days he recalled Cojo's words — he remembered his absurd words with amusement — about his ending up as a friar, and how Ramiro laughed at the prediction. 'Nevertheless, what I am doing — the revelation and definition of an aspect of evil — seems more like a Christian moralist's task than a revolutionary's.' To try to define evil, he believed, was man's first duty in the present time, and with this idea in mind he went on gathering details.

With Cojo's leaflet in his hand Ramiro said to himself: 'These pamphlets are edited by men who resemble rather unscrupulous geographers making a map. The map will be useless if the relation between the sketched distances and those of the real mountain, river, or highway, is not exact. The geographer must establish his measurements accurately. The error of a centimeter on paper is equivalent to an error of fifty or a hundred kilometers on land. This is the kind of error made by the editors of that pamphlet when reckoning up the possibilities. A trivial assertion could be turned by reality into a catastrophe with rivers of blood for dogs to drink.

Ramiro considered his mission in Benalup finished, and returned to Medina Sidonia in the same mail coach that had taken him there. The Jérez delegate met him at the inn. Although he had heard no concrete details, he had a rough idea of what had occurred. Ramiro smiled bitterly and thought: 'Kill, murder, shed blood — here is the fatality from which we will never escape. A system capable of avoiding it still does not exist in all the world.'

The Jérez delegate took Ramiro to the casino of Medina Sidonia. There he had a drink with several rich landowners. One of them said:

'Did you know that Jiménez the gipsy gave himself up?'

Ramiro asked who Jiménez was, and the other replied:

'Nobody. A poor imbecile.'

Then he added:

'They say his mother died. From the shock.'

As he said 'the shock' he made a gesture of beating with his hand. The euphemism must have been amusing because several snorted with laughter. In all fairness, however, they did seem a little ashamed, but even so still went on laughing. Ramiro left, nauseated, but not surprised.

Again on a corner of the main street he saw María Mármol, the graceful statue, indifferent and secure in her gray stone niche. The street ended in the country, facing the side of a mountain, but it had the gentle harmony, the blue and fluid air, of streets overlooking the sea. María Mármol was born long before the church of Jesus, and before Jesus himself. She had known other temples, other vaulted niches. Before the girls of Medina Sidonia called her María Mármol she had had other Phoenician, Greek and Roman names. In the name of all gods and all laws she had seen men shedding blood for thirty centuries. Then those who shed blood fell in their turn, struck down by the iron of vengeance or justice. The conflict between the justice of God and men made new victims every day. The last, for the moment, were the peasants of Benalup. The little curate had remained in his parish perplexed and confused, also.

The only one who might have understood it all was Miguel de Molinos.

From Medina Sidonia to Jérez Ramiro was accompanied by the district delegate. This man had a wife and children, and they all lived in a petty bourgeois social atmosphere, placid and agreeable. His political ideas were no more dangerous than the liberalism of so many other countries where the democratic revolution has taken place: the conservative French politicians, the English liberals, the founders of the American democracy. But in this corner of Andalusia those same liberals would be regarded as ferocious criminals and would have been obliged, like Curro Cruz, to die killing. The delegate, after listening to Ramiro's report, remarked:

'That Curro Cruz will be a popular hero some day, a national hero. Don't you think so?'

Ramiro believed that every day the generosity of an isolated man had less chance of victory, confronted by a society based on utilitarian skepticism and provided with every means of defense. The Jérez delegate was still dazzled by the heroism of Curro Cruz, repeating that men would make him an example worthy of eternal memory. Ramiro said that eternal memory did not exist in our universe, and that it was more likely the people would feel compassion for Curro, perhaps along with the disdain some feel towards violent action and brutality. In that disdain the Moscow communists, the Catholics of Rome, and New York liberals would concur.

Ramiro stopped in Jérez to see Cojo, but was told that he was in Sevilla. He learned that the Zumayos had not yet gone down to the river and that the old blue-eyed gipsy was not there. Some said she was in Sevilla, others in Perpignan.

In Sevilla Ramiro registered under an assumed name at an inn in a central street. He had the address of a man and went to see him. There he met a family of industrial workers. The son's name was Helios, and he was dark and gipsy-like. The news brought by Ramiro from Benalup did not surprise him. What he could not understand was how Ramiro had been able

231

to get out of it all so easily. Ramiro was beginning to realize that he could have been in the same danger as some of those who were shot. The worker told him that at night he would take him to a place where he could meet high-class men of fashion, loafers, typical Andalusians.

Ramiro's insistent questions about the blue-eyed old gipsy Helios could not answer. He knew nothing. As for Cojo he knew where he was, but Ramiro must not try to see him.

14

AFTER supper they went to a bar, entering a large room frequented only by a fashionable clientele. The walls were decorated with stuffed bulls' heads, saddles and saddle-bags, giving it the general appearance of a farmhouse patio. Helios introduced Ramiro to some of the people. At first they seemed frank and amiable enough, but this impression began to change in the course of the conversation. There was a young man who blushed easily, and was a nervous chatterbox none the less. Others found their own cleverness so amusing that Ramiro had no need to pretend to be amused. After two hours of this drinking and joking, and vain inquiry about the old Zumaya, he found it all deplorably stupid. Nobody knew anything about what had happened in the Jérez countryside, or about La Zumaya either.

Ramiro stayed in Sevilla for several days. Helios was expecting news from Madrid regarding him. As he waited Ramiro repeated to himself: 'All is violence. Before he is twenty, every man unconsciously lays the foundation for his violence of tomorrow. When I was in jail I saw that not only I, but everybody else — with the conscience awake or sleeping — was guilty of murder. What I saw in Benalup is just one more incident in the great fatality. My hallucinations of the night of the hundred heads as I slept with Lydia revealed to me the vanity of things, and at the same time their inevitable horror. Cojo killed in the name of social justice, the Guards kill in the name of the law, the entranced lover in the name of love, and the avenger in the name of hate. Ramiro felt a growing indifference toward everything. 'Wouldn't it be better,' he concluded, 'to play deaf, refusing to hear and see, while accepting natural villainy and waiting in it for the action of God, if indeed there is any, and He chooses to intervene? Sometimes he saw life as a monstrous pretext for everyone to establish some kind of relation between his natural wickedness and God's mercy. 'The rest,' he muttered, 'is probably immaterial.' In this sense Miguel de Molinos seemed to him a virtuous and wise man.

While he waited in Sevilla he also read some books by popular Spanish writers from a circulating library. Unamuno he found pretentious and obvious; Baroja, false and rather ludicrous in his obsession with social importance and rank. He could not read more than eight or ten pages.

His friends never called on him at his hotel. They met in the bar, and each day Helios understood Ramiro less and less, sometimes looking at him with a questioning expression. At night Ramiro listened for Graco's voice in the wind, but did not hear it. He told himself that man was crime, that he could not escape from crime, and that he himself, Ramiro, was up to his neck in crime.

The only thing he really wanted at that moment was to talk to the old gipsy woman and ask her the ultimate truths concerning himself.

In an effort to hide the truth rather than reveal it the newspapers of Sevilla reported nothing but generalities about Benalup. Only Ramiro possessed the whole truth, but what could he do with it.

He wandered about the Santa Cruz district where the narrow streets, plazas, arches and crosses gave him a sensation of ineffable calm. He felt too much alone, however, and wished he had La Cañamón beside him. Everything was white in these narrow streets, and in the midst of so much whiteness the shadows were blue. The overhanging branches were so fresh they looked like crystal with light inside. There was something like a secret and palpitating justification of life everywhere. Out of each of these little things one could create a delight, and from each delight sprang the beginning of another. Each one contained within itself the total sense of life. Maybe one could isolate himself here with his own moral sense, but would it be legitimate?

He longed to go into one of those houses whose silence under the cold blue sky seemed to be inviting him. He entered a house at random and stood in the vestibule. On the wall to the left was an image in a niche, and underneath it a little olive branch, now dry. At one side of the inner door of the vestibule, giving on to an open patio, there was hanging a chain tipped with a small copper ring. On the other side of the closed door Ramiro heard the murmur of a fountain, always the same yet always different. From the sound he judged that the jet came up from the ground, with blue tiles or bricks around it. Or perhaps a marble basin. The sound led him to believe the patio was small.

He pulled the ring gently and a bell tinkled in the distance. In a moment the lock clicked and Ramiro pushed open the door. No one was about. He entered a small open patio. The blue sky framed on the right and left by irregular tiled roofs, and in front by flower-filled balconies and windows, looked different from in the street. There was an ancient purity about it.

Facing the door on the other side of the patio were stairs decorated with glazed blue tiles. In the center, forming a semi-circle, were many flower-pots, most of them with flowers in bloom. Among the geraniums was a rare plant Ramiro had never seen before, one with tiny flowers of exquisite design. The fountain splashed on the bricks of the pavement which were laid vertically in a circle to form a little pool. Those that were wet had a blood-red color, the others were gray. On one side, at the foot of an arch, climbing ivy was growing in an immense black earthen jar.

He was beginning to think how old all this was when he heard the voice of a woman no longer young:

'Close the door, child of God.'

Ramiro saw no one. The voice seemed to come down out of the sky. The opposite balcony as well as the side windows were closed. He decided to wait, watching the little stream of water rising and falling in the air. The same voice again spoke:

'Who are you looking for?'

Ramiro meant to ask for the strangest name possible:

'For Don Pantaleón.'

The voice from the sky did not answer. Ramiro was able to wander over the little patio at his pleasure, under the arcade, near the stairs of blue and rose mosaics. 'How happy I could be here,' he thought, 'with no need to get into the game.' The same voice now descended from some hidden spot up above:

'You say you are looking for Don Pantaleón?'

He was sure that it was a woman's voice. Ramiro could not see her, but she must be old. After her last words Ramiro heard a distant clicking of heels as if someone were withdrawing to the back part of the house. He looked for someone to appear on the stairs. He sat down. The little spout of water animated this monastic silence, giving a voluptuous meaning to every color and shadow. 'And still,' Ramiro was thinking, 'that woman who spoke to me from up there could be a sister of Curro Cruz, and these flowers, perhaps, are watered by a captain of the State Police.' In his back hip pocket he carried a book full of notes about the happenings of Benalup.

Again he heard steps in the upper part of the house. The mysterious woman had evidently gone to consult someone. Before long he heard her voice again:

'Aren't you Don Pascual?'

Finally, beside the roof-tiles, Ramiro managed to see the head of a woman peering through a small sky-light framed with red curtains.

'No,' replied Ramiro, 'I am not Don Pascual, but Don Pedro.'

Again the woman's steps receded toward the back of the house, possibly to confer with someone about the new phase of the problem. The murmur of the water seemed to be talking to him in rising and falling notes, whispers, questions, eager to tell him everything all at once. But what was it saying? Ramiro knew that the dream of life had infinite resources, but he had no illusions. The same voice again called out from above:

'And whom did you say you were looking for?'

'Don Pantaleón.'

The woman commented in a whisper: 'Mother of God, what a name!' Then she said:

'Well, no sir, this is not the place. Nor in fifty years can I ever recall anybody with that name living here.'

Ramiro left. When he reached the inn he found in an envelope a scribbled note, unsigned: 'From Madrid they advise that you are to turn the papers over to the assistant driver of the express locomotive. His name is Julio. The delegate of the district committee of Jérez is in jail. Cojo has left Sevilla and the police are looking for you. Your house in Madrid is being watched. Good luck.'

Ramiro took the train on which the assistant driver worked, and to him he delivered the papers. In his third class compartment he was thinking: 'Maybe the Madrid police are also tapping my telephone and have taken Lydia by surprise when she called, and bothered her with questionings.' But that did not worry him. Neither did he care if the Duke had once more found out about his escapades.

He reached Madrid the following day. The police had closed the clubrooms. He did not know what to do. He was not interested in meeting anyone, nor was there anything significant in the world except his own sensation of insecurity. Cojo and his friends struck him as inspired children, unconsciously playing with terrible objects. 'And nevertheless,' he repeated to himself, 'they are the best I have found up till now among those who have accepted the game. The terrible game of faith.'

He went to the tavern where the final meeting with the

Graco plan had taken place. In the back room he found Cojo. He was alone, and had just finished his supper. He was now wearing an artificial leg which gave him a normal appearance, and had let his mustache and a little pointed beard grow. All this disguised him somewhat. He congratulated Ramiro on his work, about which he had already heard. Ramiro insisted on the savagery of the repression, but Cojo said that nothing else was to be expected.

The lights of the small room, unfurnished save for a table and two chairs, were too bright. There were at least fifteen light bulbs around a wooden hoop hanging from the ceiling.

'I believe,' said Ramiro, 'that you miscalculated when preparing the Graco plan.'

Cojo was rather pensive:

'What can one do? Error is inevitable. We work as we can — persecuted, with insufficient means of information. But Curro Cruz himself represents a great victory. There are various ways of winning a battle. I don't consider Benalup a defeat. Many comrades say the same thing. You can be sure that no one intended to sacrifice Curro Cruz or any of his heroic companions, and that I grieve over his death as much as anyone can. What we wanted was for them to impose their will, not give their blood. But after what has happened, it seems to me more practical to think of the consequences of the sacrifice, and the positive side, if there is one. Human blood is not shed in vain. Lacking a triumphant peasant revolution, we will have a moral victory which will also bear its fruits. You will see.'

Everything was ready for the publication of the reports, he added. When the entire country was acquainted with them, the workers of the cities would show their solidarity with the peasants, and the whole country would head the protest repeating the watchwords against the semi-feudal system of agrarian property. Cojo was sure that no government could resist the pressure of the masses. After having said 'the masses' he rectified: 'The people, I mean.' 'The masses' was a communist expression, and Cojo hated the communists, whom he considered bourgeois with no faith at all in the workers whom they consciously deceived. Communistic Machiavellianism seemed to him the greatest of all obstacles when it came to trying to impose the popular will.

'Have you got my Benalup report?' Ramiro asked.

'No. The police know me too well. But it is safe, don't worry. No one can keep it from being published and distributed. Even the rats are going to find out.'

He seemed pleased at this.

'And the district committee?'

'Still at liberty. They are meeting tonight. Do you want to come?'

'No.'

'Just as well. Unless it is indispensable you should not attend any meeting. Each one must watch out for his own health.'

Ramiro was thinking about the general strike. He had no faith in its results.

'The protest,' he said, 'will mean more blood, more sacrifice. I am very much afraid,' he added with melancholy, 'that great moral victories still lie in store for us. Horrible moral victories. Do you think the bourgeoisie loses sleep over any moral problem?'

'No, but I believe they are afraid and will be obliged to make concessions.'

Cojo assumed a tolerant and protecting attitude that irritated Ramiro. Blinking his eyes against the light, and thinking of his nightmare about the dolmen and the nude men, Ramiro said:

'Don't be surprised by what I'm going to ask.'

Cojo took out a cigarette and held it between his lips without lighting it, waiting for the question. Ramiro asked:

'Do you know if there is a hill with a dolmen anywhere around Madrid?'

'A dolmen?'

'Yes. One of those prehistoric monuments.'

238

Cojo looked amazed and said:

'No. Why?'

Since Ramiro did not care to explain why he asked the question, he dwelt insistently on the horrors of the Benalup repression. After a pause, Cojo said:

'You are obsessed with violence and blood. I think you ought to go away to some quiet place for a while. But not alone. That would be worse. With a woman you like. A little fling is an easy and healthy solution.'

'A woman?'

'Yes. Just look around and take your pick. I know one who . . .'

'Thanks,' said Ramiro, with a certain irony. 'I'll look for her myself.'

He was thinking of La Cañamón and after a long pause said that he would like to know where the old gipsy was.

'La Zumaya?'

Cojo burst out laughing, spitting out a fine spray of saliva that sparked in the light. Then he said:

'I think she's in Madrid,' and added: 'Do you know what I'm telling you? That you're the perfect natural man. You tolerate no doctrine. You do only what your nature prompts you to do every single moment. In everything. Even superstitions. But, seriously, I don't believe in the old gipsy, even though she did for a fact drive Zacarías Col de Jou out of his mind.'

There was a wooden box with mah-jongg pieces, the Chinese game then the fashion, at the end of the table. Ramiro picked up a handful and scattered them over the table. He was attracted by the figures and their strange symbolisms: the dragon, mandarin, chrysanthemum, lotus. . . .

'When one is born,' said Ramiro, 'he finds a natural law already made. If we are virtuous and gentle and want to be faithful to that natural law, they will crucify us as they crucified Jesus. If we are not virtuous or gentle but want to be just, we

239

will end up like Curro Cruz. Which means that in one way or another, if we are faithful to that natural law, they will kill us.'

'And also if we are not faithful to it,' added Cojo.

Ramiro got up and said that he intended to follow his advice. He would go away to his native village for a while.

'What will you do there?'

'Look at the clouds.'

'With your girl friend, I hope.'

He added that he was not sure that Ramiro's house in Madrid was being watched, or even that the police were shadowing him. Instead of going out by the main tavern door Ramiro crossed the kitchen and left by the service door opening on to another street. He walked along thinking that his whole problem, like everyone else's, began and ended within his own consciousness. This was not a pretext for egoism. 'I don't mean,' he thought, 'that I am incapable of giving my life for something or someone.' But he realized that everybody gave his life for someone or something, whether he wanted to or not. The most God-fearing and prudent give it for the boss who signs the monthly cheque, or for their neighbor's good opinion.

At a loss for something to do he went to a wretched café on the Calle de Embajadores where he had formerly seen gipsies. He entered, ordered a glass of anisette, and after a little while went up to a stranger with a copper colored face and asked if he knew the Zumayos from Jérez. The gipsy looked at him as if he were drunk and said no, but that he had an aunt in Alcalá.

Seeing that he was not going to find out anything, Ramiro left. He walked about Madrid, making pessimistic reflections to himself. He thought about the victims of Benalup. Because he had telephoned the countersign in code, weeks before, from his house, he felt more responsible than his companions. But responsibility did not keep him from smiling, thinking that one day he would also die violently, and that it would first be well to try to discover the meaning of life, or at least an interpretation of life that would satisfy him. For we all need to comprehend. Comprehend what? In the first place to understand, each in his own way, the need felt by all who live to go on living. And then to understand the obligation to comprehend. Beyond laughter and tears; beyond virtue and crime.

He decided to go to the Ateneo, hoping to find a letter there. And he found one, covered with stamp cancellations of different cities in Asia. He glanced at the signature and saw that it was from Ignacio de Juan. En route to the Philippines, where his father was sending him, he had escaped from the boat when it reached Calcutta. From Calcutta he had gone to Yunanfu, where the letter was dated. Since Ignacio had become an artillery officer in the reserves during his military service, he offered his services to the South Chinese and had been promoted, having been fortunate in two or three engagements.

With the letter there was a photograph with Ignacio in the center of a group of soldiers. Above one of them Ignacio had put a cross, explaining at the foot of the picture, with some arrogance, that this was his private hangman. He got along with the Chinese chiefs, he said, by speaking pidgin English.

Things like this were never surprising in the Ateneo, whose habitués were the most amazingly gifted people. It made an extraordinary impression on Ramiro. He spent over an hour in the library looking at those Chinese faces with a magnifying glass. Only the hangman smiled. The rest were very solemn, and Ignacio himself wore the distracted and grave expression of those days when he used to be looking for money to retrieve his father's dress uniform.

Ramiro went to see La Cañamón, but she was not in. Doña Paca, when she saw him, recalled his having been in jail. She had read about it in the newspapers several months ago. As if she were trying to reassure him, she added that no one in the house knew anything about that adventure.

'Not even La Cañamón?'

'No. I'm the only one in this house who reads the papers.'

Although Ramiro had seen La Cañamón after his release and she had said nothing to him, he took it for granted that she would have found out later. For Doña Paca, being in jail was nothing to be ashamed of, but she insisted that it was better for the girls not to know about it. Ramiro realized that she believed him to be an accomplice in the bank robbery and he decided not to undeceive her.

La Cañamón arrived not knowing Ramiro was there, and seemed very glad to see him. They spent the night together and Ramiro suggested that she should go away with him to the country for a while. La Cañamón had never been outside Madrid. To leave the city seemed like a very exciting adventure to her. She went to Doña Paca's room and they talked together for a long time. When she returned she told Ramiro:

'Doña Paca says I can go to the end of the world with you. But I must always let her know where we are.'

While La Cañamón was packing her bags Ramiro went out to send his mother a telegram announcing his arrival. He liked the idea of spending the rest of the winter in the old village house, snow-bound perhaps, building great fires in the fireplace, and forgotten by the rest of the world. In the telegram he said that he had married and was on his honeymoon. Then he went to the station and bought two first class tickets. He had little money left, but enough to live on for a couple of months in the village. He would write to the Duke from there.

La Cañamón said goodbye to the girls and gave them all presents, as if she were going away for ever. The servant, who was very sentimental, wandered around repeating:

'Heavens, it's like a real wedding.'

On the train La Cañamón took a blue envelope out of her purse and gave it to Ramiro:

'Keep it for me. It's a little money.'

'How much?'

'I don't know. I didn't count it. It must be between one and two thousand pesetas.'

Taking Ramiro by the arm she said that she wished to give the impression everywhere that they were married, and that she would be an exemplary wife. She told him her real name — Paquita — because hereafter he should not call her by her nickname.

'Do you know something?' she asked. 'We girls, if we decide to be honest, can't be equalled.'

Ramiro felt happy too. Paquita had not the least curiosity about the landscape, and when she looked out of the windows she frowned as if she could not comprehend so much free and uninhabited space.

At night Ramiro began to talk to her about what they would do in the village. He warned her about his mother's character, and she was touched by the fact that he would take her to live in the old family house. Ramiro felt sure of his mother's welcome after his long absence and because of his having contributed toward her nun's dowry for the convent of Sigena.

15

IN the provincial capital where they left the train Ramiro hired a car, and by lunch time that same day they were in the village. Along the way La Cañamón, whom Ramiro was now calling by her real name, had been looking at the fields and, paying a somewhat fearful attention, occasionally repeated:

'There are even goats. Real goats.'

The chauffeur looked at her out of the corner of his eye and Ramiro laughed, amused. He was finding it easy to forget his Andalusian adventures. The car entered the main street slowly to avoid running over a pig meandering along ahead of it. Paquita had never seen a pig either, except in pictures, and when the chauffeur blew his horn and the frightened animal started to run, she stuck out her head, astonished. The car came to a stop in front of Ramiro's house.

The plaza was deserted. The few villagers who had seen them pass showed no surprise. After knocking at the door and getting no response, a neighbor appeared saying that Ramiro's mother had sold the house and gone to Sigena. Seeing them hesitant, she reminded Ramiro that he had other relatives in the town. Ramiro remembered a cousin of his mother's — a widow, with two daughters. The neighbor finished her report saying that the widow had married a retired Catalonian merchant.

'Hadn't you heard about it?' she asked. 'On their wedding night they were serenaded with a charivari long to be remembered in all this part of the country. They call her house the "house of the five letters".'

'What is a charivari?' Paquita asked.

'Go on, dark eyes. The young lady doesn't know what a charivari is?' the neighbor asked grinning.

At that moment the children came running out of the schoolhouse, which was also in the plaza. Behind them came the school-master, who stopped a moment, looked at the group until he recognized Ramiro, then went up to him with open arms. Ramiro introduced Paquita as his wife, and after the introduction he felt that they were really married. Paquita thought that to behave like a wife the most important thing was to appear reserved and say little.

After the first exchange of greetings they started toward the teacher's house, followed by the chauffeur. On the way they stopped in at the Valencian's shop. Across the street was the pharmacy with its windows decorated as ever with a blue glass globe, a Mercury with winged helmet and heels, and a stone bust with disclosed brain and an inscription: *Mens sana in corpore sano.*

Ramiro remembered Aurora and imagined her blonde and fat, with cotton in her ears.

In a corner of the Valencian's shop there were three or four pine tables with bottles and glasses. The schoolmaster made several purchases. Before leaving, Ramiro told the tavern-keeper that the taxi-driver would stay there to eat and that he should give him whatever he liked. At that moment the tavern-keeper recognized Ramiro and, calling him Ramirico, shook his hand.

In the schoolmaster's home there was goodwill but few delicacies. Paquita, however, seemed delighted. After dinner the

244

schoolmaster's wife, also a teacher, showed Paquita the household objects of which she was most proud. Ramiro stayed with the schoolmaster, who, smoking his pipe, told Ramiro that his mother was in the convent of Sigena.

Ramiro, who had decided to leave with Paquita in the same car in which they had come, changed his mind when he heard the teacher say they could live in a summer house two kilometers outside the town, a house called El Tomillar. It was furnished, including bedding, and the rent would not be high. The schoolmaster had the key.

'But we would need a servant,' said Ramiro.

'The Delabitch family can let you have one of their girls. Aren't you relatives?'

'Delabitch?'

The schoolmaster told him that this was the Catalonian who had married the widow. He laughed on hearing what the neighbor had said and acknowledged that the people, instead of repeating that name, said 'the five letters', and called their home 'the house of the five letters'.

'When did you get married?' the schoolmaster asked.

Ramiro said a few days ago and that they were on their honeymoon. After a pause the teacher added:

'I think you'd better not stay in the village tonight.'

'Why?'

'I'm not advising you to return to Madrid, but to take the Tomillar house. I said it is two kilometers away, but it's over three. You know the customs of the villagers with certain marriages.'

'What custom?'

'The charivaris.'

'They have them in all the district, it's true, but only for widows and widowers when they remarry.'

The schoolmaster seemed displeased to have to be more explicit. Finally he said:

'You know that I don't think the way these barbarians do.

But widowers and also illegitimate sons are serenaded with charivaris. I imagine that this could be unpleasant for your wife and I recommend your going to El Tomillar this very day.'

They went to the house of the five letters a little later. The women received them cordially, although old Mr. Delabitch seemed distrustful. They already knew that Ramiro had arrived in a car, that he was married to a woman who had never seen a goat, and that the chauffeur had eaten at the Valencian's. Ramiro was astounded. Mrs. Delabitch sent Lucía, her younger daughter to fetch the older one, who lived with her husband and mother-in-law. When she arrived Ramiro recalled that they had played together as children. They chatted gaily for a while and laughed, re-living the old days. Ramiro asked:

'How does it happen that I don't remember Lucía?'

'She was always a solitary and stay-in-the-corner,' the mother replied. 'As a child I had to give her a push to make her go out and play.'

Old Mr. Delabitch continued staring at Ramiro, and finally asked him if it was true that he had been in jail. Ramiro said:

'Why do you ask?'

'No reason.'

Shortly afterward Ramiro thanked the mother for having promised him that Lucía would go to his house to work, and left with the teacher. In the street they found the schoolmaster's wife and Paquita. Ramiro tried to guess Paquita's state of mind by her expression, and was surprised to see her gloomy and nervous. He imagined that she had heard something disagreeable.

The schoolmaster's wife left for her school and Ramiro, Paquita and the schoolmaster drove out to El Tomillar. When they arrived Paquita saw a forsaken little garden on the south side of the house, and on the north, the remains of the night frost. The day was sunny and the teacher said that the month of January in this latitude was mild and almost always pleasant.

The house had a wall surrounding the corral. For more than a kilometer all around there was not a single tree. Once inside,

Paquita seemed surprised and delighted. The house looked as if it had been lived in the day before, but it was very cold. There were three fireplaces, and firewood in the corral. Ramiro made a fire and the flames cheered the room with their flickering reflections. The view from the side windows was very beautiful. One could see the whole river bank, for more than ten miles. Paquita became enthusiastic again, but as she approached the bedroom she let out a shriek:

'An animal,' she said, 'I saw an animal. It jumped over the bed and into the fireplace.'

The teacher ran out into the corral.

'There it is, there it is,' he cried, pointing to the roof.

'But, what is it?' asked Paquita.

'A squirrel,' answered the teacher. 'A beautiful squirrel.'

The frightened animal fled over the opposite side of the house. Ramiro built fires in all the fireplaces, to chase out any other possible animal visitors. In one there were two bats that had doubtless been sleeping. Suffocated by the smoke, they fell into the fire and were burned up. Paquita was afraid to open the wardrobes. She expected surprises everywhere.

With the fires burning the house seemed more comfortable, but was still cold. Paquita asked if there were a telephone. The schoolmaster said no, not in the house, but that there was one in the town. They turned on the water to make sure the taps were working.

Ramiro was beginning to regret his return to the village, but once there nothing in the world would make him leave. At the heart of his obscure decision there was a curious stimulus. 'Paquita will find out some day that I am a bastard,' he mused, 'and that my family is held in contempt in the region. Then she will not feel inferior to me, but my equal.'

He gave the chauffeur a list of things to buy, but fearing that he might bungle the order Ramiro went with him. He bought almost half the Valencian's store. Helped by the chauffeur and the teacher he carried the provisions to the house. The schoolmaster asked:

'Do you intend to go and see the priest?'

'No. If you see him tell him that I send greetings.'

The teacher hesitated:

'We don't get along very well. The same old squabbling.'

Ramiro paid the chauffeur who was in a hurry to be on his way, and when they were alone the teacher remarked:

'It looks as if what they were saying in town is true, that your affairs are prospering.'

'I suppose,' said Ramiro smiling, 'that they say I held up a bank and am enjoying the millions I stole.'

Ramiro paid a month's rent, the schoolmaster gave him a receipt, and aware that the young couple wished to be alone, he left. It was still light, but the sun was low. Ramiro felt happy knowing that he was out of the village and safe from the charivari. Paquita was now bold enough to open the wardrobes.

'Do you know,' she said, 'that I thought we were going to live in a castle?'

'Why?'

'Because of what Doña Paca told me.'

'There is a castle near here, it's true.'

'Yours?'

'No. But it once belonged to my grandparents.'

'Why don't we live there?'

'It's in ruins. But if you like we will go and see it some day.'

'Will it be enchanted like the castle of "Go and you will not return"?'

'No. From this castle you do return. At least I think so.'

Ramiro was paying more attention to what he was reading in Paquita's expression than to what she was saying, because he had surprised her shortly before in an attitude of somber meditation.

'This must be the place,' she had said frowning, 'where Christ uttered his three cries.'

In a moment she added:

'Will we stay here very long?'

Ramiro wondered what had gone wrong when she was with the schoolmaster's wife and asked her to tell him about it.

'You're right,' Paquita said. 'She told me that even though you had been in prison, you were just the same as ever for them.'

Ramiro did not reply. She asked:

'Is it true that you were in jail?'

'Yes.'

'Did Doña Paca know?'

'Yes. But she warned me not to tell you because you wouldn't understand.'

'And what does she know about my understanding or not? The teacher's wife also told me that they don't like you in the town. If this is so, why have we come? And why did your mother become a nun without telling you? Didn't you get along together?'

Ramiro took his time answering.

'I see now,' he finally said, 'that you wish you hadn't come.'

They were pensive. Paquita said that she had a hunch that sooner or later they would find out in the village what she was in Madrid. 'It won't be long,' she said, 'until they're calling me "La Cañamón".' Ramiro considered this more than probable. Paquita added:

'But if they would just leave us alone, I wouldn't care.'

Ramiro held her on his knees near the fire. She said:

'Tomorrow a servant will come. What a pity. I would like to be alone with you.'

Ramiro liked that. He also liked her not having asked why he had been in prison. He told her that the servant would return to the village every night to sleep in her parent's home. Night had fallen. The shadows gathered round the house, and Paquita said:

'I never thought the night could be so black.'

There was no moon, but the sky was starry. Ramiro closed the shutters and turned on the lights. The silence was complete, inside the house and out. He went to the corral for firewood

and Paquita declared that one had to be very brave to go outside the house. Ramiro explained that life was safer here than
in Madrid, and that outside the house there was nothing but
an occasional squirrel or lizard.

'On the nights when there is a moon,' he added, 'you will
see how beautiful everything is.'

He saw some books on a shelf and two shotguns in a rack.
He even found three dozen cartridges in a drawer. When she
was used to country life they would go hunting, he told her,
laughing.

They ate and sat down by the fire again. Outside an owl
was hooting.

'What's that?' Paquita asked. 'A lizard?'

'No. An owl.'

'You said there were only squirrels and lizards.'

Ramiro explained what an owl was. When she finally understood she arched her brows and said:

'That is the animal of death.'

Ramiro decided it would be best to go to bed at once. With
the fatigue of the journey Paquita would soon sleep, and the
next day everything would be easier. He lit a fire in the bedroom and they went to bed. It was a large double bed. Paquita
insisted the sheets were damp. Ramiro said they were only
cold. He tried to convince her that it almost never rained there.
The owl kept hooting on the roof and Paquita made a futile
effort not to hear it. The flames on the hearth, which were
dying, illuminated the ceiling with wavering reflections. At times
the room was buried in shadows and the fire seemed to be out,
then suddenly a little blue flame appeared, licked a log along
one side, disappeared, and flared up again. The air was filled
with quick flames. Ramiro was enjoying that immense silence
with Paquita in his arms when suddenly, in the calm of the
night, he heard a distant noise that seemed to be coming closer.
Paquita also heard it and whispered:

'They are coming. There are people outside and they are
coming closer and closer.'

The noise ceased. A little later a bell was heard, quite near, one of those big bells that cows sometimes wear around their necks.

'Nothing, it is nothing,' said Ramiro. 'A straying cow.'

Then, still nearer, the clanging sound of a caldron dragged over the stony ground. Ramiro no longer had any doubt. The charivari. The peasants had left the village in spite of the distance and cold and were surrounding the house. Ramiro, with a resigned air, sat up in bed.

'Don't be frightened,' he told her. 'They will make noise, a lot of noise, perhaps, but there is no danger whatsoever.'

Fifteen or twenty cow-bells rang out at the same time near the windows on every side. The din was infernal. Simultaneously there were whistles, braying, caldrons dragged over the rocks — evidently those huge caldrons used in preparing threshers' meals in the summertime; *arrobaderas* — the immense metal shovels which, drawn by horses, were used to gather up the wheat on the threshing floor; and copper mortars beaten with pestles of the same metal. Amidst all the racket horses were whinnying. Ramiro knew that he would be unable to reassure Paquita.

'They are coming to kill us,' she whispered again and again.

The noise was now like that of an ancient army, and in the midst of such turmoil the cow-bells, rhythmically rung, suddenly resounded with a strange and almost musical note. Savage laughter was heard. And mighty brayings, imitated by the peasants themselves. Over the uproar the bellowing of a hunter's horn rose. There were several, and they answered each other from here and there, just as in the chase. Ramiro knew that these horns could keep up long conversations, and that they meant one thing or another, depending on the tone. That dialogue in the wild depths of the night made him uneasy. Although he could not understand what they were saying, he knew that some of the bellowings were directed at him with a provocative and insulting intention. Paquita thought her last hour had come.

'Why do they want to kill us? What have we done to them?' she repeated.

251

Exasperated, Ramiro leaped out of bed, loaded one of the shotguns, and went to the vestibule. He shoved the barrel through a half-opened window, and assuming that no one would be there, he fired both barrels, one after the other. The report caused such a vibration inside the house that a picture fell off the wall, breaking the glass. Startled, Ramiro ran to the bedroom. Paquita was sobbing and screaming in a fit of nerves.

Ramiro returned to the window with the shotgun loaded. The din was louder and nearer. The hunting horns were answering each other from different places in the night, and one of them was saying distinctly: 'ca ... brón — he-goat, cuckold — ca ... brón.' Ramiro hurled back insults at the peasants, forgetting they could not hear. He fired again — both barrels at once — and heard a scream in the bedroom. He ran to Paquita's side. She had fainted. He wet her temples, warmed a towel on the hearth and wrapped it around her legs. Outside the tumult was increasing. In the vestibule itself, on the other side of the outside door, a multitude of cow-bells jangled. Paquita regained consciousness and asked:

'Did they wound you?'

'No. I told you there is no danger at all. I fired the shots.'

She started calling for her mother and weeping. Just then more than thirty horses and mules dragging the great threshing shovels, iron caldrons, zinc pails, etc., over the stony ground, must have passed by. The cow-bells clanged rhythmically again, and the hunting horns continued to insult him: 'ca ... brón, ca ... brón'. Above the clamor two or three motorcycle sirens screamed. Paquita's imagination worked in vain. Why all this and what for, if they did not wish to kill them?

Ramiro saw that the charivari was going to last all night. The village had been waiting a long time for an opportunity like this. Again he heard the insults of the hunting horns, and possessed by rage he loaded the gun once more, stuck it out of a window and fired, desiring now to make a killing. After the shots there was sudden silence on that side of the house and Ramiro thought joyfully: 'I got somebody.' Again he loaded the gun, saying to himself: 'I could gladly kill them all, even if they hanged me tomorrow.' And then, in a lucid moment he added: 'I've got into the game. And I have entered into it in the most grotesque conditions imaginable.'

Ramiro exhausted the ammunition, firing more than thirty haphazard shots without seeing anyone. He remembered Benalup and Curro Cruz and felt an ancient fury that quickened his breathing, although he considered himself rather ridiculous for the disproportionate intensity of his reactions, since nobody thought of attacking him, much less burning him alive. He had got into the game.

It was probably long after midnight when he saw Paquita sitting beside the hearth, wrapped in a blanket covering her from head to toe and giving her a pathetic appearance. Her feet were very cold. Ramiro kissed them, tucked the blanket around them, and sat down beside her. He had the fixed idea that he had killed someone and that the next day they would surely arrest him. He was thinking only of how he could get Paquita out of all this.

The din died down for a while. Paquita ran to dress, saying:

'They've gone. If we leave now we'll be able to escape somewhere.'

'Where?'

'To another town. But we'll have to go through the village and I don't want to go through the village.'

And then the charivari began again. The uproar was greater still. Paquita, wide-eyed, said:

'They have picked up the people you killed and now they are coming to set fire to the house.'

Absurd as these words were, they had a measure of probability. But it was only the last part of the charivari, and the noisiest. It must have been about three in the morning, when the moon was rising, that the peasants, their purpose accomplished, disappeared. Ramiro opened the shutters facing the south and said to Paquita:

'Look, see how beautiful the country is in the moonlight.'

She approached fearfully, asking when the charivari people would come back. Ramiro tried to be reassuring and told her to go to bed and sleep, but she was sure those 'black beasts' would return. Ramiro finally succeeded in calming her and making her comfortable in bed. Then he took a kitchen knife and went out to reconnoiter the surroundings. He found no one, although a dead dog lay in a pool of blood near the porch. 'Perhaps the master fell, too,' he thought. He seized the animal by the tail and dragged it behind some bushes, some fifty yards away. He planned to ask for a car from the city as soon as morning came. 'The schoolmaster can telephone for it from the village,' he decided. Before returning to the bedroom he totaled up the expenses and discovered that besides his own money he had spent some fifteen pesetas of Paquita's. If she left he would not be able to give her back the full amount. All this he was thinking, taking for granted that some of his shots had found victims. He was sorry, and remembering the old blue-eyed gipsy he muttered: 'If she had prophesied this, perhaps I could have avoided it.'

He went to Paquita's side. She was quietly weeping, and as soon as she saw him she asked again:

'Did you kill anyone?'

'I don't know. I didn't see anything around the house.'

Dawn came without their having slept. Paquita got up, and not daring to go out of the house she looked through the windows in the direction away from the town and said:

'Through there, walking straight, one must arrive somewhere.'

'At the river.'

'And isn't there a bridge?'

'Not in that direction.'

When she seemed calm enough to think rationally about what had happened, she started explaining that life would be impossible for them there. Ramiro listened, thinking that she could be right. At eight o'clock Lucía, Delabitch's stepdaughter, arrived. Seeing traces of blood on the porch she asked:

'Has there been an accident?'

'No. I had to kill a dog last night, that's all.'

The girl set to work. Paquita looked at her, trying to guess something from her expression, but without success. The presence of this silent woman, who all day long spoke only the words indispensable to her work, and who in her look revealed neither friendship nor distrust, puzzled Paquita.

When Lucía left that night she was carrying two letters, one for the schoolmaster and another to be posted, addressed to the Duke of L. Ramiro was agreeably surprised not to be molested by the police. He did not go to the village because Paquita refused either to stay alone or accompany him. When it was dark she began to tremble and see threats everywhere.

'Tell me, Ramiro. I always saw something mysterious in you. Tell me the truth.'

'I have always told you the truth!'

'No. That isn't so. Tell me the truth: Who are you? There are noises again in the direction of the river. Why do they want to kill you? Who are you?'

'A man, like any other.'

'No. You are more or you are less. You are something else. You were in prison. You are like a monk. They want to kill you. And now...'

In the direction of the river the din was increasing. Ramiro resigned himself to the idea of a charivari that would last three days. Far away the first hunting horn sounded: *'ca...brón'*. Slowly he walked over to Paquita, asking:

'But, Paquita, weren't we agreed that you wanted to be with me?'

'No. I'm going to Madrid or Barcelona and live honorably as I did before at Doña Paca's. But tell me, Ramiro; who are you that you go to jail, and wish to marry a prostitute like me? Now I understand something I could never explain. I was afraid of you and I loved you. But I thought the fear was silly. Now I see it wasn't. Leave me, Ramiro. Let me go away. Or have you brought me here to take me alive to a place you don't come back from? I have not been bad, Ramiro. Those people surrounding the house want to take me to a place no one comes back from, and now I understand that you want this too. What for? I have only done what other women do. We are all the same, Ramiro. We like to please, and be loved. I am very young. What could I have done? I please a man, he wants to go to bed with me and does. I please another, and the same thing all over again. We women are neither good nor bad. We are just women. Why do you want to punish me? Why did you bring me here?'

Ramiro backed away, sat down beside the fire again, and seeing Paquita on her knees he asked her to get up and come near the hearth. She refused. The house was cold. Outside the din increased in every direction. Ramiro sighed:

'Do you really wish to go away?'

'Yes.'

'You don't want to live with me any longer?'

'Don't you see, Ramiro, that it's impossible?'

'Very well. You will have to wait until daylight.'

'Then, Ramiro, leave me alone in my room. Let me lock myself in my room.'

She got to her feet and left the room. Ramiro was astonished at this sudden reaction. He thought of leaving the town also, but what for, if he did not go with her? He got up and started toward the bedroom door. He heard Paquita crying. He went to another room and to bed. The charivari ended about midnight. Later, in the silence of the house, he heard Paquita crying.

Before Lucía arrived Ramiro was up and preparing breakfast, careful to make no noise. When the servant came he invited her to have a cup of coffee, and as soon as he thought she was rested he asked her to go back to the village and tell the schoolmaster to order a car from the city.

Lucía had probably been gone half an hour when the pair of Civil Guards arrived. Again Ramiro suspected that the first night of the charivari he had wounded someone. One of the Guards looked at the spots of fresh blood on the threshold.

Then he asked Ramiro if he had asked for a car from the capital. Ramiro said yes, thinking: 'They met Lucía on the road and asked her where she was going.'

'What do you want the car for?' the corporal asked.

'My wife is not feeling well,' he answered, 'and is going to take the train to Madrid.'

From a portfolio they drew out a paper which they handed him. While Ramiro read it the corporal asked:

'You fired several shotgun blasts night before last, didn't you'?

'Yes. In self-defense.'

'A charivari is not an attack from which one has to defend himself with arms.'

'Is that so? Was anyone wounded?'

'There could have been. Do you have a license for the use of firearms?'

'No.'

'You will have to answer a summons for the illegal use of firearms. Where is the gun?'

Ramiro took him to the gun rack. The Guard took the shotgun and opened it. The two burned cartridges were still inside.

'It isn't mine,' Ramiro declared.

'That doesn't matter. We will impound it for the time being.'

At the sound of voices Paquita had opened the door of her room, but seeing the Civil Guards she closed it again. When the Guards left she came out, surprised to find Ramiro. She thought they had taken him away. Ramiro was glad to learn he had not killed anyone, and seeing Paquita more calm he felt some optimism. 'Perhaps,' he thought, 'I can still convince her.' But as soon as they had exchanged the first words he realized that her serenity came from an irrevocable decision. Ramiro took out his notecase, saying:

'I don't advise you to travel with all this money on you.'

'What do you think I should do?'

'Take a hundred pesetas, and the rest I can send to Doña Paca or to you yourself by mail.'

'No, don't bother. I'll take it.'

257

He gave it to her. A small amount was missing and he dared not tell her. He must have a few coins left in his pockets and he hoped that perhaps the Duke would send his cheque. In any case he did not care.

Ramiro went outside and found new traces of the charivari nearby. An old hat, a woman's garter. 'Ah,' he said to himself 'so women also came. They take advantage of these occasions to have a good time. He went back to the house with that ludicrous trophy. He was going to show it to Paquita, but decided not to and put in his pocket. As he did so he discovered a piece of paper. He pulled it half way out and saw that it was a fifty peseta note. It had evidently been there, overlooked, when he bought the groceries in the Valencian's store. Paquita was moving about, finishing her packing.

Lucía returned saying that the teacher had done what he asked. She saw Paquita's preparations without surprise. At midday the car arrived, and for the first time Ramiro felt the sadness of the separation. He still wished to keep her, but she shook her head and whispered, so that Lucía could not hear:

'No, Ramiro. I love you, but don't know who or what you are. I see in you something like a bottomless pit.'

'In everyone there is always a bottomless pit.'

'I don't know. I just want to live like the rest. Simply and honorably. Some day I will be old like Doña Paca and I will have an ivory-headed cane. And I will talk to the young people about you with affection and a little fear. Doña Paca also has a little fear in her memory of Prim.'

Ramiro said that he would go with her as far as the town and spend the day with the schoolmaster, but she repeated with stubborn energy:

'No, Ramiro. I don't want to go through the town.'

Ramiro told the chauffeur that the *señora* wished to go by a different road and see the village on the other side of the river. The chauffeur said that it was only four or five kilometers out of the way and that the highway was very good. And sorrowfully Ramiro watched La Cañamón depart.

He told Lucía that she would only have to come once a week to clean. Without any comment she went on polishing the windows. Alone once more Ramiro felt inclined to excuse the peasants. 'They know that any day they can have done to them what happened in Benalup,' he was thinking. 'Meanwhile they take advantage of every opportunity to molest people from the city. The city is civilization, law, the enemy. Paquita and I are the city.'

Late in the afternoon, after Lucía had gone, the schoolmaster arrived full of curiosity. He apologized, as if he had been responsible for the charivari. Ramiro appeared indifferent and said that his wife had gone home to her mother. Soon afterwards the priest arrived. He inquired about his wife and Ramiro replied impatiently:

'Señor cura, you don't need to pretend you don't know. My wife, annoyed by the barbarity of the town, has gone to her family in Madrid. That's all.'

The priest regretted that she had gone without giving the ladies of the village the opportunity to become acquainted with her and be friendly. Then he asked:

'Are you going to live here alone?'

Ramiro did not answer. As soon as the priest arrived the schoolmaster had ceased talking. The priest talked enough for both of them. In loquacity that priest found voluptuous pleasure such as other priests find in smoking or at the table.

'Gossip has circulated at your expense, my son,' he said. 'And since you had the misfortune to leave the town under rather odd circumstances the people are inclined to believe the worst.'

Ramiro said calmly:

'They are right, for everything is true.'

The priest hesitated. He did not know what to say, but added, half jesting:

'They say that you made money by non sanctus means. This, my son, I do not believe.'

Ramiro thought that if he confessed to still being poor he would give him too much satisfaction. He preferred to leave him in doubt. The priest waited for his reply — the schoolmaster too — but Ramiro maintained silence. The priest engaged in long oratorical exercises in an effort to suggest a reply to him, but it was all futile. When they realized that Ramiro was on guard the conversation languished, and the rest of the evening until sunset passed in a slow and boring fashion. Ramiro served them wine and cakes. The teacher told him that in his new situation it might be better for him to leave the house and live in the village. The priest agreed. Ramiro decided they might be right. The priest and teacher left with words of sympathy, as if they were taking leave of a bereaved family. They seemed to have had a reconciliation. Ramiro had the feeling that they were sacrificing their old grudges for the moment in honor of the sensational event they had before them.

He made a fire and sat in front of the fireplace, eating what was left on a tray, and drinking wine. He had gone to the bedroom, still fragrant with Paquita's scent. Suddenly he realized that what had happened was natural. Taking La Cañamón out of Madrid had been a stupid blunder. But the stupidest blunder of all he saw in the fact that he had wanted — as he said — to get into the game.

'But what harm did I do anyone?' he wondered.

He did not go to bed. All night long he stoked the fire and drank. He thought of all the propitious or contrary things that had left an imprint in his memory. Passing in review all the circumstances of his new situation, he also thought of his mother. He tried to imagine the nickname the organist would give her in Sigena.

In the morning he walked to the village.

The teacher told him that if he left the Tomillar house he would refund him the rent money, deducing only the cost of washing the bed-clothes. Ramiro thought this was fair. He said nothing, however, except that he had no intention of leaving the town. The schoolmaster reminded him that he could live with the Delabitches.

16

RAMIRO wandered through the village like a sleepwalker.
Although no one apparently bothered to look at him, he
felt that he was being watched. He was sure all the townspeople knew that the Civil Guard had served him with a summons, and that he had tried to keep Paquita and failed. But
no one showed the least interest. The schoolmaster's wife looked
at him in silence, pityingly, offended no doubt because he did
not confide in her.

He went to see if the Valencian still kept horses. The shop-
keeper told him there were four in the stable and that he had
only to choose. Ramiro planned to accept the offer some day
soon. 'Perhaps the Valencian himself took part in the charivari,'
he said to himself, 'but peasant tradition concerning bastards
and second marriages is one thing and friendship another.'

Late in the day, at a loss for something to do, he went to the
Delabitch house. His cousin told him that he would be wel-
come, if he wished to stay there, for they had a spare room. Mr.
Delabitch added:

'I have nothing to say against it.'

When it was dark Ramiro returned to the Tomillar house.
He slept well, but every time he waked he heard strange sounds
— the hooting of owls, and squirrels or rats running in the garrets. He thought of what had happened at Benalup, of Cojo.
He was still astounded by Cojo's being the Niño de Arcos. Toward the end of his musing he realized that he was trying to
keep from thinking about Paquita. On the vacant space the
bed felt empty and cold.

The next day he asked the Valencian for a horse and rode
aimlessly out into the country. He followed the river in its
winding course and toward nightfall, weary, returned to the
Valencian's, where he had supper. Then he walked to El To-

millar. He slept well, but woke up thinking that it would be more comfortable, as well as cheaper, to live in the village.

He went to see the Delabitch family. Although they had invited him to live with them, they seemed somewhat taken aback when he accepted. Mr. Delabitch looked at him glumly. Finally he said:

'So your wife has gone to Madrid and won't be coming back?'

The old man added: 'That's the rumor circulating in the town.'

Ramiro moved in with his relatives. He stayed in his room for days at a time, then tired of solitude he would on occasion go out. Paying no attention to the weather, rain, snow or wind, he would head for the mountain, without any fixed course. It was impossible to talk to old Mr. Delabitch because he never listened. He only stared when anyone spoke to him. Stared like an owl.

In view of the sullenness of the three people in this household Ramiro sometimes wondered: 'Why did they invite me to stay here?' One day he asked the question aloud and old Mr. Delabitch told him that they had invited him because of his mother, and that as a moral duty they would do this and a great deal more, even though he paid nothing. But if he did pay, no one would object either. Ramiro promised to pay. The old man said with emphasis:

'You will have to discuss money matters with the mistress.'

Ramiro spent two or three days in his room thinking about Miguel de Molinos, what had happened at Benalup, and about the peasants' gossip. He often thought about the greatness of the consciously abject man. The superiority of Miguel de Molinos.

After a few days, his capacity for silence and solitude exhausted, he began to take an interest in the members of the family. He was becoming conscious of the fact that the unmarried daughter, Lucía, was behaving in an extraordinary way. Her brother-in-law, the husband of her sister Joaquina, was a handsome young man who almost never came to the house. In the village he had the reputation of being a liberal in his thinking and on not very good terms with the priest.

Ramiro thought about the charivari and remembered his own shots and the peasants' insults with their hunting horns. No one mentioned this to him or referred to his wife's having left him. The memory of all these incidents was fading away in a decorous silence.

He spent the evening with his hosts, and since no one said anything Ramiro was easily abstracted. Looking at the flames he felt utterly immersed in that passive non-resistance advised by Miguel de Molinos. His reflections were occasionally interrupted by Señora Delabitch exclaiming in great alarm when she saw Ramiro so melancholy:

'What are you thinking about so deeply? So much deep thinking can't be a good thing.'

Ramiro called on the schoolmaster who gave him back almost all the money he had received as rental for El Tomillar. Ramiro realized that the townspeople had had a change of heart toward him. The teacher's wife would ask him now and then:

'When will your wife be back?'

She had been gone a month now, but apparently everybody was still thinking about her. Because of his staying on alone, and leaving the Tomillar house to go and live with the Delabitch family, they felt that something like a great calamity surrounded him. Ramiro knew this, but did not mind.

In mid-afternoon he went to the Valencian's to ask for a horse. The Valencian gave him the same one as before, and Ramiro left town at a trot. Shunning roads he roamed over the roughest and wildest places. Night soon fell, but there was a moon and he rode on. Two hours later he saw in the distance some ruins so tall they seemed to disappear in the clouds. 'A castle,' he muttered. He went nearer. When he reached the foot of the hill which served as a foundation to the ruins, he suddenly realized that this was the castle of Rocafría.

He climbed the hill. At the top he found himself on a broad

esplanade before the crumbling main entrance. Above the gate two battlemented towers were still standing and behind them, rising toward the sky, the homage tower, or keep, a part of which — the north side — was in a state of good preservation although the rest seemed to be in ruins. Motionless, the horse and rider looked at the stones in silence. The horse neighed and the echo rebounded from the castle. Ramiro cried:

'Here am I.'

He repeated it, shouting with all his might:

'Here am I!'

The echo repeated his words. Ramiro felt something familiar, but disintegrated and downfallen, in these stones. The space between him and the main entrance was paved with wide, well-leveled flagstones, with grass growing in between them. The so carefully leveled pavement, as well as other details, made it evident that men like him had organized their life here, and that this life was worthy of a respect which Ramiro could not succeed in defining. His shouting had awakened a bird of prey which was cawing from a crack in the keep. The echoes of the cawing ricocheted through the inner courts, revealing the profundity of those shadowy spaces.

'Here am I!' Ramiro repeated.

He had heard that in the fourteenth century a woman of his family with twenty thousand men had defended this castle for more than three years against the forces of the king. The name of the anti-pope Luna figured in these chronicles. Ramiro had the curiosity actually to inquire about it.

He urged his horse forward. He intended dismounting to walk to the gate, but there was no place to tether the animal. He went a little closer. It was cold. The horse from the climb was blown and sweating. His neck was covered with foam. Ramiro walked him. On the flagstones the animal's hooves made a muffled sound which echoed on the castle façade. The moon illumined everything, but for an instant Ramiro entered the zone of shadow cast by the main tower. He felt that he ought to say something and repeated, for the sake of the echo:

'Here am I!'

But the echo seemed to say something else, to answer things he had not said. These stones, he thought, had witnessed the passions of several generations of hangmen. Men of the helmet and shield, men of the axe and black hood. No, red. The red hood. They too had thought, dreamed, tried to comprehend. He shouted again:

'I, Ramiro Vallemediano y Azcona, have returned and here I am!'

He hoped that someone would come out, but no one did. He went back to the place which in the past must have been the parade-ground. He thought of Cojo, Chino, Graco, muttering: 'Are you perhaps all together now?' He, on the other hand, was free. What kind of freedom was it? 'In my freedom,' he said, 'I am accompanied by the dead of Benalup and the memory of La Cañamón, whom I allowed to escape, thinking that it would be better for her to go on living in Madrid "honorably", as she said, than to bind her to the fate of the Vallemedianos.' Remembering the apothecary's daughter he decided to visit the hermitage. The bell had been ringing all day long in the wind. Turning his horse around he started down the hill. Again he reined in his horse and, raising his voice, cried:

'Who tells me, Ramiro Vallemediano, what I can do? I who want to live without entering into life, who want to go on living on the margin?'

There was no echo. Ramiro went on down. From the plain, the high and distant ruins looked fragile as a stage setting. He started galloping toward the hermitage. It was closed, so he rode around it slowly. Inside, painted on a cupola, with her angel wings and bare thighs, was the apothecary's daughter who afterwards swelled up like a caterpillar and married someone else.

He returned to the village, letting the reins drop over the horse's neck. It was very late when he arrived, and the Valencian received him cursing, thus demonstrating his friendly concern that something might have happened to him. Ramiro ate a piece of bread and cheese and drank a glass of wine with him. Then he went home to bed.

The rest of the winter he spent in bitter solitude. People continued talking about him. No one understood how, being recently married and having nothing to do in the village, he preferred to live separated from a pretty young wife. Old Mr. Delabitch looked at him with his glum eyes and sometimes said:

'You're not a very loving husband. Or that's the way it looks, I must say.'

Ramiro did not answer and they exchanged long and silent looks.

The townspeople gave up trying to understand and the atmosphere of mystery thickened around Ramiro. He received money from the Duke from time to time, and in the village they took to saying that Ramiro's wife was rich and paying him a certain amount each month to be left alone. This was quite scandalous and satisfied the peasants' craving for something sensational.

In the spring he had an argument with the priest who insisted on his complying with church practice regarding confession and communion. Ramiro went to Mass occasionally, but not to confession. The priest ascribed this to a delinquent's prudence, and told him again and again that he could talk to him without fear since the secret of confession was inviolable. But Ramiro thought that the priest was curious and felt still further estranged. One day he did say to him:

'But I have no faith. What do you want me to do, *señor cura?*'

The priest took offense:

'You are a Protestant at heart, Ramiro,' he told him. 'Without knowing it, of course.'

A few days later Ramiro received a letter written in the following manner: 'In the name of God I entreat you by His five wounds to submit to the law of your elders and not drag my name through the mire of impiety. The Anti-Christ is approaching and you are following him, and the only thing you have

266

not done is to threaten your poor martyred mother at the point of a knife. Confess your sins, renegade. Humble yourself at the feet of the minister of God, vile worm.' It went on in this hysterical vein until the signature. A postscript said: 'At the present writing I inform you that you are not to come to see me if you have any respect for your mother's good name.' Ramiro laughed, thinking that the purpose of the letter was in the postscript. 'She has forgotten,' he also muttered, 'that it is thanks to my help that she was able to enter the convent.'

The next time the priest saw him he repeated that he was behaving like a Protestant. What had at first seemed only a joke took on special meaning with the arrival of summer. In July the most unexpected things started happening. Ramiro, who did not read the papers, understood nothing until much later. Groups of *señoritos* — young bloods — came to the village and started killing peasants known for their liberal ideas and religious skepticism. The priest, who seemed to be in on the secret, said to Ramiro:

'Look, my son, get out of the village and don't come back until everything quiets down.'

'Why?'

'People are saying that you are a Protestant and I had to intervene to spare you trouble.'

'All right, I'll go,' said Ramiro, recalling that the first one to speak of his 'Protestantism' had been the priest.

But where? He went to the provincial capital. Along the way he saw murdered men in the culverts beside the highway. Sometimes as the bus left a village two young men in red berets would come up and say:

'You'll find fresh meat on the road up ahead.'

They were referring to the men they themselves had killed the night before. Ramiro finally understood that it was a question of insurrection in all the country, but those who had risen in rebellion were not Cojo or the other revolutionaries, but those with power, the same ones who had killed Curro Cruz in Benalup. Ramiro did not know where to go to escape from those people who seemed to be springing up out of the forest and roads, cities and villages, like mushrooms after a storm. They swaggered with their red berets and arms stuck in their belts: a pistol, a knife, sometimes a whip in their hands.

He stayed in the provincial capital, but the streets were a riot of skirmishes, shouts, huzzas and shots. People saluted raising their arm in the Roman manner. In front of the cathedral one day he saw several bishops and the cardinal of the archdiocese giving this salute, dressed in their pontifical robes. Ramiro was also thinking: 'That is the salute the pagans gave before the Christian era. The salute given by the centurion who wounded Christ. How can this be?' Ramiro felt that he was in a baffling situation, with no way out and no solutions. Every time he decided to make the effort to comprehend he stumbled upon crime. He wanted to go to Madrid but was told he could not because that city was in the hands of 'the reds'. Trains were not running. He wanted to try to get out of Spain, but the roads to the frontier were also cut off. Furthermore the wireless was repeating every day: 'Let everyone stay where he is. Whoever changes his residence and location without reason does so because he has something to hide or fear from his neighbors.'

One day he found himself with a gun in his hand and sergeant's stripes on his sleeve. Other young men like himself were pushing him along and making him go to political gatherings and meetings. They were talking against capitalism just as Cojo's friends used to do, but at the same time they were murdering workers and men of liberal profession like doctors, lawyers, teachers. Especially teachers. Ramiro let himself be swept along without understanding what he was hearing or seeing, and he thought about his friends in Madrid. When he found out that the unions to which Cojo belonged were the organizations most despised by the people in red berets, he began to see things clearly. But Ramiro also had a red beret that someone had given him, and that beret obliged him to go to a militia barracks where, with others, he was receiving training. One night they took him along when, as they said, they were taking a group of men *for a ride,* and although he tried to get out of it, he could not.

They were going to kill five individuals and they took them in a truck to the edge of the city. All five had been prisoners in the militia barracks. Ramiro asked if these individuals had been tried and condemned by a judge and the question met with jesting and sneers. A young barber-shop employee who had sewed lieutenant's insignia on his sleeve said: 'History has tried them.' Another who wore no insignia repeated like a madman: 'God has judged them.' The prisoners looked indifferent, like men without hope. In their faces there was neither hate nor love, neither faith nor despair. Only a kind of frozen curiosity about what was to happen to them. Ramiro felt that he was in the same moral situation as they. But he had a red beret. And a gun.

As they left the city he saw a gipsy encampment near the river. As always when he saw those nomadic people he thought of the old Zumaya and had the impression that life — his life — had lost its true meaning because he did not know what was going to happen beforehand, because of not having heard the blue-eyed gipsy's prophecies.

When they were some four miles out of the city the truck stopped and they started firing on the prisoners then and there. No one knew who began. No one gave any order. There was a great deal of confusion in the darkness and one of the militiamen who was carrying a rifle — the others had short arms — and who moved about inside the vehicle with difficulty because the gun was too long, fired unexpectedly at close range, and the bullet, after mortally wounding one of the workers, embedded itself in Ramiro's left elbow. For a moment Ramiro thought that they had done it on purpose to kill him.

Because of the shock and pain of the wound he knew nothing more about what took place there. He held his arm with his hand and sat down in the front seat, beside the wheel. He heard shouts, groans, more shots. Ramiro stayed motionless in the darkness and felt the warm blood oozing between his fingers. 'Criminals,' he whispered to himself. 'Common murderers.' But a new reflection left him confused: 'I didn't think they were real criminals or murderers until this instant, until I saw myself wounded.'

When it was all over two men with pistols in their hands came up to him. Again Ramiro feared an instant for his life. One of the militiamen asked him:

'What are you doing here? What's wrong with you? Don't you want to get your hands dirty?'

Ramiro showed his hands red with his own blood. He said that he was wounded, whereupon they all began accusing each other for not having taken the victims out of the truck before starting to shoot. In the light of the headlights they bandaged him and promised to take him to a hospital. They seemed overwhelmed by the mishap. That act compromised them all, said the chief of the patrol. How would they justify the wound? The one wearing lieutenant's insignia with sudden determination advised:

'We will say that he was wounded at the front and take him to the military hospital.'

Ramiro could not bend his arm. They asked him if he had taken a shot at the 'little reds', and although it was a lie he said yes. He saw some danger in the fact that he had not fired. Then he was ashamed of his lie. At times he thought that they were watching him with distrust. He felt for the dying and for those who killed. He had not been able to understand when he was with Cojo in Madrid, either. Or when he worked with the travelling circus. Or in the now far off days when he was in Sigena. Or when he talked with his mother.

On the way to the city they all seemed very excited. Ramiro was thinking: 'They feel important because they killed five men.' And they started singing a hymn called *Cara al Sol* — Face to Sun. According to them heroes fell face to the sun, in action. Workers, peasants, liberals, evidently fell facing the moon and were buried in a shameful way, without the gravediggers knowing their names or daring to ask. One of the militiamen put a scapulary with an image of the Virgin Mary on Ramiro's chest to avoid hemorrhage, he said.

In the hospital Ramiro received excellent treatment. They asked him to tell how he was wounded, and Ramiro pretended not to hear and refused to answer, thus adding a halo of modesty to his prestige.

His companions on the nocturnal adventure visited him occasionally and told tales of prowess, battles won, cities captured, prisoners shot. They all seemed drunk and not on wine but on danger, on words. Ramiro realized that the whole country was fighting, divided into two parties, whose contrary interests he could not comprehend. He wondered if Cojo, the Duke, La Cañamón, Lydia, were alive. Those men who were killing their fellow-men still kept on talking against capitalism. He could not understand. Things that were formerly considered ridiculous, such as arrogance, petulance, gesticulation, impudence, braggartism, had become virtues, and his friends, the employees in the hospital and those with the red berets, were singing the praises of 'Spanish petulance', Castilian braggartism, Iberian gaudiness, mixing them all up with the imperial will and service to the Caudillo. The Caudillo was a small, potbellied little general, with an empty smug face and the eyes of a gazelle. Ramiro looked around more bewildered than ever and thought with pain of Graco, Chino and Cojo. The victims of Benalup were multiplied by thousands every day. Ramiro had reached a state of total apathy toward good and evil, hatred and love, life and death. He was not afraid. Neither did he hope. And Ramiro stayed quiet with his bandaged arm and the sensation of being on the margin.

One day several ladies and a bishop came to visit the wounded. They gave them religious prints and reminded them to confess and receive communion. One of the ladies made a speech before Ramiro: 'Contemplating this young man who has given his blood for his country, I remember the great heroes of the past, the Cortés, Pizarros, the Gran Capitán and Agustina of

271

Aragon, forgers of our glorious nationality. The cross and the sword, the sword and the cross, will again give our fatherland days of unfading glory. Before the exemplary sacrifice of these heroes I bow'—and she really bowed—'and take pride in being Spanish.' Then she gave fifty pesetas to the hospital superintendent for the improvement of the rations. Ramiro looked at her thinking that she very much resembled Aurora, the apothecary's daughter, and wondering: 'Can she have taken strychnine too?'

The bishop blessed Ramiro and the other wounded men and, when it looked as if they were about to leave, the barber-lieutenant of the militiamen arrived with a personage in civilian dress who turned out to be the provincial governor. He also made his speech. In that part of the hospital ward many people had been gathering, including newspaper men and photographers. The governor spoke in a pompous tone. In Barcelona, he said, the mobs had shot the finest patricians, and among the bloody incidents of which he had received notice there was one which showed to what extent the legions of evil had been unleased in the glorious fatherland of Viriato, the Cid, St. Ignatius, the Gran Capitán, and the Miralles brothers. A red patrol were about to shoot a group of priests, among whom there was a prelate, no less. (At this point the bishop turned his face and seemed to start listening with his round, bright eyes.) Six priests and a bishop. The execution picket was made up of about twenty men. At the order to fire they all shot, but only one of the group of victims fell: the bishop. The twenty men had all aimed at the poor prelate because, set to kill, they doubtless wished to bag the biggest game. A sense of scandal and horror went round, on hearing this. And in the midst of it all a hearty laugh was heard. It was Ramiro, for whom the incident had a certain comical character. The more horrified the others became, the harder Ramiro laughed. He finally apologized and said that he did not know what was wrong with him, that his laughter was involuntary and he could not control it. The bishop said that perhaps the boy needed to go to a psychiatric hospital.

When he was left alone Ramiro began to feel concerned. What consequences could that laughter have for him?

Two weeks later, his wound healed; they X-rayed it and discharged him after decorating him. Ramiro could not quite stretch his arm out straight and pretended that the trouble was worse than it was, hoping that this defect would incapacitate him for military service. Every time he thought about the shooting of the bishop he started laughing again.

He wanted to go to his village. When he arrived with his arm in a sling and his decoration he caused real astonishment. The priest asked him if his military cross carried a pension with it. Since Spain was geographically and ideologically divided into two camps, everyone wanted to know if Ramiro's wife had remained on the red or the national side. Ramiro said he did not know and did not care. This reply provoked still more astonishment. Some said that Ramiro was not well in the head, which was not strange since there had been insanity in the Vallemediano family.

Ramiro told the priest about the shooting of the bishop and at the end, as always, burst out laughing. The priest also thought that this laughter revealed mental disorder. The greater the astonishment of the priest, the harder Ramiro laughed. He couldn't help it. 'Pardon me,' he said to him. 'I understand that it is stupid, but it's stronger than I am.'

The physician had advised him to exercise his arm to regain the use of it, and Ramiro did the opposite. He held it motionless and when they asked him if it was better he said no, and that since he could not straighten it he was resigned to being maimed for the rest of his life. During the first year of the civil war Ramiro was considered a hero. He did not abuse his prestige. He shunned people. He took walks through the countryside, always alone, and sat down somewhere to sun himself.

In the village they had killed the doctor, the new apothecary, two engineers who had come to study a waterfall, and some forty more persons suspected of having voted for the republic in recent years. They also killed the last two mayors. Delabitch's son-in-law and Lucía's brother-in-law, who had been an alderman with liberal ideals, had been in hiding for many months. The people in red berets looked for him, but couldn't find him. Finally they trapped him—some one must have informed on him — and shot him dead. After that Joaquina, his widow, who continued to live with her mother-in-law, began to act piously and was so devout that she almost lived at church. Lucía, on the other hand, did not go to Mass and her melancholy silence became so gloomy that everyone began to worry. Lucía let weeks go by without speaking to a soul, always busy with household tasks. Mute as a sphinx, she was the first to get up and the last to go to bed, so she would not have to say good morning or good night to anyone, perhaps. Old Mr. Delabitch looked at her with his little round eyes and sometimes said:

'At her age it seems a pity for a person to live so much for others.'

Since the beginning of the terror thirty peasant suspects had disappeared from the village. Some said they were in the red camp, others that they were in the mountains. Among them were two or three childhood friends of Ramiro.

Ramiro occasionally thought about the Duke of L. The Duke was in his home in Navarra when the war broke out and the major-domo sent Ramiro his monthly cheque from there, as if nothing had happened. When the aristocrat learned that Ramiro had been wounded he sent him a cheque for double the usual amount and three scapularies, one with the apostolic blessing.

But the priest had Ramiro's laughter ringing in his ears and in his memory the incident of the shooting of the bishop in Barcelona.

Troops sometimes passed through the town on their way to the battlefronts. A column of Moors, another of Germans, three of Italians. The Moors had lice, the Germans machines, and the Italians songs. Ramiro saw it all from his window in the Delabitch house and said: 'Isn't the whole world mad? But with what kind of madness?' Words had lost their ordinary meaning. Stupidity, madness, virtue, crime, had new meanings. In the capital the newspapers reported a speech by the local head of the party, and the orator was described in these terms: 'Before beginning he made a display of arrogance and of that admirable petulance which the Hispanic legions carried everywhere with the banner of the empire.' Ramiro, nonplussed, began to make fun of such phrases to his friends. But his jesting did not prosper, finding no echo.

Old Mr. Delabitch said to him:

'One hears round about what one hears, but it would be better if you thought twice before talking because you can do us relatives harm.'

The weeks and months passed faster than ever and in a fearful silence. Only the priest and the three or four most important land-owners dared speak in all the village. They naturally talked more than ever. The others said nothing.

The second year of the civil war the Civil Guard succeeded in arresting the thirty fugitive villagers in the mountains and on the road. Twenty-seven, that is, because three had died of hunger and cold. No one defended himself or thought of offering resistance. Seeing his childhood playmates Ramiro had not the slightest desire to do anything for or against them. The priest seemed sorry for what was happening but did nothing to prevent it either, and when he talked about the Moorish troops, Hitler's regiments or Mussolini's division, he called them 'phalanxes of redeemers'.

The twenty-seven men were locked up in the prison cell in the basement of the town hall. Ramiro had been there years before because of the suspicions of the villagers regarding the apothecary's death. Recalling the dimensions of the cell Ramiro said to himself: 'How is it possible for twenty-seven men to be in it! There's not even room for them to stand up.'

Ramiro was surprised to see that the schoolmaster, who had behaved cautiously during the first period of alarm, was again talking to him, although in private, with his customary liberal tone, and lent him a book of Floridablanca, the prime minister of Carlos III — at the end of the eighteenth century — where Ramiro read that after the king succeeded in getting Pope Clement XIV to dissolve and suppress the Society of Jesus, the pontiff was afraid that the Jesuits would poison him, and never had another day of peace until his death. He died poisoned. But the autopsy revealed that he had been poisoned by the antidote he took against the poisons of the Jesuits. And he died of his own precautions. This time Ramiro did not laugh. He was wondering if his efforts to stay *on the margin* might not in the end act like an antidote, also poisonous. The schoolmaster looked all around, and convinced that he was not being overheard, made scandalous comments.

The prisoners' families, all of them poor peasants, went to see them from time to time and took them food. The priest also went to make them a speech and talk to them about the justice of God, the need for order and the defence of institutions. The peasants did not know what the institutions were, but they thought about the count, the bishop, and the men in red berets.

The Civil Guard had advised regional headquarters which sent out more Guards, and with them eight or ten militiamen, volunteers for the executions. The only thing against those peasants was their flight from the town. As old Mr. Delabitch said, he who does nothing has nothing to fear.

In those days the nationalists had a memorable victory. Ramiro, seeing around him the elation of the people, felt cheated. A nationalist victory hurt him. Soon afterwards the victory was for the republicans, who took Teruel. Ramiro regretted that also. It seemed to him that any reason for rejoicing on either side took away something from him. From him? Ramiro knew that he had nothing and wanted to have nothing in his life, but they were robbing him of the possibilities or at least making it difficult for him to continue outside the 'river of life.' The nationalists had taken Castellón? Everyone was delirious with enthusiasm. The republicans had taken Teruel?

276

The sadness of the others attempted to coerce him, but he was completely indifferent.

For Ramiro life had been one long day — ever the same — of covered and sullen sky, misting, with the sound of water in the gutters. A gurgling sound. This gave him a contented feeling: without illusions and without despair. Without fear or hope. Without memories or tomorrows. Physical life? Very well. Animals have the right to life, as do rocks and trees. Emotional life? Yes, he liked La Cañamón, and still remembered Aurora, his childhood sweetheart, with a mixture of repugnance and attraction. But moral life? What moral life? Spiritual life? Where is the spirit? Life for him would have been comprehensible if from childhood on no one had ever told him that he had to conform to the ways of others. He liked the solitude of low sky and rain. He continued as alone as before he was born, when he was in the maternal womb where he had been more lonely still, because his mother was ashamed of him and did not want him to be born. When he was born it must have been raining and windy. Wind and rain had been with him always.

Old Mr. Delabitch would sometimes say, staring at him with expressionless eyes:

'What must be done is to maintain order and let every mast carry a stiff sail.'

'What for?' asked Ramiro.

'So that money can circulate and the honest man accumulate his savings.'

His wife spent her days sighing. Both of them took an interest in the condition of his arm and Ramiro said to himself: 'They want me to get well and be sent to the front to see if they shoot me in the other arm.' He asked about the twenty-seven arrested peasants and wanted to go to the jail to see them, but gave up the idea when he saw the old man's alarm. What worried Ramiro was not the possibility of their being killed, but their being obliged — the twenty-seven of them — to live in such a small cell.

One evening the priest called him to say that they were talking about his apathy and isolation in the town. The priest did not say that this was bad. He had paid his tribute in blood, and nothing more could be asked of him, but the way he told the story about the priests shot in Barcelona had given rise to suspicion. The priest recommended caution, said that Ramiro should go to church *to set an example*. Ramiro ended up by going to Mass and putting on a devout mien. People seemed to be reassured, the priest also, but the schoolmaster — who never missed Mass — said to him privately: 'It's incredible, Ramiro. I thought you were a stronger man than I. I had faith in you.' Ramiro was bewildered.

Sometimes the priest would say to him:

'I had news from your mother. She is a saint. She only asks about you to find out if you are at the front doing your duty. She says she regrets not having ten sons' lives to give to the cause. Isn't she admirable?'

Early one morning two of the young strangers in red berets presented themselves at the Delabitch house. Ramiro received them, discreetly exaggerating the lameness of his bent arm and stiffened hand. One of the young men was named Antero. He had a violent look and in the effort he made to control himself appeared uncomfortable and nervous. He wanted to know if Ramiro was in condition to be of some service. Ramiro agreed to everything, although without the least conviction. Antero made a speech in which veiled threats intermingled with friendly words. Ramiro said to himself: 'Why do they threaten me?' Before leaving, already at the door, Antero engaged him for three o'clock that afternoon in the mayor's office. He said that they were going to solve the problem of the prisoners because feeding them was costing the municipality too much.

At three o'clock all those with the red berets were already in the mayor's office with Antero. Four Civil Guards were also present. They received Ramiro coldly, paying impertinent attention to his bent arm. After a brief period of general talk (the nationalists were advancing on Barcelona and victory was considered imminent) there was sudden silence. Antero began shouting epileptically: 'Spain — one — Spain great — Spain — imperial,' etcetera, etcetera. And then he said:

'The enemies of the fatherland who are down below must be liquidated. Without firing a shot. What for? Shooting is a death for the brave. Once again I propose the solution known to all of you: the dry well of El Ventorrillo — the country inn. Do you agree? Let those twenty-seven cowards go to join their cronies and wait there for the sentence of supreme justice.

They all gave the Roman salute to indicate their assent. Ramiro said nothing.

In front of the entrance to the town hall was a canvas-covered truck. The prisoners were brought out and made to climb into the vehicle. They were handcuffed. Some made a sorry impression, with long beards and darting eyes. No one dared say anything. Most of them were barefooted, their shoes or sandals having worn out during their time in the mountains.

After them those with the red berets got in. Antero and Ramiro sat in front with the driver. Ramiro said to himself: 'Those three who played with me as children did not recognize me. None is in condition to recognize a childhood friend because neither childhood nor friendship has any meaning for them now. All right. Nothing matters to me either.'

Ramiro was not thinking of the imminent death of those men, but of the insubstantiality of his own life from beginning to end. And he was glad he was unarmed. He was obliged to go along to make himself responsible, if only as a passive witness. But we are all witnesses of everything by virtue of the simple act of living, and for that very reason we are all responsible. The curious thing was that this responsibility was also a matter of indifference to Ramiro, neither unpleasant nor pleasing.

It did not take them long to reach El Ventorrillo. The building was in ruins as if it had been bombed, although there had been no military action there. Antero said that the owners of El Ventorrillo were Reds and that they had been killed when the inn had been stormed with hand grenades. This had happened

279

two years before. They had thrown the whole family into the dry well, visible a hundred steps or so away; two old men, the young married couple and three children, one eleven years old. Antero added: 'There is a large cavern below, like a room. It is quite deep and without a ladder it is impossible to get out. Even though they were all wounded they still lived on for some days and their cries and moans could be heard. These are going to suffer the same fate.'

They had parked the truck so that from inside the prisoners could not see the well. The first three were thrown in on their backs. Their cries came up from below. The others were told to go down and help their companions get out, and although they knew this was a lie, since they were handcuffed and could not defend themselves, one after the other they disappeared into the dark abyss. The last ones struggled, hearing the screams of those down below, but Antero shot at their feet with his pistol, and amidst insults and kicks they were all thrown alive into the well. When the last ones fell a Civil Guard returned to the truck. He came back with two or three dynamite cartridges which he lighted and threw into the well. The explosions shook the ground and dense columns of smoke rose from the mouth of the well. A part of the curb of the well was shattered and the stones fell down below. Those that fell outside they kicked down and soon the well was almost filled with rocks and earth.

They waited. There were shrieks and screams. Satisfied with their work, they went away. Cries continued to be heard for two or three days.

On the way back Ramiro was thinking: 'This is more cruel than what they did to Curro Cruz and the peasants of Benalup. And the Duke, the priest of my town, the mayor, the judges know it or take it for granted. Everyone knows it and no one does anything about it.' They returned in silence. It suddenly occurred to Ramiro that it had been a good thing for him to make himself responsible for all that. He wanted to be even more so. The word responsibility rang out inside him in an urgent way and with tremendous force. It was an obsession. Antero was smoking a strong-smelling cigar and saying: 'They do worse things on the other side.'

He told the anecdote of the shot bishop and Ramiro thought: 'He doesn't know that I was the first to tell that in the village.' He could not keep from laughing thinking of the childish vanity which, in such a tragic hour, made each one pick out the most important victim with his rifle. They were merely obeying the law of nature according to which everything is done to economize energy. The greatest possible result with the minimum of effort. 'Ready to fire, at least let it be at an object that is worth the trouble,' they must have reasoned. And Ramiro laughed. With that laugh he believed that he was also acquiring and sharing responsibilities. Antero could not understand why he laughed.

When they reached the village they went together to eat and soon afterwards the young men in the red berets and the two pairs of Civil Guards, who had arrived several weeks ago, left town, saying that the village had been mopped up and their presence was no longer necessary.

Ramiro, in the village again, went to bed as if he were ill and stayed there for several days. He spent most of the time reading. Now and then he realized that he had read a page mechanically, unconsciously, and was unaware of what he had read.

17

THE Ventorrillo well episode passed unnoticed in the Delabitch household. Lucía made no comment whatsoever. The mother, from time to time, sighed quietly.

Extraordinary things were still happening and this time in the Delabitch family. One morning Lucía, who almost never spoke, awakened, and in the early dawn saw the town covered with snow. The white earth looked dead under the sky. The smoke from the chimneys rose slowly in the still air. Leaving her bed, she walked naked, around the room. Then she opened the door and went down to the kitchen. Insensitive to the chill she sat down beside the cold hearth. Noticing the scythe on the wall she got up, took it down, and stared at the blade. Then with the scythe on her shoulder she went out into the street, treading the snow. In the middle of the plaza she looked around. No one was about. Amidst the snow her nudity had the whiteness of warm wax under the gloomy sky.

'The clouds couldn't cross the sierra,' she murmured.

Measuring her movements to the rhythm of the scythe, she 'mowed the snow'. In the windows of the houses around the plaza peasant faces clustered. She went on 'mowing the snow' beneath a sky that could almost be touched with the hands. The twisted gargoyles on the eaves, and coats of arms of heraldic stone, were crowned with cotton. Grave and serene, Lucía slowly continued mowing the snow, which rose like the wing of a swan at the touch of the steel blade. Behind their windows the peasants crossed themselves, not daring to intervene.

It was Ramiro who cautiously went down with a blanket in his arms. He was able to approach Lucía from behind, cover her and grab hold of her at the same time. Lucía struggled, but when she let go of the scythe Ramiro succeeded in wrapping the blanket around her and carrying her into the house. Lucía kicked her bare legs, bit Ramiro's arm through the blanket, but did not say a word.

A few days later the physician had her taken to an asylum and again the village was calm. Ramiro, remembering that nude and desirable body in its purity and young beauty, said to himself: 'I could never have imagined that she would be so beautiful.'

With the idea of consoling the old couple he left his room now and then to sit with them by the fire. The wind moaned in the fireplace flue, that wind in which Ramiro no longer heard Graco but Curro Cruz, while outside the rain beat down heralding the spring. At night, inside the house, Ramiro heard the rain falling on the zinc gutter and making a sound that lulled him. He wondered if this sound, perhaps, had not been the first he heard when he was born, and had lingered in his mind, associated with other circumstances attending his birth.

No one spoke of Lucía in the house. Her mother spent her days in church. Although the peasants spoke of nothing else, no one mentioned the incident before Ramiro or his relatives. Old Mr. Delabitch once spoke of his stepdaughter as if she were dead.

Two weeks later the war came to an end. Ramiro started going out, and his arm began to recover its usefulness. He exercised it every day and before long he could straighten it entirely. Old Mr. Delabitch looked at him in silence. One day he said:

'Looks like the oar mended as soon as the war ended.'

Ramiro made no reply. He went to the Valencian's tavern and sometimes told what had happened at the Ventorrillo well, but without either cruel boasting or modesty. Simply, and just as it had happened.

Life in the village was unchanged. The winter gloomy, and the sky sadder than ever. People passed each other in the streets without speaking. No one said anything to Ramiro and he liked that indifference or animosity or whatever it might be. Mrs. Delabitch occasionally remarked:

'Many people are getting government jobs now.'

Ramiro said nothing. He thought about going to Sigena to see his mother, but the priest dissuaded him, to spare her shame 'now that she seems to have entered the contemplative life by holy roads'. Again Ramiro was trying to figure out what nickname the organist nun in the convent would have given her. And he thought about Pope Clement XIV who involuntarily killed himself.

He learned that the Duke had returned to Madrid and that order had been more or less re-established everywhere. During the war only military tribunals had existed, but civil courts were re-appearing, formed, naturally, by people addicted to what they called the glorious movement. Ramiro spent long days walking in the outskirts of the town, and mud, cold, snow and rain did not deter him. He avoided passing the ruins of the Ventorrillo inn where people said they had seen will-o'-the-wisps. Others spoke of ghosts and apparitions. There must have been something, thought Ramiro, for one day when he was taking the Delabitch dog for a walk and they came to the place on the highway nearest the dry well the dog stopped, looked towards the ruins, finally leaving the road and circling around very fearfully. Ramiro wondered: 'What does that animal see on the well curb-stone?'

One day he decided to leave the village. But where would he go? Where could a man like him go in Spain? He didn't want a new way of life to mean his getting into the game. But if he refused to get into the game, where could he go? What could he do? He thought of the men thrown into the well and of the two or three who had played with him when they were children.

In the town everyone was beginning to believe that the first and perhaps only one responsible for the death of those men was Ramiro, and he liked that. 'I would like to make myself responsible for all the crimes in the world,' he muttered to himself. 'But how?' Then he remembered Lucía naked amidst the snow and he found her appealing. He liked not only her body but the disorder of her mind.

Once in a while Ramiro dropped in to see the secretary of the town council, who kept, neatly stacked on a table, the copies of the *Gaceta de Madrid*. The reading of this official daily was for the secretary an obligation he scrupulously fulfilled, as he said.

Ramiro had written the Duke again, telling him that his mother was in the convent. Almost by return mail he received a reply full of encouragement for him to follow the 'wise example of your mother, although in your case', he added, 'it would not be surprising if you came out with some form of heresy or sacrilege'. Ramiro thought: 'The Duke wants me to become a monk not for my sake, but his. To leave him in peace. But how can he be tranquil with all that has just happened in Spain?'

One day in the town hall office he picked up the *Gaceta* by chance, and it opened up at the first page of the section of the Ministry of Justice. Heading the page was an announcement, by the General Superintendent of Prisons, of two vacancies for the office of executioner. The candidates were required to be Spaniards, free of military service, able to read and write, and of age. Ramiro had a feeling of repugnance and left the *Gaceta* on the table. The memory of that announcement, however, stayed with him. During the next few days as he wandered about the countryside, he kept thinking about it and recalling his yearning for responsibility.

One day he visited the hermitage, to see his own work as a painter. Time had softened and blended the colors, everything looked better than he had expected. Under the cupola where the angel — the apothecary's daughter — was prominently placed, he lingered for more than an hour, thinking about friends and the fact that he had none. "No one has any,' he reflected. 'Neither friends nor enemies exist. In life there are only accomplices.' Gazing at the angel, he told himself, 'After eighteen days spent in painting that body there and after dreaming of her for two years, I kissed her on the mouth. Disillusioning experience! I was conscious only of our noses bumping together and that her cheeks near her eyes turned rose-colored, then red like old velvet . . . The truth is there are no windows opening upon life as I see it; those windows have never existed.' And with a sigh he reflected, 'But reality has always been as I expected. Everyone shuns responsibility, and this is what is bad. Why is this so?'

There was another late snow. After walking over the countryside blinded by the reflections from the snow, he went to the town hall. He sat down beside the big wood stove and watched the secretary working at his table under the cone of light cast by a green tulip-shaped globe. As always the secretary inquired after his wife.

At one side were the *Gacetas* for the current month of January. Ramiro glanced through them inattentively. Again he had in his hands the number about which he had thought so much, and again it opened up at the page headed by the announcement from the office of the Superintendent of Prisons. Ramiro fixed in his mind the final date for filing applications.

Since the time was only two weeks off, Ramiro wrote an application and sent it by registered post. He had no sooner done this than he felt himself involved in an immense scandal, but after thinking about it all day long he finally concluded: 'I am not mad. The office of hangman will make me unhappy, but I will sacrifice happiness to truth. The entire social order rests on the hangman, yet no one wants the responsibility of being hangman. Why?'

Four days later he received a note acknowledging receipt of his application and telling him that in case he was recommended for the appointment he would be notified within a month. They had written no title of courtesy before his name. Neither *Señor* nor *Don*. This detail intrigued him. He began to chuckle and was in a good humor all day long, which did not prevent his making the following reflection, however: 'When I am a hangman I will unconsciously reduce my person, and the idea that I have of my person, to the proper plane, to the plane rightfully belonging to every one.' The prospect of moral annihilation appealed to him, as he thought about the Duke, Cojo and Miguel de Molinos.

He had been praying before going to sleep at night, since applying for the hangman's job, and as he prayed he felt more easily detached than ever from the natural misery of his being. It was not that his soul was soaring, but that 'all the rest' was descending within himself, as he realized that he might become an executioner. Alone he reflected: 'To soar is not easy, but to break loose from one's own vileness, sinking to the very depths of our natural misery and leaving at its normal level our ideal aspirations, yes, that is easy indeed.' The phenomenon was like purifying a liquid by decanting it through a filter. And that was what Miguel de Molinos did with his own wretchedness.

A week later Ramiro received another communication, asking for six photographs: two left profiles, two right, and two front views. They also wanted other physical details: height, weight, etc. This suggested that his appointment was a definite possibility. Ramiro went to the provincial capital. He sent the photographs, and his new address in the city where he intended to remain until he was notified one way or the other. His days were troubled, his nights sleepless. Two weeks later he received the news. They did not tell him that he had been appointed executioner, but that he should report to the Prison Warden in Ocaña. The expenses of the journey would be paid by the Prison administration offices. Ramiro told himself that everything was finished, and tried to comprehend the source of his gladness.

He had a month in which to make the move to Ocaña. From the communication he judged that his entrance into the services would coincide with his reporting to the penitentiary. First he returned to the village. That winter had seen the recurrence of an old superstition: that the bells in the tower rang by themselves at night announcing someone's death. Ramiro heard them.

During the last evening with old Mr. Delabitch the Catalonian appeared talkative for the first time, undoubtedly pleased at Ramiro's departure. He believed in witches and said he had known one, years back, who wrought havoc among the herds. When she died they went to her house and on opening an old trunk a number of little human figures no larger than salt-cellars jumped out — at least that is how the old man put it — and started dancing on top of a table. Among these figures were three monks, and the parish priest had to go to the bishop and minutely describe the habits of these friars so that they could tell to what order they belonged. Afterwards the priest promised the bishop not to mention it to anyone.

'And what happened to those little figures?' Ramiro asked.

'They ran away, screeching, down the kitchen drain.'

Ramiro listening to him was thinking: 'In this town I was born. Why in this town and not another? Why on this planet and not on Jupiter? Why in the form of a human being and not in a noble plant form like the poplar or pine? And who was interested in my coming?' He thought of everything he had done 'unwillingly', of what he had seen others doing, of what the Duke had told him about his ancestors, of the crimes of Benalup, the charivari, Lucía's madness, the hundreds of thousands of men who, according to the schoolmaster, had been murdered throughout Spain, and he asked himself: 'All this, what for?'

The next day Señora Delabitch prepared a lunch for him for the train, and tearfully bade him goodbye. The old man borrowed a neighbor's horse and two-wheeled cart to drive Ramiro to the distant railway station. The company of old Mr. Delabitch, who did not open his mouth the whole way, made the journey a sad one.

To go to Ocaña Ramiro had to pass through Madrid, where he arrived next day. He went to see La Cañamón, but she was not in. Paca la Encajera had died during the war.

Then he went to call on the Duke. Along the way he noticed many soldiers and priests in the streets. The workers had a sullen, evasive look, and most of them were poorly dressed. The Duke received him with astonishment. He talked to him about Father Anglada — the deaf canon — and said that they had won the war thanks to his prayers. Then he looked at Ramiro saying:

'Your life was saved because God is reserving a great mission for you.'

They talked for a long time, but Ramiro told him nothing about his employment.

18

AS the train for Ocaña did not leave until night he went to a tearoom where Lydia had sometimes gone. It was a fashionable place with a Russian name, and very expensive. A doorman dressed like a Cossack stood by the entrance. When it rained he received the clients under a large umbrella.

Ramiro recognized no one until, as he was about to leave, he noticed at some distance, Lydia and her friend Emilia, paying their bill and preparing to go. They looked friendly and happy, and passed Ramiro without seeing him, or at least pretending not to see him.

'I am sorry,' thought Ramiro. 'Perhaps I am now the only thing lacking in Lydia's collection: a hangman.'

On his way to the station he was glad that he had not run across any old acquaintances. 'Cojo was right,' he thought, when he said that I would end up as a monk or *something like that.* The hangman is the priest of an esoteric religion which only a chosen few can attain. At that moment he felt like one who renounces the world while taking upon himself the world's responsibilities.

Ramiro boarded his train at dusk and reached Ocaña in the middle of the night. He slept at the station inn. During the journey he had felt a growing sadness, which he mastered as well as he could. In the hotel he realized that the letter in his pocket from the Superintendent of Prisons definitely cut him off from society. He paced back and forth in his room asking himself: 'But have I ever been inside what is called society?' He saw his reflection in the mirror. He thought he saw a certain bestiality in his face, an ancient and atavistic hardness. He read the letter again and said to himself: 'Now there is nothing that can be done. Even if I resign now, take the first train and go away to another country, I will always be a hangman.'

He was physically weary, as if during those days he had been walking long distances. He went to bed and slept well, contrary to his expectation, and woke next morning refreshed and contented. At the prison where he went to report to the warden with the letter from the general superintendent's office, he passed through patios framed in walls of gray brick, cement corridors. Doors opened before him and closed again after him. 'No one ever knows what a door is,' he reflected, 'until he is in a prison.'

289

The warden was a thin and colorless man with an evasive look. He wore civilian dress, although on the table was a uniform cap, undoubtedly there to make some show of authority. He looked very surprised when he saw Ramiro. As he talked to him he stared at a newspaper on the table, at the inkwells, at the map hanging on the wall. Like the circus manager—the Frenchman with the moustache — he seemed not to have his mind on what he was saying. He avoided the word 'hangman'. Aware of this, Ramiro asked:

'Then I am now the hangman of Ocaña?'

'Yes. Your appointment is here,' the warden answered, somewhat confused, and taking a folder out of a drawer. From it he extracted several papers, one of which he handed to Ramiro. 'This is your appointment. The other is a printed form for payment of your traveling expenses.'

Another individual arrived, a man about seventy, strong, stocky, dressed in a dark gray suit he seemed to have outgrown. His shoulders were beginning to sag with age. Ramiro understood that this was the retiring hangman. The warden introduced them, but he had forgotten Ramiro's name and had to read it from a memorandum. The retiring hangman's name was Urbaleta. The warden jokingly offered him a glass of wine, knowing that he did not drink. The old man warned that he could not drink because of 'the diabetes'. He pronounced the word in a mysterious and important tone, as if having diabetes were a privilege. He did not laugh. He looked as if he had never laughed. He turned towards Ramiro, explaining:

'The "diabetes" is because of the fine living I've given myself at table.'

Ramiro could not escape a certain feeling of repugnance every time he looked at him. The bestiality that he had noticed in his own face shortly before was so marked in Urbaleta's that it was difficult to look him in the eye. The warden said that they should compare notes. With these words he ordered Urbaleta to coach Ramiro and insinuated that they were both free to go.

290

'Don't worry,' Urbaleta said to Ramiro. 'The work is soon learned.'

Urbaleta had made his remark without any humor whatever. The old hangman touched Ramiro on the shoulder and asked him to follow. The warden remained in his office, but did not fail to advise Ramiro that he could count on his secrecy regarding his employment. Ramiro said:

'Secrecy? What for?'

They went out. Ramiro felt humiliated, but more so because of his association with Urbaleta than because of the warden's disdain.

The old hangman had dressed in his best to welcome Ramiro. Ramiro understood at once that he was not the kind of person with whom he could ever be on intimate terms. When they passed the door of the prison chapel the old hangman crossed himself. He seemed astonished that Ramiro did not do so, and explained:

'That's the chapel.'

There all the condemned men garrotted by Urbaleta in this penitentiary had awaited execution. Ramiro tried to think about something that could reassure him: 'Here I come seeking responsibility, the responsibility that no one wants to assume.' He kept on trying to justify his new situation: 'I could stay on the level of honest citizenship, like one more petty bourgeois, or a mediocre painter, like Santolalla. But that would be worse. Everything urges me to sanction murder, drawing some moral of material benefit from my tolerance. All right. Here I am. I will kill honestly, drawing upon my hands the scorn deserved by all, and shunned by all.' After these reflections he felt more bewildered than ever, as if he were conscious of trying to deceive himself. 'I have not entered into life,' he concluded. 'I have not got into the game, but into the mystery of the last secret truth governing it.'

Extending his arm with an operatic gesture Urbaleta pointed to the space in front of the chapel, a corner where two bare walls of brick came together on the floor of fine sand.

'There,' he said, 'is where I usually set up the posts. Many an execution have I performed. I keep count in my memory. Eighty-one. So will you. I have realized from bonuses and travelling expenses an elegant sum.'

'How much?' Ramiro asked, conscious that this was a hangman's question.

'Over twenty thousand pesetas. Not counting my salary. In forty years. I was older than you when I began. It is not a profession to be proud of. But one retires with three-fourths of the salary as pension.'

The old man, although he had already been introduced by the warden of the penitentiary, repeated his name, extending his hand. Ramiro shook hands with him. Urbaleta clung to Ramiro's hand, unwilling to let go. For over forty years he had not had occasion to shake hands with anyone. Still gripping Ramiro's hand and pumping it up and down, he explained:

'In our neighborhood they think I'm well-to-do. I own my house and garden and they see me working in it. The garden is good for the "diabetes", because one's profession really does not require much exercise. The 'iron collar" does it all.'

He finally dropped Ramiro's hand and they continued walking. Then he looked at him, half pleased, half disappointed, and said:

'But how young you are! You will be able to retire with four-fifths some day.'

They had left the penitentiary and were walking along different streets. Ramiro was so nervous he didn't notice what direction they were taking. He only realized that they were making for the edge of the city. When someone stepped off the pavement to make room for them Ramiro imagined that it was done to avoid contact with the old hangman. Urbaleta continued talking about his career. Every five years his salary had been increased. Those increases were called quinquennia. He explained what each quinquennium represented.

They stopped in front of a rather old house, of peasant style. The old man took a large key out of his pocket and opened the door. First he pointed to two flower-pots of rue in the windows:

'All in the profession,' he explained, 'have rue at the door. I don't say that rue frightens away the evil spell, but one only has to do what the others do.'

Ramiro had noticed that the old man was fond of saying 'one' instead of 'I'. They entered a large covered patio with stairs leading up to the right and to the left. In the left-hand corner there was a lighted fireplace, also used for cooking. The floor was paved with small round stones.

'My wife and daughter,' Urbaleta said, 'have gone to market.'

Ramiro's throat was dry.

'One was a bachelor for many years,' Urbaleta continued, 'but in this profession it is better to marry. I married late. One liked to live alone. One didn't need anybody to care for one. Oh, I had good health then!'

When he said 'good' he raised his left eyebrow, squinting a little. This, for some unknown reason, gave Ramiro the impression that the old man was really ill.

'Why is it advisable to marry soon?'

'Because a man living alone attracts attention.'

They were both silent. Urbaleta added: And for other reasons that I will explain to you some day. It is not that one is ashamed of one's work. Someone has to do it, and nowadays they don't mistreat the *pobreto* — poor wretch — as before, but dispatch him neatly and rapidly.'

After a short pause, he went on:

'The secret of the trick lies in the nimbleness of the hands. Without undue modesty I can say that I had elegant hands for the profession.'

Again he raised his eyebrow and squinted. Ramiro thought that the expression *pobreto* must be part of the professional jargon and dated from a long way back in history. The old man continued:

'Now the machine does everything. Easy, but delicate work. To tell you the truth, with every execution one's stomach heaves. That's why among those of the profession it is the custom, after an execution, to take a heavy meal with meat and other things that stick to the ribs. Even so, one's stomach is in his throat and one breathes with difficulty at times. The doctor calls this dyspnoea. He advises me to work only in the garden.' As he said this the hangman smiled with a blitheness that made Ramiro pale. 'And that is why they have advanced my retirement. Because I could yet work for some years longer. See, then,' and again he squinted and smiled, 'how you can thank my "diabetes" for your employment.'

Ramiro had not seen him laugh. His smile was only a painful proof of his incapacity for laughter.

'I have finished some *pobretos* in less than a minute. But when I unhang the defunct and take him out of the clamp I become a little nervous. That is the part of the work that settles in one here.'

With two fingers he pointed to where his spleen should be. Ramiro was recalling arguments heard in the patio of the Madrid jail concerning the virtues of the hangmen of Burgos and Ocaña. Suddenly Urbaleta changed the subject, saying that later he would pass on his knowledge to him in the basement, where he kept his tools. Besides, when the first execution came up, Urbaleta offered to attend as assistant. 'One job done, they are all done,' he repeated, adding: 'I close their eyes through the veronica before uncovering their face, because it is precisely the *pobreto's* stare, when he is finished, that sometimes sticks to one there.' Saying this he pointed with two fingers to Ramiro's spleen. Ramiro dared not ask what the veronica was. He would have taken a little liquor with real pleasure and said so to Urbaleta who got up and went to a cupboard, but without hiding some vexation. He took out a bottle of anisette and said, serving Ramiro a glass:

'They don't allow me to drink. This bottle has been here for six years.'

Ramiro drained his glass and helped himself to another. He praised Urbaleta's house and the old man said that all of this—

the garden, furniture, plus some small savings in government bonds—was the product of forty years' work, 'not counting meat and drink.' The salary was not large, but there had been years with four or five executions in different parts of Spain, and then he had an 'elegant' income. For each execution he received a two hundred and fifty peseta bonus plus travel expenses, and of this 'something always sticks to one', although he kept honest expense accounts. He went on talking for the pleasure of talking. Ramiro asked what inns there were in the city and Urbaleta said:

'One doesn't like to meddle in the private lives of others, but I can't recommend the lodging houses to you.'

With two fingers he tugged at his shirt-collar and stretched it as he took a deep breath and said:

'The best thing would be for you not to think about that. Doña Tadea said that she would charge twenty duros per month for board, room and laundry, less than it would cost you anywhere else. If you stay here you will be able to save two hundred and sixty pesetas every month besides the bonuses for executions and daily traveling expenses. It is necessary to be alert in all matters because the times are harder today than when I was young. In my youth, a peseta was still a peseta.'

He repeated many of the things he had said before. Ramiro was tired of listening. They climbed some stairs leading to a room on the entresol between the first and second floor. The rest of the house was reached by another stairway below an arch on the opposite side of the patio. This patio was both dining-room and kitchen, and spacious enough to pace back and forth in while engaged in conversation, as Urbaleta was accustomed to do since it tired him, he said, to look at people directly. This fatigue he blamed on his diabetes. While they were climbing the stairs Ramiro counted the steps and found that there were not thirteen, but only twelve. The room was large and comfortable. Urbaleta continued praising his home.

'Here, a balcony to the west. Here, a window to the south. What you see in front is the slaughter-house. Once an ox got

295

out and butted four or five persons. Because oxen are like people and know what's going to happen to them. In summer this room is the coolest in the house, and in winter when a flash of sunlight comes in through that window, it warms the bricks of the floor.'

Aware that his presence in this house was like a gift from heaven for the old hangman, Ramiro accepted Urbaleta's offer. They were on their way down to the patio again when they heard feminine voices in the entry.

Ramiro met Doña Tadea and her daughter, whose name he did not catch. When he asked for it to be repeated Urbaleta, very pleased, explained:

'The name Federica Blanca occurred to me. Federica, for a German king. Germany is the best country in the world and there the executers of justice are esteemed as they deserve to be. Blanca is the name of an old queen of Navarre, my country. I put them together. One enjoys reading history.'

He pointed to a thick, grimy volume between a casserole and egg-beater on the sideboard near the fireplace.

The daughter must have been fourteen or fifteen years old. She looked at Ramiro, without listening to her father. Doña Tadea, greatly excited by Ramiro's presence, left a package of food on the table.

'Any name,' she said, as talkative as the hangman, 'is better than mine. Mine is a burlesque name.'

She was trying to be witty. Federica Blanca, impassive, kept staring at Ramiro, with something like an accusing innocence in her eyes. Urbaleta called his wife 'Doña Tadea'. Turning to Ramiro, she said:

'We will introduce you as our nephew. All right? That is, the girl's cousin.'

Ramiro was wondering: 'Introduce me? To whom?' And just then Federica Blanca put this precise question into words.

'To whom must it be?' said Doña Tadea, trying to laugh. 'To the people.'

The girl insisted:

296

'To what people?'

'To our acquaintances,' the mother insisted, trying to make Ramiro feel comfortable.

Federica Blanca laughed sarcastically and then looked at Ramiro. He saw that Doña Tadea was blushing. The old man was silent, with his left eyebrow raised and squinting his eye.

After dinner, which was substantial and heavy, old Urbaleta was telling how all royal courts had their hangmen. The republics, which at first clamored against the death penalty, appointed their hangmen, too, as soon as their governments were established. The countries where 'the omelette had turned over', like Russia, had more hangmen than the rest, because besides the professionals they had an infinite number of amateurs. 'Judging from appearances,' he concluded, 'it is something that goes with civilization.'

Ramiro wrote to the Duke, thanking him for his help and telling him that it would not be necessary in the future. Nevertheless four days later Ramiro received the cheque from the major-domo 'by orders of his Excellency'. No letter came from the Duke, which did not surprise Ramiro.

Federica Blanca stared at him in an odd way. Ramiro avoided these looks, which disconcerted him. Doña Tadea said that the girl would be fifteen in May. Ramiro remembered the line of a poem read somewhere:

And maidens who in Maytime turn to women . . . '

The girl went to the movies frequently and had her own personal ideas of virtue, nobility, beauty and distinction. She had not gone to school. She had learned to write and read at home, and the prison teacher had taught her something about history and arithmetic.

Ramiro stroked his forehead and said to himself: 'Will my health be as "good" as Urbaleta's?' Doña Tadea took advantage of every opportunity to tell him that she came from a well-to-do bourgeois family.

Ramiro found himself so flush with money he did not know

297

how to spend that he decided to make a present to the girl. He had heard her ask her mother for a spring coat with a blue hood and 'wide pocket-like cuffs," that she had seen in a shop window. Ramiro bought it for her and took it home in a box tied with pretty silver ribbons. The surprise did not improve the girl's expression. She only looked at Ramiro with still greater curiosity. The one who seemed to be touched was the mother.

In the newspapers Ramiro was following the course of some important trials with interest, calculating the possibilities of a death penalty, but still he dared not ask Urbaleta to coach him.

Once he heard Federica Blanca speaking with her mother, alone. Doña Tadea asked her if she had ever thought about the fact that some day she would have to marry, and she answered that she wished to marry a naval officer dressed in a white uniform.

When Doña Tadea's husband left on a journey, she arranged to leave the two young people alone all one afternoon. Ramiro understood the intention and resolved to be careful and discreet. He said to the girl:

'Did you see, Federica Blanca? Your mother left us alone intentionally. She is thinking that I might be a good husband for you. What do you say?'

The girl looked at him sadly:

'Me? What woman in the world would marry a hangman?'

'Your mother.'

The girl made a grimace of scorn and again they were still.

'Of course you're not a hangman yet,' she said, 'since you haven't executed anybody, but you will be. Just like my father. And you will marry like my father and have a daughter, perhaps, like me.'

Ramiro said gloomily:

'No. I will have no children.'

'And you, what do you know about that?' she asked, very determined. Children are given by God.'

Ramiro stretched himself and asked:

298

'What could we do?'

'We can play cards, if you like, but I only know one game.'

'All right,' he said smiling. 'Let's play.'

She brought out the cards, saying:

'It's a game my father plays with the hangmen from Burgos and Madrid when they get together.'

'What's it called?'

'The Tooth of the *Pobreto*.'

'Do other hangmen from so far away come to visit you?'

'Sometimes. When there are several condemned men the one from Burgos comes. He is the most important. The dean, my father says. Sometimes the one from the Dueso prison comes too. For my baptism they came from all over Spain.'

In spite of everything, she said this with a certain pride.

'How many hangmen are there in Spain?'

'Thirteen I've heard. Everything is thirteen in this business. Cards too. Take thirteen cards.'

She reserved another thirteen for herself, adding:

'There are also thirteen stairs to your room. And I was born the thirteenth day of February. That certainly was good!'

Ramiro said there were not thirteen stairs to his room but she insisted, so they went to check. Federica Blanca was right. As they counted them they became good friends. They returned to the card table. She explained the game to him. She told him what to do every move, but Ramiro learned quickly and won. When she lost Federica Blanca cursed with expressions she had heard the hangmen use.

'Curses on your wicked iron collar!'

Then she looked at Ramiro, blushing, and started dealing out the cards again. Ramiro looked at her silently, with tenderness. Again he won and out came another hangman's curse:

'May San Blas shroud you and the whore cut out your shroud!'

By 'the whore' she meant the queen of spades. Ramiro realized that the girl had no idea what the word meant. He asked:

'Why San Blas?'

'He's the hangman's patron saint because he is also the patron of everything good and bad related to the throat. Haven't you heard people say. 'San Blas, cough no more'?'

Ramiro continued looking at her with the same tenderness and the girl, aware of it, picked up the cards, shuffling them angrily. Then she dealt out the cards, but before she had finished threw them on the table, crossed her arms, put her head down, and began to cry. Ramiro touched her shoulder and said:

'Come on, Federica Blanca, you are not a child.'

Her weeping became louder and more disconsolate. Although Ramiro was very young his experience warned him what these tears could mean. He patted her on the shoulder. She raised her head, then leaned it against his chest. Her hair brushed Ramiro's chin. He observed something that made him smile. Federica Blanca's hair rose in the air and stuck to his cheek. Ramiro caressed her shoulder, her back.

'Look at me, Federica Blanca.'

She lifted her face and he kissed her lightly on the lips, which were moist and warm. She cried a little more, then weary she gradually seemed to be soothed, leaning against his chest. She spoke a few confused words. Ramiro did not understand:

'What are you saying?'

She raised her head again and he kissed her. Indifferent to the kiss she said, with Ramiro's lips on hers:

'I love my mother. Not much, but after all a mother is a mother.'

'And your father?'

'My father, no. I wish he would die!'

Ramiro held her on his knees. She buried her face in his shoulder and Ramiro curbed his own desires and continued caressing her hair and shoulder. Tired of weeping the girl took a deep breath. Ramiro said:

'You kiss me.'

'Why?'

'Don't you want to kiss me?'

She kissed his cheek. Then she caressed his face saying that

300

it looked as if he had never shaved yet. Ramiro remembered
past experiencs: Lydia, the village, La Cañamón.

'Would you like to marry me?' he asked.

She was slow to answer, but finally said:

'Let's run away to another country. If you don't have any
money, that doesn't matter. My mother will look for some. And
if she doesn't find it I can steal it somewhere.'

'But . . . why run away?'

Federica Blanca looked at him attentively, without the
faintest show of coquetry.

'Would you really like to marry me?' she asked.

'Yes.'

'When I'm of age?'

'You're of age. Aren't you fifteen now?'

Lowering her voice and stroking his tie, she said:

'I will have a white wedding dress and at night black transparent pyjamas. It would be fun, to marry so young. Do you
know? That's my mother's dream.'

Ramiro thought the girl was remembering things seen in
the cinema. He saw that her eyes had the same changing color
— light chestnut — as her hair. She repeated, as if she were concentrating: 'My father is on a journey. I wish the train would
be derailed and he would be killed.'

Ramiro kissed her again, but Doña Tadea was returning,
and when she saw them with shining and evasive eyes she
began to laugh. She put one arm around Ramiro and the other
around Federica Blanca. Later, alone with Ramiro, she told
him that she had realized they loved each other, and was sure
this love would make them very happy. She had arranged
things so that during Urbaleta's absence — he would not be
back for four or five days — they could have an advance honeymoon. From joy Doña Tadea passed to tears:

'My children, enjoy youth and love. Forget about me. I
will be your servant, I will prepare your food, I will wait on
you.'

Listening to Doña Tadea gave one the impression that the

301

natural inclination between man and woman sanctified and purified everything. For Ramiro there was a natural element of fraud in love, of clandestine enjoyment and deceit, while for her sexual attraction was sacred, with or without the sacrament. Doña Tadea went up to her daughter and lifted her face with her hand. The girl closed her eyes. Ramiro heard them moving about, joking and laughing. He went out into the street for some fresh air and returned with a bouquet of flowers. As he bought them he had watched the gestures and looks of the florist, uneasy but not fearful that they suspected his hangman's profession in the city. He was sure that Urbaleta's illusions about passing unnoticed had no foundation. Ramiro sensed an immense new solitude around him. It was like living on a desert isle, freed from concepts of virtue and vice.

Doña Tadea took the flowers, moved.

'What a boon life is!' she said, going to her daughter's room.

Ramiro lived with Federica Blanca the five days of Urbaleta's absence. The 'first time' the girl had resisted, repeating what she had said before:

'Why don't we run away?'

But later they both forgot everything except joy and physical ecstasy.

When Urbaleta returned the normal regime was re-established. He had attended, he said, an assembly of hangmen. He seemed pleased with the way things had gone, and talked to Ramiro more boldly than before about professional matters. He told him that, continuing an old tradition also existent in Germany, France, as well as other countries, the executioners met every two years to exchange impressions and also to destroy the execution instruments that had been used thirteen times. In Germany, where the mode of execution was beheading, the hangmen buried the axe that had killed thirteen condemned men, wrapping it in a white scarf as if it were a person. In England the rope with which thirteen condemned men had been hanged was burned, and here also the executioners had a special ceremony. In Russia, no. They kept on using the same

302

pistols after killing thirteen condemned men, but this, he added, could do no less than bring about the ultimate downfall of the regime.

In Spain the hangmen met in an abandoned forge they kept for the purpose, and melted down the 'iron collars' that had been used thirteen times.

'And in France?' Ramiro asked, thinking of the guillotine.

'In France they change the cleaver.'

Since Doña Tadea, Federica Blanca, and Ramiro shared an important secret concealed from Urbaleta, he occasionally sensed something strange in the air which he could not define.

Ramiro spent one night — the whole night — awake, obsessed with the irremediableness of his fate and his concern over not entering into life and yet making himself responsible for the lives of others. He was happy, nevertheless. 'I am happy,' he said to himself, 'in the way that a rock or a tree can be happy. Without will. Without any desire to exercise my will in a moral direction.' He saw the castle of Rocafría. Sometimes he saw it outside himself, sometimes within.

Federica Blanca behaved with the coquetry of a satisfied lover and her father, unable to imagine the reasons for this attitude, took it as disrespect or blameworthy provocation. He scolded Federica Blanca constantly. The fact that they were deceiving Urbaleta made him more contemptible in his daughter's eyes.

One night Urbaleta took Ramiro down to the basement. They went down a wooden stairway that had not thirteen, but fifteen steps. The room was square and unfurnished except for a small carpenter's bench with a lathe at one end. The walls on the other hand were covered with tools and small instruments hanging in careful order. Ramiro was reminded of the wagon where he slept when he worked in the circus.

In a corner, on the dirt floor, there was a dark green metal box with a wide black strap round it. Here the iron collars were kept. The old man cleaned and greased them frequently. They were covered with a film of some lubricant, yellow as butter. According to the hangman, the rats were too fond of this grease. For this reason, and another which he would tell him later, he always kept the iron collars locked in the box.

'I have five complete sets,' he said contentedly. 'Each with its straps and veronicas. They will all become your property.

He pulled one out carefully, as if he were extracting a live crab. At the foot of the stairs was a wooden post that reached to the ceiling and supported the end of the railing. Urbaleta fitted the little frame on the post, which was easily done with three screws. Then he worked the apparatus, pushing the back part of the frame over the front part.

'The neck goes in here,' he said, 'between these two clamps.'

They would perform the first execution together. One execution seen, he said, and they are all seen. Any kind of innovation was shunned in the profession. There was only one on record, initiated forty years ago. Ramiro saw a copy of the royal order on a sheet of yellow and very dry paper nailed to the wall.

The innovation came about in the following manner. The Burgos hangman, by tradition considered the most important in Spain, decided that it was not necessary to make the condemned man recite the Creed when he sat down on the little garrotte seat. Until then the condemned man, once his neck was inside the iron collar, had to recite it. The chaplain ordered him to do so. And the condemned man began: 'I believe in God the Father Almighty, Maker of heaven and earth, and in Jesus Christ His only Son our Lord: Who was conceived by the Holy . . .' At this point the hangman would turn the screw so that the 'h' of 'holy' would break in his throat, prolonged into a rattle. What the condemned then said was 'hhhhhho . . . ' until the pressure of the iron collar silenced him. The purpose in making the condemned man recite the Creed was not only religious. With it they planned to lessen the terror, for as he prayed the condemned felt sure of living until the end of the prayer, and strangulation began suddenly and unexpectedly.

The innovation consisted in suppressing the Creed. At first

there was opposition in some of the prisons and two parties were formed, the traditionalist and the progressive. The bishop of Madrid-Alcalá took the traditionalist side, but the Burgos hangman won because he had a genial argument, according to Urbaleta. He said that it might be that they would have to execute a Jew, Moslem or Protestant some day. And then what would happen?

'The Burgos executioner,' said Urbaleta filled with admiration, 'was always a man of light.'

He added, lowering his voice, that in this profession very strange things happen. There were women who liked hang-men, and he had had some experiences that he preferred not to recall.

'Why?'

'They are too indecent.'

Ramiro was very curious:

'What kind of women? Prostitutes?'

'No, no. Nothing like that. Quite the contrary. Women from good families.'

Lowering his voice he added:

'Aristocrats. Almost always artistocrats. A Marquise of Madrid was looking for me for over a year . . . before she found me. I was a bachelor then. The Marquise did not look for one for his handsome face, naturally, but because of his office: and one is not vicious, but neither is one made of stone. It was an elegant experience.'

This time Ramiro did not doubt it. And Urbaleta continued:

'What can you expect? Depravity!'

Ramiro felt curiosity, but dared ask no more questions because he realized that Urbaleta had to force himself and do violence to his own personal principles of honesty to talk about it. Urbaleta showed him his different iron collars, taking them out carefully one by one. On one side of the collars Ramiro noticed small notches cut with a chisel. After each execution Urbaleta took the iron collar to the basement, fastened it on the

305

lathe, and cut another notch. When there were thirteen the mechanism was 'amortized'. He put it in another metal box, fastened down the cover with double straps—this process Urbaleta called 'condemning'—and there it stayed until the day of the meeting in the forge. Urbaleta added that for a year he had had a 'contaminated' iron collar which he melted down some days back. Ramiro asked:

'What kind of "contamination" is that?'

'The iron collar that has performed thirteen times opens and closes by itself at night, they say, and there are even those who insist that it escapes from the box and floats through the air. They also say that after thirteen executions the iron collar talks. The Burgos hangman claims he heard it. I don't believe it. I only repeat what I have heard.'

'But . . . what did it say?'

'The Burgos hangman insists he heard a voice mewing like a cat and saying: "Ay, my teeth, ay, how my teeth ache." '

Again he explained: 'I don't say I heard it. Another, from Dueso, says that he has also heard an amortized iron collar talk. But he says he only heard it say: "Here I am. Here am I. Here you have me . . ." The same words repeated over and over.'

'What do you think about that?' Ramiro asked.

'I respect what others say, and just in case, when thirteen executions have been performed, I lock up the iron collars in the box and wait for the day of the meeting. The truth is that I have only heard a crackling of the metal inside the box occasionally, and I think it can be due to temperature changes.'

Just the same Urbaleta advised him not to forget these customs. 'I have even come to the point of not using the same iron collar twice in succession, so as not to tire it.'

He took a little book out of a cupboard. It was probably not over fifty pages long and bound in leather. The pages were of coarse paper, yellowed around the edges. On the first Ramiro read: *'The Hangman of Amsterdam* — Drama by Victor Ducagne — Translated into the Spanish — Madrid — Imprenta de L. Martínez — 1828.' There was a short preface which Urbaleta read, saying that the work was based on historical fact: the noble gesture of a hangman who, when it came time to execute a condemned man whose guilt he questioned, had preferred to chop off his own hand with the axe. The condemned man was pardoned. Urbaleta, very proud, said:

'That was really an elegant deed of integrity.'

The fact is that Ramiro also felt a little satisfaction, which might now be called professional, in this story from Amsterdam. Urbaleta carelessly repeated the word *hangman* except when referring to Ramiro. Then he used the expression *executer of justice*. It was one of his forms of courtesy. They went upstairs and Urbaleta double-locked the basement door.

At times Ramiro wondered if he did not over-rate himself, believing himself capable of acting as hangman.

Federica Blanca told him once more when they were alone:

'I hate my father, and if it is true that hate kills from a distance, then one day soon he will die. When he dies everything will be ours. The house, garden, savings. You earn more than he because you have an income they send you by post every month, or so my mother says. In ten years we will be rich and we will go away to another country.'

'To what country?'

'Wherever you like. To Bolivia, for instance.'

Doña Tadea had been gradually ignoring her husband, and living almost exclusively for the young people. But one day Urbaleta announced that the Burgos hangman was arriving to spend a week with them. Years before he had thought about marrying Federica Blanca to the son of that hangman, and Doña Tadea, alarmed, now told him that Ramiro and the girl were engaged. Urbaleta was indignant, although he admitted that Ramiro seemed to him a man worthy of his daughter, more worthy than the young man from Burgos. Suddenly he asked for paper and pen and sat down and wrote a letter. He went out to post it, and when he returned called the family together and asked Ramiro:

'Have you something to tell me?'

307

Ramiro was thinking: 'Am I going to get into the game?'
But he realized that in marrying Urbaleta's daughter he was
going farther away *from the game.* He was going away, for ever
and irredeemably.

19

TIME passed too slowly, but finally the wedding day arrived.
Ramiro had refused to invite anyone, but he could not keep
them from sending announcements to the executioners at other
prisons. They received gifts from all of them, some quite luxurious. As a whimsical gesture Ramiro had sent the Duke notice
of his marriage, saying nothing about the bride's family. He
received a cheque from the Duke, and the bride a Pompeian
mirror with a frame of silver and mother-of-pearl. This gift
impressed both Federica Blanca and her mother.

After the wedding Ramiro opened a bank account, deposit-
ing several cheques from the Duke, none of which he had cashed
recently; his own salary, of which he had spent very little; and
the dowry he received when the marriage contract was signed.
With all this the account added up to twenty-one thousand
pesetas. On learning this Urbaleta repeatedly made a suggestion that seemed to obsess him:

'With that capital you could devote yourself to commerce. I
would not object.'

Federica Blanca said:

'It is useless to talk about that any more. I am the daughter
of the hangman, the wife of the hangman, and some day I will
be the mother and grandmother of the hangman.'

Urbaleta sometimes paced back and forth with the slender
volume of *The Hangman of Amsterdam* in his hands. He told
Ramiro that this was the figure which had impressed him most
in all history. When Ramiro heard this he thought of Pope
Clement XIV, who died from the antidotes he had taken to
counteract poisons.

One night Urbaleta fell down the basement stairs and frac

tured his hip. Because of his diabetes complications set in, and a few days later he died, begging forgiveness of his daughter, and talking with a person seen by no one but who appeared to be in a corner of the bedroom.

Federica Blanca said that she could not feign grief. But she went to the corner of the room where her father had thought he saw the phantom, and put consecrated candles there which she left burning all night. Doña Tadea wept and kept repeating that she had been unfair to Urbaleta. No one attended the hangman's burial but a lowly official of the prison. The news of his death was telegraphed to the other executioners, however, and they all sent wreaths.

Toward the end of summer there were two executions. The Burgos hangman was sent for to coach Ramiro. He was a massive man, neither fair nor dark, but gray. Lead-gray or light-gray, depending on his mood. His bones looked ill-adjusted or crooked in some places. He had lived in Mexico in his youth, he said, and telling it obviously made him feel cosmopolitan and important. His first remark had been:

'*Compadre* Urbaleta died a natural death in his honorable bed. May he have many a year to wait for us in the other world.'

He kept on repeating something about natural death, explaining to Ramiro that few executers of justice died in such a way, and that his father-in-law's case was exceptional.

'Then what do they die of?'

The Burgos hangman said that there were cases of suicide as well as accidental deaths. Almost always the accident took place in the basement where they kept their tools. Just as Ramiro was on the point of explaining about Urbaleta's accident he sensed that the 'natural death' version gave the family a certain prestige, and kept still.

The visiting hangman took the carpenter's bench out of the basement into the garden, and on it set up his own instruments. Ramiro went out to have a look, but his colleague covered the apparatus with his body as well as he could, saying:

309

'Pardon me, *compadre*, but it is a personal method of my own.'

Ramiro apologized. As he withdrew the Burgos hangman called after him:

'If you had asked: "*Compadre*, may I see and so learn about your personal system?"—I would have thought about how I ought to answer. But suddenly like this, you understand, it looks as if you were coming to steal my secret from me.'

Ramiro repeated his apologies and left him alone. But the Burgos hangman called him back. Ramiro returned, impatient, and the visitor commented very courteously:

'In view of your great interest, *compadre*, I have no objection to revealing my secret to you.'

This concerned the famous arrangement of the steel needle that penetrated under the condemned man's jaw. He added that this did not make the execution more rapid or less painful. It was an improvement that had only what might be called 'aesthetic ends'. This phrase, he said, occurred in the report that the warden of the Burgos prison had sent to the main offices when recommending the innovation.

The execution day was cloudy and very warm.

At dawn everything was ready and Ramiro saw that there was nothing to do but imitate his companion. The Burgos hangman worked skilfully with the condemned man until he had him ready, and in less than two minutes he had strangled him. Then the second was brought out. Ramiro, also formally dressed, waited behind his post, very pale. He did just as he had seen his colleague do, and when the condemned man's head was covered with the black cloth — it was this cloth they called the 'veronica' — he turned the screw. The mechanism struck the verterbrae without breaking them. The Burgos hangman, seeing that Ramiro was confused and repeating the movement, went over to him, took hold of the screw, and with the first movement disarticulated the base of the condemned man's skull. Then he looked at Ramiro and returned to his post, gravely leaning against the wall.

The executions over, they returned home. That night, after supper, which was unenjoyable, they played cards. They had a jar of wine and a dish of hot peppers in the middle of the table. All this — like the roast meat — was to keep the stomach from 'rising', as had happened to old Urbaleta in spite of everything. The Burgos hangman took a human tooth out of his vest pocket and laid it on the table in front of his cards. It brought him good luck, he said.

Only after the Burgos visitor had left did Ramiro realize, from some remarks of Doña Tadea's, that his colleague felt resentful toward the deceased Urbaleta for not having married Federica Blanca to his son. From the door the Burgos hangman had shouted that he wished to be godfather to the first child.

20

MANY years later Ramiro was called to Madrid to take charge of two of the four executions on the dawn of that same day when I, Juan Echenique, attended as a witness in the name of the city.

Ramiro and I had walked through the Retiro under a gray sky of broad, high clouds. A light breeze skimmed the ground whirling the sand along the deserted avenues. He told me what I have reconstructed in the preceding pages. We had been sauntering all the afternoon and evening and when night fell we found that we were locked inside the park. In order not to attract attention of the guards we went behind the observatory to the same spot where Ramiro had gone so often during his first days in Madrid. Seeing the same lighted window and the same white curtain, as well as hearing piano music, moved him. He finished his story at dawn. We had not eaten, nor had he slept, for two days. He told me that the night before executions he could not sleep, although he usually slept very well the following night.

'And the Duke?' I asked.

'He is still alive. He is over eighty years old.'

When they opened the park we started for the center of the city. Without having agreed on any plan we were going toward the café where we had met on the preceding day. I looked at Ramiro in the bleak morning light. He had the expressive face of a mature actor, with something like a patina of kindness marked by a certain distinction. I asked him why he had troubled to confide in me to such an extent, and he answered:

'Because I was conscious of your need to understand.'

I nodded. After a pause he asked:

'Did you?'

I hesitated, and finally, with a painful sincerity, said:

'No.'

'I realize,' he said, excusing me. 'It is difficult.'

It was a sunny and fragrant spring day. There were flower-sellers at the café entrances. The newspaper stands had sweet-smelling lilacs in cool pails of water. An early-rising girl looked at us, looked a second time at Ramiro and mechanically wet her lips with the tip of her tongue. I smiled at the idea of Ramiro's being successful with women.

Soon after passing the Puerta de Alcalá I heard a car stop beside us with a sharp screeching of its brakes. The face of a very old man peered out of the door, calling my friend:

'Ramiro, is it you?'

The hangman stopped, with a timid and displeased expression:

'You?'

'Climb in the car. Come on, climb in the car!'

Ramiro hesitated:

'I am with a friend.'

Ramiro and I looked at each other, wavering. The Duke — it was the Duke of L. — was saying, as he looked at me:

'Who is this young man? Let the young man get in too.'

It was unavoidable and the Duke, looking at us with marked curiosity, asked where we wished to be dropped. Since Ramiro and I had no plans, and not caring whether I went to one place or another, I gave the address of the San Ginés café. The Duke relayed it to his chauffeur. Then he explained that he got up very early every day to go to a farm near the city where he drank a glass of fresh asses' milk, still warm. He assured us that he had found it very salutary. Ramiro looked uncomfortable. The Duke, discussing the qualities of asses' milk, looked at him again and again.

'You don't have to tell me a thing, Ramiro. I know everything. Everything. I know that your mother died in the convent like a saint.'

He looked at me hesitantly, unable to decide whether to say anything to me or not, and added, addressing Ramiro:

'I know everything. Everything about you, I know. I talked to Father Anglada. I talked to others. I talked to everybody.'

He put his hand on Ramiro's, and in a fit of senile enthusiasm grasped it, raised it to his lips, and kissed it. Ramiro was silent. The Duke regretted reaching the café and parting so soon, but he said that they would see each other again that very morning, and that Ramiro should not leave the café until he received further news. The footman opened the car door and we got out. Ramiro said:

'For twenty years he has been sending me a remittance every month, but hardly ever a line. He never writes letters. I doubt if he has written more than half a dozen in his whole life.'

Nervously, we heard the Duke giving orders to the chauffeur. The car started off at high speed.

Seated at the same table as the day before, Ramiro and I looked around the empty café. It had the coldness of closed places that have just been opened up for cleaning, it was a cold more uncomfortable than that of the street.

'I had imagined the Duke as a different type,' I said.

'The poor man is so old that I myself would never have recognized him.'

I ordered a big breakfast. I was thinking that I ought to leave Ramiro, but I did not know how. Taking leave of a hangman is not easy. Meanwhile I was eating hungrily. Ramiro only

313

sipped his coffee and watched the glassed-in fish at different heights on the walls moving up or down with slow and silent movements. In one corner of the café, next to the bar, an old waiter was polishing silver candelabra. Near the door communicating with the kitchens a four-year-old child was gazing at Ramiro with his big clear eyes. I noticed that he never looked at me.

The door facing Caballero de Gracia Street — through which we had entered — was half open. Two policemen in gala uniform approached it from the outside, closed it with their white gloved hands, and stationed themselves one on each side, like porters instead of policemen. Ramiro saw the same thing happening at the entrance opening on to the Avenida del Conde Peñalver. We never gave it a second thought and went on talking. Ramiro was telling me that he had two children. He had wished to avoid it but he understood that his obligation was to be a father, without trying to interpret the moral meaning of paternity.

Neither of us made any attempt to leave. The bells of a neighboring church began to ring. I asked Ramiro if it was a holiday and he said not so far as he knew. Perhaps it was the feast day of the patron saint of that church, of the feast of San Ginés. Soon we noticed a multitude of women slowly coming up the Calle de Alcalá with shuffling feet, scapularies on their breasts, and in their hands wax candles that had been snuffed out by the wind. They formed two rows, one on either side of the street, while in the center priests in black cassocks and white rochets, with strange sergeant-like movements, marched back and forth.

'You see?' I said to Ramiro. 'There must be a religious holiday in the parish.'

'Yes, a procession.'

Streetcar bells clanged in the distance and policemen whistled directing traffic. The procession came up Caballero de Gracia Street stopping near the San Ginés café with an expectant air. Ramiro said:

'How odd!'

Another procession, this one only of men, was moving up the Avenida del Conde Peñalver. They were carrying a banner half unfurled in the breeze with the words 'Association of Heads of Families' embroidered on it. A priest dressed like the others paced back and forth, the lower edge of his cassock whipping his heavy shoes. The one carrying the banner wrinkled his nose as if something were wrong with it and he wished to rub it against his shoulder. Unable to do this he finally rubbed it on the mast of the banner with the same movement birds make when sharpening their beaks on a branch. Not only the bells of San Ginés but those of other churches nearby were now ringing in the wind. I asked Ramiro if he were sure that it was not Corpus or Holy Saturday or some other memorial day.

'No, I don't think so,' he said.

We paid the bill and got up to leave, but before reaching the door, which was still being guarded by policemen in gala uniform, the telephone on the counter rang and the old waiter who was polishing the candelabra called the hangman:

'Are you Don Ramiro Vallemediano?'

My friend answered the telephone and talked for some time. Or, to put it more correctly, he listened. I tried to hear in vain. I went up to one of the aquarium-windows through which I kept looking out into the street. Along Caballero de Gracia Street came a group of middle-aged men, not of religious appearance, although they too were carrying a banner. They walked solemnly. Almost all of them wore slight beards which gave them a certain air of distinction and authority. On the banner, embroidered in gold, were the words 'Brotherhood of Peace and Charity.' I realized, as I looked in every direction, that this kind of civil-religious procession would never end. New standards, new bands of musicians appeared at the end of the streets. The musicians were not playing, although they were lined up in broad ranks, their brass instruments shining. Behind them were still more rows of men and women, of all ages, apparently. I went up to a door and tried to open it, but the policeman would not allow it, although there was nothing whatever violent in his manner. I had succeeded, however, in half opening one of the doors and asking what it was all about.

'A jubilee,' one of the policemen answered.

'A jubilee? What for?'

They looked at each other, surprised.

'We don't know. We are just repeating what we heard.'

Ramiro came away from the telephone rather excited.

'We can't leave,' he said.

'Why?'

'Do you see those doors? They are under guard. All those people with banners and scapularies have something to do with me. I don't know exactly what they are planning, but they are coming because of me. Something terrible is happening. The Duke's major-domo told me that his master is on his way and that I must wait for him here and not be surprised at anything I see. Father Anglada is evidently coming too. Or we are going to see him. I could not hear well. All this is horrible and there is no way to get out of it. They are talking about many unexpected things. I'll have to admit that these people have a sense of organization. Look. In two hours.'

He pointed with his outstretched arm to the processions that seemed to be surrounding and blockading the building where we were. Ramiro, extremely worried, said:

'I should have returned to Ocaña yesterday. And what about you? What are you going to do?'

The old waiter kept on polishing the silver candelabra, indifferent to everything going on outside. Ramiro was very pale. His voice trembled. I would have liked to escape, but how? When I tried the other door the policeman asked:

'Are you Señor Vallemediano?'

'No, I'm not.'

'In any case you cannot leave yet.'

'How long will I have to wait?'

'I don't know. We are here to see that no one leaves or enters.'

I went back to Ramiro's side:

'We are prisoners.'

We saw long and patient lines of people making themselves comfortable all round the building, on the pavement in front and on the three sides. The café was on an octagonal plaza, with entrances on three streets.

'Is this because of me?' Ramiro muttered aloud. 'What for? Look, look there!'

The Duke's car drove up and started to park in front of one of the entrances. Inside, the Duke as well as other persons could be seen. No one left the car.

Other vehicles were parked in front and behind, and their occupants did not get out either. They were all old, large, heavy cars, so well cared for that the smallest bit of nickel shone like crystal.

'But why all this?' I repeated, sensing an immense scandal in it all.

'I don't know. In any case it concerns me alone. Don't you worry, it's only because of me. It apparently has nothing to do with you.'

He was more afraid than I. He looked at the cars lined up, at the patient crowd, and said very nervously:

'There is no doubt about it. It is the end. This is the end. Or the beginning. Who knows?'

Everyone seemed to be waiting. Ramiro went from one window to another and toward the doors, discovering once again that any attempt to leave was useless. I said:

'The policemen know your name. They asked me if I were Señor Vallemediano. Why don't you try to talk to the Duke? He is outside there in his car. At least make signs to him from here.'

The Duke did not look in our direction. Finally the person they seemed to be waiting for arrived, and the band that had been hidden from view started playing a hymn in which an occasional phrase of the national anthem was recognizable. Then someone opened the door facing the Avenida del Conde de Peñalver and eight grave citizens approached, bearing a luxurious canopy bordered with gold and silver fringe. Each of the eight men, severely dressed in black, held one of the supports of the canopy. Others held golden ribbons attached to both sides. No one was under the canopy. They placed it next to the door and waited. Ramiro decided to go out and speak to the Duke. I had retreated to the back of the café, afraid of finding myself physically involved in all this. Ramiro, after great hesitation, crossed the threshold, slowly. At that moment the Duke and others left the car and surrounded him. They kept him under the canopy, all of them talking to him at the same time. Outside the bells kept ringing and the din was such that even though the Duke and other dignitaries spoke in loud voices I, inside the café, could only catch an isolated word: *fatherland*. *Jubilee*. Father Anglada's name was also heard. Ramiro asked questions to the right and to the left of him, but no one seemed to give a satisfactory answer.

The procession was formed. The bands continued playing. Ramiro started marching under the canopy. I retreated farther, approaching the café counter where the old waiter was still polishing silver candelabra.

'Behind the band are the guilds,' he remarked. 'But where are they taking him?' I asked.

Without ceasing to rub the base of a candlestick, the waiter replied:

'I heard that they are taking him to Chamartin to see Father Anglada, a famous priest. Do you see? The guilds are also carrying their banners. Not all of them, of course.'